Dear Reader:

I have to give you the background of how I discovered R. Kayeen Thomas and this novel, *Antebellum*. I volunteered to teach high school English one day at my daughter's school and Mr. Thomas was the teacher. During the lunch break, he told me that he had written a couple of novels and had one published work. I asked him could I see them. His first book, *Light: Stories of Urban Resurrection*, immediately caught my attention. TWO of my male friends had given me copies of the book a few years before but I never got a chance to read them. Both of them said he was an excellent writer and that I was sleeping on him.

That evening, my youngest son had Little League practice. I was sitting there watching him and decided to grab the binder that Mr. Thomas had given me at lunch. I started reading *Antebellum* and got so caught up that I went home that night and finished reading the entire manuscript. I was amazed at his gift of storytelling and his ability to give readers a much-needed wakeup call. The one word that sums up his talent is "gifted." After reading this book, I am sure you will agree. Be prepared to become completely submerged from the first page because this is one of the most innovative novels that I have ever read, or published.

As always, thanks for supporting my authors and Strebor Books. We strive to bring you prolific authors who think outside of the box and lift our imaginations to a higher level. For more information on our titles, please visit www.zanestore.com and you can find me on my personal website: www.eroticanoir.com. You can also join my online social network at www.planetzane.org.

Blessings,

Zane

Zane
Publisher
Strebor Books
www.simonandschuster.com/streborbooks

ZANE PRESENTS

ANTEBELLUM

R. Kayeen Thomas

STREBOR BOOKS

NEW YORK LONDON TORONTO SYDNEY

Strebor Books
P.O. Box 6505
Largo, MD 20792
http://www.streborbooks.com

ISBN 978-1-59309-425-6
ISBN 978-1-4516-5998-6 (e-book)
LCCN 2011938443

First Strebor Books trade paperback edition June 2012

Cover design: www.mariondesigns.com
Cover photograph: © Keith Saunders/Marion Designs

10 9 8 7 6 5 4 3 2 1

Manufactured in the United States of America

For information regarding special discounts for bulk purchases, please contact Simon & Schuster Special Sales at 1-866-506-1949 or business@simonandschuster.com

The Simon & Schuster Speakers Bureau can bring authors to your live event. For more information or to book an event, contact the Simon & Schuster Speakers Bureau at 1-866-248-3049 or visit our website at www.simonspeakers.com.

This book is dedicated to the trinity of women in my life –
Marilyn, Monee, and Zion

Acknowledgments

I would first like to thank God, who saw fit to give me these words. I am honored to be a vessel, and I pray I do not disappoint you. I would like to thank my wife and my best friend, Monee, for always supporting me and encouraging me in any and all situations. Truly, without you, this book would not have been possible. To my daughter, Zion, who has had to share her father with a laptop, I thank you for always making me smile, even when the words don't come. To my parents, Marilyn and Weldon, whose support and love in the months leading up to this book has been nothing short of miraculous, I thank you for all you have done. To my brother, Daniel, the master chef, I thank you for reminding me to never take life too seriously. To Zane, who will never know how nervous I was when I handed her this manuscript, I thank you for believing in me enough to make my dreams come true. To Charmaine, my publishing director, who has put up with my missed deadlines with the utmost charm and grace, I thank you for all your support. To Strebor Books and Simon & Schuster, thank you for taking a chance on me. To Dr. Helton, who predicted my success and stood by my inspirations, I thank you. To my church family at Israel Metropolitan CME, who has shown me more love than I sometimes feel I deserve, I thank you. And to everyone over the years who told me not to quit, to keep writing because the world needs to hear what you have to say, I owe you all everything. Thank you all.

Prologue

"He's a'comin', y'hear? He's a'comin'!"

The crowd of slaves threw their bodies to and fro with reckless abandon, sending their petitions up to heaven.

The dark sky welcomed their pain, their shouts, their moans and groans, with open arms. It wrapped around them, hugged them as they lost themselves in the frenzy. The only light came from the few torches that were brought, and it jumped around with the slaves, casting its glow on whomever it chose. The faces highlighted were frozen in expressions that would haunt any child's nightmare. There was agony chiseled in cheekbones and jawlines. Despair coated women's faces like over-applied make-up. And the cries...there were no words for the cries...

And yet hope stood, standing slightly hunched over, on a large mound in front of the masses. Life shouted over the cries of the tormented. She told them to hold on, told them that their time was almost finished; that their sufferings were almost over.

The slaves breathed in Elizabeth's words, and ignited with the fires of Pentecost.

Elizabeth was exhausted. Spitting fire from her mouth to revive the damned was a job with a very short life expectancy. Yet she was the only one who could do it. The decades of whips and cotton and lost babies had dimmed the brightness in her eyes and replaced it with embers resting in her ribcage. Every so often, when things fell to their worst, she would bring her people, under the darkness of night, to this clearing in the forest. It was here that she spat those embers over her children. It was here that she gave them back their will to live.

Elizabeth fought through her fatigue as she stepped down from the makeshift podium and made her way through the crowd until she found the two she'd been looking for. She grabbed them both by the hands and yanked them, tugging and pulling them through the throng, leading them back into the woods. The woman was still shouting, trying to push her despair out through the pores of her skin. The man was silent, but wanted the same, and found it hard to see through his tears.

They trusted Elizabeth completely, and allowed her to drag them through the brush until she saw fit to stop.

After they'd composed themselves, they realized they were at the riverbank. They calmed down enough to hear what their leader had to say.

"You two's been chosen by da Lawd! You two's been chosen! A man's comin,' y'hear? And when he get here, it mark da end! It mark freedom! But he gon' need you's two! He gon' need you, or we's all damned!"

"Wh...why us, 'Lizabeth?" The woman shook her head, full of doubt. "I'se nobody to be helpin' no savior..."

"You shut up now, Sarah! Dis here ain't your choice...be God's choice!"

"What me do?" the man said, his voice seasoned with the melodies of Africa.

"Roka, he gon' need you to show 'im how to be strong, and Sarah, he gon' need you to bring 'im back t'life. He gon' need you both, or he gon' die!"

Elizabeth bent down and reached into the darkness. She emerged with a white towel and a white wooden staff, six feet long. She held it in front of Sarah's and Roka's faces.

"Dis be yo' sign, says da Lawd!" Elizabeth raised her voice, even though the two slaves were standing right in front of her. "Dis be yo' sign! When dese things come back to you, it be time! Y'hear me? It be time!"

She flung both her arms forward and threw both the cloth and the staff into the river. When she spoke again, her voice was almost a whisper.

"Lissen good, chirren…he gon' come, but he ain't gonna be ready. You gotta make 'im ready. You gotta, or he gon' die. He gon' die…"

Elizabeth fell into tears, and Roka grabbed her before she collapsed to the ground.

"You gotta make 'im ready…" she managed, speaking in a delirium now, while her head hung limp over Roka's arm. "You gots ta make 'im ready…"

Sarah, having found new strength from her mission, stood tall and walked over to the edge of the riverbank. She cupped some water in her hands, walked back over to Roka and Elizabeth, and poured it over Elizabeth's forehead.

"Don't worry yo'self no more, 'Lizabeth." She spoke with an assurance that made Roka look up.

"We makes 'im ready. We makes 'im, or we's die tryin'."

Roka bent down and picked up Elizabeth, carrying her full weight in his arms. He looked at Sarah, and she looked back at him, and they both made their way back through the brush to the other frenzied slaves.

PART ONE

1

"Yo, what's your name?"

I was staring at the back of a snoring stranger's head. Her weave fell disheveled against the pillow as her torso rose up and down. The hair was fake, but who cared? It was just another way of hiding. The makeup that was no doubt smeared on her face, the designer jeans and heels that lay on the ground, the sweet smelling perfume that coated the sheets—it was all fake, but I had bought into it anyway. I guess because deep down inside, I was fake, too. Everybody's got a hustle, right? My façade earned me money, and hers earned her my bed for the night.

I heard knuckles rap rhythmically against the door. *It must be eight*, I thought. The bedside clock verified my guess. I tried to jump out of bed, but the bricks in my head wouldn't allow me to. Instead, I moved slowly, with my hand against the wall to steady myself. A condom hung from me, but I was too dizzy to take it off.

The noise on the door stirred my guest. She moaned slightly and turned her head in my direction.

Her face was okay, from what I could tell. I'd seen better. I studied her long and hard and wondered why I'd brought her up here.

"Hey ma, you gotta get up," I said.

My voice might as well have been the Liberty Bell. All at once she opened her eyes and realized where she was and who was speaking. If there were bricks in her head, too, then they all shattered against one another as she hurtled from the bed.

Turned out she was naked under the sheets. All that smooth white satin was hiding an Amazon donkey booty. My mouth fell open as she galloped into the bathroom and slammed the door. I was surprised it didn't pull her to the ground.

"No wonder she got the key," I said aloud as I made my way to the door and looked through the peephole. A petite little cutie stood outside with short dreads, wearing a tight-fitting T-shirt and jeans. I opened the door and smiled as best I could, considering the demolition going on in my temporal lobe. She spoke before I could greet her.

"The one with the butt, right?"

SaTia knew me too well. She's wasn't even swayed by the fact that I was standing in front of her Butterball naked. She sidestepped me and made her way into the room.

"At least take the condom off, Moe. That's just nasty. Is she gone yet?"

"Naw, she's in the bathroom."

"Damn. I thought we agreed you'd have them out by eight? I don't get paid enough to deal with these crazy…"

"I know, I know. My bad. I slept late, aight? I just woke up."

"Can you get her out before I start, please? And I swear to God, if she even thinks about coming at me wrong…"

"I'll get her out, aight? I promise. Just sit down and relax."

There must have been an *Extreme Makeover* crew hidden in my bathroom. When the mystery girl came out, she looked nothing like the woman who had jumped from the bed a few minutes ago. Her makeup was on point, her hair was straight, and her skirt made her butt look even bigger. I couldn't figure out if it was the material or the fact that she wasn't wearing any panties.

She would definitely be in my next video.

"Hey, baby." She spoke as if we'd been dating for two years. SaTia rolled her eyes and sat down on the couch. The makeup magician cocked her head to the side and quickly let her attitude show. She pointed to SaTia as if she was an ugly dress on the clearance rack at Old Navy.

"Ummm, who is that?"

I spoke up before SaTia could.

"That's my manager, sweetheart. Look, you fine as hell, but I got business to handle. Leave me ya number so I can hit you when I'm back in town. Oh, I almost forgot, you wanna be in my next video?"

She looked as if I had given her the key to paradise. I turned around just to make sure there wasn't a white man behind me with a check the size of a big-screen television.

"Oh my God...you want me in your video?"

"Yeah. Like I said, leave ya number. I'll hit you next week to let you know the details."

She covered her mouth as she screamed, then jumped around like a sixth grader who discovered school was cancelled. It was all expected. I smiled my usual congratulations-you-should-be-proud smile as she walked up to me and held my hand palm up. With the other hand, she pulled a pen from her bra.

"You make sure you don't lose this, daddy."

She finished writing her number on my palm and put the pen back in her bra. Then, without warning, she put my hand under her skirt. It felt like an undercooked cinnamon roll with too much icing.

"You got all this waiting for you when you come back," she whispered. "I don't care how long it takes, Nigga, I ain't letting nobody near it till you beat it up again. This right here will always be your pussy."

She was bold; I had to give her that. If SaTia hadn't been in the room, her words and action would've been enough to convince me to throw her back on the bed. Instead, I played a makeshift guitar with my pointer and index fingers as I responded.

"I'll keep that in mind, ma. Matter a' fact, keep ya phone by you this afternoon. I may get lonely."

I don't know if she heard me over her moaning. I took my hand back and she kept going like it was still there.

"Uh...oooo...why'd you stop, daddy?"

I looked over at SaTia. She looked back at me like I was driving the wrong way on a one-way street.

"Business," I said as I turned around and sat down beside my manager.

The woman seemed confused for a second, but when she looked over and saw SaTia's smug face, she got the picture. She shot one last I-will-rip-out-your-windpipe look at SaTia and then made her way toward the door.

"Don't forget to call me, baby. I promise, you won't regret it."

And she walked out the door.

SaTia sighed with relief. You never knew how the groupies would react to her in the morning. Even though she had beaten down her share of anonymous females, I could tell she was glad that this one was relatively calm.

"You really know how to pick 'em," she said as she reached for her computer bag.

"What? She had a phat butt! Come on, you know I can't be held responsible..."

"Yeah, right. You do have a light schedule today. You gonna call her back?"

"Sure, why not? I don't even remember what happened last night. With a booty like that, I gotta have a memory to tell the crew about."

SaTia set the laptop on her thighs and powered it up. "Well, good luck trying to reach her."

"What do you mean? She left her name and number right here..."

I lifted up my palm and saw a piece of abstract art. SaTia tried to stifle her chuckles.

"She wrote her number on the same hand that you just put in her cookie jar," she said, and giggled. "Man, those must have been some soggy Oreos."

I jumped up and sprinted toward the door. SaTia gave in to her laughter. I forgot I was naked as I threw open the door. The same maid who had delivered my *Washington Post* for the last three mornings was standing in the hall like clockwork. You would've thought my penis kicked her in the stomach. She threw her hands up, screamed and crashed into the wall.

I jumped back inside the room and slammed the door behind me. SaTia had set her laptop to the side and was now on the floor howling and smacking the soft carpet with her hand.

I came back to the couch and smiled sheepishly. Maybe this wouldn't be a story for the crew after all.

My audience of one composed herself as best she could. She made her way back up to the couch and wiped the tears from her eyes.

"Go wash your hands and put some clothes on, please."

Defeated, with my head still throbbing, I did as I was told.

Twenty minutes later I came back to the couch adorned in an overly stylish outfit for a Wednesday morning. I was trying to make up for the embarrassment from less than an hour ago.

Superficial as it was, it helped knowing I looked fly. If SaTia noticed, she didn't let on. She drummed away on her laptop as if it was some sort of musical instrument. When she finished her symphony, she turned her attention toward me.

"Like I said earlier, you've got a light day today. Mr. Rose is in the city on business, and he wants to do breakfast."

"Why breakfast, man? Don't white dudes ever sleep late?"

"Not when they have meetings in four cities within twenty-four hours. I'm glad you got dressed, 'cause you have to leave for that soon."

"Aight, what else is goin' on?"

"At three o'clock, the local radio station will be set up at Birchtown Mall. You're going to be on air with them for about an hour, to give the kids getting out of school a chance to come and see you. After that, you'll sign some autographs and leave."

She paused to make sure I was cool with everything she'd said before she continued.

"The concert tonight is going to be a small one. The club is tiny compared to some of the others where we've been. They're already sold out of tickets."

"If the club is so small, why am I performing there?" I wrinkled my brow. The image of performing in a one-room shack popped into my head.

"The owner has a lot of contacts and the club is the most popular one in town. The cover charge is really high and drink prices are ridiculous, but that's how he can afford you."

The massive crowds and seas of fanatical women had spoiled me. I wasn't feeling in the mood for a tiny crowd, no matter how much they were paying me.

"I don't know, I'm thinking maybe I should cancel it. We could call 'em and say I'm sick or somethin'. Have you seen the place?"

SaTia responded without turning her eyes from her laptop screen. I hated it when she did that, even though I never told her so.

"Of course I've been there. I go to all the locations where you're supposed to perform beforehand."

"What did you think?"

"What the guy lacks in size he makes up for with presentation. It's amazing inside. It's definitely worth it, despite the small crowd."

I nodded my head and walked over to make some coffee. I could hear SaTia's fingers gradually slow down and then stop tapping on her keyboard, as if something was grabbing more and more of her attention. She tried to disguise her hurt feelings with an attitude as she spoke, but I had known her for too long to be fooled.

"So what, you don't trust me to schedule good shows for you anymore? Is that it?"

My sidekick had her own way of letting me know she cared. With my back turned to her, I grinned. By the time I turned to face her, black coffee in hand, my mouth had formed a slight, almost insignificant smirk.

"No, I still trust you. I was just feeling a little full of myself. It's all good, though. I'll kill 'em like always."

"Good. 'Cause you know, if you don't trust me to look out for you, you can always find another manager."

She played this game every once in a while, and I have to say, she was always more direct than I was. She knew I wouldn't hire another manager as long as she made herself available. And I knew that she would always put more effort into looking out for me than she needed to.

Though the thought of not having her around made my stomach knot up, I pretended to shrug off the comment like I always did.

"Whatever. Can we just get down to the limo?"

She briefly cut her eyes at me, then softly closed her laptop and began to pack it away. I put on my designer Dolce & Gabbana shades, brushed off my limited-edition Nikes and put in the diamond-and-platinum grill I had custom-made a few months back.

No sooner than we'd stood up, ready to walk side by side as always, SaTia's BlackBerry rang. I was content in knowing that she was always taking care of my business. She spoke briefly to one of my endorsers about rescheduling a commercial shoot, and had her technology back in her pocket by the time we reached the elevator.

"You don't have those stupid teeth in, do you?"

The elevator door opened and we both stepped in. The car looked like the shrunken bedroom of a king. I took in the beauty surrounding me while feeling my stomach drop from the descent. SaTia glanced up and saw our reflections in the mirror that doubled as a ceiling. I looked up as well, pressed my teeth together, and opened my lips to show off the precious metal and stones temporarily filling my mouth.

I thought briefly about how stupid I would look doing that if there wasn't $100,000 worth of shiny stuff behind my lips.

SaTia cringed and dropped her eyes to look forward again.

"I don't think you will ever know how ridiculous those things make you look."

"Image sells and ordinary is boring. My fans want me to be the star they made me."

The line rolled off my tongue like a bowling ball gliding down a lane. It had become my get-out-of-jail-free card for the last two years.

That's what the execs—Mr. Rose included—told me when I first started out, and that's what I lived by. Always be the person your fans want you to be.

"The guys should be in the lobby waiting for you." SaTia glanced over at me. "Orlando texted me and let me know the cameras are already down there, so be prepared for pictures. All the guys know you have a meeting to go to, so we're going to drop them off at the local mall before we head to the restaurant."

"Why is it that my boys get to have more fun than me?"

"Because you're working."

"So what are they doing?"

"Living off of you."

As if on cue, the elevator stopped and the door opened. Three men and one woman, each armed with a high quality camera and a persistent ability to never leave me alone, started flashing pictures. The first two snaps would have blinded me if it wasn't for the shades I was wearing. The next two hundred or so were a breeze. I turned on the swagger and walked out of the elevator as if I owned the world and everything in it.

Brian, Henry, Ray, and Orlando were sitting on the lush couches in front of the door. They appeared to be even more sluggish than I was, but when they heard all the commotion and the cameras flashing, they rushed over to me.

"What's good?" I said as I gave them dap.

They were guys I'd grown up with. We rhymed together in high school. So, as was the rule, when I got big, I brought them with me. I made sure that they were each working toward a solo album, but for now they just backed me up on stage. In order to set themselves apart, they all had alter egos—Brian was Ballin-B, Henry was HardKnock, Ray was Reason, and Orlando was O-Dog.

"What happened to the chick from last night?" Orlando asked as he walked beside me. The other three were pushing the camera people back so we could move.

I shook my head and looked down at my undecorated palm.

"I'll tell you in the limo."

The one white reporter, Allen, had been following me since before I made it big. For that, he was always either the first to get his questions answered, or the only one I responded to. He stood away from the vultures, but still in the path between the elevator entrance and the door. A taller Middle Eastern man held the camera while Allen controlled the microphone.

All my boys knew Allen, so they let him through to me when he walked up to us.

"Moe…Moe. Why don't you say hello to some of your fans out here in Miami?"

I always laughed to myself when Allen asked me questions. He'd been on the job a long time, and I'd seen him cover a lot of different artists. Every other celebrity he interviewed, he addressed by their stage name. Not with me, though. He didn't want to risk it.

I took a deep breath and made sure my mask was on nice and tight. Then I leaned in to the microphone.

"Yea, yea, yea! Dis here is Da Nigga, and you been knowed what it do, baby! Deez Nutz records foreva! Knowhatimsayin! I'm da sickest ta eva sneeze out a rhyme and da hottest ta eva burn up a track! Call all da ladies wid da phat bootie back and double D rack and tell 'em holla at ya BOY! YEA!"

I guess a little bit of me died inside as I spoke, but I was rich, so it didn't matter.

2

A limousine is the most magical thing in the world. It's like a portal into an alternate reality. I've known hustle-on-the-corner-Uzi-carrying thugs who've stepped into a limousine and climbed out as reformed members of an upper-class society. There's just something about those long, shiny monstrosities that convinces you that you're important, that the world needs you to succeed. Limousines are so magical that people don't even have to see who's riding inside. All it takes is for one to slowly roll past, taunting you with the tinted windows up, for you to think, "Wow, whoever is in that thing must be really special."

In the end, they're the only things on earth that can change a man's social status while air-conditioning him and providing him with free alcohol. That's why I always had SaTia order one to meet us at the airport of whatever city I'm visiting, and drive us everywhere until I leave. Unless I was back home in D.C., whenever you saw me traveling it would be in a limo.

The one we were all in now looked like someone had knocked over a spaceship and put chrome rims and Goodyear tires underneath it. I didn't even know they made limos like it. I gave SaTia a nod of approval when we first got in and she shrugged her shoulders as if it wasn't anything special. I guess that's why I kept her around.

As the limo pulled away from the hotel, I tried to take my mind off of the meeting I had coming up. Ray, Brian, and Orlando sat on the seat that stretched down the middle of the limo. I sat at the back, with Henry on one side of me and SaTia on the other.

If I knew my manager, she wouldn't say a word until the guys were out of the car. Meanwhile, my homeboys started their conversation, even before they had a chance to get comfortable.

"Yo, last night? Last night was off da chain!" Ray gave dap to the guys sitting beside him as he spoke with a grin. "What da hell did those white boys give us?"

Orlando exhaled slowly as he sat back and nursed his crotch.

"I think it was X, dude. That or Viagra. I ran through at least six chicks last night. My dick feel like a skinned knee."

"Naw, they had a bunch a' different stuff." Ray still seemed excited from the previous night's escapades. "I was on some straight-up, whacked-out, psychedelic stuff. I swear I banged out an angel last night, homie. Wings and halo and all! And I gave her da business!"

"That's gotta be some kinda sin or somethin'," Henry said, laughing along with the rest of us as he spoke. "You goin' to hell, dude."

"Naw, I ain't. I mean, she was an angel, so I was real nice to her. Ain't cuss at her or nothing."

"But you still blew da back out, right?"

"Most def."

"So you goin' to hell."

Ray turned to me for support. I was still laughing.

"Moe, man, tell dis nigga just cause you give a' angel da pipe don't mean you automatically goin' to hell."

"It's common sense, though." Henry turned to me as well. "You cain't have rough sex wid no angel and still go to heaven…"

I looked back at Ray, who looked genuinely concerned about his fate in the afterlife, and I fell out of my seat. I laughed so hard that I strained my stomach muscles. Brian and Orlando were both leaning over, too. Brian was slapping the seat with his palm while Orlando was trying to catch his breath.

By the time I composed myself, my eyes were bloodshot. I looked at Ray again and saw two of him instead of one.

"You...you do know that you ain't really screw an angel last night, right?"

"I mean, yeah... I know...but still, you shoulda seen her, dogg..."

I shook my head. Ray was pitiful.

"Don't let no drugs fool you, dude. It was probably a crack-head."

Orlando cracked up again, but not as hard. His lungs couldn't take it, and his crotch was still on fire. When he finished catching his breath, he looked up at me.

"So what'd you end up trippin' off of?"

I shrugged my shoulders.

"I 'ont know, man. Probably X. I ended up wid this chick wid a donkey booty."

Brian shot straight up in his seat.

"So Phatback found you, huh?"

I must've looked confused, because Orlando stepped in and clarified.

"Phatback was the name we gave the chick you got with. She got to the hotel 'round two in the afternoon wid her girls yesterday. All she did was ask where you was at. We partied a lil bit while you was still at the photo shoot. We even broke her girls off. But she had dat radar on, boy. Soon as you came back, it was a wrap."

"Why I cain't remember her from last night then?"

"'Cause you was high all day yesterday. You told me have a blunt ready fo' when you came back from da shoot, so I gave it to you soon as the limo pulled up. We got blazed 'fore you even got back in da hotel. And dat was before we met da white boys."

I was getting ready to ask another question, but I felt the limo make a sharp right turn. When I looked out the window, I saw the mall entrance.

"Alright, listen guys..." SaTia finally broke her silence. "Our meeting with Mr. Rose shouldn't take any longer than an hour. You all have the credit cards, but don't overdo it. The last thing we need is to start hearing about misappropriation of funds."

Each one of my friends shut up when she spoke. When she finished, they each nodded their head, gave me dap and got out of the limo.

It had always been like that, back since junior high school. SaTia was just one of those girls nobody wanted to cross. Straight from the ghetto, but everybody recognized she was going places. All the players would make excuses about why they wouldn't holla at her—but they all realized she was out of their league. If you gave her a pickup line, she'd either treat you like a cute puppy or like an idiot. Neither one did much for the male ego.

Imagine my surprise when in the ninth grade, she told me she'd fallen in love with my words.

"Why are they so afraid of you?" I asked my manager as the last of my friends jumped out of the limo. She ignored me, giving preference to her BlackBerry. The limo began to pull off, and had gotten to the end of the parking lot when the limo driver got my attention through the intercom.

"Umm...sir?"

"Yeah, what's up?"

"There's a situation going on with one of your colleagues."

SaTia and I turned around and looked out of the back window. From a distance, we could see Ray, Brian, and Henry all standing behind Orlando, who flailed his arms wildly while gesturing down to one of the shoes he had on. We could also see the guy yelling back at him, the five guys surrounding him, and the matching gang colors they were wearing.

"Here we go again..." SaTia put her BlackBerry down and became instantly angry.

"Let me handle this." The limo pulled back around to the scene as I rolled down my window. Orlando was still yelling fearlessly as his offender began to reach back into his jeans. Orlando followed suit.

"What, nigga? You think yall the only ones dat carry hammers 'round here? What you wanna do, nigga? Pull your strap on me, nigga, you better kill me!"

Ray, Brian, and Henry had crossed from uneasiness into a fear that none of them would ever admit, but loyalty held them in place. They each breathed a sigh of relief as I rolled back around.

"Yo, yo, yo! It's Da Nigga! What's good?"

"Yo, dat's Da Nigga? No bull? Yo! Yo, dat's Da Nigga right there!"

The gang members were caught between their bloodlust and being starstruck. I used the temporary lapse in tension to address my friend.

"'Lando, what da hell is goin' on, man?"

"Dis nigga stepped on my shoe!"

I looked at the guy, who still had his hands on whatever was hidden in his jeans, and looked back at Orlando.

"Did he do it on purpose?"

Orlando looked back at me like I belonged on the short yellow bus.

"What the hell is this, kindergarten? Who cares if he did it on purpose? He messed up my Air Force Ones! Niggas die for that back home, you know dat!"

"Yeah, but we not back home, 'Lando! We in Miami with platinum credit cards and weed dat smell like apple pie! Come on, man, we go through this all the time. Leave Southeast in Southeast! It's gonna be there waitin' for you when you get back."

Orlando was one of those people who thrived on confrontation, so he wasn't happy that I was ending another would-be shootout. I didn't care. I stepped out of the limo and faced the would-be gunman.

"Yo, on my strength, can we jus' dead this whole thing? My man get a lil crazy sometimes, Matter 'fact, here you go."

I looked around to make sure there was no one in uniform, climbed into the limo, and beckoned the guy to follow me. After he'd walked up to the door, I reached under the seat at the far end of the limo and grabbed a bag with two ounces of Purple Haze, the same weed we were smoking last night.

"I know my man acts stupid sometimes. This here's for yo' trouble."

Honestly, I thought he was going to start crying. Without a word, he put the bag under his shirt and walked over to his companions. After he got them to huddle around, he showed them what he'd been given and they all caught the holy ghost.

Orlando looked around, confused, before his light bulb turned on.

"Yo, I know you ain't just give 'em the cush!!!"

I turned swiftly and glared at Orlando, and then focused on Ray, Brian, and Henry behind him.

"Take him inside! Get him drunk, get him blazed, do whatever you gotta do, but make sure he don't start no more trouble!"

Grateful to still be alive, the three of them took a reluctant Orlando and went inside the mall. I jumped back into the limo with a chorus of gratitude behind me.

"Thank you, Nigga! Thank you, man! Thank you!"

Five minutes later, I was reading SaTia's mind as we were driving down the road. I decided to let her speak for herself.

"You need to get rid of him." She spoke matter-of-factly as she continued on her laptop.

"Come on, SaTia, he's like my brother. You know how many times we've gone to war together?"

"I don't care. It's just a matter of time before he gets himself into something that you can't get him out of."

"Look, I'll talk to him again tonight, aight? Now let's change the subject. What we talkin' 'bout at this meetin'?"

"Remember to reassure Mr. Rose about finishing the next album…" She said some other things as well, but I wasn't paying attention to her. We were the only two people in a rolling palace that must've comfortably sat twenty people, and tense situations always made me think of sex afterward. I began to imagine what the girls would look like who'd fill the limo seats later tonight.

"Moe! Moe, are you listening? Take your mind off your dick for a second and pay attention!"

I hated it when she read my mind.

"Aight, man! Okay! What is it?"

"I said, remember to tell Mr. Rose you'll be done with the album by next month. They're worried about you missing the deadline."

I showed SaTia the resentfulness I had yet to show Mr. Rose.

"To hell with them! Look, I'm the CEO of Deez Nutz Records. I make more money for these people than they can count. I'll put out an album when I wanna put out an album!"

Every once in a while, all the hype surrounding a celebrity goes to their head. They begin to believe they're invincible because it's their name people are screaming when they come to a concert or see them in public. This was one of those moments that SaTia called "lapses." She had long since taken it upon herself to be my wake-up call.

She stopped typing long enough to reach over and slap the back of my head.

"Shut up," she said as if she were teaching me a lesson.

"Why you…?"

"'Cause I'm not gonna keep preaching the same sermon to you over and over again, Moe!"

"What sermon?"

I already knew the monologue well enough to mouth it by heart, but it still pissed me off when she recited it. When you feel like you own the world, there's something piercing about someone telling you what you can't do.

She turned away from me and back to her laptop.

"I'm not gonna say it again."

"Why not? You never believed in me from the start, did you? You kill my dream all the rest of the time, you might as well go ahead and do it again now."

SaTia slammed her laptop closed. I could tell she considered throwing it at me. When she turned to me again, she looked like a bull preparing to charge.

"You are such an idiot! If I didn't believe in you, why in the hell would I still be here?"

I decided not to respond. Even when I was mad, I'd long since decided there was only so far I was willing to push this woman.

"I'm only telling you the truth, Moe! Deez Nutz is your crew. Brian, Orlando, Ray, and Henry—all dudes we grew up with who could rap. You got signed by Cosmos Records and Cosmos Records let you form Deez Nutz and bring your friends along, but they still own you. You signed a contract, Moe. Legally binding! When it's up, then you can talk about trying to do your own thing. Until then, you jump when they tell you to jump."

An image of Mr. Rose popped into my head. He was telling me to jump, and I was hopping from one foot to the other like a monkey. Eventually, he fell to the ground and started rolling with laughter.

"Forget that! Da Nigga don't jump for nobody!"

"You already have, Moe. You remember the first song you ever wrote? Back in seventh grade? You remember what it was about?"

Suddenly, I wanted the conversation to end. I looked at my childhood friend and shook my head, begging her to stop talking. I knew she wouldn't, though. That was never her style. I'd opened up Pandora's Box, and she was going to make sure everything got out.

"You don't remember, Moe? Huh? 'Cause I do. It was about Kia Morris, in the eighth grade. About how her dad had molested her and how she tried to kill herself. Remember you spit the lyrics for her and she started crying in the library? And then she asked you to do it again at the talent show. Nobody in the school knew what to say to her until you performed that song. You made everybody know how she felt. You remember that?"

I began to feel like SaTia had her hands around my neck. I rolled the window down to try and get some fresh air.

"You remember your second song? About the homeless guy who was always on MLK Avenue when we caught the bus home from school? Or the third one, about the slaves we had talked about during Black History Month? You remember any of those, Moe? 'Cause last I remember, Da Nigga's latest single was

'Hoes In Da Attic.' So don't tell me Da Nigga don't jump for nobody!"

I hit the intercom button and the driver answered immediately.

"Yes, sir?"

"Pull over!"

"Yes, sir!"

The limo cut sharply to the right and pulled up against the curb in a suburban area. Cookie cutter homes welcomed me as I bolted from the limousine cabin. Anyone who saw me jump out would've expected flames from the sunroof as well.

SaTia waited a few seconds after I had jumped out, and then followed me. I was sitting on the curb, coughing and trying to regulate my breathing when she joined me.

"I'm sorry," she said after a long silence.

Though I already knew what I wanted to ask her, I hadn't regained enough air to speak without wheezing. We spent another fifteen minutes just sitting there, waiting for my lungs to relax.

Once I ceased to sound like a fat man on a stair climber, I turned to her. As I opened my mouth, I wondered if she knew what I was going to ask. Better yet, I wondered if she knew how many times I wanted to ask her before. I spoke as though I was afraid of my own words. "Why are you still here, SaTia? If you're so disappointed in me, then why are you still here?"

She smirked and chuckled to herself. "You pay well."

"Yeah, I do, but that's not why you're still here."

She started looking around, taking in all her surroundings. I learned in middle school that was what she did when she was really thinking hard about something.

I can't even count the number of times I'd wanted to ask that question in the past, but I'd always been afraid of that moment. Of her looking around and thinking hard, and then looking back and realizing that she shouldn't still be here with me. She should've been off reuniting with the boyfriend she had in college or trying to earn her master's and doctorate degrees. She should've been off heading the missionary society of a church somewhere. There were a million and one other things she could've been doing with her life.

In fact, there wasn't one logical reason I could think of for her to stay. As my manager of three years, I was sure she had saved enough money to pay for tuition in any graduate program she wanted to go to, and even after that, she'd still have enough to live comfortably. And if she ever needed anything, I'd be happier to give it than she'd be to receive it.

This is it, I thought to myself. *She's going to leave.*

After what seemed like millennia, she finally turned back to me.

"I guess…I'm still here because no matter what you say in your songs, or how many of those ridiculous teeth you wear, or even how many women you sleep with, in the end, I still see the little boy rapping offbeat in seventh grade."

Her words raped me. I couldn't have been more penetrated in a jailhouse shower.

"I may be the last person on earth who knows who you really are," she added.

Men (urban men especially) have a whole repertoire of things we do to keep from crying. I pulled out an old favorite and bit down hard on my bottom lip.

"Excuse me, sir? Is everything okay?"

The driver had gotten out from his seat behind the wheel. He was younger than I expected. In another time he would have been called a half-breed or a mulatto. As it stood now, he was a pretty boy with good hair. He was obviously nervous about confronting me, but his curiosity had gotten the best of him.

I turned Da Nigga back on instinctively.

"Yeah, we good, man! Lil' bit a privacy'd be cool, though."

His embarrassment began to show through his cheeks and perspiration. Most of the time I never saw the full faces of my limo drivers, just the shot of their eyes reflecting in the rearview mirror when they were paying too much attention to the party in back.

I was known for giving my chauffeurs a story to tell the next morning.

"I'm sorry, sir…I…thought I heard you choking or crying or something…"

"Naw, youngin, you heard wrong. You musta smoked more than me dis mornin'. Go 'head and get back behind the wheel so we can roll out—we getting up right now."

"Yes, sir!"

The driver jogged back over to the driver's-side door and leaped in. SaTia looked at me and shook her head slightly. She debated in her mind for a half-second before she threw caution to the wind.

"I want to tell you something, but after I say it, you have to pretend like you never heard it. You can't ask any questions about it or anything. It was never said."

"Like we used to do in high school?"

"Yeah, just like that. Deal?"

I acted as if I was thinking about it, but I'd have given up a hit record to hear what she was going to say.

"Umm…yeah, sure. What's up?"

SaTia surveyed her surroundings again, and then turned her head and looked straight at me.

"At some point, you're going to have to decide whether you're Da Nigga or Moses Jenkins. When that day comes, I'll either marry you or quit."

She was back in the limo tapping away on her laptop before I closed my mouth. I had more questions than an insecure spouse, but I knew the rules all too well. She'd never said it. The words had never come out of her mouth. That's how we got away with telling other people's secrets in high school, and that's how she was getting away with torturing me now.

By the time I stood back up, I could see the driver getting antsy again. I didn't care. I slowly walked up to the door of the limo and climbed in like a sore tennis player.

"I hate you," I said.

"I know."

She gave me a quick glance, hit the intercom button, and put her focus back on her e-mail. The enthusiastic driver responded in record time.

"Yes, sir?"

"Hi...this is SaTia. I'm Da Nigga's manager. Can you get us to The Marbury restaurant as quickly as possible, please? We're late for a very important meeting."

"Right away, ma'am!"

As our chauffeur pretended he was behind the wheel of an ambulance, I pretended I wasn't sitting beside a person who could turn my world like a nauseous stomach.

I had thought a lot of things before SaTia and I walked into that restaurant, but there were two things I thought I was sure of. First, I thought I had been to some of the best restaurants anyone had ever seen. I figured that was one of the perks of being rich.

Ironically, that was the second. I thought I was rich.

I had never seen anything like The Marbury. It looked like a place out of one of those black and white movies where a man and woman always end up dancing the night away. The floors sparkled, the glasses sparkled, the cups sparkled, the plates sparkled—I couldn't figure out how someone could eat here and not be depressed by what they would have to go home to. All the waiters had skin colors that contrasted with their white tuxedoes. There was lady in a black gown playing the harp, and a man in a black tuxedo playing the piano beside her. Their skin colors contrasted with their clothes as well.

I saw the patrons talking to one another, but I quickly realized that they were all speaking a language I wasn't wealthy enough to understand. To me it all sounded like "*Moneymoneymoney? Moneymoney…Moneymoneymoneymoney.*"

I wondered if I'd ventured off to the bathroom, would I find unflushed hundred dollar bills floating in the toilet.

SaTia spotted Mr. Rose sitting at the back of the restaurant. She nudged my shoulder and motioned toward his table. He had a plate of culinary art sitting in front of him, and was focused on trying to eat as much of it as he could without ruining its beauty. After taking three steps in his direction, he managed to glance up long enough to notice our approach. His attention quickly shifted from his postmodern plate to the two urbanites coming his way. He stood up and spoke with a jovial seriousness.

"Nigger! Where have you been? I thought we were going to be able to eat, but we'll have to make this quick now. Come on here and take a seat!"

Sometimes people get killed for a reason no one ever finds out. You can question the person who did it for hours and hours, and even if they admit that they committed the murder, they won't tell you the reason. They'll get sentenced and go to jail and spend huge chunks of their lives behind bars, but will never tell you what motivated them. They won't tell you, because a lot of times even they don't know. A normal guy may have never had any interaction with a gay person, until one day he gets hit on by a flamboyant man in a miniskirt and blows his brains into his wig. Or a girl completely suppresses her memory of being raped until a drunken guy shoves his hand under her skirt and ends up with an ice pick in his larynx. Someone says or does something that touches an unknown, unforgiving button, and in the blink of an eye a college athlete or a petite secretary is standing over a dead body wondering what kind of computer glitch just altered their reality…

Standing there, in that restaurant, with billionaire couples smirking at the privilege of hearing a racial epithet in public, I found out I had a button that could be pushed. And if I had a gun, Mr. Rose would have died where he stood.

Rage glued my Nikes to the plush carpet and held me there. Just as I resolved to do something violent, SaTia leaned over and whispered to me.

"You chose the name, Moe. I told you from the beginning that a lot of white folks don't know the difference. It was bound to happen sometime." She paused and glanced up to see my top row of teeth sinking into my lower lip. "You better chill out. If you kirk out in here, you can kiss all your money goodbye."

I swear having her around was like having a walking reality check.

All the black waiters had paused just long enough to see how I would react. A black guy in urban clothing with dark sunglasses and a grill in his mouth had just been called a nigger in front of about thirty rich white people. Two of the waiters looked poised to dive onto the ground. They glanced from me and to one another, smirking at the possibility of an oppressor being massacred.

It was too late, though. The image of me back in the hood, broke, with a dirty wifebeater and a malfunctioning Tech-9 had sobered me up. SaTia's inconvenient truth had left me flaccid.

After a few seconds passed, each member of the serving staff took turns calling me an Uncle Tom with their eyes before they returned to gently placing beautiful cloth napkins on the laps of rich white people.

"Let's just sit at the table so you can calm down," SaTia said. "I'll do all the talking, you just pull yourself together."

We walked up to Mr. Rose's table and sat down in front of him. As he opened his mouth, I found myself again trying to tame the wild animal trapped inside of me.

"I assume you all got tied up back at the hotel? I guess when it comes to making stars, we know what we're doing, huh?"

He looked at me, expecting some sort of jovial gratitude. I just stared back at him, trying not to envision blood squirting from his throat.

Not getting the reaction he was looking for, his eyes betrayed the smile on his face. At that moment, I was nothing but an ungrateful nigger. I reached out for the salt shaker with the worst of intentions. Before I could even get a good grasp on it, SaTia reached over and took it out of my hand.

"Thank you." She smiled at me, but somehow whispered the word "stop" through her grinning teeth. Then she turned back to Mr. Rose. "I go completely postal if I don't have enough salt in my food, so he always makes sure I have it on my side of the table."

SaTia always pressed what she called her "inner white girl button" when we went to meetings with execs. She said she learned how to do it in college. It was more annoying than hearing someone scrape the end of a fork against a plate, but it worked. We always came out with more money, or the promise of more money, than we had before.

I could tell by the word "postal" that she had hit her button, but I was too angry to care.

Mr. Rose glanced suspiciously from me to SaTia, and then back to me. SaTia cut his thoughts short.

"Getting down to business, Mr. Rose, Mr. Jenkins has been very pleased with his success since signing with your company."

"Well, good. He doesn't seem like it at all."

"It's been a considerably hectic morning, Mr. Rose. I requested that he quiet his thoughts a bit before coming into this meeting. He's just trying to pull himself together. Oh...and by the way, Mr. Rose, Mr. Jenkins likes to be called Moe or Moses when he's dealing with business."

Mr. Rose glanced at me one more time. I kept the same stone expression on my canvas. He shrugged his shoulders and looked back at SaTia.

"Okay, fair enough. We're starting late, so let's jump right into it, shall we? How's the second project going?"

SaTia turned on her white girl excitement.

"It's going wonderfully! We're making progress quicker than we expected to. Mr. Jenkins has really learned a lot from the completion of his first album."

Mr. Rose nodded his head as he methodically picked apart the sculpture on his plate.

"Good, because we're going to need to kick up the deadline."

My righteous indignation went limp. "Whoa, what? You cain't just kick up the deadline without lettin' me know!"

"He speaks!" Mr. Rose chuckled to himself. I tried to grab at my butter knife, but SaTia had already moved it.

I looked over at her as she leaned forward, clasped her hands together, and stared directly at Mr. Rose, and I knew I had nothing to worry about.

The inner white girl button had been turned off again. Now she was just plain old SaTia.

"Mr. Rose, we discussed a clear timeline in our last meeting and agreed that the dates that were set would be permanent. May I ask the reason our previously agreed upon deadline is no longer sufficient?"

Mr. Rose finished chewing the food in his mouth before he answered. He seemed vaguely amused at her, but he was too smart to underestimate her.

"Riggs and Baker, the head guys at Infiniti, got wind of our scheduled release dates. They kicked up all of No Parole's rap LPs by at least a month."

SaTia started to respond, but I cut her off.

"But I outsell all them nigg...umm...bastards at No Parole! Cain't none of 'em touch me! Why I gotta move my stuff up 'cause of them?"

"They've got some new guys signed who are supposed to be pretty decent. They call themselves 'P.' Silencers, 'p' as in potato. Apparently they had quite a buzz around them in Idaho before hitting big."

SaTia and I sang out in unison, "Idaho?"

Mr. Rose smirked at our ignorance.

"Yes, Idaho. There is a hip-hop scene everywhere in this country, and in most places outside of it. Idaho is no different."

One of the waiters who had eyeballed me earlier now came and put water in front of SaTia and me. She picked hers up as she spoke.

"I'm still having trouble understanding how this affects my client?"

"It's a precautionary measure, Ms. Brooks. Just to make sure they don't get one up on us."

"And will Mr. Jenkins be compensated for this precautionary measure?"

"Of course. We recognize the extra studio and production time he'll have to put in, and we'll make sure it translates into cash. We'll even throw in a $100,000 bonus at the end of the quarter."

I didn't care if it was a wise man or a crackhead who first said it, but they're the truest words ever spoken—money heals all wounds. I raised my hand to signal for the waiter, and when he came around I gave him the biggest grin that the muscles in my jaw could manage.

"Yes, sir?"

I pointed to the almost empty plate in front of Mr. Rose. "I'll have whatever he's having."

"Yes, sir."

The waiter shot me another resentful glance as he left, and I smiled even harder. Mr. Rose laughed out loud.

"I see that put you in a better mood."

"You know it!"

SaTia kicked me under the table to tell me to get hold of myself, and I reduced my grin to a subtle smirk. Once she saw I was a little more composed, she looked back at Mr. Rose.

"Let's leave that $100,000 up for negotiation. I wouldn't want to agree right now, as we don't know exactly how hard Mr. Jenkins will have to work in order to meet his new deadline. We'll need to tie down specifics on exactly how this extra working time will 'translate' into cash."

Mr. Rose seemed annoyed and impressed at the same time. He sighed to signal that he was no longer amused.

"Agreed. As long as Moses does what is asked of him, we can negotiate the whole thing to your liking."

I could tell that SaTia and I had the same thought again. I decided it was best to let her speak.

"Exactly what is it that is being asked of my client, Mr. Rose?"

"Our plan is in two parts. First, we'll kick up the original deadline by three weeks, and release two singles instead of one for radio."

That would be easy for me. I had my first single done, and already had a song in mind that would be perfect for the second. I started to grin again, but I thought about SaTia and tried to stay calm. She kept her gaze drilled on Mr. Rose.

"I'll talk it over with my client, but that seems doable. What is the second part of your plan?"

Mr. Rose finished the last bite on his plate and slowly put his fork down. "The second part is a little more interesting…"

We glanced at each other out of the corners of our eyes. SaTia telepathically told me to shut up, but she didn't need to. I didn't trust myself enough to speak.

"Do tell, Mr. Rose." My spokeswoman was all ears.

"One of the main draws to this new group is that they are known for making battle records. We have an inside source who has informed us that their first single will be a battle record aimed at your client."

My instincts took over.

"Me? What? I don't even know these dudes!"

Mr. Rose suddenly sounded lighthearted.

"It's nothing, Moe. They're just some ex-cons trying to make a name for themselves."

SaTia almost knocked her water over.

"Ex-cons?"

Mr. Rose responded to her but kept his eyes on me.

"Yes. Apparently they met in jail and formed their group. It wouldn't be such a big deal, but you know how much a diss record can hurt a rap career. So, we would like for your second single to be a battle record against them."

"Absolutely not!" SaTia said adamantly, but Mr. Rose continued to look straight at me.

"Look, these guys are going to say all types of things about you. They've been asking people about you and getting information you would never think they could have. Girls you've slept with on the road, ex-girlfriends from D.C., old friends who are mad because you left them in the ghetto—I mean, these guys have been serious. They were going to surprise you with it—have you turn on the radio and here is this song tearing you apart—but we found out about it. We found out and now you have the chance to strike before they do!"

SaTia plucked me upside my head. She had been calling me, but I hadn't heard her. I finally turned away from Mr. Rose and looked her in the eyes.

"Don't listen to him, Moe. This is ridiculous. People get killed over this kind of stuff! We can find another label before we get involved with some mess like this."

I heard everything my best friend had said, but Mr. Rose's seed had already been planted. I was already having visions of people laughing at me when I walked onstage, reciting lines to someone else's diss record.

My pride wouldn't let me go through it. I turned back to Mr. Rose.

"How am I supposed to write a diss record against people I've never heard of before?"

"I've had my people look into them, and I have got enough

info to fill a college textbook. All you have to do is write the song and record it."

SaTia reached over and grabbed my chin, turning my head toward her. The show of affection even took Mr. Rose by surprise. His eyes went wide as he sat back in his chair.

"Listen to me, Moe. This is dangerous. People take diss records to heart. I...I don't like this..."

"Ahem..." Mr. Rose reached into his pocket and pulled out a CD case. "I was able to get a rough copy of the song. It's not mastered at all, but the words will be the same."

I looked back and forth from SaTia to the CD case. Finally, I stopped at SaTia.

"I'm gonna listen to it, okay? I just wanna hear what they say."

SaTia realized she had lost the battle. Her eyes dropped as she let go of my chin. After a few seconds, she took in a deep breath and lifted her eyes back up to Mr. Rose.

"Okay, if we do this, we are talking about a whole new level of negotiations. Scratch your bonus and try multiplying it by five, at least, in addition to hourly compensation for studio time and increased control over the production process for the entire album."

While she talked, I reached out and grabbed the CD case. This time, it was Mr. Rose's turn to grin.

"If this project is successful, you can have whatever you want."

I took the CD out of the case and played around with it in my hand.

Mr. Rose glanced at his watch and stood up. We stood up with him, and he took turns shaking both of our hands.

"Unfortunately, I have to catch a plane, but this has been a very fruitful meeting. Ms. Brooks, someone from HQ will call you within twenty-four hours. We can work out all the fine details the next time we meet. And please, stay and enjoy whatever you like from the menu, on me."

SaTia hid her distress well as she extended her hand.

"Thank you for your time, Mr. Rose."

"I'll holla at you later, man." My farewell was a bit less professional, but I had a lot on my mind.

We both turned and watched Mr. Rose walk away, then sat back down at the table. I could hear SaTia's disappointment in her breathing.

"Look, Tia, I think—"

"Stop. Just stop, okay? You're the superstar, and you made your decision. Can we please get out of here?"

"Yeah, let's go."

We stood up as the indignant waiter came around the corner with my dish. He placed it on the table as I was putting my sunglasses back on.

"You're not going to eat, sir?"

"Naw. Give my compliments to the chef, though. It looks like a million bucks."

I got one last distasteful look before SaTia and I walked back to the limo.

3

Why is every makeup artist that I've ever seen ugly? Isn't that some sort of conflict of interest?

I sent the text message to SaTia and the guys while a very scary woman tried to improve my countenance. She either got regular Botox, or someone had recently stuck her head in a freezer. Her eyes reflected emotions that her face simply couldn't show. I found myself imagining holding up a chisel and lightly tapping on her cheek. Her face would probably fall apart. Ray would walk in and think I dumped a puzzle on the floor.

Meanwhile, I sat in a chair that looked as if it was meant for a movie director and wondered if putting foundation on a man qualified him as being metrosexual. It couldn't, I thought to myself, because I was definitely not the first MC to ever be on a late-night talk show. Either Leno and Letterman only invited ambiguously gay rappers to sit on their couch, or I was in the clear and this was a necessary suspension of my manhood.

Orlando, Ray, Brian, Henry, SaTia and I had all arrived at the studio a half-hour earlier. Our days had been long since the diss record dropped. We'd been flying all over the place. I was doing TV interviews and performing in almost every major city in the U.S. This was the biggest primetime television opportunity we'd had, though.

About a month ago, I was sitting in my hotel room eating a bowl of Froot Loops when SaTia burst in with a grin on her face.

She told me the producers from the *Phil Winters Show* had just contacted her. They wanted to know if Da Nigga would be available to come to Chicago in five weeks and be a guest. *The Phil Winters Show* had been the number one late-night talk show on TV for over a decade. I almost choked on a loop.

These kinds of things had been happening regularly in the last eight months. I dropped one song, and all of a sudden I couldn't perform in clubs anymore because the crowds were overcapacity. I went from being recognized by four or five people every time I went out to having to wear a disguise and notify local police departments where I'd be going so they could have their squads on standby to deal with the mobs. It was insanity. Even my crew was changing. They'd caught the residual effects of my new-found superstardom, and had decided that they no longer wanted to be referred to by their real names. Instead, they always wanted to be known by their aliases.

"You're kidding me," I told them in the VIP section of a club in Dallas. "You want me to call all of you by your stage names? The only time you're even on stage is when you're with me!"

"We know, man," Henry said for the group. They had all seen how much pressure had been put on me lately, and they figured Henry would be the best person to approach me without getting me upset. "But with you being so famous now, people actually startin' to recognize us, too. Couple a times you did interviews and used our real names, and befo' it wasn't really no big deal, but now...well...I mean, you ain't got to if you don't want to, but we already said we was gonna start callin' each otha by our aliases, so we jus' wanted to know if you was down to do the same thing?"

Everyone was losing their minds. It seemed like the only sane person around me was SaTia, and even she had to admit that as long as nothing changed down the road, making the battle record might have been the best thing I could've done.

Lost in my own thought, I didn't even notice the porcelain lady stop what she was doing and glance over my shoulder. It took for an energetic voice approaching me from behind to snap me out of my daze. I looked up and into the mirror just in time to see Phil Winters prepare to slap his hand down on my shoulder. Even though he was over twice my age, his visage beamed with the vivaciousness of a teenager. I guess daily professional grooming and sex with younger women really is the fountain of youth. I turned my head to look into his eyes as he spoke.

"Thrilled, absolutely thrilled to have you on the show! What should I call you, huh? Should I call you Moe or 'Da N' or 'Da N-word', or what? Man, I swear you picked one helluva name!"

I had been getting this question a lot lately, and it was starting to piss me off. SaTia constantly told me I'd asked for it.

"You can call me whateva, man. Most white folk jus stick to Da N-word, though. Seem like y'all don't know the difference between nig-ga and nig-ger, so you're better off playin' it safe."

Phil vigorously nodded his head.

"I totally agree, totally agree! Is Sandy treating you okay?" He motioned to the lady with the frozen face. "She's a miracle worker with makeup. Makes me look great on my worst days…"

"Yeah, she's great," I said, as I glanced at Sandy. I could tell by her eyes she didn't care what I said one way or the other.

"Great! Listen, I'm so glad we got you on while the dissing record is still hot! It's been lighting up the airways for months now!"

I laughed to myself and shook my head. "It's called a diss record, Phil, not a dissing record. Anyone who knows anything about rap is gonna laugh at you if you say that."

Phil immediately yanked a notepad out from the inside pocket of his designer suit. He scribbled the note down, said it once out loud to himself, and then slipped the pad back into his pocket.

"Got it! Won't make that mistake on the show, I promise! And just so you know, I'll probably ask you more questions about the record tonight than anything else. Is that okay with you?"

"Yeah, it figures. Just make sure you push the new CD."

"Already covered that with your business manager, and everything's under control. Is there anything else you need? Anything at all?"

"Nope, I'm good."

"Wonderful! See you on the set!"

He slapped me on the shoulder again and briskly walked out, leaving Sandy and me to an awkward silence.

"I can finish up if you like." She talked with so little enthusiasm that I started to get sleepy.

"Yeah, that'd be good."

She made her way back over to my face and began wrapping up her masterpiece. Five minutes later, SaTia burst through the door.

"The show's starting, Moe. He's gonna call you out in ten minutes. We need to be in place."

I glanced at Sandy again, and this time she gave me a slight smile. It looked like it hurt.

"We're all done here," she declared with indistinguishable triumph.

"Thanks, Sandy," I said as I got up. She nodded, and turned to gather her equipment as I walked out with my manager.

"The set is this way," SaTia said and pointed to the right as we began speed walking. "I've already run down what he can and can't ask you, but it sounds like most of his questions will be about the record."

"I know, he told me."

"Just be careful what you say, okay? The record is out and it's done its job—there's no use in rubbing it in."

I could hear the concern in my best friend's voice.

"You not still worried about those fools, are you?"

"Just be careful what you say, okay?"

We approached an open doorway with a curtain in front of it, and two men who looked like the guys on the runway at the airport. One pulled off his headphones and turned to us while the other kept up a conversation over a walkie-talkie.

"The stage is on the other side of this curtain. You'll be coming on from the far right, and the camera will be on you from the time you emerge until the time you sit down with Phil. This is live, so please no profanity or lewd comments. Have a great show."

SaTia nodded at the stagehand and then turned to me. "I'll be waiting back here during the interview. If something goes wrong, I'll come out during the commercial break. Otherwise, see you when it's over."

I had the urge to kiss her. I always had the urge to kiss her before I went onstage, like just in case someone was waiting in the crowd with bad intentions, at least I got one in before I died. Instead, I did what I always did, which was nod at her. She nodded back, and took two steps behind me.

The ground controller began a silent countdown with his hands. When he got down to seven I took a deep breath and checked myself. My jeans and Washington Wizards jersey were on point, my Jordans were fresh, and both my chain and my grill were bright enough to power a solar vehicle. I was ready.

Three fingers…two fingers…one finger…

The guy extended his arm out toward the curtain and I walked through.

I wasn't expecting people to be so excited about seeing me. I'd always thought late-night talk shows were for rich, white insomniacs, and I figured the most I'd get was a modest applause before I made my way to the couch and sat down.

Instead, there was this huge roar that seemed to originate from everywhere. It started when I came out from the curtain, blinded by the stagelights and waving to people whose faces I couldn't make out. It was like a huge, deafening tidal wave.

By the time I made it across the stage and was sitting down beside Phil, the room seemed to be split down the middle. One side was simply yelling and cheering, while the other side was chanting my name like a mantra.

"Da Nig-ga! Da Nig-ga!..."

It took a while for Phil to quiet everyone down, but he managed to do it without breaking a sweat. We both took a seat, him behind the same desk that his nightly fans were so used to, and me on the comfortable loveseat beside it.

Phil spoke with the same energetic tone he always used.

"Well, I guess we know what side all the black people are sitting on in the audience, huh? I imagine that most of your white fans don't feel comfortable saying your stage name."

Even as I sat in front of a nationally televised audience, time seemed to freeze for a second.

The truth was that he was probably right. Now that I had reached this new superstar status, there had been this big thing about who could and couldn't say my stage name. Every white person I met acted like Phil back in the dressing room. They were terrified of saying "Da Nigga." There had even been a news report done on all the white guys who got punched in the face at my concerts for screaming it after the show.

Because it was causing so much controversy, the execs consulted an outside publicist. Mr. Rose (who, after my new album went platinum, told me to just call him Rose) called SaTia and me in one day and told us he had called in Lois Lane.

"Who?" I was high, so I figured I was trippin'.

"Lois Lane," Rose repeated. "She's the best PR consultant in the business."

"Is that her real name?" SaTia was documenting the meeting on her laptop.

"It might as well be. They call her that 'cause she's such a tough cunt she's probably the only woman who could survive screwing Superman."

She walked in the door just as he'd finished his sentence, and I couldn't contain my laughter if you'd paid me. That's a downside to being toasted and trying to do business.

SaTia elbowed me so hard I thought I'd see blood on my next trip to the bathroom, but I couldn't stop. When Lois sat down, she looked at me with my head thrown back, laughing like Heath Ledger in white face paint, and then looked at Rose.

"Told him why they call me Lois Lane, huh?"

"Yep," he said with a smile.

"I apologize for my client," SaTia started. "He's..."

"Oh please." Lois waved her hand nonchalantly. She was a middle-aged white lady whose skin had wrinkled before it was supposed to. Cigarettes had scratched up her throat like a DJ did a record. Her voice sounded like steel nails methodically grinding against sheet metal.

"I've had dreams about it. Give him a second to compose himself. I have to run to the restroom, anyway."

I had stopped laughing when she returned, but only because I'd exhausted myself. Turns out, that would be the only thing funny about our meeting. She proceeded to advise Rose, SaTia, and me that whenever possible I should deny the racial divide that my stage name caused.

"Always tell the camera that you know plenty of white people who feel comfortable saying your alias."

"Does it matter that I don't?" I inquired sarcastically. She answered seriously.

"Not at all. People expect to be lied to. Especially by celebrities. At the end of the day, your standpoint should always be that racism doesn't exist in this wonderful country anymore."

"Hell naw. Look, I know you a hotshot and all, but…"

I still had my mouth open from the sentence she wouldn't let me finish.

"But nothing!" She slammed her palm down on the cherrywood table. I was prepared to put on a spectacle for being disrespected, but when I looked up Lois was staring at me like there was a countdown to the rapture and she was trying to bring me to Jesus.

"I'm sure, Mr. Jenkins, that you're aware of the fact that the largest demographic of people buying your music is young white kids. And believe me, the last thing a white person wants to think about while zoning out to music is whether or not they're a racist. You make this statement and you neutralize the situation. Your record sales have already gone through the roof, but if you do this, they'll go through the stratosphere."

I didn't even have to look at SaTia. Lois had barely finished her sentence before she spoke up.

"My client WILL NOT compromise…"

This time, Rose cut her off.

"Ahem…umm…look, we know that this is a very sensitive situation. We feel, however, that this strategy will be lucrative for everyone involved." As he spoke, he gestured to Loen and Mytino, the other two execs who had just walked in the room. I used to call both of them Mister, too, before my new record sales.

"In fact, Moses, we've already drawn up the paperwork for a healthy bonus for you—provided that you stay within the lines of certain public relations boundaries. Of course, we would never force you to say or refrain from saying anything, but…well, the choice is yours."

Now all that past conversation had faded and I was back on the set of Phil Winters' show. He was staring at me, showing his artificially whitened teeth, and waiting for my response.

"Actually, Phil, I got plenty white fans who say my name all the time. You probably got a bunch of 'em in that all-black section you was talkin' 'bout. Plus, you forgettin' the Latinos and Asians and anybody else who digs my music. They probably in that all-black section, too. Maybe we could cut on all da lights and see who sittin' where…"

Phil Winters could have a conversation about Armageddon and still keep a smile on his face. This little conversation about race was no different. It was interesting to watch him keep his cheekbones high and his pearly whites showing, but it wasn't a surprise. The surprise was from looking in his eyes up close, during this conversation, and seeing the fear flash through them like the lights on top of a police car.

"No, no, that's not necessary," he said.

The host still had his smile, but he couldn't hide the red cheeks and forehead.

"Bottom line is—" I began to get heartburn as I was talking, "—I don't believe we got no more racism in America. All dat stuff was back in the past, man."

Phil Winters broke character for about a half a second, and looked at me completely shocked before he caught himself and put his smile back on. Clearing his throat, he took in a deep breath and kept going.

"So…getting down to business, you've had an amazing couple of months, have you not?"

He was desperate to change the subject, as was I.

"Yeah, most definitely. Last few months have been crazy."

"Can you tell us how everything got started?"

He was talking about the diss record, but I saw an opportunity to be coy. I couldn't pass it up.

"Well, it all started back when I was eight, and I heard my first rap song on the babysitter's radio..."

I could hear the chuckles from the crowd. Winters smiled at the lighthearted joke.

"As much as we'd all love to hear your life story, I was talking about your musical career. Specifically, the record you made that had such a big impact on the hip-hop world. What is it called again?"

I had to smile slightly as I recounted the name I'd given the song.

"Piss On The Silenzas."

Phil leaned forward and rested his chin in his palm.

"And we know who it was about, but tell us the story of how it came to be."

"Well, I got word one day that Trigga and Barrel were makin' a diss record 'bout me..."

"Trigga and Barrel would be the two members of P. Silenzas, right?"

"Yeah, yeah, dat's them."

"And who did you hear about their diss record from?"

"Some of my inside sources let me know 'bout it."

"Care to share any names?"

I gave Phil a look and shook my head. Not wanting to break the momentum, he picked back up with his next question.

"Okay, so, you decide to make 'Piss On The Silenzas.' Did you know when you were making it that it would be such a huge hit?"

"Naw, I had no idea. I mean, it just took off. Label put it out as a single, and it was curtains from there."

"What do you think made it such a big hit?"

I paused for a second to think.

"It was all 'bout the timing, Phil. They was getting ready to release their first single, which happened to be 'bout me. Matter-of-fact, my label was so slick wid it that we got my single put out the day after their single came out. Made it seem like we was sittin' back waitin' for these niggas to make da first move."

"And the name of their single—and I know we can't say the real name on the air—but the title of the song they made...?"

"'B-word Nigga' was the name of their song. Don't worry, Phil, I'm not gon' cuss on ya show. I'm not tryin' to get you in no trouble."

"Well, I appreciate that. Why do you think they named their song that, though?"

"Well, I'm Da Nigga, so I guess maybe they was tryin' to be creative. Somebody shoulda told 'em they was messin' with da wrong one."

"Well, I would guess that they know that now. We're going to show a quick clip from the video..."

"Oh, really?"

I wasn't expecting for them to show any clips, but I didn't have a problem with it. A large screen came out of the floor and rose up behind us. I saw Phil begin to turn, so I turned around and faced the screen as well. As it turned on, I immediately recognized the portion of the video that the clip was starting from. I bent over on the loveseat and started laughing. Phil looked at me and smirked. "You still get a kick out of seeing the video?"

I had gotten control of myself, and was wiping my eyes with my shirt sleeves.

"Hell yeah. This is classic stuff right here."

The lights faded slightly and the video began to play.

I was dressed in baggy jeans and a black hoodie that had "Silence these nuts" written on the front of it. The word "nuts" was blocked out by one of those boxes that distorts the image it covers. The scene took place in a jail, and I was standing outside of a cell while two men were on the inside petting and caressing each other. The words rang out across the studio…

Y'all some bootyhole rappers
Dick in da booty trappers
Y'all n***as drop da soap on purpose
And laugh after
Got up outta jail
Tried to battle da best rapper
Man, they ain't tell you?
I'll hang you from da rafters
Keep talkin'
Watch I put ya face through da pavement
Make you pay for da damages
And put it in my savings
It's basic
You n***as is pussies
So just face it
Came from outta nowhere and failed
Like Sarah Palin…

By the last four lines of the song, it seemed as if the entire audience was reciting the lyrics word for word.

"Wow…" I couldn't hide my shock as the lights came back up and the screen that was behind us lowered back down into oblivion.

Phil looked back over at me.

"Are you surprised that the audience knows the song so well?"

"Yeah. I mean, you would think I'd be used to it by now, right?"

The talk show host leaned forward and crossed his hands on top of his desk.

"This is how someone explained this whole phenomenon to me…well, wait…would you agree that it's a phenomenon? Your instant rise to superstardom, I mean?"

I leaned forward to meet his gaze.

"Real talk, Phil? Look, I thought I was big before. I thought I was already a superstar. But now, with this diss record—man, it's a whole other world. I cain't think of no better word for it than a phenomenon."

"Okay, good…so here's how someone explained it to me: no matter how peaceful and civilized people try and make themselves out to be, in the end those same people want to see some conflict. And it had been a really long time since rap music had any serious conflict. Small little arguments here and there, yeah, but this thing between you and P. Silenzas has gotten serious. There have been some death threats involved, correct?"

My entire demeanor changed. I shifted back in my seat, rubbed my nose with my thumb and pointer fingers and let my head hang to the side a bit. It wasn't purposeful, but my street instincts kicked in—never show fear.

"Whateva, man. Niggas just mad 'cause I ruined they career. They ain't 'bout to do nothin'."

"Do you feel as if they have a right to be mad about how things have turned out?"

"At themselves, maybe. Ain't no use in bein' mad at me when you was da one makin' battle records in da first place."

"That's a good point—they did start it. But you most definitely finished it. I mean, after your record, they couldn't perform anywhere without people reciting your lyrics. People would even call in to their radio interviews to tease them. And, of course, we all know how it turned out. The final indignity."

"Yeah, we do. They couldn't rap noways. They was gonna get dropped from that label no matter what. I just sped up the process."

"So you do admit that you played a role in P. Silenzas getting dropped from their label?"

"Look, I'ont know what the conversations sounded like on that end, 'cause I ain't signed to that label. What I'll say is the same thing I been sayin' since the whole thing started—if I ruined anybody's career, then I ruined the career of two fluke rappers who wasn't goin' nowhere to begin with."

"Well, I guess there's…"

"YOU A DEAD MAN!"

Our heads shot around so quickly, you could hear the wind breaking. I knew where the voice was coming from, but because of the stage lights shining on us, I couldn't see anyone in the audience. Phil stood from his seat.

"Who is that? Security!"

"YOU A DEAD MAN, NIGGA! YOU HEAR ME? I SWEAR TO GOD, YOU…"

I heard what could only be described as a ghetto warrior cry come from Ray or Henry, and then the sound of a grown man colliding with another grown man. They must have landed on or around some other audience members, because two ladies screamed out simultaneously, after which it sounded like nine or ten full rows of people jumped out of their seats to avoid what was happening. As the seconds rolled by, the commotion grew exponentially.

It was the two gunshots that sent everything into utter chaos.

"CUT THE FEED!!!!" I heard someone in charge yell out. Almost immediately, the screen attached to the main camera that had been recording us cut to those multicolored bars that show on public broadcasting channels late at night. The lights came up just in time for me to see three different security guards try and pick a man up from under the stomping feet of Brian and Orlando. I would find out later that Henry was the closest to the guy and had run headfirst into him. After being knocked down, the assailant managed to climb to his knees, take aim, and fire a shot at the stage before Henry pulled him back down again. The gun went off a second time as they were rolling around on the ground. Henry was bleeding from his right arm, and Ray was trying to get him some help while the studio audience rushed out through two different emergency exits like a stampede.

That's when it occurred to me that in the thirty seconds that the whole ordeal had taken place, I hadn't moved. I was frozen in fear. My eyes darted back and forth wildly, but my body wouldn't budge. Even Phil had ducked to the back after the feed was cut, but I might as well have been super glued to the loveseat. I felt like George Bush on 9-11. My heart was bursting out of my ribcage and I was wheezing to catch my breath, but I sat like a statue until I saw SaTia sprint down the aisle and leap up onto the stage.

"LET'S GO!"

As she grabbed my hand, the invisible weights fell off my legs. We bolted back through the curtain and the door that I had come through to get to the stage, and then found the side door backstage that led to the garage. The Maybach driver was singing a Whitney Houston song aloud. He choked when we jumped in the car. SaTia couldn't have cared less.

"Get us out of here!"

Still trying to clear the saliva from his windpipe, the driver nodded to show that he recognized the request. Wheezing, he floored the gas in the extravagant car and left the most expensive tire tracks anyone has ever seen.

4

Rose, Loen, and Mytino traveled around a lot, but their main offices were located in Chicago. Loen and Rose had grown up in Chicago, and they'd met Mytino at the University of Illinois. When they dropped out to form Cosmos Records, they started out in Loen's basement, and then moved into a run-down office space on the outskirts of the city. As Cosmos grew, so did their venues, until they finally decided to buy a building in the Business district and make it their headquarters. They had satellite offices in Miami and Los Angeles, but all of the major decisions came from an extravagant structure in Chicago's Loop.

Luckily, it was only about ten minutes away from the television studio where I'd almost been shot.

The lobby looked like an upscale piano bar minus the alcohol and piano. The furniture was all postmodern and perfectly matched the dark marble floors. There were 50-inch, high-definition televisions on either end of the space, and a glass waterfall that took up most of the west wall. Each of the twenty-three floors above the lobby were just as exquisite and each dealt with a different aspect of Cosmos Records' business. The second floor was dedicated to marketing and retail. The ninth was for production. The eleventh floor was where all the lawyers' offices were, and the twentieth was dedicated to staff meetings. I, as well as most of the other employees, had been on every floor up to the twentieth. I had been in the building dozens of times and never knew the building went up any higher. As far as I was concerned, the building ended at the twentieth floor. The night that SaTia and I jumped out of a screeching Maybach and knocked over three security guards on our way in the building, I found out otherwise.

"Where is Rose?" My manager slammed her hand down on the desk so hard that Lisa's—the receptionist—stapler fell onto the floor. The security guards started after us once they'd gotten up, but one of them recognized me and signaled the other two to leave us alone.

Lisa's eyes were closed and she'd had headphones on when we'd burst through the door. She'd been mouthing her favorite Beyoncé song and had no idea what was going on until SaTia scared the beautiful nightmare out of her.

"Wha...umm...what...what's the matter?" Lisa fumbled to take the headphones off of her ears while trying to compose herself.

"Just get Rose down here! No...you know what...just tell me where he is so we can see him!"

"Umm...I'm so...I'm sorry...I don't think Mr. Rose is here."

Adrenaline and fear will make you do some insane things. My crazed companion shot her hand across the desk and grabbed a handful of Lisa's blouse before I could say a word.

Truthfully, I couldn't have stopped her if I tried. The sprint from the Maybach and through the guards to the front desk had left me feeling as if I was having an asthma attack. Now I was bent over with my hands on my knees.

"I know he's here!" SaTia had just about picked Lisa up off of her feet. She brought the receptionist close enough to her face so that they could feel each other's breath. "I talked to him earlier, and he said he'd be here watching the interview. Now you get on the phone and you FIND OUT WHERE HE IS!"

By this time I was standing up, and I saw Lisa's face turn cue-ball white before a figure appeared in the shadow behind her.

"Mr. Jenkins...Ms. Brooks..."

I immediately recognized the Spanish accent. Carmen, Rose's personal assistant, stepped out into the light. Her voice was firm yet sultry, and it was tailor-made for her body. She stood upright and proud, and was completely business-like, despite her blouse being slightly low and her skirt teasingly high.

"Mr. Rose has instructed me to show you to his quarters."

We must have looked like we'd just stepped out of a tornado. SaTia's makeup was smeared, her hair was all over the place, and part of her jacket was ripped. My chain had snapped at some point between the studio and here, and was hanging open around my neck like a dead snake. My Wizards jersey was turned around backward, and I'd lost one of my Jordans.

Carmen brought a sense of calm back to the situation. SaTia released Lisa's blouse and attempted to straighten her own hair. I turned my jersey around, took off my broken chain and stuffed it into my pocket.

Lisa managed to calm herself down and not cry.

SaTia had turned back into her usual self, and muttered an apology to the traumatized receptionist as we followed Carmen into an area of the lobby that neither of us had known was there. The way the space behind the receptionist's desk was set up made it look as if there was just a wall, but in reality there was a long corridor that appeared to be a dead end. Carmen placed her finger on a groove in the wall. It miraculously lit up, and before we knew what was happening, opened up to a lavish secret elevator.

Any other time, SaTia and I would have been amazed, but after barely escaping a gunman and a television-studio-turned-death-trap, we weren't really in the mood to be awestruck.

As usual, my companion spoke for the both of us. "What the hell is this?"

"It's the elevator to Mr. Rose's private quarters. He's waiting for you."

Once we had stepped inside, Carmen pulled out a keycard and waved it in front of a blinking red sensor. There were three buttons to the left of the elevator door. One was marked with the letter L, one with R, and the last with M. Carmen hit the button marked R and then stepped out.

"You're not coming up with us?" SaTia wrinkled her forehead.

"No. He wants to speak with you alone," she said, standing motionless in front of us until the doors to the elevator closed.

The universe paused for the eight seconds that it took to get to the twenty-second floor. My cohort was silent, and the soft ride of the cabin as it ascended the floors caused me to close my eyes and inhale deeply. When I exhaled, it was as if someone had calmly whispered in my ear.

"Someone wanted you dead tonight."

I felt ice get stuck in my spinal cord. My heartbeat sped up and my chest struggled to expand. My breathing became audible.

My sidekick turned to me just as my knees were getting weak. "Moe, are you okay?"

By the time the elevator door opened, I was sitting on the floor with my head between my legs, panting like an overweight dog. SaTia was rubbing my back and telling me to calm down. When Rose saw us, he jumped up from his chair.

"What the hell happened? He didn't get hurt, did he?"

"I think he's having a panic attack...help me get him to the couch!"

Rose ran over and grabbed my right arm as SaTia kept hold of my left, and together they dragged me over to the chaise that sat by the window.

If I hadn't felt like I was dying, I'm sure I would've noticed the penthouse suite I was in. It was one whole floor of a twenty-three-story building. The only walls in the space were the four that made up the perimeter of the room. It looked like an indoor football field, with Oriental carpet instead of turf and with elaborate tapestries covering most of the space. A huge marble desk sat at the front of the room with a touch-screen HD monitor on it. Two huge oil paintings seemed to watch over the desk like bodyguards on either side, and sitting in the middle of the room, in direct line of sight from the desk, was a huge, white marble sculpture of Napoleon Bonaparte. On the east side of the room there was a Jacuzzi made of the same dark marble as the desk, and a king-sized abaca bed made up with silk linens. On the west side there were nine 62-inch, flat-screen plasma televisions. They were set up on the wall in rows and columns of threes, so that together they formed one huge rectangle. Rose could either watch the one of the televisions in the rectangle, or have the entire group form one huge picture.

As of now, all of the screens came together to form an image of an attractive woman reporting in front of the Phil Winters' studio building. The headline "Gunman Targets Rapper" ran across the bottom of the screen, while "Breaking News!" flashed in big, bold letters across at the top.

"Put your head between your legs again, Moe. It might help."

SaTia spoke softly, but couldn't hide the worry in her voice. I sat on the chaise between her and Rose, wheezing like a chain-smoker on a treadmill. I bowed my head and grabbed both of my ankles to try and get some relief.

"Ms. Brooks, for the love of God, what happened tonight? One second Moe's having a great interview, and the next there's gunshots going off and the footage is cut."

"There was a man in the audience with a gun," she said while rubbing my back. "He took a shot at Moe. The guys tackled him before he could do anything else, but I think Henry was hit."

"Do you think this has anything to do with P. Silenzas?"

SaTia jerked and stared thumbtacks at Rose from her eyes. It was as if someone had given her a booster shot of resentment. "What are you, some kind of idiot? Of course this has to do with P. Silenzas! This has everything to do with those fools! I told you in the beginning—people like them don't play! They don't have the same concept of right and wrong as you and I do! But all you care about is money! You sit up here in your little palace, and you throw money at people to get them to do what you want! And then, when reality comes back to bite and someone almost gets killed, you act as if you had nothing to do with it!"

"Now wait a minute, Ms. Brooks..."

"No. No, I will not wait a minute. You shut up and listen!"

I was still hyperventilating, but I managed to look up at SaTia as if she'd lost her mind. She walked around me and stood in Rose's face.

"My best friend was almost killed tonight because you threw so much money at him he couldn't turn it down. I blame you for this, and so help me God, you had better find a way to make this right. If he gets hurt over this foolishness..."

I wasn't looking at them, but the last time I'd heard my manager's voice reach this tone, she'd ended up pulling a girl's weave out.

"End this crap, and end it now," she barked.

My breathing was starting to slow down, and I looked up again to see my short, black friend staring down the tall white man. If I was an artist, I'd have painted a picture.

"It's...it's not that simple, Ms. Brooks..."

Rose's phone rang loudly from the top of his desk. He was all too happy to run over and hit the speakerphone button.

"Ahem...yes, Lisa, what is it?"

"Mr. Rose..." Lisa's voice sounded strained and timid. You could hear male voices in the background.

"Yes, Lisa, what do you want?"

"Ummm...three of Mr. Jenkins' friends are here in the lobby. They're asking for him and you both, and they seem pretty excited. One of them has blood all over his shirt. What should I do?"

Despite my condition, I jumped up to my feet. SaTia helped to steady me before I fell back down, while Rose closed his eyes and paused for a second to think. When he opened them again, he spoke into the phone. "Send them to the twentieth floor and tell them to wait in the conference room. We'll be right there."

"Yes, sir."

Rose clicked the button off on the phone and motioned to the elevator. "We can take it down to the conference room."

I followed slowly as he walked toward the elevator doors. SaTia was right behind me, making sure I was okay. When we arrived, Rose pressed the button and the doors instantly opened. As we stepped inside the cabin Rose made a parting request. "Very few people know about my quarters up here. I'd like to keep it that way."

"I couldn't care less who knows about your little shag pad up here, Rose," SaTia said as the elevator doors were closing. "I'd like you to finish what you were saying before—something about how it's not that simple to get my client out of all the foolishness you've gotten him into."

Rose took a deep breath, got his wits about himself, and then turned to face SaTia.

"Ms. Brooks, Moe is an adult. I am not his father, and more importantly, you are not his mother. I am sorry that things have gotten so complicated, but the bottom line is that Moe was made an offer by the company and he accepted it. Because of that acceptance, he's made more money in the last couple of months than any of us thought possible. Maybe he regrets the decision now, at this very moment, but he's been fine over the last eight months, and when all this blows over, he'll remember that he's one of the highest paid rappers in the business, and he'll know that all this was worth it."

She-Hulk wanted to come out of SaTia, but this was no low-level receptionist that my manager was impaling in her imagination. This was one of the CEOs of Cosmos Records.

SaTia stood unmoved with her fists balled, breathing sulfur out of her nostrils.

Once Rose realized the short, brown-skinned woman recognized his power the same way everyone else did, he relaxed his shoulders and began breathing easier.

"You know, I've always been intrigued by cultural differences when it comes to the concept of responsibility. It seems only logical to me that if you are upset about a decision that was made, you would direct that concern to the person who made the decision."

"You son-of-a—"

The elevator doors started to open and cut off SaTia's would-be profanity, and the ensuing chaos wiped away any traces of the previous conversation. Brian, Orlando, and Ray had made such a scene when they came into the building that the same three security guards that SaTia and I had run into followed them up to the twentieth floor. They'd exchanged words on the elevator, and consequently, Orlando had tried to swing on the tallest one while the head guard called two more up for backup. When our elevator doors opened, we saw eight grown men trying to give each other concussions.

When they saw the three of us, they all froze like ice sculptures. SaTia and Rose spoke simultaneously.

"Get in the conference room."

"Get back to your posts."

They scattered like moviegoers after a bomb threat.

I had regained most of my strength by this point, and wanting to look strong in front of my entourage, I led the way into the conference room. Though the security guards were gone, Ray, Brian, and Orlando looked as if they were still in the middle of a fight.

Brian yelled out loud first.

"Yo, we gotta get dem niggas, Moe! We gotta get dem niggas, for real!"

"Who—the guards?"

"No! Man, forget dem guards, they was pussies anyway," Ray cut in, jumping up and down. "I'm talkin 'bout P. Silenzas, man! Dem niggas gotta get dealt wid!"

For the first time, I realized that only three of my crew members were in the room with me.

"Where's Henry?"

"Dat's what I'm sayin', man!" Ray continued to hop around like a pissed off bunny. "Henry in da hospital, dogg! Orlando got through to da back while dey was workin' on him. Dey was tryin' to keep us out, but 'Lando got in and heard 'em fo' hisself. They said he got hit in one'a his arteries and he lost too much blood on the way to da 'mergency room. He in a coma!"

"What?" I would've preferred another panic attack to the way I felt when I heard those words. I couldn't decide if I wanted to throw up or pass out. Instead, I jumped out of my seat for the second time in ten minutes.

"He in a coma, dogg." Orlando scared me. He wasn't jumping

around or pacing or anything. He stood up from the wall with this cold look in his eyes and evil in his voice. "Laid up like a vegetable, dude. And I'ont know 'bout none'a y'all niggas—" He walked up to the table in the middle of the room and pulled a 9mm handgun out of his pants. "—but I'm tryin' to ride on dese niggas tonight."

He put the gun down on the glass table in front of him and kept his hand on top of it as he looked up at each of us. "What's up?"

"Whoa!" Rose and SaTia jumped back from the table.

"Hell yeah!" Ray pointed to the gun on the glass table. "Dat's what I'm talkin bout!"

"Let's lay dese niggas on the sidewalk!" Brian walked around the room, slamming his hand against the wall.

I stayed in my seat, looking at Orlando as if I was trying to pinpoint the part of his brain that had stopped functioning properly.

"What the hell are you doing?"

"Oh, so what? You Mr. Hotshot Famous Rapper now and you cain't ride for yo' homies no more? Yo' man sittin' up in the hospital half-dead and you cain't take no action? All dis fame done made you some kinda pussy?"

Without thinking, I walked over to the table, picked up the gun, turned it around in my palm so that I was holding the barrel, and smacked Orlando across the face with the handle.

"Nigga, don't you ever call me no pussy again! I could give a damn 'bout yo' lil gun! You forget who da hell you talkin' to? I'm Da Nigga; you wouldn't be nothin' without me! Nothin'! Everything you got, I bought, nigga! I'll beat da bricks off you!"

Orlando spit blood from his mouth onto the floor and looked up at me with unadulterated contempt.

"So you can pistol whip me, but you cain't go after da niggas who 'bout killed your man? Aight, Mr. Moses Jenkins, let's see how many bricks you beat off me when I get dat gun back…"

At that moment, I decided to quit everything. Doing shows, making music, interviews, I was going to quit it all.

Somehow, in only one day, a man had tried to kill me, one of my best friends was in a coma, and now another of my best friends had threatened my life. And it all related back to being in this godforsaken business. It was only one night, but that was all it had taken. It was too much for me to bear.

"I can't do this anymore..." I started.

Rose cut in before I could finish.

"Alright, look, everyone needs to calm down, okay? Moe, give me the gun so I can check to see if there's a serial number on it."

I still had my eyes nailed on Orlando as I slid the gun down the table.

When Rose got it in his hands, he examined it briefly.

"Ms. Brooks," Rose said. SaTia shook herself out of the trance of watching two best friends get ready to come to blows. She turned toward Rose. "Do you think you could continue to add some common sense to this situation? Moe put his fingerprints on this gun. I need to go and make sure it disappears."

Aligning herself with him would have been out of the question in any other situation, but she recognized the severity of the moment. She gave him a slight nod, and he quickly got up with the firearm and headed to his quarters. As soon as he was gone, SaTia turned back to us. "So, I guess it's time to pack up our stuff and move back to the ghetto, right? It was fun while it lasted, fellas. Hope your careers were worth it."

Orlando wiped some more blood away from his mouth with his wrist.

"I'ont care what dat nigga..."

SaTia turned to him instantly and stuck her finger in his face.

"Shut up! You shut up! What kind of idiot shows his gun off in front of a record executive? And what did you all think you were gonna do?" She looked back and forth between Ray, Brian, and Orlando. "You were gonna go ride for your nigga, huh? You got no proof that P. Silenzas had anything to do with what happened tonight. And even if you did, so what? Did you think you were gonna ride three blocks and pull a drive-by? They're not even in the same state as us! We're in Chicago, you dummies! They live in Idaho!"

"I'ont care where dey live at!" SaTia's insults had turned Orlando's anger to madness. He stood up and got into her face, cocked back his arm and swung.

Instinctively, I ran up behind SaTia and pushed her out of the way, putting myself in the trajectory of Orlando's fist. He missed us both, and as SaTia caught her balance from my shove, Orlando and I both stared at each other.

Turns out it was providence that had Rose take that gun upstairs. If Orlando had hit SaTia, I have no doubt I would've shot him.

No one said it, but we were all thinking the same thing. Orlando knew it, and felt the need to respond.

"All I know is dat my mans is in the hospital, and somebody gotta pay fo' it."

He sneered at me as he spoke, as if he already had a plan. I stood solid in front of him, looking him straight in the eye.

"Yo, 'Lando, dis is crazy, dude..." Brian said from the corner. "Ain't nobody in here cap Henry, man. Why you so mad at Moe?"

"'Cause Moe a punk!" My newest enemy answered Brian while still staring at me. "He won't ride, dat's why! Long as we been homies, and dis nigga won't ride! It ain't all dat surprisin' though, when you think 'bout it. We been dis nigga's slaves since we left D.C.! We cain't even take a piss without askin' dis man 'toilet or urinal?'"

Ray stood up beside Brian.

"What is you talkin' 'bout? We don't ask for nuthin' when we out here. Moe hook us up wid everything! Yo, real talk, you wildin' out. You need to be easy…"

For the first time since I stepped in for SaTia, Orlando broke his stare and looked back and forth between Brian and Ray. After a few seconds had passed, he took a step back from me and glanced around the room.

"Forget all y'all." He seemed disoriented as he spoke. "Y'all can keep on bein' dis man's field niggas if y'all want to, but I'm out."

Just then Rose emerged from around the corner. He looked like he had been rushing to get back.

"The gun will be taken care of," he said, looking directly at SaTia and me as he spoke. "And I just got off the phone with the hospital. Henry is stable, but still in a coma."

Anger is the only emotion that can make you oblivious. I was so angry with Orlando that I hadn't had the time to soak in the fact that Henry was in a coma. Now, with my partner-turned-nemesis having retreated, I sat down at the table and put my hand over my face.

"We should go back and see him," Brian said softly, but SaTia pounced on him anyway.

"Really? I thought you wanted to go bus' some caps?"

"You ain't funny."

Twenty minutes later, we were all standing in the lobby. Rose had one of his drivers give us a ride to the hospital, and the security guards from earlier were more than happy to hold Orlando until a cab arrived. I stood in front of the traitor and looked him in the eye one last time before we went down to the garage.

"Gimme my card."

He paused for a second, then reached into his pocket and pulled out the platinum Visa I had given to him and everyone else. I reached out for it and he threw it on the ground.

Rage requires energy, which I was all out of. I took two steps, picked up the card, and gave it to SaTia.

"What about the cash you gave him earlier?" she asked.

If it was up to her, I'd have left him naked on the sidewalk. I briefly looked at her, and then back over to Orlando. "You can go to da hospital, you can go home, you can go to a strip club wid sexy midgets and a one-eyed bouncer for all I care. And you can keep the two g's I gave you earlier. Dat ain't no money to me, homie. But come tomorrow, you gon' wake up in some nasty motel, laid up wid some nasty broad, and you gon' realize it's all over."

I turned to walk away, but the image of me picking his Visa card up off of the ground compelled me to leave one last thought. I turned back. "And you might wanna think 'bout how you gon' break dis whole thing to yo family, seein' as how you got 'em livin' all large off of my money. How much is your lil sister's tuition these days?"

He tried to keep a straight face, but his eyes betrayed him and began to gloss over. I had no remorse as I turned to walk away. I couldn't forgive Orlando for what he tried to do to SaTia. Emotions were high and had he merely threatened me, maybe there would have been a possibility of forgiveness. Where we're from, you fight with your boys all the time, and in the end it only makes you both stronger. But had I not been there, he would have put his fist through SaTia's jaw. There was no coming back from that.

When SaTia, Ray, Brian, and I reached the garage level and stepped out the elevator, the driver was already seated behind the wheel of a Cadillac Escalade. I guessed by the clean frame and the new-car smell of the interior that it had never been driven before. As we pulled out of the parking lot, the chauffeur behind the wheel adjusted his rearview mirror. When I looked up, he was staring right at me.

"I don't know if you're aware, sir, but for the past two hours there have been news reports running about the incident."

SaTia, Brian, and Ray all looked at me, then each other, and then back at me. I could tell they really wanted to see the news reports. Neither of them said a word, though. They knew how fragile I was.

"If you like, I can put them on, sir."

I rubbed my forehead, trying to search through the fog in my brain for an answer.

"Yeah, lemme see 'em," I said after awhile.

The driver hit a button on the information deck and the screens on the back of each seat's headrest came on. The female news reporter's voice echoed through the vehicle.

"Once again, we have breaking news that tonight, here at the Phil Winters' studio in Chicago, Illinois, a lone gunman attempted to shoot rap superstar Da Nigga, aka Moses Jenkins, while he was being interviewed live. Initial reports said that the rap star had been shot and was in critical condition at the University of Chicago Hospital. However, we now have it confirmed that the patient admitted to the hospital was Henry Baldwin, aka Hard-Knock, a member of Da Nigga's entourage. Reports say he was shot while trying to subdue the gunman and lost massive amounts of blood on his way to the hospital. In addition, fifteen studio audience members were rushed to the hospital with injuries sustained during the pandemonium. Three of them were trampled by the mob of people trying to escape, and are also in critical condition. Witnesses had this to say…"

The screen cut to two disheveled women, visibly traumatized by what they had experienced. Both women were in tears and one was close to hysteria. The more sane of the two women hugged her friend closely as she talked.

"…it was horrible, oh my God, it was horrible! We thought we were going to die! People were punching and kicking and screaming at each other, and when you looked down all you saw were people…you couldn't get out without stepping on the…oh my God, forgive me…"

A paramedic broke into the interview and ushered the two women away from the camera and toward an ambulance. The woman reporter's face appeared back on the screen.

"The whereabouts of Moses Jenkins, aka Da Nigga, are unknown at this time. Witnesses say they saw a luxury Maybach automobile speed away from the scene, however no one can confirm where the automobile went. Authorities say it's too early to call the situation a kidnapping, but many have already speculated that this attack was the work of the P. Silenzas, a rap group with whom Jenkins was feuding before their record deal was cancelled. We caught up with Reginald Bankhead, aka Trigga, one of the members of P. Silenzas, who had this to say…"

The scene cut to Trigga sitting in an old lawn chair outside of a dilapidated public housing project. He had put on every piece of jewelry he could find. The light from a leaning lamppost reflected off of his platinum chain and grill as he spoke. He looked like an oxymoron. A hesitant white reporter stood beside him and spoke into a microphone.

"Mr. Bankhead, do you have any idea who attacked Moses Jenkins tonight in Chicago?"

Trigga turned to the reporter and took his sunglasses off. "No, but I hope dey blew his f***in' head off."

For ten seconds after he said that, Trigga just stared into the camera. He didn't move, he didn't talk, and he didn't blink. His dark, cloudy eyes jumped right through the television screen at me. I felt like I was in a horror movie.

Finally, the reporter cut back in.

"Okay...thank you, Mr. Bankhead."

The lead reporter, now standing in front of the hospital, came back on the screen.

"This story keeps developing by the second. We've now received word that Moses Jenkins, aka Da Nigga, is no longer missing, but he's actually en route here, to the University of Chicago Hospital, to see his friend, Henry Baldwin, who sources now tell me has fallen into a coma as a result of his blood loss."

"Aww, what the hell!" I threw up my hands, wondering if things could get any worse.

"Rose called in to the hospital security to let them know we were coming." SaTia talked as she picked up her cell phone. "The idea was to sneak us through the cargo entrance to avoid contact with the public. Someone from security must have leaked that we were coming...hello, hospital security?"

Someone on the other end of the phone gave her a positive answer.

"I need to speak with the head of security now, please. This is an emergency."

She waited about five seconds before another voice came through the phone.

"Hello, this is SaTia Rosewood. I am Moses Jenkins' manager. He and I, as well as two colleagues, are five minutes away from the hospital, and we've just heard a news report announcing our arrival to the public."

She waited another two seconds while the head of security fired off curse words.

"Unfortunately, one of your security personnel must have leaked our arrival to the media. Mr. Jenkins is still very concerned about his friend; however, and so we need to know if there is any way possible we can still enter the hospital without causing a disturbance?"

This time, my manager listened and nodded her head. When the voice on the other end of the phone was done, she thought for a moment before responding. "Can you do it in five minutes?"

Quick answer from the other end of phone, and SaTia exhaled deeply.

"Okay, let's stick with that as the tentative plan. We're pulling up in a black Cadillac Escalade. If things look like they're going bad, I'm taking my client and leaving."

One more quick answer, and SaTia hung up.

"He says there are cameras and reporters everywhere—even at the cargo entrance. Our best bet is to just come through the front door. The local police department keeps units on standby for the hospital, so he's calling them now. The local PD plus the hospital security should be enough to keep things under control. If it's not, we're leaving."

I shook my head. "No, we not."

Everyone in the car looked at me. Even the driver fixed the rearview mirror so he could see what I was about to say.

I looked at SaTia. "No matter what, we not leavin' til I see Henry. I gotta make sure he's okay."

"Moe, you saw the news reports. You saw how crazy it got at the *Phil Winters Show*. Now, you have to trust me, okay?" She spoke softly, like a doctor does with a child before giving them a needle. "There are people out here trying to kill you. If I say it's bad, then we have to leave. It's not worth it."

I never took my eyes off of her as she spoke. She was trying to protect me, to do for me what I had done for her back at the office, but it didn't matter.

"No," I said. "We leave after I see Henry. Period."

She wanted to argue about it some more, but also realized that would be pointless. It was rare that I trusted my own judgment over hers, but the few times I had I was stubborn in my convictions. She turned her gaze to the front windshield.

"We're coming up on the hospital now," the driver said as he stopped at a red light. "I can see the television vans and lights from here. Looks like it's going to be crazy."

SaTia looked over at me again, pleading for me to change my mind with her eyes.

I looked at her and then back at the driver. "It's all good. Ain't nuthin' we ain't used to. They said they was gonna have the cops here anyways. Jus' pull up to the front."

The driver nodded his head and waited for the light to turn green.

"Even if da cops ain't here, Moe, you know we got yo' back," Brian said from the backseat. "Like you say, it ain't nuthin' we ain't used to."

As we pulled into the hospital entrance, I saw vehicles from television channels that I didn't know existed. A mob of men and women, armed with oversized television cameras and high-quality microphones adorned with media insignias, stormed the luxury SUV like a swarm of angry bees. Fortunately, the police cars had arrived before we got here, and they jumped into action. Putting their sirens on, they broke through the mob until they reached our vehicle, and then led us to the front door. As soon as they had stopped, both the police officers and the hospital security rushed out to the truck. The head of security opened the rear door and poked his head in. He looked directly at me.

"It's a madhouse out here, but we're all set up to get you in to your friend's room and back safely. It's up to you if you still want to go in."

I nodded my head. "Let's do it."

"Great. Give us thirty seconds and then come on out."

When I opened the door, the officers and security had formed a perimeter around the Escalade. None of the reporters or fans were close enough to touch me, but the onslaught of flashing lights and screaming voices took me back to the *Phil Winters Show*. I couldn't shake the idea that one of the couple hundred people standing around me could easily take out a gun, aim it at me, and pull the trigger.

The terror was crippling. It blurred my vision and muddled my hearing. My eyes darted from side to side again. Questions from the different reporters came so quickly I had trouble distinguishing one from another.

How did you get away from Phil Winters' studio?

Were you injured in any way during the incident?

How did you find out that Mr. Baldwin was injured?

Do you take responsibility for the incident?

Do you believe this was the work of the P. Silenzas?

How big of a role do you think your battle record played in the events of tonight?

Was tonight worth all the fame and fortune that you've gained over the past months?

I found myself sprinting to get inside the building.

Luckily, the cops and security had been well-trained. Without a word, they sprinted right along with me.

I was breathing heavily once we finally got inside the hospital doors. SaTia was standing alongside me while Brian and Ray were pulling up the rear. None of the camera crews had been allowed inside the actual hospital. I glanced back and saw them smashed against the sliding doors, one on top of another, flashing pictures and screaming into their microphones. I felt like I had gone through a gauntlet.

"Mr. Jenkins?"

A middle-aged doctor with olive skin and a turban stood in front of me. His white coat and stethoscope announced his professional standing, but I couldn't help thinking of the two men who ran the 7-Eleven back home. His accent enveloped his words. Trying to understand him was like trying to hold a conversation underwater.

"My name is Dr. Ahmed. I am told you have come to see Mr. Baldwin?"

I couldn't understand him. "Umm…did you ask…"

"Yes," SaTia thankfully cut in. "We are here to see Henry Baldwin."

"Very good," Dr. Ahmed responded. "Follow me."

My mother always hated going to hospitals. She would send the sick people from her church get-well cards and flowers, and call and pray with them every night, but she would never actually set foot in the hospital. Walking through the intensive care unit of the University of Chicago Hospital allowed me to understand her reservations. The whole ward smelled like sickness and death. It filled up your nostrils and lungs but wouldn't let you cough or sneeze it out. It just enveloped you, reminding you that somewhere in your immediate vicinity was a person who was more than likely going to die soon.

As we approached Henry's room, I bowed my head and prayed silently that he wouldn't be among that number.…

The lines and tubes that ran from his body and back to the machines made him look like an urban cyborg. He lay motionless in the hospital bed, his mouth partially open because of the tube that was running down his throat. A little box beside his bed beeped every time his heart pumped, and the sheets were pulled down just enough for me to see the huge bandages and gauze on his upper left arm.

SaTia couldn't contain her shock. She placed her hand over her mouth and tightly grasped my hand, cutting off the circulation.

"Oh God...oh my God..."

The hospital room took all of our energy and sent it out through the vents in the ceiling. We had to grab onto something to make our way to one of the seats. Ray's breathing became audible as he fumbled around in dismay. Brian walked over to him and put a hand on his shoulder. He spoke with glassy eyes. "You gotta stay calm, my nigga. You gotta be strong."

I realized as I sat in that room that the power I thought I had was really no power at all. Chart-topping songs and sold-out performances don't bring people out of comas. It took for me to finally be as rich as I'd always wanted to realize that there are things money simply couldn't buy. My helplessness tugged on my tears, and I wept silently.

Dr. Ahmed addressed us from the foot of the bed.

"When Mr. Baldwin was brought in, he had lost approximately 35% of his blood, and had gone into hypovolemic shock. We gave him multiple blood transfusions and other fluids to get him stable, but since that time he has not regained consciousness or been able to respond to pain, light, or sound."

Ray still seemed shaky, but he spoke up. "So what all dat mean?"

"It means that he is in a coma. Right now we do not know how long it will last. It could be a few hours, or a few days."

"But…" Brian's voice rocked back and forth as he spoke. "But… some people don't never wake up from dey comas, right? Some people stay like dis till dey die, right?"

Dr. Ahmed looked like he was having as hard of a time understanding Brian as I was having understanding him.

"I am sorry, I don't…"

SaTia took an exasperated breath. "Isn't it true, Doctor, that in some cases, people never wake up from their comas?"

"Oh, oh yes, that is true, but this condition is very unpredictable. Many coma patients awake within a few weeks. You have to take it one day at a time."

Dr. Ahmed waited a few minutes. When none of us presented any more questions, he walked over and picked up his clipboard.

"Either myself or one of the other nurses will be coming in regularly to check on Mr. Baldwin. If there is anything you need, please let us know."

None of us spoke as Dr. Ahmed left the room. We all stared at our friend, watching his chest rise and fall as if he were taking a nap. I kept thinking about the times growing up when all of us would daydream about becoming big rap stars. Now that day was here and one of us could die because of it.

It was then that I knew, sometime before I left the hospital, that I had to talk to Henry alone.

The ringing of my iPhone sharply broke the silence. I reached for it to turn it off, but looked at the screen and realized it was my mother. I got up and walked out of the room. One of the police officers waiting outside the door followed me as I paced the hallway.

"Hello?"

My mother's voice was three octaves higher than usual, and she sounded as if she was ready to jump through the phone. I could hear the news reports echoing in her background, as well as Big Mama asking her if she'd finally reached me.

"Moses? Oh my God, are you alright? They've been talking about a man trying to kill you!"

I've had friends whose mothers could never get through to them, no matter how much they tried. That was never the case with Tisha Freeman. As a child, all I had to do was hear her voice, and all my emotions would come pouring out.

As much as I'd like to deny it, the situation hadn't changed very much. I heard her fear and terror through my cell phone, and it was all I could do to make it to one of the seats in the waiting room before I dropped my head and sobbed bitterly. My mother's voice was a hurricane, and the levees that were holding all my feelings from the past several hours at bay broke at once.

"Baby? Baby, are you okay? Oh my God, please tell me you're okay..."

I couldn't even put a coherent sentence together. My body convulsed and shook, and my tears and mucus combined with each other before falling off my face in a straight line to the floor. I found myself struggling to catch my breath, inhaling five or six quick times before I could exhale once.

Hearing me cry so intensely and not knowing what was going on made my mother hysterical. For all she knew I could be on the other end of the phone bleeding to death, and I didn't have enough control over my weeping to let her know I was unharmed. I heard Big Mama talking to her, and when that wasn't enough, Big Mama took the phone and spoke to me herself.

"Moses...Moses, is that you, son?"

I couldn't answer her, but she could hear my lamentations.

"Moses, I need you to settle down, sweetheart. Me and yo' mama gotta know what's goin' on with you. We's worried sick over this way, baby. Jus' calm down enough jus' to let us know if you okay…"

Hattie Jenkins was a rock. If hearing my mother caused me to break down, then hearing Big Mama made me pull myself together. I took three or four deep breaths, and forced words out through my lips.

"I'm…I'm fine, Big Mama. I'm not hurt…I'm fine…"

"Okay, now get back on with your mama and talk to her, okay?"

"Yes, ma'am."

She gave the phone back to my mother. "Baby…"

I took another deep breath.

"I'm okay, Mama. I'm not hurt…I'm okay…"

"Oh thank God! Thank God!"

She began crying again, this time out of relief. I took the time to compose myself as best I could. After I had wiped my face with my jersey, I repeated what I had said a moment before.

"It's okay, Mom. I'm not hurt."

"But…but that man—he tried to shoot you?"

"Yeah, yeah, he tried to shoot me."

"But he didn't hurt you, right?"

"No…no, he didn't…"

Satisfied that I was safe, I could hear my mother's voice and demeanor begin to return to normal. I knew Big Mama was standing beside her, too, giving her strength through her presence. Mama cleared her throat before she spoke again.

"How is everyone else? Is it true what they're saying about Henry?"

I wiped one of the remaining tears from my right eye.

"It's true. We're sitting here at the hospital now."

"So…so he's in a coma?"

"Yes, ma'am."

Mama stopped talking to me for a moment. I heard remnants of a prayer coming through the other end of the phone. Out of habit, I closed my eyes and prayed along with her. When she was finished, she resumed our conversation.

"So what are you all gonna do now?"

It was a question I hadn't really thought about. I shook my head as I answered. "I don't know, Mama. I mean, all I can think about right now is Henry."

"I know, sweetheart, I know."

We were both silent for a few seconds, but I knew my mama well enough to know that there was something she wanted to say.

"What is it, Mama?"

I could hear her breathing on the other end, contemplating her words. Finally, she threw caution to the wind. "I want you to come home, baby."

"What?"

"I want you to come home. Things have gotten so crazy since all this rivalry mess started, and now, with everything that happened tonight, I think you should come home."

I began to get agitated, though I would never let Mama know. I had a million and one things on my mind already. I didn't need one more.

"Why, Mama? Why would I come home now?"

"I mean, it's safe here. Everyone loves you. You could have a police escort everywhere you went, if you wanted to."

"But I've got interviews and events scheduled for the next six months…"

"And you don't think you need some sort of break? Especially with everything that happened tonight?"

My agitation faded. I couldn't answer her. I honestly didn't know what I needed.

"Look, Moses, your grandmother agrees with me. You need a rest. You need to be around people who love you. And we haven't seen you in so long, sweetheart…just…please, think about it, okay, baby?"

It's funny, I hadn't thought about what life would be like after I woke up tomorrow morning. All I could see was tonight. And now that I was forced to think past the next few hours, I tried to delude myself. I tried to make myself believe that when I woke up tomorrow it would be business as usual. But that wasn't the case. I couldn't even walk into the hospital without being terror-stricken.

Mama and Big Mama were right. I had to get somewhere where I felt safe.

"Okay, Mama, look…let's see what happens with Henry first, okay? If he pulls through, then I'll clear everything and come on home to D.C. But right now, he's my first priority."

"Of course, baby, of course. I'm so glad to know you're coming."

Her grin beamed at me through the phone.

"Nothing is definite yet, Mama. We gotta see…"

"I know, I know…let me get excited though, okay? My son might be coming home!"

SaTia came around the corner. I could tell she was looking for me.

"Mama, look, I have to go, okay? I'll give you a call tomorrow to let you know if anything changes."

"Okay. I love you, Moses."

"Love you, too, Mama. Good night."

"Good night, baby."

I ended the call on my iPhone and stood up. The police officer that had come with me prepared himself to move again.

"SaTia, I'm right here."

She turned her head and saw me as I began to walk toward her. She had a hard time hiding her concern.

"Where did you go?" she asked.

"I was out here talkin' to Ma' Dukes. What's up?"

She stared hard into my eyes, noticing the mist from my emotional breakdown a moment ago.

"Are you okay, Moe?"

"Yeah, I'm fine."

I could tell she wanted to push the issue, but she let it go.

"We're all in the room trying to decide how the rest of the night is going to go. Ray and Brian can barely keep their eyes open, but you know they're not about to make any decisions without you."

"Aight, let's head back then."

We walked silently back down the hallway to Henry's room. The cop stayed two steps ahead of us, making sure that anyone who recognized me was hesitant to try and interact. I did my best to make sure the mist in my eyes that SaTia had seen was gone when I reentered the room.

"Yo, you good, dogg?" Brian opened his eyes and sat up in his chair, shaking the cobwebs out of his brain. "You was gone for a minute. We ain't know where you was."

"Yeah, I'm straight." I went back to the seat I was in before and plopped down. "Moms was on the phone trippin' 'cause she saw the news reports. Had to let her know things was all good."

"Yo, we ain't mean to pass out, Moe." Ray was pulling himself up from dozing off as well. "Jus' that it's been a crazy day, dude. You don't even realize how tired you is 'til you fall 'sleep an don't even know it."

They were right. The day had seemed long even before I'd even stepped foot on the Phil Winters' set. Now that the adrenaline from the shooting had passed, my friends were fighting a losing battle. Even SaTia's eyelids looked weighed down.

"Look, y'all niggas go back to da hotel."

"Hell naw!" Brian seemed offended that I would even suggest that they leave me.

I got up and walked back over to the door where the police officer stood guard.

"Homie, how long you gon' be out here keepin' watch?"

"As long as you're here, sir. My assignment is to keep you safe as long as you're in the hospital."

I nodded my head and went back inside.

"Look, the cops is gon' be here as long as I'm here. I got some personal stuff I need to talk to Henry 'bout anyway. If he gon' die 'cause he took a bullet for me, then I got some stuff I need ta tell him. Y'all niggas ain't gon' do nothin' but go to sleep anyways, man. You, too, SaTia."

My manager looked at me as if I'd just cursed at her.

"Ain't no reason in you stayin' here, is all I'm sayin'. All y'all go back to da hotel, get some sleep and come back in the mornin' fresh."

I looked at all of their faces. None of them were buying it. But I needed to be able to think, and I needed Henry to know how sorry I was, and I wouldn't be able to do either with SaTia and the guys around.

I changed the tone of my voice from apologetic to adamant when I spoke up again.

"I know y'all don't like it, but that's what I need to happen tonight. Go back to the villa and come through in the mornin'. I need to be here alone."

It was an historic occasion when SaTia showed chinks in her armor, and tonight her face almost made me change my mind.

She didn't speak but her eyes begged me to let her stay. Ray and Brian stood up and walked over, gave me dap, and waited by the door. SaTia continued to stare at me, pleading silently. Maybe she felt as though she needed to stay to protect me, or maybe she didn't feel as protected without me. The night's events could provide evidence for both. Either way, I was standing my ground.

"I'm sorry, but I gotta do this by myself."

When she dropped her eyes, I knew she'd accepted it. I got up and walked over to the officer outside the door again. "Yo, weren't there two of y'all?"

"Yes, sir. The other officer is posted by the elevator."

"Aight, thanks."

As I walked out of the room, my three companions followed me. I rounded two corners and there was the other officer, standing by the elevators.

"Yo, can you make sure my people get back to the car safe? The driver should be waitin' in the garage."

"Yes, sir."

I nodded at him, and then gave Ray and Brian dap once more as the elevator opened. SaTia was standing in front of me, waiting for some type of gesture to show that she still had that unspoken place in my heart. I couldn't think of anything else to do, so I hugged her.

Most people think of kissing as the physical interaction that ignites passion between people. The first kiss is always the one people scribble about in their diaries and get weak in the knees over. But when someone who you're actively in love with squeezes themselves into you so tight that your chests expand against one another's as you breathe, and then refuses to let you go, it sets off a different kind of reaction in your body. It was like having an orgasm without being touched in your sweet spot.

I had no words when we separated, only a deep breath that took the fragrance of her perfume and pumped it through my body like lifeblood.

"I'll see you tomorrow," she said as she stepped onto the elevator. Our eyes were still locked as the doors closed.

Unfortunately, her being out of sight reminded me that one of my best friends was lying in a coma. The switch from ecstasy to grief was physically painful. I held my chest as I walked back.

"You okay, sir?"

The officer in front of Henry's door had seen me dealing with the discomfort. It had almost faded by the time I got to him, but he still made sure everything was in order.

"Yeah, yeah, I'm good. Jus' some lil chest pains…"

He went to open the door for me, but I stopped him.

"What's your name, bro?"

"Jones, sir. Officer Jones."

"I 'preciate you watchin' out for me, man."

"Not a problem, sir. Just doing my job."

"You married, Officer Jones?"

"Yes, sir. Eight years next month."

"Tell you what…" I reached into my pocket, pulled out my money clip, and took out seven or eight hundred-dollar bills. "Tell ya' wife I'm sorry for takin' her husband for the night. Get her somethin' nice and take her out to dinner on me."

Officer Jones was a good man. He tried hard not to look at the amount of money I was giving him. When I put it in his hand, he put it straight in his pocket.

"Thank you, sir."

I nodded at him, and then went back in the room. I immediately regretted my decision to send everyone home. I felt naked, standing in there by myself. My feeling of helplessness was now a garment, covering me from head to toe. I started to panic, and sat down in the seat that SaTia had occupied. Her perfume still lingered in the air. It caused my muscles to relax.

I had to do this. One of my best friends could be nearing death on account of me. I owed him this much.

I took the chair with SaTia's scent on it and moved up alongside Henry's bed. I sat down close enough to lay my own head down, but instead I crossed my hands and lay them on the mattress. Someone walking in would have thought I was preparing to pray, and in a way I was.

"'Sup, Henry. This is Moses…" I took a second to gather my wits so I wouldn't lose my nerve. I put my forehead in my palms and then took my hands and ran them down my face, turning my head from side to side like I was looking at people who weren't there. When I looked up though, I still saw the same comatose Henry.

I figured there was no use in stalling for any more time.

"They say that sometimes people in a coma can hear people talking to them, even though they can't respond. I don't know if you can hear me or not, but there's somethin' I gotta tell you. Just in case…well, just in case we don't get to talk again. I want to tell you that I know why you did it. I know why you went after that guy with the gun. You did it 'cause…'cause you think I'm something I'm not. You did it 'cause you believe I'm a hero. All these people come yellin' and screamin' wherever we go, sendin' fan mail and passin' out at the concerts, and somewhere along the line, you began thinkin' that maybe I was worth savin'. But the truth is, I'm not. The truth, man, is that I'm just a slave. As long as they pay me, I do what the white folks at Cosmos tell me to do. I'm in it for the money, dogg. Point blank. Period. It ain't about the people in the ghetto and it ain't about the struggle. It's about the money. But I never thought…"

I turned my head away. Even though his eyes were closed, I couldn't look at him. My voice cracked as I tried to speak again.

"…I never thought anything like this would ever happen, man. I swear. It was all supposed to be fun and games. I get my four best friends together and we all go ballin' from state to state. I record some albums, do some shows, do some interviews, and make more money than any of us had ever seen in our lives. What nigga don't wanna keep himself and his mans iced out, huh? And we find dat sticky in ev'ry city, homie! E'rywhere we go, we blazed—and we da flashiest niggas around, right? Ha ha!"

When I realized I had been laughing, I thought I'd lost my mind. My smile slowly dissolved into a sea of confusion. I had to go inside my head and separate reality from fantasy before I could keep talking.

My friend was in a coma, and I was sitting beside him trying to figure out if I was alive or dead myself.

"It wasn't worth it, Henry." I could tell my sanity was back, because my words felt like needles. "None of this, none of it was worth it. I took it too far, homie. They threw some money at me and I jumped into this beef headfirst. You lyin' here in this bed 'cause I couldn't turn down a bonus. You lyin' here 'cause of my greed. So you see? That's why you gotta wake up, man. 'Cause I'm not worth givin' your life for, dogg. I never was."

My words exhausted me. I leaned forward and lay my forehead on the edge of the mattress.

Before I could whisper, "I'm sorry," I was asleep.

5

"Yo, I just had this wild dream, cuz. Yo, wake up, man, I just had this crazy dream…"

Coming out of a deep sleep makes the world seem like a damaged CD. Before you awake fully, everything scratches and skips, and you can't really tell whether you're coming or going. Add waking up in a strange place to the equation, and you run the risk of being downright delusional.

I felt my head and shoulders shake before I actually opened my eyes and I found myself wondering what was going on. I didn't smell the fresh hotel linen scent that I was so used to, and I was fairly sure that I was bent over the edge of a bed instead of lying flat on a pillow.

Either something wasn't right, or I had gotten seriously wasted last night.

Still, I wasn't fully awake yet. I tried to ask where I was, but my words came out as a mumbling mess. Someone was still pushing on my head and shoulders, trying to wake me up. I blindly reached out a hand to push the person away, but they persisted.

Annoyed, I finally lifted my head up. Everything was in doubles for a few seconds, and I couldn't make out the person in front of me. I looked around and realized I wasn't in a hotel room at all.

"Where…where in da hell…"

My vision started to clear. I saw the chairs and all the medical equipment, and memories from last night started to come back in small drops. I was in a hospital...*Phil Winters Show*...guy with a gun...Orlando went crazy...I was in a hospital...

And I looked up to see Henry sitting up in his bed, staring back at me.

Olympic long jumpers have never been airborne as long as I was. I jumped clear across the room, knocking over two chairs and a small table.

"WHAT THE HELL? WHAT THE HELL, HENRY? WHAT THE HELL?"

A nurse outside heard the commotion and came into the room.

"Is everything okay, Mister...Oh my God, he's awake!" She ran out of the room, yelling out loud. "Dr. Ahmed, Dr. Ahmed, come quick! He's awake! Baldwin is awake!"

I still had my back against the window on the opposite side of the room. Henry looked at me as if I'd sprouted a second head and was singing a duet, and I returned the gaze.

"What's up with you, man?" Henry always spoke with his eyebrows cocked upwards when he was confused about something. "Why you actin' all funny? And..." He stopped mid-sentence and looked at his garments, and then hesitantly looked around the room. He tried to hold his arms up, but the pain from his gunshot wound shot through his left one. He screamed out.

"What the hell is wrong with my arm, man? And why am I in da hospital?"

Dr. Ahmed burst into the room, followed by another doctor and three different nurses. They all seemed to be stampeding toward Henry, who instinctively jumped out of bed. I winced as I watched his face. It contorted like a cartoon character in slow motion. He'd forgotten about his arm just that quickly. As soon as he got both feet back on the floor, he used them to collapse beside the bed, pulling one of the machines that was attached to him down to the floor with a crash.

The doctors and nurses all ran over to help him, but he had used his one good arm to pull himself up to his knees. He balled up his one working fist and looked straight at the hesitant medical staff.

"Hold up, homie, hold up! Back up, nigga! Don't touch me!"

I jumped in front of my friend before he socked one of the nurses in the eye.

"Yo, yo, Henry, chill, dogg, it's me, Moe! Be easy, homie!"

"Moe, what'ss goin' on, man?" His eyes darted from side to side like a crackhead's.

"You 'member anything 'bout last night?"

"What? What you talkin' 'bout? What's goin' on?"

"I'm tryin'a tell you, dogg. You remember anything 'bout last night or not?"

He lowered his fists two inches and paused for a moment.

"Naw, man. Last I remember we was sittin' at the TV show watchin' you onstage…" His eyebrows cocked upwards again.

"Aight, listen, man, don't worry 'bout it, aight? I'm gonna explain everything, but you gotta trust me, though. The doctor's gotta come in and take a look at you, man. Go 'head and lay back down in the bed, and I'm gonna go call Brian and 'em and tell 'em to come through. Soon's I get back, I'm gonna fill you in on what went down, aight?"

He turned and looked me in the eye. He wanted to trust me, but he was still uncertain.

"Aight, look, you lay down, and I'm gonna call dem niggas

from right here beside the bed, aight? That way I ain't gotta go nowhere, cool?"

"And you gonna tell me how I got here, right?"

"Hell yeah! I'm only callin' them first 'cause the whole conversation probably gonna take like three or four hours, and if they find out you was up all that time and they ain't know, they gon' be mad hurt! We was thinkin' you might die, dude!"

That last part must have hit him pretty hard because he dropped his fist and climbed back into the bed without any hesitation. No sooner had his head hit the pillow than I was on the phone speed-dialing SaTia. I could tell she was already up when she answered.

"How's Henry?" she asked.

"This nigga awake like he jus' had a fresh night sleep!"

SaTia dropped whatever else she was holding. I heard it thud against the carpet on the floor of the villa. "What?"

"He awake, man! Straight up, he's right here layin' in bed talkin' to the doctors! See?"

I held the phone up against Henry's ear, which clearly got in the way of a test one of the nurses was trying to administer. She gave me a dirty look as SaTia's voice echoed out of the receiver.

"Henry? Henry, are you alright?"

"What the hell happened last night, SaTia?"

I put the phone back up to my ear just as she was beginning to explain.

"He awake, but he don't remember nothin' from the show or the rest of the night."

"Oh wow…"

"Yeah, I know! Y'all need to get down here quick!"

"We're on our way, Moe. The driver's outside waiting. We'll be there in ten minutes."

Two hours later, Dr. Ahmed seemed to have checked everything on Henry, from his breathing to his muscle reflexes. He said that this type of retrograde amnesia was fairly common in people who had been through a traumatic ordeal, and there was really no telling how long it would last. He made sure the nurses cleaned and dressed his wound regularly, and placed his arm in a sling so that he wouldn't try to use it.

When he was done, Dr. Ahmed gave Henry a clean bill of health. He said they would hold him for another few hours, and nurses would come in periodically just for observation, but after that, Henry was free to go.

We spent the time trying to explain everything that had happened last night. Henry was sitting up in bed, a little sluggish from the pain medication, and careful not to move the left side of his body between his neck and waist.

I didn't think his eyebrows would ever come down.

"Wait…so…I got shot?"

"Yeah, man!" Brian answered like he was announcing a movie. "You, me, and 'Lando ran up on dude while he was pullin' his gun out! You was the first one to him, and you tackled that nigga like a linebacker! When y'all was rollin' 'round on the floor, the gun went off and hit you in your arm."

"And after that I came here?"

"Yep. You was bleedin' all over the place, dogg. It was like somebody turned on a water hose! It was squirtin' and sprayin' all over people…yo, it was crazy!"

Henry's memories seemed to be on the tip of his tongue, like a random forgotten fact that bugs you all day. "Anybody else get hurt?"

"No, Mr. Hero," SaTia chimed in, in good spirits. "Just you."

"Then where's 'Lando?"

We all looked back and forth between each other. It was the one question we were hoping Henry wouldn't ask. I decided it should be me who answered it. "'Lando flipped out."

"What you mean, 'Lando flipped out? Like he in jail?"

"Naw, I mean like he flippped out on me."

Henry shook his head. "That don't make no type'a sense, man."

"Yeah, I know. That's what I thought when he did it, too. But he flipped out, dude. He found out you was in a coma and he came through the office wid a hammer. I tried to tell 'em he was trippin' and he started callin' me a pussy for not tryin' to go after P. Silenzas."

Henry knew that wasn't enough to prevent Orlando from being here in the room.

"Okay…then what happened?"

"I pistol-whipped him for talkin' trash."

"You pistol-whipped Orlando? What the hell, Moe? That's yo' mans! We all boys, man! Why would you do that?"

I stood by what I had done.

"You wasn't there, dogg. 'Lando wasn't himself. He tried to punch SaTia."

"What? What did you say?"

"He tried to punch SaTia, man."

You could see when Henry's expression changed—he knew that was the straw that had done it. Everyone who knew me was aware that there was always something between SaTia and me, but Henry, Orlando, Ray, and Brian knew better than anyone. We had all been together since I got famous. They assumed we would get married as soon as I decided to stop bagging groupie chicks.

"So where is he now?"

"I don't know. I made him gimme back the Visa and we left him with security at the office."

Henry closed his eyes and shook his head again, massaging his temple with his one good arm.

"I don't believe this, man. This is too much. I got blasted, my homie flipped out, my arm is busted…what da hell am I s'posed to do now?"

"I'll tell you what *we* doin' now…" I stood up from the bed, figuring this was a good enough time to tell everyone what I'd already decided. "Soon as we get Henry up outta here, we headin' straight to the airport and we goin' back home."

The shock hit everyone at the same time. SaTia mouthed a whole sentence before a word actually came from her mouth.

"You…you mean…you mean back home to D.C.?"

"Yeah, back to D.C."

"Umm…I hate to break this to you, Moe, but you're booked up with shows and appearances for at least the next six months…"

"I'm cancellin' everything till further notice."

"You can't. It's in your contract. Failure to…"

The last thing I wanted to hear about was a contract. My voice got louder than I meant for it to. "I don't care what's in the contract, SaTia!"

My outburst caught her with her mouth still open. She glared at me for a second, then closed her mouth and turned her head away.

"My bad," I said after I had gotten control of myself. "I ain't mean to yell. But I don't…I don't care 'bout no contract. SaTia…" I waited for her to turn and look at me again. She was stubborn, but I finally connected with her eyes again.

"SaTia, look around, man. We in a hospital 'cause some niggas is mad at my battle record and wanna kill me. One'a my mans is lyin' here busted up, and another one went nuts. I gotta get someplace safe—where I can get my head on straight." I turned from her and looked around at everyone. "We been travelin' for months now, y'all. It's the same routine, right? Get to the city, bag chicks, blow they backs out, find da dope boy and get twisted, do a show or two, drop a few G's at the mall and strip club and leave. It ain't just me that needs a break; it's all of us."

It was hard reading their faces. I couldn't tell if they were mad that I would even consider stopping, or if they were dumbfounded that I finally decided to do so.

"I'm sayin', in the end, y'all all grown people. Really, y'all can do whateva y'all want. But I'm gettin' on a plane and goin' back to Chocolate City. If y'all wanna use this as some vacation time or somethin,' do you. I'll let you know what's good."

"What we look like goin' on some vacation when niggas is after you, man?" Ray stood up from his seat. "You already know, my nigga, we goin' wherever you goin'."

I looked from Ray over to Brian, Henry, and SaTia.

"Y'all feel the same way? It's cool if you don't."

They all nodded in agreement.

"Aight, cool. Let's go home."

Six hours later, we were all sitting in first-class seats of a Boeing 787. Henry's arm was wrapped up in a sling and pulled closely to his body. The pain medicine they had given him made him giggle at the passengers as they walked by.

Although it was funny watching him make a fool of himself, I couldn't enjoy the moment. Two things were taking up my thoughts. The first was a conversation I'd had with Henry on the way to the airport. I was sitting in the back of the Escalade, starting to doze off, while Henry came and sat gingerly beside me. This was before he had taken the Vicodin that the doctor prescribed for him. It seemed as if his every movement was a labor. The fact that he made the effort told me he wanted to talk about something important.

"Yo, you up, man?"

I'd had my dark glasses on, and he couldn't tell if I was just sitting quietly or crossing over into sleep.

Though Henry was almost back to his old self, it was hard forgetting how he looked while unconscious in the hospital bed. The memory made me really appreciate his presence. I sat up to let him know I was listening. "Yeah, man, I'm up. What's good?"

"You 'member me sayin' anything in da hospital 'bout a dream I had?"

I thought for a moment.

"Umm…yeah…when you woke me up you was talkin' somethin' 'bout some dream you had to tell me. I was so shocked to see you conscious, I don't think I let you finish."

"Aight, well, check this out—when I was out, right, I had this dream that you was a slave…"

Henry stopped and I imagined flashes of his dream came up in his mind. Each one seemed to prick him like a sewing needle. When he looked back at me, he seemed like he had just come from a funeral. "Yo…I could see your face when they was beatin' you, dogg. I could hear your screams…"

Immediately I thought back to the words I'd told Henry while he was still unconscious. His dream was probably just a manifestation of the things I'd said. I thought briefly about telling him of my confessions, but decided against it. There'd be plenty of time for that back home. For now, I just laughed quietly and turned back to my friend.

"You sure they wasn't giving you no drugs befo' you came out the coma?"

I could tell by his face that my humor wouldn't be reciprocated.

"Naw, man, I'm serious."

"Don't be, cuz. I know where it came from."

My nonchalant attitude caused my injured friend to get frustrated. I could see the firmness in his gaze, and I figured it was the just the pain in his arm showing through.

"Aight, man, look, if the dream was what I think it was, then it happened 'cause I took some time last night and spilled my guts at your bedside. I only did it 'cause we ain't know if you was gonna die or not, but I put out some real talk. I don't really feel like talkin' 'bout it right now, but when we get back to D.C., I'll tell you everything I said. It fits with what you're tellin' me, though. That's why I'm sayin' don't stress it. I know where it came from."

Henry seemed uneasy about letting it go. I leaned over closer to him and pulled my sunglasses off.

"I promise, man, soon as we get settled in D.C., we'll talk about it. Aight?"

He hesitantly nodded his head.

"Cool." I put my sunglasses back on and settled back in my seat again. Henry waited a few seconds, and then started to move to his seat.

"Hey…" I called out to him, and he stopped and turned around.

"It's good havin' you back, my nigga."

"Thanks, man…" He waited there, looking at me while something on his tongue held his legs in place. Finally, he let it go and went to sit down.

The second assailant of my peace of mind was the reality that I was actually going back home. Back to the realities of my life before music, money, drugs, cars, and women had become my day-to-day routine.

And if I ever tried to come home and forget who I was, my family would be quick about jogging my memory.

To me, home meant a couple of things. It meant the two-floor brick house that had been in my family since my great-grand-parents took their blood and sweat to the bank in a pillowcase. My grandmother was thirteen when they moved in. She took one look at her parents' faces when that balding white man grudgingly handed them the keys, and she vowed to herself right there that she would die before she let anything happen to the house. When my great-grandmother died, Big Mama's husband had already been killed in the war. She moved back into the house to help take care of Papa Jenkins, and she brought Marcus Jenkins, my father, with her.

Marcus Jenkins was a genius. Big Mama told me that her hus-band left him a saxophone that one of his war buddies brought to him personally after he came home. From that day on, my dad never went anywhere without it. When it got old and rusty, my dad worked a whole year to make enough money to get it refurbished. By the time he graduated from high school, he was making enough money playing music that he started doing it full time.

"Only two groups of people I really believe is cursed in this world," Big Mama would always say with sadness pouring from her eyes, "the Kennedys and musicians."

Tisha Freeman fell in love with Marcus Jenkins while he was playing "In A Sentimental Mood" with his band in a local club. Her love was thick and sweet, like honey, my dad always used to say. She was smart enough to know what his twitches meant, but too smitten to care. He brought her home one day to meet Big

Mama, and when he came back from dropping her off, Big Mama told him to marry her.

Mama says I kicked her so hard during the wedding that she had to hold on to the pews as she walked down the aisle.

Seven years after my parents married, my mom decided she couldn't take care of my dad on her own. He'd been hospitalized more times than she could count, and she was terrified of waking up one morning and finding him dead beside her. Mama and Big Mama had a long talk one afternoon, and the next week mama packed us all up and we moved from our apartment into the family house. The day we moved in, Mama put all of my dad's stuff into his childhood room and told him they wouldn't sleep in the same bed again until he was clean.

In the end, it was Big Mama who made the difference. To this day, she won't tell us what she told him, but after Mama took the last of my dad's stuff in the room, Big Mama went in and closed the door behind her. When she came out, my dad swore to us that he wouldn't leave the house until he got better.

About three days in, my father called me into his room. In between the shaking and cold sweats, he told me stories about Big Mama cleaning up feces off the bed and floor when my great-grandfather would have accidents. He told me how she would bathe Papa Jenkins and put him in her bed while she stayed up bleaching the floor and mattress, only to have to go bathe herself and head out to the Whitfield house to scrub and wash and scrape and soak all day.

"Why didn't y'all just take him to an old people's home?" I asked.

"Sh...she...she could've," my father told me. It was the middle of July, and he shivered like he was caught naked in a blizzard. "I...I asked her the same thing...one day, when the...the whole house smelled like a toilet... 'cause Granddaddy had the stomach flu..."

I went and got a warm cloth to put on his forehead.

"What did she say?" I asked when I came back.

"Sh...she slapped me...'cross the face."

"Dang."

"Then...she looked at me...and said that without him, n...n... none of us would b...b...b...be here. She said he...he gave his s...ss...soul to white folks so he could feed her mother and her, and anything else he had left over he g...gave up for this house...."

"Wow, Daddy..."

Marcus Jenkins did all he could to sit up in his bed. Dripping sweat like an icicle when the sun comes out, he looked me in the eye and cupped the back of my neck with his hand.

"That's...why I called you in here, Moses. My grand...my granddaddy died before his time...tryin' to make sure this family had something...and my daddy...di...died in the war doin' the same...thing. It ain't a day that g...goes by that I ain't proud of both of 'em. I'm in bondage right now...but I swear...Moses... soon as I get...get...this monkey off my back...I'ma make you just as proud...just as proud of me."

I was only seven years old, and I didn't understand what was happening to my father. All I knew was that he was sick and confused. I couldn't do anything about him being sick, but I knew I could cure his confusion.

"But, Daddy..." I said as I looked back up at him. "I am proud of you."

It was the only time I'd ever seen my father cry.

Two weeks later, when he walked out of his room, it was as if someone had turned on a lightbulb under his skin. That week was the best one of my life. He asked me whether there was something I always wished we could do when he was sick, and after I told him, he found a way to make it happen. I felt like Richie Rich.

His first gig after sobering up was that Saturday. At 1 a.m. on Sunday morning, Rico, the drummer in my dad's band, handed him a small case with a needle in it.

The following Monday night, Rico came to our house and wept on our couch. "I was jealous," he struggled to speak through his tears. "He looked so young, so healthy, and the rest of us was still junkies...I just wanted to show him the demon was still there... that he wasn't no better...I swear...I ain't know he'd do it all..."

By 2 a.m. Sunday morning, Marcus Jenkins, my father, was dead. Big Mama had Jeremiah 9:4 engraved on his tombstone.

Beware of your friends; do not trust your brothers...

My mother loved my dad to the point of insanity. When he died, she tried on two separate occasions to commit suicide. After the second time, Big Mama went out and bought a gun. She filled it with bullets and took it up to Mama's room. Mama's wails echoed through the door as Hattie Jenkins rested the gun on my mother's lap, and told her that if she didn't love her son enough to stay alive, then go ahead and put herself out of her misery and stop costing the family money by running back and forth to the hospital. But if she decided she did love me enough, then come downstairs tomorrow morning ready to start living again.

"Black girls born wid pain in they blood..." Big Mama said as she walked out of the door. "They cain't help it. Each one a' us get to a point where pain so deep it seem to set our souls afire. And we each gotta choose whether we wanna live o' die. Time to make yo' choice, girl."

The next morning, Mama got up early and made pancakes for

breakfast. Since that day, it had always been Big Mama, Mama, and myself. That's how it had been from the time I was seven years old to the time I left D.C. as a signed rap artist. And I was sure that back home nothing had changed.

I had tried five different times to get Big Mama and Mama to move. I knew they would never sell the house, and that was never my intention. I just wanted to give them what they deserved. I had realtors waiting nervously with mortgages for huge mansions in their hands, knowing that depending on a yea or nay from the women in my life, they stood to make enough commission to take the rest of the year off. Mama and Big Mama would come see the properties, marvel at their size, rave about their beauty, and still politely decline. The realtors always left disappointed. Tisha and Hattie Jenkins had their home, and no Jacuzzis or indoor pools or guest houses were going to replace that.

They wouldn't even spend the money I sent them. The few times I got to drop into D.C. for a few hours, I would never notice anything different about the way they lived. When I asked where all the money was going, Mama showed me a statement from a money market account with upwards of $5 million in it.

"We keepin' it for a rainy day," Big Mama nonchalantly commented as she stood over the stove. "You cain't never have too much saved up, you know."

Mama and Big Mama were never too happy about my rapping. Mama was just scared that I would end up like my daddy. I tried to tell her that things were different and I would never be addicted to anything except rhymes, but she stayed worried. She, of course, never heard about the narcotics that I'd become so fond of.

Big Mama's problem was on another level. When I first started rhyming, and talked about everything going on around me and in the streets, all she would tell me was that she wished I wouldn't curse so much. When the first single under Cosmos Records was released, and she found out that my stage name was Da Nigga, Hattie waited until I flew back to D.C. to sit me down.

"Boy, don't you know you got the blood of slaves in yo' veins? You gone off and lost yo' mind, hangin' 'round these folks!"

We were at the kitchen table, sitting across from one another. My mother sat beside my grandmother, but her thoughts weren't aligned with my grandmother's. Mama was just happy to have her son, the big star, home again.

"Big Mama, listen, it's just a name, okay? Just a fake name to set me apart from everyone else who's trying to get rich rapping. It doesn't mean anything."

"That's a load of manure, Moses. Who you got feedin' you these lies? A man's name tell the world who he is! It tell 'em who his family is—what kinda stock he come from!"

"I know, Big Mama, and everyone will know that my real name is Moses Jenkins. Everybody will know the name Mama and Daddy gave me."

"Don' lie to me, boy. I ain't dumb. People get rich and they pick who they wanna be. You tellin' people you don' wanna be Moses no mo'. And you replacing it with the worst name you could think of…"

"Naw, Big Mama, you don't understand. That's not what I'm tellin' people…"

She raised her hand just slightly off the table with her palm facing me, and I shut up. I could tell it wasn't something she wanted to discuss further—she simply needed me to know how she felt about it.

After a few seconds, she looked back up at me, perplexed.

"I...I jus' don't understand...you really want every white folk you meet the rest a' your life callin' you nigger?"

"No, Big Mama...it's not nigger, it's nigga. My name is Da Nigga. You see the difference?"

"No."

I gave some thought to how I should explain to her.

"You see, 'nigger' is a racist term. It's the name that white people used to call black people during the Civil Rights Movement and slavery and everything. But 'nigga' is like calling someone your friend or your homie. It's like, we took the word, and turned the whole thing around."

Big Mama dropped her eyes and pondered what I said. She pressed her lips together like she did when she read the Bible, and I looked at her from my seat and waited for her to get my point.

Finally, she raised her eyes to me again. Her face was resolute.

"That's the dumbest thing I ever heard in my life, baby."

It was my turn to be perplexed. She turned and looked at my mother, who was just as shocked as I was to hear her mother-in-law speak so bluntly.

"It is, Tisha. It's jus' dumb...but the youngins, they believe it...they really do..."

She turned back to me with sympathy in her face.

"Nigger is nigger, no matter how you say it, baby. You can roll it 'round in yo' mouth and gargle it like Listerine, but when you spit it out, it still gonna be nigger. You youngins might not understand that now, but you will. In the meantime, far be it for me to tell you something you believe ain't right. Jus' promise me, when you learn the truth, you'll come on back here and tell me."

Her words were a code that I wasn't able to crack. I nodded my

head, not knowing what else to do. She gave a weak smile in
return, and retired up to her room.

I suspected that Big Mama's disapproval of my name was one
of the reasons they never really spent the money I sent them, but
I'd never asked.

We sat at the front of the plane, listening to Henry sing nursery
rhymes and waiting for the attendants to shut the door. SaTia's
phone rang just as she was about to turn it off. I already knew
who it was, but looked over at SaTia to confirm my suspicion.

"It's Rose," she said, and looked from her phone to me, and
back to her phone.

"Tell him the same thing you told him last time."

This was the sixth time Rose had called since learning of our
spontaneous plans. The first three calls were full of threats of
contract cancellations and breach lawsuits. The only good thing
that had come from the last twenty-four hours was the fact that
I was now dinner table discussion for any family with a television.
Rose knew how much money he stood to gain from my misfor-
tunes, but he also knew how much he stood to lose if I bailed
from the company. He tried to act as if he didn't, but after the
third call, which contained threats to make sure I was penniless
and blacklisted, SaTia quickly reminded him of what he already
knew, and then hung up on him.

The fourth call was an apology for the first three, and the last
two calls consisted of him pleading with me to stay on the schedule.

"My client has already made up his mind on this issue, Mr.
Rose. When we arrive in Washington and he has a chance to clear
his head, we will be in touch to figure out how best to proceed

from there. In the meantime, I don't have to remind you that your competitors would love an opportunity to steal Mr. Jenkins, especially given the current situation. We plan on giving them that opportunity if Cosmos Records retaliates in any way, shape, or form against the act of self-preservation that Mr. Jenkins is currently undertaking."

I imagined SaTia dressed in a business suit with her incisors sunk into Rose's carotid artery.

Nervousness seems to make time speed by and slow down simultaneously. Our plane ride seemed as if it took both eight hours and eight minutes. I found myself staring out of window into nothingness, and without knowing, I drifted into a fitful sleep.

Had I been awake, I would've seen Henry, his medicine having worn off, walking lightly up to SaTia. He tried his best to keep the left side of his body still, but with the plane swaying back and forth, his muffled cries of pain became rhythmical. SaTia heard him as he approached, and turned to face him as he slowly knelt down beside her.

"Hey, Henry. How are you feeling?"

"I'll be a lot better once I pop another pill."

"What's stopping you?"

Henry hesitated a moment.

"I wanted to talk to you about something while I was still clear-headed."

SaTia turned her body more in Henry's direction to show that he had her full attention.

"What's up?"

Henry looked over at me to make sure I was still asleep, and then back to SaTia.

"'Lando called me yesterday."

SaTia's body tensed up, but she kept her face calm.

"Really?"

"Yeah. He said he heard I was out the coma, and he wanted to check for himself."

"Okay…well, that's not a big deal."

"Yeah, that's what I was thinkin' 'til I saw this…"

Henry reached SaTia his smartphone. There was a news report from BET News that had been paused on the screen. SaTia took the phone, glanced at Henry, and then hit play on his touchscreen.

"As you know, we have been following the attempted murder of Moses "Da Nigga" Jenkins, and its aftermath, since it occurred two nights ago. The developments in this story seem to get more and more bizarre. Earlier this morning, we reported that Orlando "O-Dogg" Brown, a known member of Da Nigga's entourage, had been ousted from the group…"

"How did they…?"

Henry shrugged his shoulders, winced in pain, and motioned for SaTia to look back at the screen.

"Speculations have been flying about the reason for this break, and Brown's possible involvement with P. Silenzas, who many think orga- nized the murder attempt. These speculations hit a fever pitch tonight, however, when just a few hours ago, Brown was seen leaving his hotel and getting into an SUV driven by Simon "Ounces" Taylor, a former bodyguard and known associate of the rival rap group…"

SaTia dropped Henry's phone. It hit the ground with a deep thud as she put her hand over her mouth.

"Oh my God."

Henry looked back up at SaTia.

"See…see, that's what I was thinkin', right? But then I stopped. I mean, we talkin' 'bout 'Lando here. We been boys since high school. Ain't no way he teamed up with no Silenzas. There must have been some kinda mistake."

SaTia hadn't heard anything Henry said. She sat in shock, trying to pull her thoughts together as I snoozed beside her.

Finally, she whipped her head over to Henry.

"Did you tell him we were coming to D.C?"

"What?"

"Did you tell him we were coming to D.C?"

Henry stumbled over his words, and then dropped his head.

"I didn't know, SaTia. I didn't know. All I said was that we were comin' home to clear our heads for a while."

SaTia threw her arms up, pressed her palms against her forehead, and tried not to panic.

"Why? Why would you do that, Henry?"

"I thought maybe him and Moe could work stuff out. It ain't feel the same without 'im, you know?"

SaTia resisted the urge to grab Henry by the neck as she forced her brain to think clearly. When she spoke out loud again, it was to herself.

"Okay…I've already got a uniformed cop at the house at all times. There's another hour and a half left in the flight—use the Skyphone and call back and see if I can get two uniforms and a plain clothes. Also, contact Danny, get him to contract four personal bodyguards as soon as possible, and don't let Moe leave the house without them…"

"SaTia? SaTia?"

Henry was disturbing her concentration. She couldn't hide her annoyance.

"What???"

"Do you think we should tell 'im?"

"What are you talking about?"

"Moe. You think we should tell Moe?"

The agitation fell off of SaTia's face as she looked over at me.

"No…for God's sake, no! We don't know anything for sure, and he's got enough on him already. And don't tell the guys either! Just let me handle it, okay? Pretend like we never had this conversation."

Henry raised his one good arm up in surrender as he stood.

"You the boss."

SaTia stopped him before he could move.

"Thank you. And don't worry, okay? Everything's going to be fine."

The plane jerked me awake as it landed, and beads of sweat appeared on my brow as the wheels of the plane turned down the runway. I had no idea what being back home would feel like. Worse yet, I didn't know if my troubles would follow me. The thought of putting my mother and Big Mama in danger never crossed my mind. I'd come home to feel safe and secure, but there were too many unknowns. I began thinking that maybe this had been a mistake.

Scared of my shadow, I turned to SaTia, who was hiding worries of her own "What if…"

"Don't worry, Moses, everything will be fine. Local cops are gonna be around 24/7 for as long as we're here, and you'll have four bodyguards on your detail starting tomorrow. Plus, the people in this city would shoot anyone on sight who spoke against you."

It was as if my thoughts sent her brain a text message.

"How did you…"

"I could see it in your eyes," she lied. I thought she was sensing my fears, but really she was addressing her own.

It took a few seconds for my amazement to wear off.

"These guys, SaTia…they tried to kill me in a television studio! In front of a live audience! What's to stop 'em from goin' after Mama or Big Mama?"

"Your mother is the widow of the legendary Marcus Jenkins, and your grandmother taught half the thugs in the city at Sunday School. Between the cops and the grassroots security you'll no doubt receive, I'm telling you, you don't have anything to worry about. I'm sure everyone will be fine." She looked out the window at the other planes coming and going, and then turned back to me. "You know, it may not have been the smartest business decision to come here, but if you take money out of the equation, you couldn't have made a better choice."

Take money out of the equation—those words didn't sound too good to me.

"Maybe, while I'm here, we could find a way to…"

Our conversation was cut short by airport security, who had made their way onto the plane. They were one of the calls SaTia made before we landed. They were already set up at the gate, and as soon as they were able, five of them filed onto the plane to act as our personal escorts.

The officers tried their best to stand so that no one could see us, but it didn't work. Ten seconds in the terminal and a mob of people had formed. They screamed and clawed and scratched while Ray and Brian used their bodies to protect SaTia and me. Luckily, there were fifteen other airport security officers waiting. They held off the mob while our escorts quickly got us onto three separate golf carts and took off down the hall and into a locked VIP corridor two terminals over.

The space looked like a hotel suite. Four well-dressed attendants sat us down in our prospective leather lounge chairs and handed us glasses of water and dinner menus.

"Do you have transportation?" One of the larger attendants asked the question as the security officers rushed back outside to disperse the crowd.

"Yes," SaTia said. She was sitting in one of the lounge chairs against the wall. "The driver should be here shortly."

"There's a glass door at the end of that corridor." The attendant pointed toward the hallway in front of him. "It leads to the VIP parking lot. Tell the driver to pull into the VIP parking lot and up to the door marked 'C'. When you walk out, he should be right there. In the meantime…" He motioned again, but this time toward the open bar that sat to his right. "Help yourselves to anything you like. It's on the house, compliments of the airport. Did you need anything else?"

I looked around. SaTia was getting her feet rubbed. Ray, Brian, and Henry were flirting with one of the attendants. She looked to be Japanese. I caught sight of a cigar box, and before I could open my mouth one of the attendants had it open and a cigar out and cut, lit, and in between my thumb and forefinger. I decided to speak for everyone. "I think we aight."

He nodded at the other attendants who weren't busy serving myself or my friends, and they proceeded to leave out the door, one by one.

"If you need anything," he said as he moved toward the door himself, "just hit the buzzer on the wall and someone will respond within a few seconds."

"Thanks, man."

He nodded, then stepped out of the room.

Ray spoke to me, but kept his eyes on the Japanese attendant. If she was offended by my friend's ogling, she didn't show it.

"Man, this is even better than the setup at LAX."

"Don't get too comfortable," SaTia said, glancing down as her cell phone rang. "We're leaving."

SaTia's statement was confirmed when she answered her Black-Berry. The Oriental bombshell, who'd been the object of Ray's attention, quickly scribbled her number on a napkin as we all stood up and gathered our things. Ray and Brian held their hands out in anticipation, but she walked past them both and handed it to Henry. "I promise I can make you forget all about that arm," she told him.

Henry kept a smile on his face up until we climbed into the limo. The driver waited for me to get in and settled before he spoke.

"On behalf of the entire city, sir, welcome home. It will be my pleasure to take you anywhere you want to go tonight."

I looked out the window and saw the Washington Monument off in the distance. The same one that my father had decided, when I was in elementary school, to take me to the top of. This despite his bloodshot eyes and legs as fragile as uncooked spaghetti. He was almost hyperventilating when we made it to the top, but smiled at me, even as he wheezed. It was my first time feeling as if I owned the world.

"I just want to go home, man. Take me to Southeast."

"As you wish, sir."

6

Tisha Jenkins was sitting on the porch, half asleep. The random but regular sirens echoing through the air kept her eyelids from closing completely. Instead, they hovered like helicopters, fluttering sometimes but never landing, and the whites that showed as a result had scared away many children who were out too late to begin with.

The sound of our large automobile woke Mama. She stood straight up, showing no signs that she had been drifting away. When the headlights of the luxury vehicle got close enough, she came down off the porch and stood beside the curb.

We pulled up beside her. I was barely out of the door when Mama threw her arms around me and tried to squeeze my arms and my chest together.

"Oh, my baby…my baby…my baby…"

She wept as she continued to squeeze me. Her sobs echoed off of the lamp posts and barred glass windows. I didn't mind.

"Lord, I wanna thank you…thank you for keepin' my baby safe…"

Mama prayed out loud as she continued to cut off my circulation. There were more sirens in the distance, but her sobbing nearly drowned them out. My eyes glossed over as I hugged my mother, returning the love she was drenching me with. It was one of those feelings I hadn't realized I'd missed.

I stood wrapped in her cocoon for what seemed like decades. When she finally let me go, SaTia moved beside me.

"Hello, Mrs. Jenkins."

"Hey, sweetheart. I'm so glad y'all back! Y'all come on in."

SaTia shook her head apologetically.

"No, ma'am, we better head on to our homes, too." No sooner had she finished talking did a police car ride up smoothly and park directly in front of the house. I looked at Mama to see if there was anything she was expecting the police for. SaTia spoke up as we exchanged uncomfortable glances. "The chief has agreed to have two uniformed officers in a patrol car, and one plain-clothes officer in an unmarked car, with you for however long you decide to stay."

"So, I'ma have two cops with me all the time?"

"Three. One you should never know is there, though."

I looked around at all the cars parked on the block, and then looked back at SaTia.

"Is the undercover one here already?"

"Yep, he's here."

"Do you know where he is?"

"No, and I don't want to know. As long as he's keeping you safe, that's all that matters."

I looked around at all the dark sedans and SUVs parked on the block, and wondered which one contained the person charged with my protection.

"Well…" Mama wiped her tears and nose as she spoke. "Tomorrow me and yo' Big Mama makin' a huge meal. We already invited all the family from Maryland. Even yo' Uncle Boney s'posed to be comin'." She began the conversation talking to me, but then shifted her eyes to SaTia. "You and the boys are more than welcome to come on through tomorrow. Y'all family, too, now."

Brian poked his head out of the rear window of the limousine.

"I'll be here fo' sure, Mrs. Jenkins!"

"Well, hey, Brian…how are you?"

"I'm great, now that I know you and Big Mama cookin'!"

"Is Henry in there?"

Brian put his head back inside the limo, and Henry came to the window.

"Henry, are you alright? We was so worried about you!"

"Yes, ma'am, I'm fine. My arm is sore, but it's nothin' I can't handle."

"Well, then you gon' be even better tomorrow. Y'all come on through at four o'clock, okay?"

All three of my friends sounded off at the same time.

"Yes, ma'am!"

SaTia turned to make her way to the limo, but stopped short. When she turned back around, her eyes locked with mine.

"I…I'll see you tomorrow…"

Defenseless, I nodded my head. "Yeah…tomorrow…"

She pulled her eyes away and climbed back into the limo. It pulled off slowly down the street.

Mama looked at me and chuckled.

"Hmmm, some things don't never change."

"Huh? What do you mean?"

"I mean you and that girl. She look at you the way I used to look at yo' daddy. Been like that since y'all was in school."

I must have felt the way a gay person feels when they come out to their family and everyone tells them it was common knowledge.

Mama looked at my face and laughed again.

"What, you been gone so long, you forgot you my flesh and blood? I know things 'bout you that you won't find out till you forty."

She walked past me, cleaning the last of the tears off her face.

"Come on in, Moses," she yelled behind her. "I got a plate in the fridge for you; jus' lemme pop it in the microwave."

I moved behind her, still amazed at her insight on a topic I didn't fully understand. I decided I had to ask her at least one question. "Mama, if you knew there was somethin' between SaTia and me, why...?"

She knew my question, so she cut me off.

"'Cause the feelings y'all had, you wasn't ready for yet. Neither one of you was. Maybe you still ain't."

Maybe that's the real reason I was scared to come home. I had spent so long being famous and perfect, I had forgotten what it felt like to have someone tell me the truth about myself. Just that little bit stopped me in my tracks.

I resolved not to ask any more questions about SaTia until I was ready to know the answers. In the meantime, I could smell the fried chicken, ham, stuffing, yams, and greens warming up in the microwave. The aroma would put any five-star restaurant to shame.

The microwave beeped, indicating the food was ready, and I snatched it as if someone else was after it. Mama gave me a fork, and I had two yams four inches from my mouth when a voice stopped me cold.

"You ain't forgot to give the Lord what He due, has you? You been gone that long?"

Big Mama's voice always sounded as if it had come down from the clouds. I put my fork back down on my plate and stood up to face her.

"No ma'am, I haven't."

She looked the same as I remembered, except more of her hair had turned gray.

"Come 'ere, Moses. Let me take a look at you."

I walked over to her and stood straight up while she looked me over. When she was done, I could see her face soften. Her eyes tried to blink away the emotion she felt. She pursed her lips and shook her head slightly. "You look just like yo' daddy."

I reached out and hugged her tight, blinking a few extra times myself.

That night I dreamed of my father. He was tall and broad-shouldered, and walked to his own soundtrack. I was sitting in the audience, and he winked at me as he climbed onstage and began playing his saxophone in a local club. Every few minutes he would look over at me to check and see if I was still there. I never moved from the spot I was sitting in, but each time he looked for me, his eyes would go wide with concern until he found me, and then he would smile and continue playing.

Then, suddenly, the music sped up. One moment I was tapping to the rhythm, and the next, my foot couldn't hit the ground fast enough. I looked around to see how everyone else was reacting to the change in the music, and realized that they had somehow changed from their nice, fancy suits and dresses to dingy cotton pants, shirts, and overalls. No one was in their seat anymore, either. Everyone was up and dancing, and the faster the music got, the more they danced like wild animals. I grabbed the person closest to me, a dark-skinned man about ten years my senior, and shook him out of a trance.

"Why does everybody in here look like a slave? Why don't they put their nice clothes back on?"

The man smiled at me, revealing missing and rotted teeth.

"Dey was always slaves, son," the man answered. "They was jus' hidin' it with those nice clothes, but they was always slaves. Here—come enjoy yo'self…"

He went right back to dancing like a madman, and my foot tapping turned into head nodding, and then body swaying. Before I knew it, I was flailing my arms and jumping around like everyone else.

My dad tried to look for me again, but this time he couldn't find me. He got so worried that he stopped playing the sax, threw it to the side, and walked to the edge of the stage, screaming my name.

I couldn't answer him. I could hear him, but whatever had gotten a hold of everyone else had gotten an extra tight hold on me as well. He screamed until his voice gave out.

"MOSES! MOSES! God, please…MOSES!…"

Then, defeated, he sat back down in his seat.

"Be strong, son."

He whispered it, but I heard it as clear as water.

I woke up the next morning to the faint sound of chanting. It crept into my slumber like a termite and gnawed away at my snores until I could no longer keep my eyes closed. Both eyelids popped open at the same time, and for a split second, I couldn't remember where I was and how I'd gotten there.

It took the smell of ham and apple pie to remind me.

Everyone was already at the house. I could hear the different voices traveling up through the air vents. The digital clock on the dresser flashed 12:30 p.m. across its LCD screen, and I thought to myself that my dad must have kept me asleep so I could finish my dream. Then I shook my head and laughed at myself. "Man, this house must really be screwin' with my head," I said aloud.

I pushed the covers to the side and climbed out of the bed with the images from the dream fading in and out like the opening credits of a movie. As I stretched by the foot of the mattress, I realized I was still hearing the chanting noises that woke me up in the first place. They were coming from the window beside my old dresser. I yawned as I walked up to it, sleepily glanced outside, and then dove back onto the floor.

There were about two hundred people congregated outside the house. Most were standing. Some had lawn chairs and blankets, and were sitting either on the grass or on the sidewalk. There was a group of about ten pimped-out, customized sports cars sitting on the street, and another group of customized sport motorcycles. All the drivers were standing beside their vehicles. All the men were outside in all their freshest gear, and most of the women were wearing clothes that you could pluck off with a pair of tweezers. They all chanted the same thing.

"DA-NIG-GA! DA-NIG-GA! DA-NIG-GA!"

The police had formed a barrier so that no one could pass. I crawled on the floor over to my suitcase and begin to search frantically for something to put on. Just as I was taking out my jeans, someone knocked three times at the door.

"Who is it?" I said with more frustration than I meant to.

"SaTia."

If it had been anyone else, I would have told them to wait for me downstairs.

"Aight, come in."

I was in the middle of throwing my jeans on when she walked in. She made me stop with them around my ankles, as if I was preparing for a ride on the toilet. She looked like she used to look, back in the day when we'd pass notes in class. She didn't have on any makeup, no Bluetooth headset looped over her ear; no dark sunglasses; no laptop in her hands; nothing. She'd put her hair in a ponytail with a scrunchie, and she wore the same jean skirt and tank top that used to make my boys ask if I would mind if they tried to get with her.

"Good luck," I'd always answer. They never did have any.

She walked into the room and shut the door.

"I heard some noise up here and figured you had woken up. I told everyone to let you sleep; that's why no one came and got you when the crowd showed up."

"You don't have no makeup on?" I felt like an idiot, but it was either that or "I love you," and it was too early in the day for confessions.

"I'm home too, Moe. When I woke up this morning, I didn't feel like a famous rapper's manager. I felt like…me."

I pulled myself away from her eyes and reached down to pull my pants up.

"Well, you look…you look like you used to back when we was in school."

"I don't know if that's a compliment or an insult."

Wanting to change the subject, I motioned to the window. "When did they get here?"

"The guys and I got here two hours ago, and there were about ten people out there. It's grown since then, though. It's ridiculous out there now. I'm trying to get the cops to make everyone leave."

"Why would you do that?"

"Because we didn't come back here for a concert, Moe."

I chose to ignore her as I made my way across the room.

"Can you believe I walked up to the window with almost no

clothes on? What was I thinking? People could've seen me without my shades, my grill, my chains…man, I musta been trippin'."

SaTia walked over and sat down on the foot of my bed.

"You're not thinking about going out there, are you?"

"Hell yeah, I'm goin' out there! Those are my fans!"

"Moe—people are trying to kill you!"

"What? I'm supposed to be scared of these niggas for the rest of my life?"

SaTia stood in front of me defiantly.

"The bodyguards will be here in two hours. You can go outside after they get here."

I glanced out of the window at the sea of people who came to support me, and I decided not to wait.

"These people shouldn't have to wait no two hours, SaTia."

"*These people* should have never shown up here in the first place!"

SaTia was getting upset. Her voice was getting shaky and the chinks in her armor were starting to show again. She turned her eyes away from me and tried to compose herself. I lowered my voice and placed my hand on her shoulder.

"Aight, look, I'll just go out on the porch, okay? I won't even leave the house. I'll take Ray, Brian, and Henry with me, we'll stand out there for a couple seconds, hype up the crowd, and come back. And I won't do nothin' else without the bodyguards. Cool?"

She still would've preferred that I stay in the house, but she knew this was the best deal she was going to get. She nodded her head, conceding to my plan, and walked back over to the bed.

I began putting the rest of my clothes and jewelry back on. It wasn't until I turned around that I noticed the look she was giving me.

"What?"

"I don't want you to go out there, but if you insist on it, please give these people more credit. Moe, the people outside are here because they love you. Most of them probably remember you from high school battling and freestyling in the park. Honestly, I don't think they care about your chains. They want to make sure you're okay."

"Whatever. They want the same Nigga everybody else want."

"Why don't you go out there and see for yourself?"

I put my shades down and looked at her. "That's what I plan to do."

"I mean, go out there with nothin' but some jeans and a T-shirt on, and see how much love you get."

"Now you trippin'," I said as I grabbed my shades and put them back on. I was reaching for my cap when I felt a hand stop me. I turned my head just in time to see SaTia's hands reaching up to grab my shades and pull them back off of my head. With my eyes now exposed, she looked right into them. "You're home, Moe. Stop being Da Nigga for just one second. Show them the real you."

Something inside me began to ache. I reached out slowly and grabbed my shades once again. They were heavier than bricks.

"This is the real me. In front of you, in front of Mama and Big Mama, yeah, I can be somebody different. But in front of them, this is all I know. Moses Jenkins ain't no multi-platinum recordin' artist, SaTia. Da Nigga is."

I reached for my suitcase as SaTia's gaze began to melt the self-respect off of my skin. Her face grew more and more somber as I put on the shades, chains, and pinky ring. When I reached for my grill, she turned toward the door.

"See you downstairs, Nigga."

She might as well have spit acid in my eyes.

When I got downstairs, Big Mama took one look at me and put her attention back on her chicken and dumplings. She whispered just loud enough for God, Mama, and me, who was next to her making gravy, to hear.

"...be damned if he comin' to the table like that..."

Ray was sitting in front of the television with a coaster under his glass of Kool-Aid. He was laughing at SpongeBob on the screen as I walked over.

"We been in six-star hotels where they got diamond dust sprinkled in the walls, and I ain't never seen you use a coaster for nothing," I said as I walked up behind him. "What you doin' with one now?"

Ray jumped up from his seat when he heard my voice. He looked at me, then down at the coaster. When he looked back up, he shrugged his shoulders.

"I got mad respect for your moms, Moe. She tell me to use a coaster, then I'm usin' a coaster."

I reached out my hand to give him dap. He clasped my hand and we both leaned forward to tap each other on the back.

"I 'preciate the love, man."

"No problem, Moe. You know your peoples is my peoples, real talk."

"Get everybody together for me, dogg. Think it's 'bout time we stepped outside and said hello."

"We...umm...we was waitin' on you." Henry and Brian came from around the corner with their mouths full of food. Brian spoke up for the both of them.

"Hope you ain't want us to wait on you to eat. Since you was sleep so long and SaTia wasn't letting nobody wake you up, Ma Dukes fixed us a plate to hold us over."

"Naw, it's cool. Fix yourself up, though; we gettin' ready to go outside."

"What we gonna do outside?" Henry's arm was still in a sling, and his face didn't reflect the excitement of the other two.

"Just hype the crowd up a bit, probably sign some autographs. You know, just show 'em some love," I answered, and then looked back at Henry. His face hadn't changed."Why? Is there somethin' wrong?"

He took a step toward me and lowered his voice.

"Somebody's tryin' to kill you, Moe. You came back here for a break, right? What's the point, if you gonna keep feedin' the public?"

I was starting to get frustrated with people telling me what was best for me, even if they were telling the truth.

"They out there yellin' my name, man! What you want me to do?"

"Send us out there. We'll tell 'em you came here to be with your fam and get your head on straight. Won't be no special appearances or nothing like that."

"Naw…naw. I got my start here. My fans from D.C. put me on the map, man! And I'm supposed to ignore 'em now when they need me?"

Henry looked over at SaTia. She shrugged her shoulders and shook her head, as if to say, "I tried to tell him, but he wouldn't listen." Clearly, they had some information that I was not privy to.

Henry raised his voice level to reach mine when he responded. "Don't nobody out there need you, Moe. Everybody that need you is right here in the house. I mean, what if P. Silenzas got another nigga out there with a gun, waiting for you to come out on the front step? What then, huh?"

The thought of being shot on my front step cut my next statement short. Mama and Big Mama came out to the living room to see what all the noise was about, and SaTia was staring at us from the steps. The entire house went silent. Henry looked around at everyone, then walked up to me and whispered in my ear. "Look… you know I'ma follow you wherever you go. If you wanna go out and hype up the fans, then do you. Just know that you ain't doin' it for them—you doin' it for Da Nigga."

When he finished, he took enough steps back to leave me by myself in the middle of the room. I felt like a bull's-eye as the clock on the mantle continued to count seconds away.

"So…umm," Brian said, breaking the silence with his anxiousness. "What we doin,' Moe?"

"Get your gear on. We goin' outside."

Ray, Brian, and Henry all put on their shades, chains, and caps. Henry moved a little slower than usual, but when I walked toward the door, he was right beside me. SaTia took a seat on the steps while Mama and Big Mama returned to their cooking.

I stopped at the door. I could still hear the chants of the people outside, daring me to put myself in harm's way to prove I was still a superstar.

I glanced over at Henry. I couldn't see his eyes through his shades, but I sensed he was looking at me.

He was right. Moses wanted, even needed, to stay inside and figure his life out. But Da Nigga needed to be fed.

That's what they don't realize, I thought to myself as I took hold of the doorknob; *If he starves, everybody starves.*

I twisted the doorknob, counted to three, and threw the door open.

"AY YO D.C.! CHOCOLATE CITY, WHAT'S POPPIN'!"

Thunder echoed through the air. The crowd's roar made the house shake. I soaked it all in like sunlight. The electricity went into my chest and through my entire body. It ran down my legs and stopped at my toes. It ran through my arms and lingered in my fingertips. I stood there with my arms outstretched and my eyes closed, and it felt as though lightening was pulsing through my veins.

"To hell with the Silenzas!" I spoke to myself as the crowd turned me back into a superhuman. "I run this right here! I run this!"

The mass of people almost broke through the line of cops at the front lawn. The officers waiting in their cars jumped out to help. I could hear Ray, Brian, and Henry screaming and jumping around, feeding off of the same energy I was. I couldn't make out their words, and I didn't care. They were here for me. Everyone was here for me.

I opened my eyes and realized I ruled the world. For the first time since the *Phil Winters Show*, I was invincible again.

I didn't have a mic, but I belted out the hook to my latest single anyway. Miraculously, the crowd heard me, and began rapping it along with me.

"HOES IN DA ATTIC, YEAH! HOES IN THE ATTIC, YEAH! COME TO MY CRIB, I GOT SOME HOES IN DA ATTIC, YEAH!"

Now that I was back to being indestructible, I scanned the crowd for the female I was going to sleep with tonight.

That's when I saw Orlando standing off to the right.

We caught eyes for two seconds before he turned around and made a gesture to the upstairs window of Mrs. Marble's house, across the street.

He gave a speech with his eyes in those two seconds. He told me I'd broken his heart. He told me I forgot about the streets, and I forgot what it meant to be down for my niggas. He told me

I'd chosen a female over him, and he couldn't let that slide. He told me I should've been down to ride on the Silenzas no matter what, and he couldn't let that slide either. He told me he didn't know what he was doing, but he was so angry that it didn't matter, and even if he regretted it afterward, I still deserved what I got.

And right before he pivoted on his front foot and turned his back toward me, he told me that he was sorry.

I realized what was going to happen before I had time to react to it.

The first shot knocked me back about two steps. Everything went quiet after that. I could see the crowd going mad, but I couldn't hear them.

The second shot knocked me clear back into the house and turned all the sound on again.

I could only hear the screams of the masses. My eyes were fixed on no particular spot on the ceiling, and I couldn't seem to move them. I lay on my back in the hallway where my father had come and gone so many times, and I could start to feel my blood pooling under my back.

There was a hole in my chest. I could feel air in places other than my lungs. I didn't feel any pain, though. It felt more like my body was a puzzle, and my core had been removed from the board.

I heard Big Mama's good china fall and shatter on the floor as she and Mama hurtled across the kitchen. SaTia's scream pierced the chaos. She had stayed on the steps while the guys and I went outside. After the second shot, my body flew past her before it landed on the floor. She got to me before anyone else did and cradled my head in her lap.

"Oh my...oh my God...Moe...MOE! MOE!"

I couldn't answer her. I began to feel blood in my throat, choking me. I gagged and coughed it up. When I saw how thick it was, I recognized that I was in trouble.

I could hear Mama screaming now, but her hysteria made her words hard to understand.

Big Mama came up and put a towel over the crater in my torso before she kneeled beside me. I believe she wanted to touch me, but her hands shook in mid-air. Her face seemed to melt into one big tear as she rocked back and forth.

"Here…here, baby…you gon' be okay. Lord, he gonna be okay…Lord, I cain't take another one…You save him, Lord… You save him 'cause I'm askin'!…and I ain't done nothing but right by you! I ain't done nothin' to deserve losin' my son and my grandson! You owes me, so you repay me now! You saves my baby!"

Henry, Ray, and Brian came in the doorway and slammed it behind them. Henry was the first to get a good look at me.

"Oh no…no…God…"

"CALL AN AMBULANCE!" SaTia screamed through her tears.

Ray already had his cell phone out, but sirens were coming down the street before he even pressed a button.

I only remember flashes after that. My memories turned into strobe lights. Being put on a stretcher, lying face down in a field, being in an ambulance, picking cotton seeds out of my finger-nails, rushing through the hospital, aiming a rifle through my tears, all of it went by like a blurry movie with bad sound. The last flash was of SaTia, with makeup melting down her face, praying on the right side of my bed. My dad was on the left side, doing the same thing. Then everything went dark.

PART TWO

PART TWO

7

It felt as if someone had stuck an adrenaline needle in my heart. My head jerked up so fast from being facedown in the dirt that it threw me onto my back. I scrambled around, using my hands and feet to propel me, for about ten seconds before I realized I didn't know who I was running from. There was no one around me. In fact, there didn't seem to be anyone in the area at all. Just a big open field with golden grass and no shade.

I patted my chest lightly, expecting to be able to feel shredded clothes and flesh, but there was nothing there. No gunshot wounds. No blood. Nothing. I didn't have a scratch on me. It was as if I had dreamed it all.

"What the hell is goin' on?" I stood up as I spoke aloud.

The field stretched as far as I could see. There was nothing else around but grass and a scorching hot sun.

"SaTia? Ray? Brian? Henry? Where y'all at?"

I spoke but no one responded.

I began walking in an unknown direction. The sun was beating down against my body. When it gets this hot, your grill starts to give you cottonmouth. I could feel sweat gathering in my Air Force Ones and dripping down my face underneath my shades. I tried to wipe it away from my eyes and scratched my cheek with my pinky ring. My confusion took the sting away.

How had I gotten here? The last thing I remembered was lying half-dead on a hospital bed. People don't get shot and then wake up in the middle of nowhere with the sun cooking their hair grease. I stopped and looked around again. Scanning all around me, again, all I could see were fields.

"Well, it's too hot to be heaven..." I said aloud. "And too peaceful to be hell. And I'm not Catholic, so this can't be purgatory. Where am I?"

I continued to walk through the field. After a while, I quit trying to wipe the sweat away from my face and dealt with the sting of it in my eyes. My white tee was completely soaked and I had puddles in my Nikes. It got harder to put one foot in front of the other, and my path through the field began to zig-zag like a piece of artwork done by a two-year-old.

Maybe this is hell... I began to think as I staggered from left to right. Before I could finish the thought, I was back on the ground again.

"SATIA!" I screamed out as I rolled around on the ground. "BRIAN, HENRY, RAY...WHAT'S GOING ON?"

I began reaching out for something—clawing at the ground as if it would somehow provide me with an answer to my question. When I stopped, I considered lying there and letting whatever was going to happen to me play itself out. Then I remembered... I'm Da Nigga. I don't lay down for nothing.

The thought itself wasn't strong enough to get me back up to my feet, so I began repeating it aloud.

"I'm...Da...Nigga," I coughed out as I got up to my knees. "I don't...lie down...for nothing."

As I swayed back and forth on my feet, I forced myself to begin thinking rationally.

I'll probably pass out in a few minutes, I thought. *I might as well get as far as I can get before I go down for good.*

I could barely lift my head, but I took a step, and then another, and then one more. By the time I got to nine or ten, I lifted my head, expecting to still see an eternity of fields. Instead I saw a road. It looked like one of the back country roads that people have on their farms—as if someone had cleared all the grass and plants out of the way, but forgot to put down any pavement. I didn't care, though. A road meant that someone would be coming by sooner or later. They'd recognize me and get me back to some type of civilization.

By the time I reached the road, I could vaguely see something approaching in the distance. My vision was blurred from all the sweat that had found its way into my eyes, so I wasn't surprised when the figure began to look more like a horse than a car.

"I'm trippin'," I said aloud as I began to wave down the car.

"Yo, yo, I need some help! Yo, stop the car, man! I need some help! I don't even know where the hell I am, dogg! You gotta help me!"

There was something wrong with the car's engine. As it pulled up, it sounded like some type of animal. Even with blurred vision, I could tell I had never seen any car like this before. And it stunk.

"Yo, what's wrong with your....never mind, man. You got any water?"

I took off my shades and wiped my eyes with the back of my hands. Before I put the shades back on, I looked up. There were two horses in front of me, with two white guys on them that looked as if they were straight out of an old Western movie.

"Wow," I said, looking at the men, then at the horses, then back at them.

Before I could say another word, the first guy hit me in the mouth with a rifle butt. I fell to the ground, stunned.

"Where you come from, nigger?" The shorter of the two men

jumped off of his horse and walked up to me. The taller one, the one who'd hit me with the gun, did the same.

My mind was going eighty miles per hour. So these country rednecks obviously knew me, or at least knew my stage name. Maybe they were hired by the P. Silenzas. Maybe they were the ones who'd somehow gotten me out of the hospital and over here to No Man's Land. Whatever the case, they had guns and I didn't. This wasn't the time to be acting gangsta.

"Aight, look, fellas," I said as I started to get back up. It took longer than usual, considering how weak I already was. By the time I got back to my feet, the right side of my mouth was dripping blood onto the dirt. "There's obviously been some kinda misunderstandin'. Ain't no need for the guns, though. Look, whatever the Silenzas is payin' y'all, I'll double it. You know I got more money than them niggas. Just take me to the nearest bank, let me pay y'all off, and we'll pretend like none of this ever happened, aight?"

I looked both of them in the eye, waiting for a response. What I got was another gun butt to my mouth. I felt a tooth come loose when I hit the ground.

"Yo, what's your problem, man? What's wrong with you?"

The shorter one slowly walked up to me, observed me for about three seconds, and then kicked me in the side of my head.

I couldn't have gotten back up if I'd tried. I could barely open my eyes. Pain radiated through my skull as I began to drift in and out of consciousness.

"Looks like we got ourselves an uppity nigger here, Mr. Talbert." The tall one who'd hit me with the gun spit as he spoke.

My vision was going from different shades of purple to pitch black. I listened as well as I could in between consciousness.

"Yes, we do. But he's strange, though. Look at all this stuff he's

got on, Bradley. Looks like something out of a child's nightmare."
He stopped and used his foot to turn me over, and I plopped onto
my back like a ragdoll. Eventually, he shrugged his shoulders.

"Oh, well, a nigger's a nigger. Bradley, string him up on the
horse and bring him back with us. I don't know where he came
from, but he obviously hasn't been properly broken."

"Lemme have the honor, Mr. Talbert. I'll have him kissin' my
toes by the time I'm done with 'im."

Mr. Talbert shook his head slightly.

"This fella right here is foreign, Bradley. You don't want bucks
like this stirring up the rest. Might be best to hang him soon as
we get back—set an example for the others. I'll decide by the time
we arrive home."

Bradley nodded, bent down and picked me up like a sack of
flour. I was still going in and out of consciousness as he tied me
to the back of the horse. When he began riding, my body flopped
around uncontrollably. It had suffered all it could take. I blacked
out while looking at the behind of a horse.

8

When a person comes back from being unconscious, they usually come back in segments. The way all your senses come back to you, piece by piece, is like an orchestra. I was moaning incoherently for the better part of my masterpiece. The crescendo would be me coming back to being fully aware again, but as with any good musical work, my mind couldn't just jump to the climax. There had to be a lead up to the final moment.

The first thing I recognized was that the place where I was smelled like someone was trying to broil a dirty sock. It reminded me of my old high school locker room, when we'd all come back in after basketball practice and figure out whose gym bag was rank enough to kill a small child.

The second thing I recognized was that I was on a dirt floor. I knew this, because my mouth had been open during my unconsciousness, and now that I was coming to, I could taste the soil that my tongue rested on. I rolled myself around slowly, still unable to see straight or to speak anything intelligible. The same dirt that was on my tongue had caked itself against the side of my head where the blood had dried. The mixture of the liquid and earth created a paste that covered half of my face. I must have looked like something out of a low-budget horror movie as I started to sit up.

I heard whispers as I slowly began to get all my faculties back.

My eyesight was getting better, I had gone from seeing one continuous piece of art around me to now seeing everything in double. There were people standing all around, looking down at me as if I'd been the subject of some experiment. My head still pounded from the boot that had collided with it earlier. I tried to stand up, but only got a third of the way before I went back down again.

Everything was clear now; as I looked around again, I noticed that everyone around me was dressed in the same type of clothing as the two guys on the side of the road. They all looked like characters out of a Civil War movie. The people that were standing around me must have been picked to play the slaves. They were blacker than Biggie.

Now that I was looking back at them, the whispering stopped.

"Am...." It took a great deal of effort to try and talk straight, and my grill was hanging halfway out of my mouth. I took out the shiny metal piece, which seemed to be shocking to my spectators, and gained control over my tongue.

"Am I on a movie set? Why is everybody dressed like this?"

Nobody said a word.

Despite the bass drum beating against the inside of my skull, I stood up and tried to think through my situation. Maybe they were working with the guys who'd kidnapped me in the field. Maybe I really was on some sort of movie set. Did these people even recognize me? I put my fingers up and rubbed my cheek. The nastiness on my fingertips covered it like face paint. I decided I needed to get some answers and get the hell out of there—not necessarily in that order.

"Come on, man. Where...where am I?" I stood up straight to give the impression that I wasn't hurt anymore. Truth be told, I'd have fallen if one of them sneezed on me. "Who was those guys that attacked me? Somebody gotta tell me somethin'. Stop standin' there looking stupid...don't y'all know who I am? I'm Da Nigga! Somebody better tell me somethin'!"

Again, nobody said anything.

"Look, man, I don't know what y'all supposed to be doin', but you gotta let me go. Like I told the white boys, I'll get you all the money you want. I'll pay double what the P. Silenzas's payin' y'all. You know them niggas broke anyways! I killed they career, remember? Take me to da nearest bank, let me cash y'all out, and let me get up outta here!"

One of the actors stepped out from the group and walked up to me. He had a physique that made me think carefully about what I'd do if he attacked me. He was at least 6-foot-4 inches tall, and had eyes that reminded me of a homeless woman who used to be on the corner of Pennsylvania Avenue every day.

You can always tell the difference between guys who built themselves up by going to the gym and those who were lumberjacks or worked construction. The gym guys were usually pretty boys. They couldn't fight, but most people would stay away from them strictly because of their size. The guys who got huge unintentionally were the ones that even the shoot-first dope boys should think twice about bothering. There was something about hard labor that earned a man his respect.

The man who stood in front of me looked as though he was paid to chew bricks. Like I said, I thought carefully about what I would do if he attacked me.

"Where come from?" He had an accent that I couldn't place to any particular region. His voice rang off the walls like a bullhorn. It took a second for me to get my wits before I answered.

"You tell me, cuz? One second I'm in the hospital, next I'm dying of dehydration in a field, and now I'm here. Can you please lemme know where I am?"

He looked as if he had just as much trouble understanding me as I did understanding him. He thought about it for a second, and then pointed at the ground.

"Dis?" He pointed to the ground repeatedly. "Dis Massa Talbert plantation. Who you?"

I took a good, long look at the man in front of me. He seemed to be dead serious. I took a good, long look at the people standing around me as well. Men, women, and children, all staring straight at me, all dressed exactly as I imagined slaves would've looked. I looked at each and every one of them, stared at them, studied them, and when I was done, I looked back at the human tree trunk standing in front of me.

And then I fell into side-splitting laughter.

It made my head pound even harder than before, but I couldn't stop. It was like having someone crack a joke in a quiet place.. I was obviously on a movie set, how I got here I didn't know, and these actors and actresses were way too into their roles. Or maybe they were filming right now. Either way, the fact that they were so serious about it made me almost bust my gut wide open. I was slapping the floor and everything. The only thing that stopped me was my double vision coming back.

It took me another few minutes, but I finally regained my composure.

"You guys are too funny," I said, catching my breath.

Nobody laughed along with me.

"Why you laugh?" the man in front of me asked again. "Massa Talbert say you be hung or you go wid Bradley. Ain't no time to laugh. You go!"

For a reason I couldn't explain, I didn't feel threatened by the people around me anymore. They were so committed to their roles, they were almost pathetic. I would've felt sorry for them if we weren't on set.

I walked up to the dark-skinned colossus and put a hand on his shoulder. He started to pull away, but stopped. "Look, umm... what's your name, dude?"

He pointed to himself with a question on his face.

"Yeah, yeah, you. What's your name?"

"Roka...me Roka."...

"Aight, look, Roka...I understand you bein' committed to your role and everything, but I gotta find out how I got here. I'm gonna go find a place to get all this crap off my face. Take a few seconds to come outta your character, and when I get back, we can talk."

"How you get here?" Roka asked me.

"Yeah, I gotta find out how I got here."

"Massa Talbert bring you...now you—"

"Massa Talbert, huh?" I cut him off, still feeling the effects of my laughing binge. "Yeah, I'm suing that dude. Being in character is one thing, but if he kick me again, I'ma find a shovel or a rake or somethin' 'round dis..."

"STOP!" This time, Roka cut me off. He grabbed me firmly by the shoulders and shook me. I tried to shrug away from him, but realized I couldn't move.

"You leave now! Can't stay fo' Massa Talbert come back! You run now! You different! You run now!"

I looked into his eyes and knew he was serious. I began to think that maybe this wasn't a movie, but then again there was no other explanation for what was happening. Nothing else made sense.

Roka finally loosened his grip on my shoulders and I jerked myself away from him.

"Aight man, damn! I don't know what the hell kinda actors y'all are, but y'all crazy! I promise you that. I'm outta here!"

I took two steps toward the door and Bradley threw it open. All the actors jumped back as if they'd seen the devil. I stood up straight and stared him in the eye.

"Look, I don't know what kinda movie y'all s'posed to be shootin' here, but when my lawyer gets through you gonna be shootin' porno flicks with crossdressing midgets! Who in the hell you think you is kickin' me? I don't care who you workin' for...I'm Da Nigga, you rat bastard! You done lost your mind! Now get the hell outta my way so I can find a phone!"

The black people behind me stopped breathing. I might as well have been Superman with lasers coming out of my eyes.

"He different..." Roka whispered to the closest dark-skinned person in proximity to him.

Bradley stopped in his tracks and stared at me. He looked intently at me for longer than I had the patience for. His eyes held both fear and confusion, and I could tell he didn't know what to do. Finally, I heard another set of footsteps coming, and Mr. Talbert appeared at the door as well.

"Well, I see you've awakened. We had a time trying to figure out what to do with you. It will be a shame to kill you, since you obviously aren't from here. But as I told my wife and children, I can't risk you getting the rest of my niggers in an uproar. Bradley, if you'd be so kind..."

I was still lost as to what was happening and why. I did understand, however, that someone had made the decision to kill me. Movie or not, these were the same two men who had knocked me unconscious earlier. I'd worry about suing them for everything they owned when I was back in a hotel room with SaTia. For now, I wasn't willing to wait around to see if someone would yell "Cut!" from behind a tree. I sprinted forward without warning and threw my entire body into the space that separated Bradley from Mr. Talbert, forcing them apart and knocking them down. Then I ran out into the open sun.

I had no idea where I was going, but I ran with all the speed my legs could muster. Whoever these people were, they were definitely crazy. My best move was to get away from them and find someone who had some common sense. I didn't have any money, but I still had my diamond and platinum chain on. I quickly made the decision to hand it over to the first person I met who could take me back to some sort of recognizable civilization.

When I got off of the movie set plantation, I turned onto a dirt road and kept running hard. It would be great, I thought, if someone would pull up in a car and give me a ride, but something told me that wasn't going to happen. If I was on some sort of island, maybe I'd come across someone with a plane or boat. Whatever happened, I had to keep running and make my way back to the real world. The people here were crazy.

Behind me, Mr. Talbert and Bradley were getting back up to their feet. Mr. Talbert yelled for Bradley to chase after me, and he quickly ran over to his horse and jumped on, galloping away. Mr. Talbert jumped on his horse, too, but he went back toward the mansion. When I finally thought to turn around, I saw Bradley on his horse, riding hard and gaining on me quick. I also saw four other men, including Mr. Talbert, riding up behind him. They were coming up too fast, and I'd be caught in the next minute if I didn't do something. With my lungs burning, I made a hard right turn and ran headlong into the woods that were on the side of the road.

A few seconds in the thick brush made me regret my decision. Every tree limb, shrub, and leaf that touched my skin seemed to slice it open. After feeling as if I'd gotten a million paper cuts, I crossed my arms over my face to try and keep the forest from attacking my eyes. I tripped over something every few steps, but I always made it back up and kept running. But a few moments later, I fell down hard on my forearm and couldn't find the air to rise. I lay there, breathing in the fresh dirt that was inches away from face, wondering again where I was and how I could get away. Exhaustion began to sweep over me, and I was startled to find that, as I was lying there, my eyelids were trying to close. I forced them open and pulled myself up to my knees. I didn't hear anyone else coming through the woods, and I began to think that maybe I'd lost my pursuers. Relieved, I began to daydream about my Bentley sportscar. I hadn't had the chance to drive it yet. It was waiting for me at a lot in Tysons Corner, with all the modifications I'd asked for. I'd stopped by to see it on the way to a concert one night, and sat in the driver's seat for a while. It felt as though I was sitting inside a missle.

"I gotta get outta here," I thought I was thinking to myself, but I ended up saying it aloud. I tried to pull myself up from off of my knees, but my body told me it wasn't quite ready yet. "Okay..." I spoke back to it. "They ain't chasing me no more, so we can rest here awhile."

It was then that I heard the sound. It was muffled at first, like when someone calls out a name from a distance and you turn around to make sure they weren't talking to you. It got louder with every breath I took, though, and I knew as the echoes jumped from the trees that this wasn't my imagination. My body may have been uninspired by the thought of the Bentley, but it got a shot of adrenaline from this new threat.

"Dogs..." Again, I spoke aloud without meaning to. Instinct trumped my exhaustion, and I jumped back up my feet and began running again.

The dogs kept getting closer. I tried to zig-zag through the woods, but they were so near, I could hear the men's voices that accompanied them. They sounded wild and excited, as if this was some hunting expedition. I tried to run faster, but the fuel I was burning had its limits. My vision blurred and my hands started to shake, but I kept going. Suddenly, I heard one of the men yell out, his voice laced with a hatred I couldn't understand. "There he is! Let the dogs go!"

I began to panic. The terror in my chest felt like an animal trying to force its way out. I looked around and saw a tree with a branch low enough for me to grab on to. Without thinking, I leaped over and grabbed it.

As soon as I had a hold, I felt a set of teeth sink into my ankle. I screamed and tried to kick the dog off, but the harder I kicked, the deeper its teeth sank into my flesh. I could hear the other dogs growling and barking up at me. Two of them began jumping up and nipping at my pant leg. They were anticipating the meal they'd get when I fell, but I was determined to disappoint them. I reached up to the next highest branch of the tree, and began to pull myself up. The weight of the dog that was biting me pulled down on my ankle, and I thought my entire foot would tear from the rest of my leg. I screamed out again, but continued to try and climb. The dog that was tasting my ankle loosened its grip a bit. His legs dangled off the ground and his growls turned to yelps of confusion. I kicked one last time and the dog released his jaws entirely and fell back to earth. I checked to see if I still had an ankle attached to my right leg, and in my periphery, caught the image of a man running up to me with something in his hand.

I quickly tried to make my way up to the next highest branch, but the man hit me so hard in my side with his object that I almost fell. I looked down and saw his eyes, filled with satisfaction because of the pain he had inflicted. I was high enough off of the ground now that he had to swing as if he was trying to break a piñata. The thick stick he had in his hand had some sort of thorns on it. When he hit me again, they bit into my side and my eyes began to water. I couldn't take another blow and still hold onto the tree. I tried to kick at him, but my range of motion was too limited. He easily dodged my foot and cocked back for another swing. Desperate, I tried to throw myself around the trunk of the tree, hoping it would hold on to me better than I could hold onto it.

When the thorny stick hit me again, it connected with my lower back. My body jerked in pain, and I felt my grip around the tree release. I fell and landed on my back, hitting my head against something that made my skull feel like Play-Doh. My vision almost went blurry again, but five sets of fangs found a home in my flesh and brought it back to clarity.

"Ahhh! Get these...get these dogs off me, man!"

One of the beasts had torn away the chunk of flesh it was biting, and had come back for more. I couldn't tell how much I was bleeding, but the leg of my jeans began to feel moist. I tried to ignore the five white men that stood over me, watching as I tried to scamper away. When it seemed as if I might have gotten my feet under me, I felt the sharp stick come back across my legs again. I fell down once more, and as I hit the ground, one of the white men called the dogs back to him. When I turned around, I saw the muzzle of an old gun pointed at my mouth.

"What the hell is wrong with you people, man? What y'all want?"

Each of the men looked around at each other, and then at Bradley.

"You was right," the man who held the gun told Bradley. "This ain't no regular nigger. Ah well..."

The gunslinger raised his hand a few inches up to my forehead, and pulled the trigger.

Barely able to register what was happening, I saw the flash

come from the front of the gun as I lay there on the ground. I squeezed my eyelids shut and waited for my life to go by in a flash.

After five seconds, I figured either my death had been painless or something had gone wrong. I opened my eyes and saw Bradley with his hand on the shooter's wrist. He had pushed the shooter's hand up so that the bullet had gone up in the air instead of into my brain. The man looked at Bradley with both confusion and anger painting his face.

"What're you doing, Bradley?"

Bradley let the shooter's wrist go and stood in front of him.

"This nigger ain't from 'round here, Finch. He somethin' differen'. He talk differen', he walk differen'. Missus Talbert, she flap her mouth from here straight'a the ocean if you let her. Boss told her 'bout dis here nigger, and you know half the town gotta know bout 'im by now. Now, Finch, what if I take this here nigger, and break 'em so bad that he weep when he sees himself a white man? What you reckon that'll do for ol' Bradley's reputation?"

"Mista Talbert say to kill 'im," Finch replied.

"I know that, but jus' hear me a second. Lemme talk to the boss before we kill 'im. If he still want the nigger dead, we'll leave him side of the road. But if he says I can have 'im, I'll letcha help me teach 'im some manners. We both be the most famous nigger breakers for miles! Whatcha say?"

I could tell Finch was thinking hard about his decision. I had no idea what they were talking about, but I tried my best to jump up and run away. The furthest I got was my hands and knees, and my reward for that was a quick kick in my head. I passed out, thinking that I must have suffered some type of brain damage by now.

When I came to, I was being dragged up the road that I had run down during my attempted escape. Two of the men that had chased me were holding me under either arm. The rest of my body was limp. I was too weak to pick up my head, but I let my eyes flutter open. I was leaving a steady trail of blood behind me, and my Nikes dragged the ground and left a parallel path on either side of the thin red line. As we moved, I heard snatches of conversation.

"I don't like it, Bradley."

"And I knows it, Mr. Talbert. I knows you feelin' uncomfortable 'bout this nigger here. But sir, you give me one month with 'im, and I swear I'll have 'im lined up perfect! He'll be da best slave you ever laid eyes on when I'm done with 'im!"

"And if he's not, Bradley? What happens if you can't break him, and he rouses up all my other niggers? Do you know how much money a field full of slaves is worth, Bradley? Do you have enough money to purchase replacements for runaway slaves? No, you don't. I know this because I pay you."

"I knows it, sir, and you absolutely right, but I can—"

"Shut up, Bradley. I don't care about what you can and cannot do. I don't appreciate you convincing Finch to disobey my orders, and I don't appreciate you trying to use this situation for your personal gain. Do as I say, and shoot this nigger in the head."

"What if you cut my pay, sir?"

"What?"

"Cut my pay, sir. You can cut my pay, and in return, I can keep the nigger. You needin' another cotton gin, Mr. Talbert. You can take the extra monies and get equipment, get yourself a strong buck, you can do whatevers you want, sir. Jus' lemme have the nigger, sir, please..."

Mr. Talbert stopped short for a moment.

"Why do you want him so bad, Bradley?"

Bradley's voice became quiet, almost somber.

"Half the town already know 'bout this nigger we found, sir. People sayin' everything—from him bein' from 'cross the ocean to him bein' from out in space somewheres. If I break 'im, and break 'im good, I'll be famous, sir. Be known for miles out. Get me a big 'ol mansion and lots a land jus' like you, Mr. Talbert. Feel like a real white man, 'stead of havin' to be 'round these niggers all the time. God help me, sir...getting so's that I cain't stand the sight of 'em no more."

Mr. Talbert was quiet for another moment.

"Well, I guess you can't knock a man for having ambition. And you're right about the niggers—any halfway civilized man can only tolerate them in small doses. That's why we hire people like you, Bradley. But again...you can't knock a man for having ambition..."

"And I knows you can use the money, sir."

"You are correct, Bradley. I could use the money."

Bradley leaned in close and whispered, so that only Mr. Talbert could hear him. "Maggie ain't fresh no more, sir. Maybe you'se take your pick from the next ship come in..."

Mr. Talbert whispered back with acid in his voice.

"I do not wish for my indiscretions to be thrown back in my face, you irreputable heathen! I should have you thrown in jail for that!"

"I'm sorry, sir...I'm sorry...please forgive me..."

"You'd better be!" Mr. Talbert glanced hatefully at Bradley, then softened his look and his voice. "But as much as I hate to admit it, Maggie is worn out. She's had more children than I can count. It would be nice to have a fresh wench around here."

Bradley bit his thumbnails in anticipation.

"Alright, Bradley. I will take your next payment in full. I trust you have enough saved up to be able to cover it?"

"Yes, sir, I do."

"You may have the nigger, but I want daily reports on him. The moment something goes wrong, I'll hang him myself. And I'll be coming by your quarters regularly to check on your progress. Do you understand?"

"Yes, sir."

"I still have a bad feeling about this, Bradley. I really do. Unfortunately, there are certain sins that I continue to struggle with. We all have a little nigger in us, Bradley. That's why we ask God for forgiveness. Do you understand?"

"Yes, sir."

"Good."

I was dropped on the ground, and kicked in my side for good measure. My head jerked up in response to the pain, and I saw that I was back on the same plantation that I had run away from. All the slaves filed out from the warehouse to see what was happening.

Mr. Talbert turned back to Bradley.

"You break him, and you break him good. If he ruins my slaves, I'll have you hung."

Shock echoed across Bradley's face, but he tried to keep his composure. "Sir?"

"You will never have enough money to restock my slaves, Bradley. If you fail with this nigger, then that is on you and you alone. But if your failure ruins my investments, you don't have the capital to back it, and I won't want you around here to try and repay your debt. I will simply have you hung, and move on. You understand that, don't you, Bradley?"

Bradley's voice lowered. "Yes, sir."

"Good. I'm going in the house. Dudley!"

One of the white men who had captured me ran up to meet Mr. Talbert. "Yes, sir."

"Run down to the docks and see when the next shipment comes in, won't you?"

"Yes, sir."

All the men dispersed except Bradley and Finch, who waited until Mr. Talbert went back inside of his house before taking the thickest rope I had ever seen and tying it around my wrists. I fought as best I could, but my energy was gone and my muscles just wouldn't work. All I could do was mumble.

"Wait...till I...get back...to D.C. Forget...suing...I'ma have... y'all...murcked...in da...street..."

Bradley and Finch laughed as they grabbed the other end of the rope and tugged until it was upright. I felt my arms being pulled above my head, and pretty soon my body was supported only by my wrists. My feet dangled and my torso was stretched like rubber. Gravity pulled on my legs like a barbell, and each second became more and more painful. I tried to scream, but all that came out were short yelps. I figured after a while, my body would rip apart.

I could only lift my head enough to have it fall right back down again. I could still see the slaves staring at me, and suddenly Roka broke out from the crowd and screamed out.

"DON'T LET THEM TAKE DIFFERENT! DON'T LET THEM TAKE DIFFERENT!"

"You shut up, you black bastard!" Bradley pointed at Roka as he yelled. "I had enough of you! Talbert say next time you act up

I can gut ya myself. Say another word, goddammit. I'll feed your heart to the pigs."

I turned my head toward Roka. He stood with his fist clenched, his teeth grinding together, but he kept his mouth closed.

"You!" Bradley stared at Roka, but walked over to the crowd of slaves that stood at the warehouse door. "Y'all take a good look at this here nigger."

He pointed up at me. I tried to kick him, but it was torture to try and use any of my muscles. I gathered as much saliva as I could, which wasn't much, and spit it out. Three tiny drops hit the ground in front of me. The spit wouldn't reach him, but the familiar hocking sound made the slaves gasp. Bradley turned and stared at me in disbelief.

"Go...call...my lawyer..."

Bradley began chuckling uneasily, but eventually fell into a rolling laughter. Finch looked confused, but took his cue from his partner and made himself laugh as well. When Bradley was done, he looked back at the slaves.

"Let this nigger be a lesson for all a' you! I control niggers on this here plantation. You cain't take a squat in a hole without my permission."

He paused to let his message sink in.

"Talbert been protectin' you niggers till now. That black piece a' trash right here—" Bradley pointed again at Roka "—you shoulda been dead, but you pick mo' cotton than any two niggers out here combined. You thinkin' ol Bradley can't get to you 'cause Talbert say so, huh? But watch...you'se watch what happen after I crush this here nigger. Watch how much respect I get...hell, I buy all of you myself!" Again, Bradley pointed at Roka. "First thing I'ma do is cut off your balls and eat 'em for supper."

Bradley broke into a wild, fanatical sort of laughter as he walked over and picked up a whip that had been rolled into a coil. He grabbed the handle and flung the coil so that the whip stretched out to its full length, and grinned menacingly as he prepared to cock his arm back. His laughter didn't move me. I'd already felt as if I was about to die. There was nothing more fearful than what I had already experienced.

Finch reached up and ripped off my shirt. More gasps came from the slaves. I was too weary to wonder what the big deal was.

"Bradley..." Finch kept looking back and forth from me to his partner. "Bradley...looka here...this nigger's back...he ain't...he ain't never been whipped."

Bradley dropped the whip, then walked over and clawed at the flesh on my back. I screamed inside my head. My throat wasn't strong enough to make it audible.

"Where the hell did you come from?" Bradley stared up at me, letting his uneasiness show for a second before he placed his mask back on. He walked back over to the whip he had dropped, and picked it up with a large grin. Squatting down slightly on his knees, he turned back toward me and stopped.

"Don't matter where you came from, you mine now, boy..."

He lifted the whip and cracked it toward me.

Hanging there by my wrists, I was certain that I was in more pain than I could ever express. My body hung limp and swayed with the nudging of the wind, and gravity continued to make an attempt at separating my torso from my legs. My head was pounding, as it had been for several hours now, and my exhaustion prevented me from doing much else other than moaning and swallowing spit. I figured there wasn't anything that could be done to me that was more painful than what I'd already felt.

I was wrong.

Fire from hell ripped the skin from my back. My eyes went

from fluttering to shooting open wider than I'd ever known they could go. My bone-dry tonsils pulsed and released a sound of pure agony.

"UhhhhggghhhhaaaAAAHHH..."

Bradley laughed out loud.

"Finch, I do believe you was right. This boy ain't never felt a whip before! Jesus must be smilin down on me today—give me this good luck."

"Must be," Finch said, and grinned.

I heard the long cord be pulled back and snatched forward, and felt the fire rip more flesh from my back. Cries came up and out from my gut, and had I heard a recording of these sounds, I wouldn't have believed they'd come from me. Every time the whip touched me, it took a piece of life with it. I began to suffocate on my own screams.

"DON'T LET THEM TAKE DIFFERENT!" I could barely make out Roka's voice, even though he yelled loudly.

"Goddammit..." Bradley reached into his pants with his free hand, pulled out his revolver and fired a shot at Roka. It missed Roka and hit an older woman beside him. She staggered backward two or three steps, and then fell down dead.

Three women with cloths wrapped around their heads ran up to the corpse.

"Awww, nooo...NOOOO..."

"Elizabeth...speak t'me, honey...please..."

"Please, Lord, no, please..."

A collective choir of sorrow began. Roka dropped to his knees and picked up the woman's body, and the multitude of slaves carried her back into the warehouse.

"Mr. Talbert ain't gonna be happy about that, Bradley..."

"Just another dead nigger," Bradley said, and pulled the whip back again.

And suddenly it hit me, just as my eyes began to roll to the back of my head. This was no movie. These people weren't actors. No one was going to pop out of the bushes and shout that I had been punked. These weren't kidnappers or people wanting ransom, and this was not an elaborate movie set. This was real. These people were real, the whip was real, and the torture was real. There was nothing fake about any of it.

My body, in an act of genuine mercy, allowed me to pass out.

9

I stared at the face in the mirror with confusion, and then grinned as the sound of the crowd echoed outside the door. The face in the mirror grinned back at me as if its ridiculously large smile was all there was to life.

I felt as if I'd just arrived where I was, although I knew I'd been here for hours. The soundchecks, the makeup, the wardrobe choice, it all felt like it happened in a cloud of time that blew away without ever being noticed. I stood up and looked at myself in the mirror once again. Custom Nikes, skinny jeans, Armani T-shirt and a Burberry jacket draped from my frame. A fresh shape-up outlined my face, and the waves above my hairline were flawless. I was ready to take on the world.

The crowd kept chanting "Nigga....Nigga......Nigga.....!"

I was starting to get hyped up from the crowd. I began bouncing up and down on my toes, throwing punches at my friend in the mirror.

"Hey, Henry, we gonna kill 'em tonight, dogg!"

No one answered. I look around the room, and it was empty. Not one breathing soul between the four walls but me.

I don't remember seeing anyone leave, though, I thought to myself.

After figuring out that everyone would probably burst through the door in any minute to try and get me onstage, I considered sitting down and relaxing for a few minutes. Most of my concerts went for two hours, and even though Henry, Brian, Ray, and Orlando could fill in for me if I got tired, the people paid to see me. I had to give them what they paid for. Most nights I needed a Red Bull and an E pill to enjoy the afterparty.

I sat back down in the plush leather seat and stared again at the grinning face in the mirror. The more I stared at his grin, the more I hated it. He wasn't grinning because he was happy. He was grinning because there was something hurting him, like a paper cut or a broken fingernail. Whatever it was, grinning was the only way he could fight it. If you stared at him long enough, as I had, you could see that the smiling was hurting him more than the affliction.

I reached out my hand to try and move the mirror so that I wouldn't have to look at the face anymore. The person in the glass reached back toward me, as if I held the key to his tears. I jumped back out of the seat.

"Jesus...Is that me?"

"Yes, it is."

I heard the voice, but fear kept me from turning around immediately.

"Who...who are you...?"

"You know who I am, son."

I spun around and my father stood in front of me.

"Dad!"

I ran up to him before I could remember that I wasn't a kindergartener anymore. When I reached him, I threw my arms around his neck and pulled him close enough to smell his cologne. He hugged me back, and almost took the breath out of me. I didn't care, though. I would've gladly suffocated there in his arms.

"Dad...what....where....where have you been?"

"I've been away, son. I've been far, far away."

And we both cried like toddlers after dropping their candy.

After leaving puddles on the floor for us to leave our shoe prints in, my father slowly pulled away from me. I tried to pull him back, but he easily broke away from me. He was always stronger than I was.

"Son, listen to me, okay? Are you listening?"

"Yes, Dad," I said, wiping the mucus from under my nose.

And suddenly his tears stopped and he stared me straight in the eye.

"Son, you can't go out there tonight."

I stopped wiping my nose and looked at my father with shock.

"What do you mean, I can't go out there?"

"I mean, you can't, Moses. You don't know what you're doing. You got power you don't know how to use yet. You can't go out there..."

"The hell I can't, Dad!" I wasn't sure when my joy had turned to irrational anger. I just knew I was seeing red through my blurry eyes.

"You just a boy, son. You don't know..."

"Look, nigga, I took care of Mama and Big Mama when you died! I'm the reason don't neither of 'em have to work no more in they life!"

"Listen to me, son. It's not worth it."

"Ain't worth what? Ain't worth savin' your mama and wife? Whatever, man. Get outta my face."

Dad sighed long and hard, as though he was trying to find a reason not to give up. Finally, he gestured his hand to something behind my back.

I turned around to see SaTia in an outfit that made my jaw fall so that my goatee nearly hit the plush carpet.

"SaTia...what...where did you come from?"

"I just got here, Moe. I came just for you."

I didn't try to hide my confusion.

"SaTia, what are you talkin' about?"

"I think it's time we made things more serious, Moe. I know how you feel about me, and I've loved you since high school. I don't think we should waste any more time."

"Wow...you saying we should...like...get married?"

"Yes, I think we should."

"Where did this come from, SaTia?"

"You do love me, right, Moe?"

I couldn't lie to her anymore. I dropped my head and felt my walls collapse. "More than anything. I...I just never thought..."

"It doesn't matter now, Moe. We can be together now. You will marry me, right?"

My head was spinning. I took a step back and put my hands up to my forehead, trying to steady myself. "I...I don't know what's goin' on."

SaTia took a step toward me and grabbed me by the shoulders.

"Moe. will you marry me? Yes or no?"

I stared her in the eyes. "Yeah, yeah, of course I'll marry you."

She wiped a tear from her left cheek and gave me a deep, passionate hug.

"I'll always love you, Moe, I'll always treat you right, and I'll always be there for you. There's just one thing you have to do..."

Still not completely sure of what was happening, I found myself starting to get excited by the idea of marrying SaTia.

"Yeah, okay, anything. What is it?"

She pulled me back to arm's length from her, so I could see that her face was no longer emotional. It was dead serious.

"You can't go out there tonight."

I don't know where my anger came from. One second I heard

wedding bells, and the next I was ready to put my fist through a wall.

"What the hell is wrong with you people?" I screamed. Both SaTia and my father were taken aback. They began backing toward the wall as my father spoke.

"Listen, son. This girl loves you. All she wants is—"

"Shut up! You shut up! You don't know anything about me. And you," I said, and pointed to SaTia as she winced in pain. "You trying to use my heart to take me from the only thing I love! Take me from the only thing that's ever mattered to me."

SaTia winced again, but this time from a different sort of pain.

"The hell with both of you! You listen and listen good...I will never stop! Out there, that crowd, they waitin' on me. They paid their good money to come see your boy, right here. I'll be damned if I disappoint 'em!"

SaTia and my father were now standing with their backs flat against the wall. They looked terrified. My dad looked at me as if I was pointing a gun to my head.

"Son, please, just hear us out..."

"No! No! This is finished! I'm going out there! Period!"

Both my father and SaTia dropped their heads and began sobbing, but my anger wouldn't allow me to care. I turned to the door, prepared to storm out, but Orlando, Brian, Ray, and Henry stood in front of it. They had the same grins on their faces that the man staring at me through the mirror had. They each had on a pair of old, worn down cotton overalls with no shirt underneath. And they each had a thick noose hanging around their necks. The ropes from the nooses hung down at their sides and dragged the floor.

I walked up to them slowly.

"Yo, y'all aight?"

"We good," Orlando said through his grin.

"What y'all got on, man? You can't go onstage like that."

"This what we supposed to be wearing, right?" Ray spoke up through his clenched teeth.

Confused once again, I walked over and braced myself against the wall. I glanced to my right, and my father and sweetheart were still sobbing. Dad was trying to comfort SaTia, but his tears just made her worse. I turned back to the fellas.

"Guys, man, I have no idea what's going on right now. I'm not even sure how I got here..."

I looked at my entourage and their grins had not changed. Brian took a step toward me.

"Don't worry about it, Moe. You got a crowd out there, waitin', and you know we gonna follow you wherever you go, no matter what. Do what you do."

I nodded my head and the group of four parted, revealing the door. I turned the knob and stepped through into chaos. People in jeans with black shirts and headsets on were running around, trying to prepare for the show. They all smiled at me, but became hellbent once they passed. I looked behind me to see my crew of four still carrying widemouthed grins, and it suddenly became sickening to look at them. I looked away to keep my stomach from turning and worked my way forward.

When I approached the stairs to the stage, one of the technicians handed me a huge, gaudy microphone. I looked at it for a while, and then looked back at her.

"For those great big lips!" she commented as if she was going to pinch my cheek and give me a dollar, but instead she ran past me to take care of some other problem. A tall white man tapped me on the shoulder and began to count down.

"Three...two...one...go!"

I ran out onto the stage with the guys behind me, and the crowd erupted. I let the cheers feed me for a few seconds. I let them clear my mind of the craziness that had just happened backstage. When I was ready, I raised the mic to my mouth and began rapping.

"HOES IN DA ATTIC, YEAH! HOES IN DA ATTIC, YEAH! COME ON TO MY CRIB! I KEEPS SOME HOES IN DA ATTIC, YEAH!"

I stopped. Something wasn't right. The cheers were deafening, the music was blasting, but something was off. I listened to the crowd chant as Henry and Ray picked up my verse. Something wasn't right about it...

Then I realized the problem. How had I not heard it before? The words that the crowd was chanting. They weren't screaming "Nigga," they were chanting "Nigger."

I lowered my mic and looked out over the crowd. It took a while for my eyes to adjust to the light, but what I saw eventually made me drop the microphone. Bradley was standing in the front row, centerstage, leading the cheer. I looked around for the security guard to kick him out, and almost collapsed. Bradley wasn't just front row, centerstage—he was everywhere! It was as if he'd cloned himself a million times and given every version of himself a ticket to this concert. Everywhere I looked, all I saw was the face of the man who'd whipped me.

"NIGGER! NIGGER! NIGGER!"

"Wait a minute, who the hell is Bradley?" I yelled, but the wave of memories had already reached their peak. They came crashing down with a force that tried to drive me insane. Flashes came back like punches in a boxing ring. *The Phil Winters Show*...house in D.C. ...gunshot...empty field...slaves...Bradley...BRADLEY...

"HELP!" I cried out as my dream faded. I woke up facedown on the floor of a horse stable.

"Help..."

The plea carried over from my dream, and I said it aloud as my eyes opened. I felt a lot of sweat on my skin, and noticed how hot it was as soon as I came to. There was something else I felt as well, but I couldn't pinpoint it. Instinctively, I tried to look around to see where I was and what was going on. As it turned out, that was a mistake.

I've heard physicians say that your whole body is connected. It's one of those things you hear and forget, until something traumatic happens to one part of your frame. That's when you realize it for yourself—when you've broken your right arm and discovered that moving your left leg causes you just as much pain as trying to shoot a basketball with the broken arm.

I discovered, quite coincidentally, that if you happen to be strung up and whipped, all of your body parts react to it. I tried to lift my head to get a glimpse of my surroundings, and acid shot out from my back and into every corner and crevice of my body.

I felt a hand swiftly cover my mouth before I could release whatever was coming from my throat. The hand jerked my head slightly and made the acid run again. The pain made my fingers shoot out and the hair on my arms stand up.

I distinguished a voice through the echoing synapses in my head.

"Shhhhhh! We's here tryin' to help you, boy! You gotta be calm, though. We's friends. We jus' tryin' to help."

The agony played a constant, steady drum beat in my ear, and I could barely hear the woman speaking over it. I screamed and cried with her hand still over my mouth. She held me gently, but firm.

"I knows it hurt, son. Feel like you jus' wanna bend on over and die..."

I opened my eyes again and looked down at the hands that covered my lips. They looked like they belonged to a man, although it was a woman's voice that accompanied them. I tried my best to not move a muscle as I let my eyes scan around. I had felt hellfire shoot through my body twice now, and I would try as hard as I could not to feel it again.

Everything I saw was blurry, but I could make out two female slaves standing in front of me to either side. One looked as though she could have been my age, with caramel skin that had been beaten by the sun. The other was middle-aged, with skin the color of a dark oak tree. They both needed perms as soon as possible. I was still on my stomach, so they seemed like giants. One of them pointed to my back.

"Lord Jesus, seem like he jus' got da whip dis mornin'..."

I began to think of questions that I didn't have the strength to ask. Where was I? What day was it? What year was it? The fact that this was really happening began to throb almost as much as the pain. How was this even possible? And most importantly, how did I get out? How did I get back to the world I knew?

I spoke nonsense aloud to whoever was listening. "Cut...the... stereo...off..."

I tried my best to not move so I wouldn't cause anymore pain to go shooting through my muscles. The three women in the shed looked at me and sighed. I could no longer scream, but whimpered as I let my cheek rest on the dirt. The woman holding my mouth took this as a sign that I had stopped making noise, and let my mouth go. She stepped over my body and walked in front of me where I could see her. Her blurred figure stooped down to its knees. She was as close to my face as she could get before she spoke. "I'se Aunt Sarah. I used to be a healer fo' they put me on da ship. I'm tryin' to help you."

I looked up at her while my face still lay sideways on the ground. She was old. If I had to guess, I would've said she was in her sixties or seventies. Her charcoal skin looked as if it had been shorn and grown back a couple of times over, and the wrinkles on her face were motionless as she spoke and moved.

I wasn't used to seeing people this old doing anything other than gazing endlessly out of an institution window while waiting to die. She had kneeled down to me easy and effortlessly, and her posture made her look more like she was thirty.

She confused me, but I had neither the energy nor the will to show it. I was trying to stop my eyes from rolling in the back of my head.

"We don' know nothin' 'bout you, but you'se special. Roka been sayin' it, but we seen how you'se talked to Massa Talbert and Bradley, and we knows you ain't from 'round here. We's been guessin' dat maybe you from way up north, like up far wheres the white folk can't do nuthin to you..."

I wanted to say that I was from a place where white people didn't string up black people and rip all the skin off of their backs. That where I was from, I was a king, a person recognized everywhere I went by both black and white people. I had more money than I could count and more hoes than I could pipe, and my pinky ring (which was lost back in the forest) cost more than all of their lives put together. I wanted to say all of this, but I had just been whipped by a slave overseer. So instead I simply moaned.

"Don' you worry none, whoever you is, you jus' rest. You got da fever, and it gotta break on in its own time. It's been more n' a day now, so you may be seein' things that ain't really there. Jus' remember, if it don' make no sense to be there, then it really ain't."

"I got some salve I put on your back whiles you was sleepin'," Aunt Sarah finished. "We prays it help, if only jus' a lil bit."

She bent down and lightly patted my cheek.

"Poor thing! Bradley jus' a'soon see you dead as be in with the rest a'us. We's been prayin', though! 'Cause if you really..."

There was a noise somewhere in the distance. I didn't hear it, but all three of the women did. They looked at one another with alarmed faces and frantically began picking up their supplies.

"I thought you said Bradley was gon' be gone for hours!" the middle-aged assistant said to the younger one.

"I thought he was!" the youngest one snapped back. "He musta found himself a white girl this time!"

"Shush, both of you," Aunt Sarah snapped at both of the women, and they closed up. "Get all yo' stuff and move! We gets caught in here and we gon' be right where he layin' at!"

The women gathered everything they had brought with them, and ran over to the far east end of the stable. Aunt Sarah felt three of the wooden slabs before she located the right one. With a tug, she lifted and moved it out of the way so that the two younger women could run out, and then went through herself. Before she shut it, she peeked back through the space.

"Hang in there, son. You stay yourself alive, and I promise I be comin' back."

And then she was gone.

It seemed as if days had passed in between the slave women leaving and Bradley showing up in the stable. I knew in my mind that it couldn't have been as long as it felt, but my teeth were aching from being clenched from so long. I might have passed out again, but if I had, I was unaware. The only thing that seemed real anymore was pain.

Bradley stumbled through the door, using effort to hold himself up straight and not lying on the ground with me. I saw him, even though I hadn't moved my head at all, and my gaze followed his trajectory for as long as they could. He glanced down at me as he entered the stable, then laughed and walked over to the corner where I couldn't see him.

I realized at that moment that I hated Bradley. I had never hated anyone before in my life, but I hated the man with everything inside of me. I resolved to kill him the very first opportunity I had.

Even though Bradley was out of my sight, I still heard his footsteps shuffling around. Immediately, I began to worry about his plans. I imagined myself springing up to my feet, running headlong into his abdomen and knocking him to the floor, and then finding a way out of this warped reality I'd found myself in. I imagined the scenario all the way through, but I wasn't willing to risk the pain of moving a limb. When Bradley returned, stumbling yet again, and accompanied by a young white woman, I was in the same place he'd left me.

"Is this here the nigger?" A giggling, high-pitched voice spoke to Bradley as if it was viewing an experiment.

"Yep, this the nigger right here. I don' whipped him somethin' good..."

"He look like a regular nigger to me."

"Naw, sweetheart, he ain't no regular nigger. You heard what they been sayin' 'bout him in town, ain'tcha?"

The white woman continued to laugh as she spoke. "Yeah, but all that stuff is rubbish, Bradley. They sayin' he could take a bite outta tree and fell it to the ground! Somebody say at the market that he could jump twenty feet and devour a mule! He don't look like no special nigger whiles I'm lookin' at 'em."

"But you wasn't here when we caught 'em, Susie. I'm tellin' ya, the nigger got the strength a' ten men!"

Susie laughed at first, but then looked at Bradley, who was keeping as taut a face as he could while being drunk. Her giggles slowed from constant to sporadic, and then stopped altogether as she began to back up.

"Why don't you kill 'im then, Bradley?" The concern in her eyes was glossed over from the alcohol. "He could be dangerous."

"That's why I'm breakin' 'em so hard, sweetheart. See, this nigger could rip me to tiny pieces, but I ain't yellow, see? And I knows that if we can break a nigger like this, he be worth twenty times any ordinary nigger off the boat. He could do the work of ten bucks in a day!"

Susie nodded her head in understanding.

"Mr. Talbert went 'round lookin' fo' men brave enough to take on the challenge of this here nigger, and I'm the only one accepted. And by God, I'ma break this here nigger, or I'm gonna die tryin'!"

Susie leaned against Bradley's arm in a clumsy attempt at affection. Her voice turned to admiration as she spoke.

"You so brave, Bradley...I never knew you was so brave..."

Bradley wrapped an arm around her shoulder and they fell against each other and into a kiss. I still lay on the ground, hearing everything in a barely coherent wave of sounds. When Bradley finally broke away from her, he walked back over to the corner again.

"Watch this here, sweetheart. Call it a lesson in tamin' the savage nigger, eh? Then I'm gon', uh, show you where I be sleepin'."

Susie's giggle came back as she stumbled and nodded her head.

I heard Bradley continue to fumble around. A hollow metal sound echoed around the barn. I thought, for a second, that I should be nervous, but the bass wave from the stereo sent another rush of heat across my body. I gritted my teeth and kept my body still, trying to imagine a way to get back to my reality and out of this hell.

I heard three footsteps and saw Bradley's shadow out of the corner of my eye. He was standing right over top of me with something in his hand. He looked over at Susie and shook his head.

"You betta get yo'self back, sweetheart. Dis here nigger ain't ta be played with. What you 'bout to see ain't fo' the faint of heart..."

"I'm a big girl," Susie said in a tone you'd expect from a three-year-old.

"Aight then..."

Whatever Bradley was holding, it wasn't a whip. He had to grab it with both hands as he towered over my frame, and I could tell by its shadow on the wall that it was some sort of pail. He took a deep breath, lifted it with both arms outstretched above his head, and turned it over.

I thought for a half second, as I watched the falling cloud through the shadow on the wall, that Bradley had sprinkled pixie dust. Everything else seemed possible in this god-forsaken place. Why not some pixie dust? I imagined myself floating up and out of the stable I was confined in, and then flying out of this dream-world like Neo in *The Matrix*. I saw myself traveling back to Mr. Rose, bursting through his window, and cursing him out for not finding me before I was tortured. And then, maybe, I could take my place again. I could go back to my old life.

But there was no pixie dust in the pail, and no escape from this place I'd found myself in. There was only desolation. And despair. And salt.

The tiny white crystals hit my back and everything else was a blur. The agony was so severe I jumped up off of the ground and leaped around like a madman. Bradley and Susie went pale and jumped behind one of the stable doors, but they could've rolled around naked in the hay as well and I would've never known it. When your body reaches a certain level of anguish, your mind shuts down. It's as if it understands that it's safer for you to go insane than to feel what your body is going through. Had I been in my right mind, I would've known that my reaction supressed all doubts that Susie ever had about me being some sort of savage super-nigger. She would leave from Bradley's place and tell her own stories about me, the heathen beast. She would recount that Bradley had dumped the salt on me and I had grown four feet, swelled to the size of an enormous gorilla, and destroyed half of the stable before I shrunk back to my normal size. Whatever transformation I'd gone through, I wound up back on the ground, bleeding all over, and mumbling some lost ancient voodoo language.

My thin line of sanity snapped under the weight of the tiny salt minerals. My body fell back to the dirt floor. In an attempt to regain his pride from cowering, Bradley had begun to beat me with the metal end of his shovel. He had no idea that I wasn't there anymore. Instead, I had been taken to a place inside my head, where I was still dressed in my chains, jewelry, and custom shoes. I stood in the middle of one of the music studios for Rage Recka Records in Miami. I didn't have the time to wonder why it felt as though I was dreaming. My fear hung on me heavier than the rope chain, and was represented by the beads of sweat that ran down my face and splashed on the floor.

I could feel it coming.

I couldn't see it yet, but I could feel it, like a newly diagnosed HIV patient. I didn't know exactly what was coming, but I knew it would kill me eventually.

I heard a loud thud against the entrance of the studio, followed

by what sounded like a tornado and Bradley's voice echoing outside the door. He sounded as though he was swinging something
downward with all the strength his drunken body could muster.

"You dirty nigger! Humph! You thinkin' you can jus' destroy
my stable! Humph! I break every bone in yo body! Humph!"

I took off running. The studio was huge, and I sprinted through
the recording room, out into the mixing room, and through the
hallway with the four office doors on either side. Finally, I rounded
the corner and found the exit. Lowering my shoulder, I burst
through the door just as the unknown force destroyed the entrance
behind me. I glanced back in horror as I saw a white cloud burst
through the room like a gusty stampede. It sounded like a million
Bradleys had jumped in a pool and began playing Marco Polo
with one another. It devoured everything in the studio just as I
slammed through the exit door. I didn't have much time. I
looked around, expecting to be outside on the sidewalk or in the
alley behind the building. I'd hail a cab and have it take me
straight to the nearest hotel. But instead I was in one of Killa
Krack Records' recording studios, staring at their wall of artists
and waving off marijuana smoke.

"How the hell...?"

And then came the thud, and the sound of tornadoes and
Bradley, and again I ran. It continued like this, with me being
chased through every recording studio I'd ever stepped foot in,
and then going back around again and again.

This is what I did, in my head, while Bradley broke me. Every
once in a while I would try and come back; my mind knowing
that if I stayed locked inside for too long I might never come
back out. I'd run through a studio door and fall down on my face,
and when I'd wake up I'd be back in the stable, or outside strung
up while the elements bullied me around, or, toward the end,
locked in a homemade cage with strange people staring at me. I'd

gain enough consciousness to feel the different types of agony that I'd been put through, and to wonder once again how I'd gotten where I was. Eventually, I'd hear Bradley's voice and begin to hyperventilate. He'd come and grab me, and take the time to prepare me for whatever sick torture he'd devised the previous night. And right before he would begin, my mind would burst back through my consciousness and drag me back down to the depths of its abyss; to the neverending chase. I would be so deep down into my subconscious that I would barely remember anything until I was allowed to re-emerge.

Later, Aunt Sarah would put me through a ritual that would unlock these memories. I'd remember being pissed and defecated on. I'd remember being whipped multiple times a day. I'd remember having my left pinky finger cut off and stuffed into my mouth. I'd remember being starved, and being made to drink pig urine, and being sodomized with a bayonet. I'd remember all of this later, when my mind could digest the thoughts and not vomit them back up. For now, there was another world inside my head where I was constantly being chased, but I was still free. I decided how fast and how long I wanted to run—no one else did. And so when Bradley approached me with the sharp metal end to his war rifle, for example, my mind would trigger the trapdoor and drop me back into oblivion. And all I did was run. From studio to studio, constantly being pursued. I never got exhausted. I never got sore. But I was always terrified. I couldn't help feeling as though I'd eventually be caught, no matter what I did.

It happened one day when my mind had released me to my consciousness, and I was trying to pick myself up from the bottom of the cage I had been locked in. It seemed as though every time I would find my way back into consciousness, the pain that my body had gone through had decided not to leave. Now, after the endless torture I'd endured, my entire body bore the weight of all the days combined. I lay on the ground and felt as if I was being stepped on, and no matter how hard I tried, I could not get up. I placed both my palms on the ground, pushed up with all the strength I had left, and went nowhere.

Before I fell back down to the earth, I heard the faintest sound of footsteps on the dry ground.

I didn't know what Bradley had in store for me, and I couldn't even lift my head to see if he had anything with him. When my mind tried to pull the trapdoor, and drop me back into my subconscious yet again, something went wrong. My mind was too weak to protect me.

I knew then that I would die. Whatever Bradley was planning would kill me.

I placed my palms flat on the ground and tried to push myself up again, but this time I heard a snap and felt a thin needle enter into my right elbow and run its way down to my wrist. I collapsed on top of it, and silently writhed as my tormentor unlocked my cage and stepped up so his boots met my earlobe.

I was no longer Da Nigga, and I had no more pride left. The rapper with the gaudy jewelry and pristine clothes was gone. What was left was a sunken-faced, malnourished skeleton. In despair and desperation, I reached out, grabbed Bradley's ankle, and wept at his feet. I had no other options, and what little bit of life I had left in my body, I wanted to save.

Slowly, I heard Bradley laugh. It began as a low, deep laughter, and then grew into a rousing, exuberant howl. I continued to hold on to him and weep as his laughter finally died down, and he crouched and patted me on the head. "Now, dat there's a good nigger..."

And after a moment he turned around, closed the cage behind him, and walked away smiling.

10

I didn't know how long I'd been in the cage that Bradley made. It was made of all wood, and the bars would've been near impossible to break if I was at my strongest. I barely had enough strength to sit up straight now, though, so escaping was not an option.

The cage sat apart from anything else, like it was the sole attraction of the field. It was long enough for me to lie flat on my chest with my legs out, which is how I stayed most of the time. It wasn't tall enough to stand up in, but my legs were broken. I couldn't have stood up anyways.

The days came and went, without even seeming to pass. I spent the time in my wooden box, huddled in the corner and trying not to look through the bars to a world I did not know. My body had changed so drastically I hardly recognized myself when I looked down at my arms, legs, torso, and feet. My skin had changed color. What used to be a caramel hue was now faded the color of moldy wheat bread. Black and white splotches were randomly situated across my body, and whenever I scratched them the skin would give way and a sore would emerge that would bleed continuously for hours. I was later told that the reason my skin seemed to be rotting off was because I had been fed a steady diet of rotten trash and pig dung. I had stopped caring about what food was given to me. I'd eat whatever was brought to me, with the knowledge that, like clockwork, my body would reject most of it within the following minutes. Whenever Aunt Sarah could, she and the girls would sneak away and bring me food that didn't stampede through my stomach and out of my crevices. I would swallow it whole, forgetting to chew or taste it, and immediately become angry for not savoring it more. Then I would huddle up again with my back against the bars.

There wasn't a square inch on the floor of that gorilla cage that I hadn't vomited, urinated, or defecated on. Avoiding contaminated areas was useless, and so I huddled and lay down anywhere. I didn't open my mouth for anything except food. There was no reason to talk, and until I figured out who, where, and what I now was, it would only come out as gibberish anyways.

In my other life, I'd once given a bunch of money to a charity dedicated to the treatment of AIDS in the inner city. At the ceremony they'd thrown in appreciation, I met a man named Jerry. Jerry was HIV positive, but was built like a bodybuilder. The founders of the organization explained that they used Jerry to drive home the point for teenagers that anyone could have HIV, no matter who they were or what they looked like. Seven months later, Jerry's HIV had turned into full-blown AIDS. Two weeks before his death, he made a request to see me again. Mr. Rose implored me to go, and sent along a TV crew to help portray me as a patron saint. I walked past Jerry's bed twice, without recognizing him, before he finally called out to me. I couldn't believe it. He looked nothing like he used to. His chiseled frame was gone, replaced with a talking skeleton that had skin covering the bones for good measure.

"That's not the same youngin' I met before," I remember telling SaTia at the time. "They switched up guys on me or somethin'. That's not the same dude."

Now, staring at my own foreign limbs and unfamiliar skin, I thought the same about myself. I was Jerry, and AIDS seemed merciful compared to what was happening to me.

I was missing a finger. I had no idea where it had gone, or how it had been taken, but the nub left behind sent vibrations through my arm. The natural movement of my body was gone as well, replaced by a limp, a stagger, and sharp pains that I was still learning to manage. If I raised my right arm too high, the right side of my torso sent an electric shock through the rest of my body. If I straightened my left knee out as far as it could go, the lower half of my body went numb and was useless for the next half-hour at least. Every move of my body had a consequence, and the only way to avoid them was to keep still.

As the days drew on, I noticed that more and more white people began coming to Bradley's little section of the plantation. I only took notice because they seemed to wander for a moment, and then come straight to my cage. They would point and stare in awe while I ignored them. If I moved for any reason, they would jump back and rise up on their toes, ready to sprint away at the slightest sign of trouble. But mostly they just pointed, stared, and carried on conversations that passed through my ears without ever being actually heard. Two or three people turned into crowds of twenty and thirty, and trickles of conversation became rivers of noise as they poked and prodded and pointed and laughed. I didn't care.

One day, both Bradley and Mr. Talbert came strolling up to my wooden abode. It had just finished raining, and the freezing dampness made my body numb. I lay on the ground, huddled in a fetal position, with green mucus smudged in with the dirt on my face. I recognized both of their voices, but I couldn't move. I don't think they would've stood so close to me and held the conversation they had under normal circumstances, but because I hadn't spoken in weeks, they'd both probably concluded that Bradley had beaten me deaf and dumb.

"How did you do this, Bradley?" Mr. Talbert said as if he was viewing a magic trick. "How did you pull this off?"

"Well, Mista Talbert, all I did was follows ya example. I sees this nigger here and I think Bradley—this yo' chance right here. Take dis nigger and show 'em what you can do!"

"I'll say! You showed everyone in this town what you could do. He doesn't even look like the same nigger anymore."

"I knows it. He was a tough one to crack. Any of these regular niggers would've been died long time ago, sir."

"He ever tell you where he was from?"

"No, sir, he never said nothin' 'bout it, and I wasn't asking."

"No, you wouldn't, would you have?"

Bradley stopped and looked at Mr. Talbert. He knew he had been insulted, but didn't understand how exactly. After a few seconds of silence, Mr. Talbert placed his hand on Bradley's shoulder. "Well, let me congratulate you, Bradley. You've managed to tame the savage beast! Susie went around telling everyone the story, and now the town thinks you're a hero."

"That story true just as I'm standing here, Mr. Talbert! The nigger—"

"Oh, please, save me the fantasies, Bradley. You may have everyone else fooled with the story, but for God's sake, give me some credit! We both know that nigger never turned into some giant ape and destroyed your stable. He was more civilized than you when we first found him."

Bradley tried to mask his hate, but he didn't have to. Mr. Talbert had never taken his emotions seriously.

"But I guess that doesn't matter, does it?" Mr. Talbert continued as he looked over and observed my mangled body. "People believed you two, and now you're a hero. You saved this town from the ape-nigger, or whatever else people are calling him these days. You've made a name for yourself. Have you gotten any clients yet?"

"Mr. Stanley say he bringin' his nigger down Monday," Bradley said through clenched teeth.

"That's wonderful! You do remember our agreement, right?"

"Yes, sir. I'll keep usin' your land, and you get part a' the money every month, sir."

"Good, Bradley. Good. You learn well. I do believe I was prepared to get little Katie out here to spell it out for you in...umm... simpler terms..."

Bradley would've killed any other man for a statement like that. He was at least twice the size of Mr. Talbert, and could easily overpower the smaller man; I imagine an invisible force must've kept him from laying a hand on Mr. Talbert, or even speaking ill of him.

He inhaled a deep breath. No, he couldn't swing a punch at Mr. Talbert, but he could attack in other ways—below the belt. He fixed his face into a smile and turned to face his tormentor. "I made myself a pretty good inves'ment keepin' this here nigger..."

"Yes, you did, Bradley. Quite good, I must say."

Bradley scrunched up his face in feigned contemplation. "You thinkin' it was stupid for me give up my wages?"

"No, no, Bradley, that wasn't stupid. Look what it got you. You're a lucky man."

Bradley pretended to ponder once again, and then turned slowly back to Mr. Talbert. "You must'a been able to buy somethin' real nice with all the money, sir."

"Well, actually, I..." Mr. Talbert stopped mid-sentence, realizing where Bradley had brought the line of questioning. He swiftly picked up his fist and brought it across Bradley's jaw. Bradley's head turned with the force of the blow. Only a keen eye would've caught the smirk on his face right before the impact.

"You insolent little prick!" Mr. Talbert spat out.

Bradley immediately shifted the features on his face, and when he turned back to Mr. Talbert, he looked like a wounded poodle.

"I'm sorry, sir! I'm sorry! I meant nothin' by what I said! Ain't meant nothin' by it!"

Mr. Talbert studied him long and hard, looking for a reason to believe his disrespect had been anything but unintentional. But Bradley wore the mask as good as any slave, and Mr. Talbert couldn't find one.

"You sure are a dumb one, Bradley. You don't even know when you're insulting a man, do you?"

Bradley rubbed his cheek and looked down sheepishly at the ground. "No sir, I was jus' thinkin' out loud when you struck me, sir. Ain't know I was offendin' you."

"Well, you need to be very careful when you're talking to a gentleman, Bradley. We offend easily, and I would've hated to punish you for something you were too ignorant to understand."

"Yes, sir."

Introspection crept over Mr. Talbert's face as his anger dissipated and he wandered into thought.

"You know, Bradley, Satan really is all about seeking whom he may devour..."

"Yes, sir. I knows it."

"That money could've been spent on a lot of things. A good many things. Gifts for my wife—my daughters...you know how the girls love the dolls from up north..."

"Yes, sir?"

"But Mr. Stanley had a wench. A wench that I had my eye on

every time I visited. She worked in his kitchen. I asked him once if he'd ever...umm...sinned against God, and he told me the midwife kept her too close..."

Bradley knew where his boss's monologue was going, but he continued to play dumb.

"Sir...I...I don't know if I'm the right one to tell this to..."

Mr. Talbert wasn't listening. His pants bulged as he continued to reminisce.

"You know what I did with all the money I saved from not paying you? I took it right down to Mr. Stanley, and gave it to him in exchange for that pretty little wench. That midwife. Boy, she put up a good fight! Stanley said it was the first he'd ever whipped her. And that little wench screamed and cried something awful, but she ended up in my carriage. Yes, she did. And when she was so far away that she couldn't see her home anymore, she sat there beside me and purred like a kitten. Christ help me, I almost threw her out and ravaged her on the side of the road...Christ help me..."

Bradley remained silent. Mr. Talbert shook in disgust with himself, and then snapped back into the present day. He looked around, and then at Bradley. When he spoke again, it was as if he was trying to keep a secret from himself. "You've had your share of nigger wenches, right?" he asked in a strained whisper.

"Yes, sir, I have."

"I think their crotches have some sort of spell in them. Some kind of African voodoo magic that makes them impossible to resist. I swear, I've never felt anything like it. No matter how much I pray and read the scriptures, no matter how much I ask Jesus Christ to take this burden from me...I...I just can't stop..."

He sighed loudly, and turned around and began making his way back to the plantation. This wasn't the first time he had confessed his sins to Bradley, and it wouldn't be the last, either. Sleeping with slaves, if the knowledge became public, would ruin a reputable man. Mr. Talbert couldn't even tell his priest about his indiscretions. But he'd told Bradley, because he knew Bradley's survival depended on his satisfaction. Bradley, in turn, knew he would never share his boss's secrets. The damage it would do to him would be far greater than any injuries suffered by Mr. Talbert. But Bradley knew how much his obsession with slave women made Mr. Talbert hate himself. The torture he put himself through was enough satisfaction to last Bradley a few years, and as long as he kept his sins consistent, they would last him for the days to come as well.

My days continued to arrive and depart, like trains traveling through a busy station. The crowds began to dwindle down to three or four people a day—most of them out-of-towners who'd been told about the community's main attraction. Sometimes a child would have a recurring ape-nigger nightmare, and the mother and father would bring them to my cage to show them that the beast was contained and, according to the way I looked and smelled, damn near dead. The child or children would take turns throwing stones and debris at me as I huddled on the floor. They'd do this until they were satisfied I wasn't hiding under their beds at night, and then they'd go home content. My mind was so fragile by this time that I had begun smiling at the children when they came. Apparently though, for someone in my condition, a smile looks more like a growl, and I would inadvertently scare both child and adult. They would promptly run away and go and get the hero, Bradley, who would swing open the cage door and quite efficiently knock me unconscious or semi-conscious. He'd then hand the shovel, or bat, or whatever the object of choice was for the day, to the first person brave enough to take it (usually a father), who would gingerly step into the cage and begin to beat me, too. The blows always started softly, because of their fear of being in the cage in the first place. After they were confident that I wouldn't jump up and eat them, however, the blows came with much more force. Mothers and children would observe the fun that Daddy was having, and inevitably they'd yell out with glee that they wanted a turn as well. My beating would turn into a family affair that, on most occasions, left me so broken Bradley would only bring me partially rotten food to eat for the next few days—until it seemed as though my strength had come back. Then it was back to fully rotten trash, pig dung, and business as usual.

Aunt Sarah still snuck me food a couple of nights a week, and so that became the time I was most active. During the day I lay flat in my cage like a deer that had been hit and laid on the side of the road to die. At night, though, I began to learn the dynamics of my new body. I learned which angles and movements caused a pain that made me faint, and which angles caused a pain that I could live with. I learned how to deal with the agony in my shoulders in order to reach out and grab whatever food was given to me. I retaught myself how to use my arms and how to operate on broken legs, and eventually I was able to push up on all fours. On the nights that Aunt Sarah or one of the girls brought me food, I would crawl from one end of the cage to the other and back before the sun came up. On the days that they didn't make it, I'd make it halfway to one side and pass out from exhaustion.

I still hadn't spoken a word to anyone. Not even Aunt Sarah.

Somewhere, in some faraway land, I had been a king. My voice had been known around the world.

I was terrified of the sounds that would come out of my mouth now.

On a particularly hot day, when the transparent heat waves could be seen off in the distance, a young white man walked up to my cage. I saw him through my half-closed eyelids, and I figured he had come to spectate like everyone else. My mouth hung open and my tongue hung limply out of the right side. I decided not to move.

When he got close enough, he found something to cover his nose and mouth to help block my stench. He looked to be about thirty years old, and he wore a solid black shirt, black pants, and a collar that I used to see the preacher from the church on the corner wear.

By this time, Bradley had gotten business from many of the slave owners in the town. If he could tame a beast, they figured, then knocking their most troublesome slaves down to size shouldn't be a problem. He had kept four slave men tied up at various places around the land, and would torture them incessantly, stopping only if they cried like babies or lost consciousness. He was becoming masterful at inducing either one....

The day the young white man came to see me, the screams of the slaves echoed off of the trees and caused the wildlife to pray. Their agony had been mine once, and I shed dry tears for them regularly.

The man walked up with anguish as his background music. When he got to my cage, the cloth still covering his mouth, he regarded me with a great deal of intrigue. Most who came had a distinct curiosity. They bathed in the danger of doing something to make me turn back into an ape, and when I didn't, they credited

Bradley for his bravery and effective nigger-breaking methods. But this man actually tried to look at me—to see who I was. He regarded me from head to toe, looking for something that was either never there or stolen along with my freedom. I allowed my eyes to fully open, spending more energy than I thought it would take. I looked back at the white man, unsure of his motives. When our eyes were locked long enough, he lowered his handkerchief and stepped up to the bars.

"Where are you from?" he whispered.

It was the first time since I had been pulled from my subconscious that I was reminded of where I had come from. I lay virtually motionless, yet my mind leaped into thoughts of jewelry and concerts and women and drugs. My mind flashed through pictures of five-star hotels and strip clubs, and for the first time since I'd lost myself, I tried to speak. Fueled by a new determination, I lifted my head about two inches off the ground. The old man noticed my slight movement and stared in disbelief.

"You...you're...you're not...are you...trying to talk?"

The young white man's eyebrows jumped up in fear and excitement. He couldn't decide whether to stay where he was or take off for the woods. I concentrated on the muscles in my lips and tongue and willed them to move to form words. I wanted to scream. I wanted to jump up and run headfirst into the bars and proclaim that this was not my world, that God had made some sort of cosmic mistake and dropped a square peg into a round hole. I pressed my lips together as tight as I could and exhaled, hoping to hear the word please come out of them.

"Mmm...mmph...mmph...mmph..."

I sounded like a wounded horse. My lips would barely separate themselves, much less form any words. The screams in the air continued to set the ambiance. Defeated and exhausted, I let my head fall back to the dirt. The excitement on the white man's face faded as I let my eyelids drop back down to half-open. I was in hell. There was no use in hoping for any sort of redemption.

"I don't know if you can hear me," the white man began. "Or if you can understand me at all, but I'm Reverend Lewis. I'm new here in Charleston. I came straight down here from Massachusetts to spread the good news of Christ Jesus!"

He spoke with an excitement that I hadn't heard since encountering my last groupie. He sounded as if he was twelve and Jesus was his new toy.

"You seem to be a local superstition around these parts. People use the story of the ape-nigger to scare their children into behaving or going to bed on time. I heard so much about you that I had to come and see for myself."

He looked at me critically again, trying to draw his own conclusions. Finally, he sighed and looked into my eye.

"Honestly, I don't know what you are. If you're a man, which you very well might be, then there's no excuse for them locking you up and treating you like an animal. If you are indeed human, then this is the most inhumane situation I've ever seen. But if you're something else...well then, I don't know. I don't know how the Lord feels about it...I've..." He paused and laughed incredulously. "I've only prayed for actual people before...never any animals, I'm sorry to say."

I could see the conflict on Reverend Lewis' face. He had come to see if there was a man here that needed to be set free. But he'd heard so many stories, and my condition was so barbaric, that he must've had a hard time separating fact from fiction. How could he be sure that what he was looking at was a human being if it held the closest resemblance to a dying beast?

"Well," he said as he prepared to leave, "everything on God's green earth needs prayer, I suppose." He stepped closer to the bars and bowed his head.

"Let us pray...Our Father, which art in heaven, hallowed be Thy name. Thy kingdom come..."

I thought my heart would leap a hurdle over my rib cage and charge through my chest. Big Mama! Big Mama used to say the Lord's Prayer at least ten times a day. She'd make us say it at the table before any meal, and she was liable to break out with it at the most unlikely and random times. When she'd said it to herself, though, when she thought no one else was listening, that was when she made it feel as if God was using her words to step down from heaven. They would hover in the air, dipped in emotion, and it was not uncommon for someone to unknowingly walk into the room and stop mid-sentence, knowing that something was in the air..

The Lord's Prayer. Big Mama. Mama. Dad. SaTia. How had I managed to forget them? The times I'd spent using my mind to take me back to my old life, I'd sustained myself with images of voluptuous women and insanely expensive cars. But now, thinking of Big Mama saying the Lord's Prayer, I realized for the first time since I'd woke up in the field all that had been taken away from me. My God, I thought to myself, I'd almost forgotten them.

I felt a pain deeper than any physical ailment. I'd almost let them go. The people closest to me, the people who'd cared the most for my well-being, I'd almost let their memories die inside of my head and heart. I'd reduced my past life to a series of sex acts and blurry hip hop performances. I'd forgotten about the Lord's Prayer, and everything else that had happened in my life before I became Da Nigga.

The pain erupted before I could try and contain it.

"....die.....die....wheel...beedone...in...earf...asssseeeettttttiiiii-isssss...en....heben..."

A tiny little weight dropped in the bottom portion of Reverend Lewis' jaw. His eyebrows shot up, but this time they stayed up and refused to come down. He took one step back, then another, and then tripped over a tree root that had sprung up from the ground. He fell backward and hit the ground, his eyes on me and his mouth open the entire time. He scrambled back a few paces on his hands and feet, then flipped his body around so that he was on all fours and scrambled back up the hill like a squirrel.

I would never see Reverend Lewis again. The pale shade of his face after hearing me had convinced me of that. But I already owed him more than I could ever repay. I lay back down on the dirt floor and let memories flood my mind. I remembered the look on Mama's face after my dad's funeral, and how Big Mama acted as if nothing had ever happened, spending entire days in church every once in a while after that. I remembered Mama dropping me off for my first day of high school, and watching SaTia walk up the steps like a prom queen. How could I have forgotten these things? How could I have lost so much of myself?

I figured that I'd never see Reverend Lewis again, but if I did, no matter how many years I'd have to wait, I'd try my best to open my mouth again and thank him for waking me up.

As it turns out, my chance came in the next half-hour.

I heard the pastor's voice before I actually saw him. The excitement that he had before was gone, replaced by a barely controlled rage. Mr. Talbert walked swiftly behind him, and Bradley walked in front of both of them with his arms outstretched on either side.

"Please! Please, Mista Talbert, you can't do this, sir! Think 'bout the business this nigger done brought in! We's becomin' rich folks!"

"You're becoming rich off of this nigger, Bradley," Mr. Talbert responded matter-of-factly, very aware of Reverend Lewis' presence. "I'm financing it, and you're able to put some spare change in my pocket. That is all."

"I don't care who's making money off of this operation, sir!" Reverend Lewis' voice bellowed over his companions. "It stops now! This nigger is a human being! There's a human behind these bars!"

"It...it ain't no human, though. You mistaken, sir! You ain't been here long 'nough to know, but this here's an ape-nigger! I seen him...!"

"Shut up!" Reverend Lewis pointed a finger straight at Bradley. "You shut up! You've got this entire community thinking he's some kind of savage beast! This nigger knows the Lord's Prayer! The Lord's Prayer! Do you know the Lord's Prayer, Mr. Bradley?"

"Yes, sir...well...some a' the words escape me, but I knows I..."

"My point exactly! I know your type, Mr. Bradley. You torture these niggers because you know you're closer to them than you'll ever be to a civilized white man. I'd reduce your entire story to hogwash if Mr. Talbert hadn't verified how you found this nigger and what he looked like. Now I don't know where he came from, but I intend to find out from his mouth. You let him out of there now!"

The three men must have caused enough commotion coming from the plantation to draw the attention of the other slaves. A few of them were sneaking into the forest one by one, hiding behind trees that were close enough for them to hear the argument taking place. Aunt Sarah and Roka had gotten so close that I could make them out when they poked their heads around the tree. They looked at each other with wide eyes when they heard Reverend Lewis' command.

Bradley shook his head from side to side like a guilty four-year-old. When he spoke he sounded the same.

"Naw, sir...I can't do that. I can't let him out for nobody. People in this town, they expects me to keep 'em safe. They expects me to protect 'em by keepin' this ape-nigger at bay, sir, and that's what I plan to do."

It was Mr. Talbert's turn to shake his head. "Bradley, my friend, I do believe you've fallen for your own trick..."

Bradley looked at Mr. Talbert with confusion, then back at Reverend Lewis with hate.

"You can't have him."

Reverend Lewis turned his gaze from Bradley back to Mr. Talbert.

"I am a man of the cloth, sir. Therefore I will not threaten physical violence against your employee. However, Mr. Talbert, you know who my father is, and you know how much his business affects cotton crops like yours down here in the south. I'm afraid, Mr. Talbert, that if we cannot come to some sort of agreement with this situation..."

"You don't have to say any more." Mr. Talbert no doubt felt the discomfort of having to play by someone else's rules. He looked back to Bradley with genuine sadness. "I'm sorry, Bradley. I know how much this nigger means to you, but you're going to have to let him go."

By this time, enough of the slaves had snuck into the woods surrounding Bradley's operation that their reaction to Mr. Talbert's words was audible. Mr. Talbert looked around in confusion, but Bradley responded before he could say anything. "No! Naw, sir! No!"

"Bradley, don't make this a harder situation than it already is. Look, if the people ask you what happened, you tell them the truth. You tell them that it was Reverend Lewis' decision..." Mr. Talbert gestured toward Reverend Lewis, who shrugged uncaring shoulders.

"Tell them that he made you set the nigger free. Everyone knows that his father is H.P Lewis. Hell, anyone with any status in this town is wearing his daddy's clothes as we speak. They'll know you didn't have a choice, Bradley. But you have to be smart. You have to let him go."

To everyone's surprise, including my own, Bradley broke down into a fistful of tears. He began mumbling through his sobbing.

"I...I...Dis...nig...nig...ger...I...cain't...cain't...wh...why...why..."

Obviously not expecting the show of emotion, Reverend Lewis and Mr. Talbert withdrew slightly and looked at each other with a shared discomfort. After a few seconds, Mr. Talbert gave a deep sigh and walked up to the basket case. "Look, Bradley...umm...it will be alright, okay? Why...umm...why don't you come into the house? I'll have some tea made for you, huh?"

Bradley continued to weep uncontrollably as Mr. Talbert gingerly placed a hand on his back and began to nudge him back up the hill. Reverend Lewis stopped them after three steps. "I'm sorry, but I'll need the key to this nigger's cage. I plan to have him loose before you return."

Bradley turned toward Reverend Lewis, his face bright red and sopping wet. He had hate glaring out of his glassy eyes. "If I had me's a gun, you would be in the ground by now, sir..."

Reverend Lewis kept a slight smirk on his face. "Well then, Mr. Bradley, I'll thank my Lord above that you can't afford one."

Bradley took the key to the cage out of his pocket and hurled it at Reverend Lewis. It struck the pastor on the side of the head, and his eyes burned with hellfire for five seconds before he calmed himself down enough to bend and pick up the key. When he looked back at Bradley, his smirk had come back, but the unholiness in his eyes still remained.

"You'll pay for that, Mr. Bradley. Sooner rather than later, I promise you."

Mr. Talbert shoved Bradley forward before he could say or do anything else, and they proceeded up the hill to the house.

After they had gotten further up the hill, and Reverend Lewis had gotten the red flashes out of his brain, he walked up to the door of my cage. I was still lying there, like a carcass out in the sun, but I'd heard the entire conversation. When the pastor stuck the key in the lock and opened the door to my prison, he realized he wasn't fully prepared for what he would find. After coming close enough to see my pulsating sores, his body betrayed him and he vomited all over me. The chunky liquid splashed down on my skin and was welcome with all of the other impurities. Staggering, Reverend Lewis made his way back out of the cage and up the hill for some fresh air. When he got to the top, he turned and faced the woods.

"You niggers who came into the woods earlier," he bellowed out into the brush. "Which one of you knows any nigger medicine?"

"I do, sah," Aunt Sarah answered as she emerged from the woods. She, Roka, and the other slaves had been creeping their way back toward the plantation, hoping to return before they were caught. She kept her eyes focused on the fallen leaves as she spoke....

"Do you know that nigger down there in the cage?"

"Yassah."

"Do you think he'll live?"

"Don't know, sah."

"Well, go grab some other niggers and take him out of that cage. Fix him up, get him cleaned up and fed."

"Yassah."

As Reverend Lewis walked away, Roka signaled for four of the slaves. They came down the hill and entered my cage. Two of them grabbed my armpits, two of them grabbed my thighs, and Roka lifted my head up by the chin. My eyes fluttered as he spoke.

"I knowed it be true..."

I had no idea what he was talking about, and I didn't care. My cage was empty. I was free.

11

"Get on outta there, all you! Bennie, Liza, y'all get movin' and fetch all daroots I done laid 'round here! Nessie, gone head and throws all dastuff off the bed and on da floor! Roka, lays 'im down right here! Lawd, we's see a miracle if he make it through da night!"

People scurried around the little hut as though it was a third-world emergency room. Roka and the other men carried me like a treasure chest. If they saw and smelled the same thing Reverend Lewis did, they didn't show it. When they brought me inside the hut, everyone else's face turned a shade of dark green, and Nessie ran outside, along with three other girls. Seconds later, their vomit left pastel colors on the ground. When Nessie came back, Aunt Sarah snatched her up with her left hand while mixing three herbs in a bowl of water with her right.

"Is you done? I gots me a life need savin'..."

"Yessum," Nessie answered with her face to the ground.

"Good. Go take these here buckets and find Bennie and Liza! Y'all head out to da creek and take up asmany leeches you c'find, hear?"

"Yessum." She kept her face to the ground as she took the buckets and ran off out the hut. Aunt Sarah turned her attention back to me.

"How he do?" Roka turned to Aunt Sarah with an eyebrow raised.

"He half dead...shoulda been all da way dead long time go. Been waitin' weeks to hear dis boy died off in dat cage. Folks don' live like dat for too long. Boy got somethin' in 'im, Roka. Don' know what, but it been keepin' 'im from passin' on."

Roka nodded his head in agreement.

"He be okay?"

"Lawd Jesus naw! Good sneeze'll send him to his maker!"

"What we do?"

"First thing's pray whatever keeping him alive keep on doin' what it doin'. Makin' roots to help 'im, but it ain't us keepin' him here. If he last long 'nough for da girls to get back, I can put da leeches to 'im."

Roka nodded his head again, and then looked over at me. After staring quietly for a few seconds, he turned back to Aunt Sarah with his index finger pointed to his chest.

"You need?"

"Naw, naw, I don't. I'm gon give 'im these here roots, but all to do nows wait. Longs I'm in here, he still alive."

Roka pointed to the small door of the hut.

"I stop dem come here."

"Yea, that's good thinkin'. Don' wan't nobody botherin' 'im. If I come out—"

Roka cut her off with a nod of his head, and made his way to the small door. After stepping outside, he sat like a boulder in front of it. He kept his back straight, his eyes fixed ahead, and he became a gargoyle until someone came near enough for him to either grab or gaze fearlessly at.

I lay in the bed with my eyes fluttering, though they refused to actually see anything. Somehow I knew I was with Aunt Sarah, even though my brain seemed to be operating in Morse Code. I wasn't conscious, but I knew, for now, that I was safe. My skin burned and I had a fever hot enough to burn a hole through the mattress. Aunt Sarah finished mixing her roots into the water, and slowly and painfully poured the bitter liquid into my mouth. She had to do it easily, or it would've backed up behind my swollen throat like a stopped-up sink. After I'd ingested half of her concoction, my body wretched and convulsed and I defecated explosively. Aunt Sarah hummed softly as she waited for me to finish, and then rolled me over like a baby and thoroughly cleaned me. When she was done, she rolled me back over again and painstakingly poured the rest of her concoction down my swollen throat.

After the second fireworks show from my bowels, Bennie, Liza, and Nessie finally returned. They would have burst through the door, had Roka not stopped them cold and permitted them to enter. They came with their pockets full of odd-looking herbs and roots, each one of them carrying a bucket full of leeches.

"Quick, bring them!" Aunt Sarah commanded before they had all stepped fully through the door. They each rushed her their bucket, and artistically she took a single leech and carefully held it to my stomach until it latched itself onto my skin and began to feed itself with my blood.

"Y'all seen what I'm doin'?" Aunt Sarah asked the ladies.

"Yessum," they replied in unison, but with uncertainty in their tones.

"Then I needs y'all to do exactly what I done. Don' do nothin' different! Save for his face, neck, an' privates, he need his whole body covered. Y'hear?"

"Yessum..." The ladies looked back and forth, waiting for the bravest one of them to reach in and grab a leech.

Aunt Sarah reached into the bucket and grabbed her second one. She bent over to place it on my body, then stopped and looked at the younger women.

"Y'all waitin' for his permission?"

"No'm."

"Move then!"……

Choosing disgust over the wrath of Aunt Sarah, each of the women plunged a hand in the bucket. Aunt Sarah ignored their muffled grunts and moans.

"Jus' like I did it," Aunt Sarah harshly reminded the women. By the time they'd reached in the bucket for a third time, the younger women had struck up a conversation.

Aunt Sarah listened, but didn't speak. She was too busy trying to save my life.

It wasn't until my upper body was completely covered in leeches before Aunt Sarah noticed one of the leeches moving. She stared in quiet horror, so as not to alarm the other women. The leech moved slowly and in a straight line, leaving a trail of transparent slime behind it. As the angle coming down my side steepened, the leech moved faster, until finally it reached the edge of my side and fell off of my body completely. Bennie screamed out as the leech thumped beside her foot, lying motionless.

"It's dead," Aunt Sarah said like a scientist. "My Jesus…it's dead…"

She looked up slowly at the other women.

"Check the leeches y'all put on 'im first…"

All the women began reaching out and checking to see if the leeches still had a hold on my skin. Almost half of them were nothing more than lifeless decorations.

"What's happenin', Aunt Sarah?" Liza looked confused. "Why they not movin'?"

"Dis boy blood got poison 'nough to kill da po' things," Aunt Sarah said, shaking her head. "Ain't never seen nothin' like dis… not in none my days…"

By the time they'd finished checking all of the creatures, more than half of whom were found to be dead or dying, Aunt Sarah took them all and dumped them into one of the buckets, and then took the bucket to the door. She turned and looked at Roka before she walked past him. His gaze fell sullenly to the floor.

"Naw! Naw, Roka, he ain't dead; just sicker than anybody I ever seen. I needs you to dig up a hole for these here leeches. They dead now, and if they stay above ground they gon' smell worse den anything you ever knowed."

Roka jumped up and began sprinting away. Aunt Sarah called after him.

"Hold a minute, boy!"

Roka stopped and turned around.

"When you comes back, needs you to go back down da creek with the girls. They gotta get mo', and I don't want 'em runnin' 'cross no white folk by theyself in this darkness."

The slightest look of defiance came across Roka's face. Aunt Sarah wouldn't have noticed it if she was standing right in front of him.

"I keep two you safe." Roka stood straight and spoke hard.

"I know you'se protectin us, Roka, but these leeches takin' so much poison outta this boy that it's killin' 'em! They cleanin' 'da blood, and if we clean da boy blood, then da rest of him get better. You knows I only ask you to go if it be important."

Roka let his eyes wander at the thought, then nodded his head at Aunt Sarah before he bounded away. Aunt Sarah turned around and went back inside the hut. The girls stared at her, awaiting her instructions.

"Roka gon' take y'all back down the creek. Get as many mo' leeches as you can, and bring 'em back."

The girls jumped up and prepared themselves to leave out into the night again. Before they left the hut, Roka was back to escort them. A large hole had been dug on the edge of the field, and a shovel rested against the nearby tree. Aunt Sarah nodded her head at Roka, he nodded back, and then he and the three women took off into the woods. Aunt Sarah came back into the house and proceeded to take out more roots and water. She mixed some more of her tonic and took a deep breath, preparing herself for my body's reaction. To her amazement, the swelling in my throat had gone down enough for me to actually swallow the liquid medicine. She poured in a little, allowed me a moment to swallow, then poured in a bit more. My body was writhing before finishing it all, but I managed to get it all down. I shook and jerked and convulsed on the bed, and Aunt Sarah prepared herself for my explosive excrement. I jerked once or twice more, and then lay flat, still, and breathless. I was as motionless as the dead leeches, and sadness began to creep over my caretaker's face until she saw the same substance I had excreted earlier rising out of my mouth this time.

She ran across the room to grab several pieces of equipment and a bucket, and then ran back to me and turned my head to the side. I had already begun choking on the bile rising up through my throat. She cleared what she could out of my mouth using something that looked like a wooden spoon, and then used a long, thin wooden piece to trigger my gag reflex and clear the rest out of my throat. My body had been still the whole time, but I sputtered and coughed as my airway opened up. Once my breathing returned to normal, she fell back into her chair, relieved.

"Thank you, Lawd...thank you, Jesus..." Her voice was a broken record until Roka and the ladies returned.

"What happened?" Nessie stared at Aunt Sarah's strained face as she came back through the door.

"Nothin', chile...nothin'...jus' bring dem leeches back here."

The girls rushed to my bedside while Roka waited at the door. He stood there silently waiting for whatever news was to come.

"He be alright," the physician said as she approached the returned women, but they all knew who she was really speaking to. As soon as she finished her statement, Roka stepped back outside the door and froze once again.

"He doin' better..." Aunt Sarah redirected her statements as she looked at the three women. "Had a close call, but he pulled on through. Go on 'head and put da leeches back on 'im."

One by one, the three women covered my body with slimy invertebrates. Aunt Sarah regularly checked to see if any of them had broken their seal. The ones that had survived the first round were now swollen with blood, and they began to detach and try to crawl away. Aunt Sarah would simply pluck them up and place them in one of the same buckets they had arrived in. Many of them still died as a result of the bad blood they had been feeding on, but some managed to stay alive long enough to anticipate a return home. Those that had been placed on after the first ones died had no problems. They latched on to me like a fresh, hungry baby and ate to their hearts' content. One by one they swelled up like balloons, and one by one Aunt Sarah picked them off and dunked them back into the bucket. She removed the last ones as the sun began poking its head through the window of the hut. Exhausted, she fell onto the bed at the other end of the hut and used all her remaining strength to hold up her smile.

"He gon' make it," she told the three women, who were so tired they were barely able to stand themselves. "Lie on the floor, get yo'selves some rest. I told Massa an' dat preachaman I needs your help to save dis boy, so thys not lookin' for you in da fields today. I wakes you up soon."

The women were already asleep before Aunt Sarah finished talking. She laughed, then heaved herself back up to her feet. She could barely walk as she made her way to the door and swung it open.

Roka sat there, eyes wide open, not moving a muscle until he saw Aunt Sarah in his periphery. He turned his head so he could face her.

"He gon' be okay?"

Aunt Sarah nodded her head. "Why don't you get no sleep?" she asked, trying to keep herself from dozing.

"No need."

"Well, me and da girls is restin', and I suggest you do same. Hard work start when we wake. Preachaman must got da fire of God behind 'im. Even got 'im to get Massa to keeps you wid me and da boy stead of in da field. Whoever he is, preachaman want dis here boy bad."

Roka broke his frozen stance and turned again to face Aunt Sarah. "We get him first."

Aunt Sarah nodded her head. "I knows it, Roka, I knows. Now get your rest..."

She turned around to go back inside, and stole a last glance at Roka. His eyelids fluttered ever so slightly as he lay his head back against the wall. Aunt Sarah couldn't smile, but contentment carried her back inside the hut and lay her down gently on her cot to rest.

"Raise yourselves up!"

The voice of the matriarch shot through the air like lightening, jerking everyone who could hear it from their slumbers and up on their feet. I heard it clearly as well, though I couldn't respond.

Whatever Aunt Sarah was doing to me was working. The voices around me were no longer distant whispers, but rather echoes off of the walls of my subconscious. I still couldn't escape the tunnel, but now, at least, I knew there was a light at the end.

"Liza, you go on down to da well and get as'much fresh water as you can carry!"

"Ma'am?" Liza was still partially asleep, and unable to comprehend what Aunt Sarah had said. Without hesitation, the boss lady trotted over and slapped Liza across the face. Liza's head turned from the force of the blow, and when she regained her balance her eyes were wide open.

"You wake now, girl?"

"Yes'm!"

"How's about da rest of you girls? Y'all wake, too?"

All three girls responded like a choir.

"Yes'm!"

"Good! Liza, you go on down to da well to fetch some fresh water! Nessie and Bennie, y'all get yourselves suds and buckets and scrub dis boy till he shine like silver! He gots skin on 'im that's dead as dis floor, and it ain't doin' 'im no good. Nessie, when Liza come back with da water, you make sure he drink every drop! Liza gon' keep bringin' it till I tells her stop, and aslong as she bring it, you make sure he drank it. Hear?"

"Yes'm!" Again, the women responded as a trio, and as soon as they heard themselves speak, they jumped up to do as they had been told.

"Don' nobody feed dis boy nothin' but what I give 'im!" The matriarch spoke up again, before the women went their separate ways. "You give 'im da water, and dat's it!"

Once again, the ladies nodded in obedience, and then rushed off to follow her orders. Aunt Sarah went to her table in the back and began lining up the different herbs and roots she would need. She spoke to each plant as if they were her babies, giving them all affectionate names and patting them gingerly with her middle finger. She soothed the nerves of each piece of foliage as she ground it in the bottom of her mud bowl and poured enough water in to make a paste out of the ingredients. As she finished her concoction, Liza burst through the door with her first pail of water.

"Good, chile. Now takes it over to them two! Y'all splits it in half and do as I told you!"

Liza ran the water over to the other two women, who had their own pails ready. Nessie poured half the water into her bowl and gave the rest to Bennie, who immediately began scrubbing my skin with a cloth that had aspirations of being a brick when it grew up. Nessie grabbed a ladle and began dipping water out of her bowl and pouring it slowly down my throat. When Liza saw that her bowl was empty, she checked with Aunt Sarah, who gave her a nod, and then ran out the door and back to the well.

The matriarch stood and walked up behind Nessie with her mud bowl in hand. The paste left a stench behind that was only rivaled by my own. Nessie finished pouring the water she had in my mouth, and then turned back to look at her instructor.

"Dis here gonna make his insides burn like fire, but it get the rest of da trash out 'im. Leeches c'only do so much. The rest too small to come out. Gotta kill 'em in da inside."

Aunt Sarah leaned forward, scooped all of the paste out of the bowl with her index and pointer fingers, and spread it all throughout my mouth. She nodded at Nessie, who grabbed her utensil and quickly dipped out some more water. Carefully, she poured it into my mouth, washing the paste down my throat.

"Keeps doin' whatcha doin', but keeps an eye on 'im. Them roots come callin' and he ain't gonna be still for much longer."

The women went back to work while Aunt Sarah returned to her table and began picking roots for another concoction. I'd heard everything, but felt nothing. I wondered if the paste that my antebellum physician had put in my mouth would actually do anything to bring me back to health.

I got my answer in the form of a gentle sting in my belly. Having existed for the last day or so entirely in my head, I was excited to feel anything at all. My jubilation was shortlived, however, as the stinging sensation turned to an all-out nuclear explosion inside of my gut. And then it began to spread, from my stomach to my sides, to my chest, to my arms and legs, my hands and feet, and finally my neck and face. Whatever Aunt Sarah had given me was waging an all-out battle against the poison that was left over in my blood. I could feel every attack, every gunshot, the maiming and disembowelment happening inside of me. It felt as if I was going to explode.

Bennie seemed to notice my slight murmur. At first, she probably dismissed it as just her hearing things. But when she heard it a second time, she stopped scrubbing and called out to Aunt Sarah. "I thinks he jus' made noise, Auntie..."

Aunt Sarah stood and walked over to me again. She felt my forehead, my hands, and my stomach, and then stood very quietly and listened.

"Mmm..." The sound escaped from my lips. The explosions inside me were so loud, I didn't realize I had made a real sound.

Aunt Sarah nodded her head in anticipation.

"Yep, he comin' back, alright. Y'all prepare yourselves now. When he gets here, ain't gonna be pretty. Dis boy gon be in more pain than you ever felt before. All you can do is' talk soft n'stay with 'im. Dat's 'bout to be our job till he let up. Gives 'im water, clean 'im, and stays wid 'im. That's gon be all we c'do."

Less than an hour later, I was back to full consciousness, but I wished with every ounce of my being that I was dead. The rising pain inside of me kept getting worse, enough to make me periodically lose consciousness, before bringing me right back to recognition. My body didn't fully react to the pain it was in because my muscles were all but destroyed. I could only move seven of my fingers and four of my toes, lift my arms about an inch, and slightly shake my legs. I couldn't even open my eyes all the way. My only saving grace was that my throat was no longer swollen, and even though I couldn't move my head, I could scream as loud as my vocal chords would allow. And so that's what I did—I screamed. I screamed until I passed out, and when I came to, I screamed some more. It was the only release I could muster.

Despite Aunt Sarah's warning, Bennie, Liza, and Nessie weren't ready for the kind of pain I was in. They seemed to brighten just before the short periods of time when I blacked out, and looked all the more weary when I would awaken and start up again. They fought their fatigue, however, and kept attending to me. Liza ran back and forth to the well as needed, which was quite frequently. Liza tried to force me to swallow the water in between screams, and Nessie sang songs to relax me as she continued scrubbing. Aunt Sarah, having known how daunting the task of my care would be, remained. She kept a close eye on each of the girls, and when it seemed as if one of them was getting ready to crack, she'd send them outside. If it happened to be Liza, she'd send her on another run to the well. If it was Nessie or Bennie, she'd have them temporarily switch jobs with Liza.

At one point in the late afternoon, Roka showed up in the doorway. After hearing my cries echo throughout the air for most of the day, he was beginning to believe I had already died and just didn't know it yet. Aunt Sarah walked over to meet him, recognizing the concern in his face. She looked up at him and spoke through her exhaustion. "Long as' he yellin' we knows he alive," she told him. He nodded his head in acceptance, and proceeded to make his way back out the door.

I suffered through the night. The supernovas in my body wouldn't let me rest. I stopped screaming, but more from exhaustion than from the subsiding of the pain. The women slept in shifts, making sure there was always two people awake to tend to my needs. By morning they were all zombies—performing their tasks as if programmed to do so and with barely enough energy to make a difference. But they were successful. The dynamite going off in my stomach had downgraded to low-grade firecrackers, and the sun's face was the last thing I saw before my body finally allowed me to sleep.

I didn't know it, but I was a new man. Nessie had repeatedly cleaned me from head to toe for almost a full day. Dead skin and dirt covered the bed, but my skin and my hair no longer looked as if it had been coated in sewage. Bennie had given me buckets upon buckets of water, but I had been so engulfed in my pain that I didn't realize when I was urinating. Many times the appearance of liquid on the lower sheets was Nessie's indication to begin her cleaning ritual, again. Now, it seemed as if the same liquid going in was what was coming out. Aunt Sarah recognized as much, despite her fatigue. When she saw that I had nearly fallen asleep, and not passed out, she turned again to address her helpers.

"Y'all need to know you saved dis here boy's life...ain't no way he be still livin' now if y'all hadn't been here. Takes yo' rest, now. We still gots work to do, but ain't nothin' gon' be harder den what you jus' did. I'm proud of you. Nows rest, chirren."

Without a word, the women collapsed as if someone had cut their power off.

The sun hung patiently in the sky during the day while my body rested in a bubble of peace that I hadn't known since my arrival. The women rose, one by one, in the late afternoon. Aunt Sarah had stolen some rest for herself after the girls fell asleep, but had awakened long before the first assistant shifted her weight on the hard floor and opened her eyes. It probably seemed to the apprentices as though their teacher never slept; just spent the hours humming Jesus songs to energize herself. She did so now, as Nessie gently shook Bennie and Liza, rousing them as well.

"What we doin' now, Aunt Sarah?" Liza wiped the sleep from her eyes as she spoke.

"Nothin', chile. Da boy restin' now, makin' himself strong. He gon' be powerful hungry when he get up, tho. We make sure we gots food for 'im to eat little by little when he come fully wake, but till then, we leave 'im alone. He fight for himself now."

Without me to focus all their attention on, the three women seemed lost. They fumbled around for a while, trying to figure out what to do. Their supervisor laughed as she observed their awkwardness.

"Listen, y'all get to cleanin' dis place up. Been filthy in here since we got da boy. After that, y'all go on to your homes. Ain't no way to tell how long he'll be sleepin'. You comes by every few hours, check to see if he woke. When that happen, I'll be needin' y'all again."

"Yessum!" Again, all three women answered in unison, and began looking around the hut for specific things to start cleaning. The dirt from my body seemed to cover everything else like soot. The area around the bed was especially foul, with a day's worth of grime collected on the bed and the floor underneath it. The women looked with new eyes at the filthiness they had been working in, and promptly began scrubbing everything from top to bottom. The job took twice as long as it should have, but each of the women knew that leaving Aunt Sarah's place was dangerous. There was a protection they had there that didn't exist anywhere else. Aunt Sarah let them clean the abode three times over before she made them stop.

"Y'all go on home, now. Da boy be needin' rest."

She saw uncertainty on the faces of her surrogate daughters.

"I can't keep you here forever, now. If you leavin' now, you come back when da boy opens his eyes. I tell Massa you left and come back, so he don't get no mind dat we's schemin'. If they know 'bout dis boy, 'bout what Elizabeth say, they kill 'im sures I standin' here. Gotta be careful..."

Each of the younger women nodded their heads in understanding.

"I know what's waitin' for you out there. Just know you gonna be back quick, y'hear?"

Each of the women nodded again, but this time with somberness that quickly flooded the room. They each walked over and gave Aunt Sarah a hug, and then they sulked out of the door. When she was sure they were gone and far enough away, Aunt Sarah slowly walked over to my bed. She looked down at me, and stood there for a long while before she let her thoughts escape. "You better be da man everybody hopes you is..."

She stood over me for a few seconds longer, then made her way back to her table, humming her Jesus music as she went.

My mind and body charged for another twenty-four hours, as I slumbered in a place where no one could reach me. My mind was too tired to dream. Unaware of what to expect next, it suspended itself in a state of partial animation. It floated within the confines of my skull, afraid to commit to any one reality anymore. If I didn't expect to wake up somewhere, then I could wake up anywhere and not be affected. Thus, my brain took the idea of home, with Big Mama and SaTia, and put it in a place where it couldn't do any harm once I awoke.

When the time came, my mind woke before my eyes opened. I slowly became aware of what was happening around me, as if someone was deliberately turning the distortion off from a sound recording. The first thing I was able to make out was sobbing—soft and low, yet pregnant with pain. Aunt Sarah was whispering just loud enough for me to hear.

"...you can't believe it were your fault, chile...dem crackas gonna do whatever dey wants to...Lawd, Nessie chile, he done beat you some terrible..."

Nessie kept on weeping, head in hands, as Aunt Sarah tried to stop some of her bleeding. She looked up once and kept herself from calling Aunt Sarah her Mama.

"I...I try...to...stop him...ma'am..."

"Chile, you ain't gotta tell me! Don' no woman return from da other side of da field lookin' like you 'less she been in a fight...."

"Don't...I don't know why he...?"

"Ain't no use in askin' what you can't answer. You hush now, girl. Lemme clean you up..."

For almost the next hour, I listened to the saddest song I'd ever heard. Nessie kept sobbing as she was being cleaned, but Aunt Sarah began humming a low, drawn out tune behind Nessie's sounds of sadness. Together they made a ballad that reached up to heaven and made the angels gasp. When my heart could take no more, I shed a tear through my closed eyes and felt it run down the side of my face and form a tiny puddle by my earlobe.

Apparently, I also moaned.

Nessie jumped up from the bed and Aunt Sarah from her seat. They ran over to me just as my eyes began to flutter.

"My Lawd!" Aunt Sarah exclaimed as she placed her hand on my forehead. "Boy, can you hear me?"

I moved my lips to speak.

"Yyyyyyeeeeee...yyyyyyyeeeeee..." My voice came out as a series of hoarse chokes.

I still couldn't speak clearly, but Aunt Sarah got the point. Before she could say anything else, Bennie and Liza popped through the door. Liza spoke first, with Bennie as her backup.

"We jus' comin' to check and see..."

"Get yourselves in here! Boy's wakin' up!"

It took the ladies a split second to let Aunt Sarah's message sink in, and then they were tripping over themselves trying to get back in the room. They each stood around my bed in anticipation.

When I opened my eyes, I saw the four ladies looking down at me with smiles on their faces. I thought, just for a second, that maybe I had just been born and these three women were midwives of some sort.

"Can you nod yo head, son?" Aunt Sarah asked me in a voice so soft I wondered if she thought her tone would hurt me. I tried to nod with the little energy I had, but was unable. My neck lay stiff and tight on the bed. I took a breath and concentrated my energy. It was bad enough I couldn't talk right. I needed to be able to do this.

Focusing solely on the muscles in my neck, I was able to slowly raise my chin. It felt as though I was lifting a barbell with my neck, but I managed to get my chin up as far as it could go and bring it back down again before letting my head fall to the pillow in exhaustion.

"That's it...that's it...good, son. You done real good. Now, let's see what else you can do..."

Aunt Sarah's soft voice disappeared, replaced by a harder, more dictatorial tone. After she realized I was conscious and improving, she made it her business to learn what she needed to do to get me back to where I was when she'd first seen me.

Over the next few hours, Aunt Sarah and the ladies found out everything that was wrong with me. Because I was now awake and responsive, they told me everything they found out. My jaw was still healing and my vocal cords had been shocked, which is why I couldn't talk right. With some practice, and continued healing, Aunt Sarah believed I'd be talking in the next few days. The rest of my body wasn't so cut and dry. My arms and legs had been broken in numerous different places during my time in the cage. I could raise both my forearms high enough off of the bed to wave hello to someone, but that required more pain than I thought it was worth. The rest of my arm and shoulder I couldn't move at all. Even though it hurt, I'd turn my head as far as it could go and look at my arms. They both looked like a little child had broken them apart and tried to put them back together again. My makeshift physician said it was because the bones had been broken and hadn't healed correctly. From what I could see of my legs, they looked the same way. I could wiggle my toes and lift my legs up about an inch, but no more than that. When Liza tried to bend my legs at the knees, it felt as if someone was trying to convince the ligaments to emancipate themselves from my leg altogether. Aunt Sarah explained that it was the same problem— broken bones that hadn't healed correctly.

"I can try and fix 'im, but ain't gonna be pretty doin' it," she said after she explained the condition of my mangled limbs.

I wanted to grab her and scream out to do whatever she had to do to get me well again. I was forced to settle for a mumble and a head nod.

I slept off and on for the next three days, continuing to feel myself get stronger. Every day I was able to keep my eyes open longer than before, and I grew familiar with my surroundings. I felt safe, which I would later discover was because I hadn't seen a white person since I'd been brought into Aunt Sarah's triage space. At times I felt as if I had forgotten something important— as if I had started to watch a movie from the middle and had forgotten about how the film started. But I was safe, and I was being cared for, and considering what I'd gone through with Bradley, that was more than enough for me.

I later found out that Mr. Talbert, Bradley, and Reverend Lewis had been by the hut numerous times since I was first brought here. Aunt Sarah, with all her wit, made up a tale of a disease that niggers could stand, but God forbid any good, pure white folk came across it, because they would surely die. The three white men, not wanting to endanger their lives, decided to stay outside the quarantine zone until they received an okay from the expert, who had already decided to keep up the façade until the last possible moment.

On my fourth day of recovery, I was able to stay awake the entire day. My pain seemed to grow with my energy, but I used Nessie, Bennie, and Liza as my medicine. They came and went, and I made sure to give them all smiles as they bathed and pampered me. Roka would come in and periodically check on me as well. He would never speak, just stare down at me as if he was trying to solve a puzzle written on my chest. I couldn't talk to him yet either, and so his visits became staring contests that he inevitably won. When he was done, he would turn his head abruptly and walk out of the space without making a sound.

On the fifth day, Aunt Sarah and her girls gingerly walked up to me after I had awakened. I was scared before either of them opened their mouths.

"It's time dat we get to fixin' your bones, son," Aunt Sarah began. "We goes any longer and you be bent down the rest of your life..."

I nodded my head in agreement. If anyone could fix my bones, Aunt Sarah could.

"We gots to break 'em again for them to heal good. We gots to break 'em and set 'em straight."

I started to nod my head again, and stopped. She had just said that she was going to break my bones again. I shook my head like a wet dog.

"I knows you scared, son, but dis da only way we can get you back up. It's da only way. You gotta decide whether you wanna stay like you is, or let me fix you."

I bent my head down again and looked at my mangled legs and arms. I'd never be any good to anyone, much less myself, if I stayed like I was. Slowly, I looked back up at Aunt Sarah and nodded my head.

"Gots me a special root. Brought it here long time ago, when I gots here. Can't give it to you till after, if you can hang on. You take it, and it be no pain. Take you somewheres only da spirits know about. When you get back in dis here world, your bones be healed. But, if you get yourself stuck dere, you gotta stay. Dey won't letcha leave. It's da only thing I gots for what you gots to go through."

"If be stuck?" Roka had come into the room while Aunt Sarah was talking, and responded to what he heard. It was my first time hearing Roka speak. I was shocked at the concern in his monstrous voice.

"If da spirits make 'im stay, dey take his soul and keeps it there. He die here."

"No," Roka responded, and his one word seemed to be final. He stared straight at Aunt Sarah as he spoke, and expected nothing said in return. She stared back at him, her face soft but determined. The power of their gazes began to send shock waves through the air, and I was sure that where their stares met each other would be the epicenter of some huge explosion if they kept it up much longer.

Finally, Aunt Sarah spoke. Her hesitation was as shocking as Roka's concern.

"Roka, listen here, son...we gots to break da boy's bones to get 'em back right. He gettin' stronger, Roka, but a far cry from bein' perfect. Gots tons mo' healing to do. We puts 'im through dat kinda pain nows, and I can't promise he gon' make it. It's just too much when he so far from a full health. Least these here roots gives 'im a chance."

Roka didn't respond, but his face softened a bit.

"Anyways you cuts it, he gon' have to fight. 'Is body ain't ready for it. Gotta take 'is chances on how strong he be on da inside. 'Sides, if he be who we's all hope, den he gotta come back, huh?"

I could see the uncertainty on Roka's face. No one said anything, but everyone's eyes bore into his wrinkled brows, and I knew the final decision was his. After some time contemplating, he turned his eyes back to Aunt Sarah.

"If he dead—"

Aunt Sarah gently cut him off.

"'Lieves me, Roka, I knows what's at stake. Dis da best way to get 'im back right again."

"But don know."

"Naw, only Jesus knowed what gon' happen. I knows dis be da

best thing fo' 'im, and I do everything I can to help 'im. It's all I can promise."

Roka took a deep breath and shut his eyes tight, whispering some kind of prayer as he exhaled. When he opened his eyes again, he turned back to Aunt Sarah and nodded.

I had all sorts of questions. What exactly would this root do to me? How did they plan to break my bones? How could they be sure I would heal the way they wanted me to? Why did I have to risk death in order to get better? Didn't Aunt Sarah have any Tylenol?

My thoughts stopped abruptly.

Tylenol...why does that sound familiar...

An alarm went off in my brain, and I felt a spotlight shift from a clearing fog back to the fact that I was getting ready to have my bones broken. I opened my mouth to protest. I needed my questions answered before I let anyone touch me.

"Drrrrrrrrriiiiiiiiivvvvvvvvvvppppppp...mmmmmm-aaaaaazzzzzzzzoooop...!"

Defeated, I let my head fall to the side. I couldn't talk and could barely move. This decision wouldn't be up to me.

Roka heard my incoherent protest, and walked up to the side of my bed. Without warning he placed one hand on my forehead and the other on my stomach, and spoke for several minutes in a language I could not understand. When he finished, he looked at me with the same wrinkled brow that he'd presented to Aunt Sarah.

"You...must...live."

He spoke each word deliberately, as if each syllable were a sermon.

"You...must...live."

He pushed his hands onto my forehead and stomach with enough pressure to cause me to wince, and then snatched them off as if my skin was on fire. Then he nodded and walked back over to Aunt Sarah. She whispered something to him, making sure that he understood everything she was saying. When she was done, he gave her a brief nod, and quickly left the room.

Aunt Sarah walked back over to her table and began rummaging through all of her roots. Normally she would hum as she worked, but this time she moved with a focus that I could hear in her footsteps....

Nessie, Bennie, and Liza remained by my side. They tried to talk and soothe me, but their voices betrayed them. Whatever was coming was bad enough to alter the melody of their beautiful voices, and every wrong chord made me more nervous.

After about an hour, four slave men walked through the door. Aunt Sarah had been working so intently at her desk that I'd almost forgotten she was there. She jumped up when the men came through the door and immediately began telling them what to do. Two of them came over to the head of the bed and stood over me. They tried not to look down, but couldn't help themselves. I was so intriguing they couldn't help visually dissecting me. The other two stood at my feet, and as far as I could tell, they did the same thing.

The medicine woman walked up beside my bed with a small bowl in her hand. She couldn't hide her worry anymore. She spoke like a woman who was sending her child to surgery.

"Dis here is da roots I tol' you 'bout. Can't give 'em to you till you at da worse, dat's when your spirit be open da most. It's gone be bad, real bad, but dis here take it all away. You jus' gots to fight. Y'stands me?"

My face was decorated with lines of panic, but I nodded anyway. She leaned down close to my ear, so that I couldn't see her face, and she spoke again with a cracked voice.

"I don't know wheres you goin', but you gots to come back. Promise me you comin' back..."

Aunt Sarah's fear began to break me, and I felt my body begin to shake as I nodded my head. She stood and looked at me with glistening eyes. I stared back with terrified pupils, and tried to convey the promise that I would be back.

She looked away from me and blinked her eyes repeatedly, refusing to let a tear drop. Then she looked at the two men at the foot of the bed and nodded. They grabbed hold of my feet and held them firmly in place.

Roka seemed to come out of the shadows. I hadn't even seen him come in. He stepped up to the bed and swung something above his head. There was no way I could know how thick or how hard that long piece of wood was, and if I had, it wouldn't have made much of a difference. Roka's body seemed as though it was made of elastic as his back arched, and he sprang forward with the log in his hand like a catapult.

The log came down on my lower legs, forcing the bone in both of my shins to pop out of my flesh. It seemed to happen in slow motion. It seemed unreal.

But then my face began to react to a pain that I hadn't yet comprehended. My eyes went bloodshot red and expanded to twice their normal size. My teeth ground against each other as my mouth opened around them, showing my bleeding gums. The skin of my face grew tight enough to rip itself, and my entire body began to twitch. I hadn't made a sound yet, but even Roka stopped when he looked down and saw who was staring back at him. He looked hesitantly at Aunt Sarah.

"Ain't no use in stoppin' now. Gots to be strong, Roka."

He turned his gaze away from her and moved up a half step to my knees. Again, he curved his back into an arch, and flung himself forward, breaking my kneecaps.

I screamed in a voice that was unfamiliar to me. Roka's log may as well have been an axe. It felt as though every limb he hit was coming off. I began moving muscles I didn't know I could, trying to get away from him.

The two slave men standing near my head grabbed me by the shoulders, and Roka threw the log off to the side. Thinking it was all over, I let my head fall back onto the bed and my eyes close. My screams came involuntarily.

Suddenly I felt my arm being raised. I figured it was to help move me to another position, and the agony I felt from my waist down prevented me from looking to see what was going on.

A firm hand ran up and down my arm until it found the spot where the previous break had been. Two hands then grabbed my arm, one on either side, and yanked it in opposite directions. I heard the snap over my own screaming.

By the time Roka had gotten over to my other arm, my eyes were already starting to roll back. I was covered in sweat, and my heart was beating fast enough to power a small engine. The breaking of my last arm came over me in a wave, like jumping into a swimming pool. The agony washed over me like ocean water on a beach.

My screaming came in short bursts because I was having a hard time catching my breath. I began seeing two of everything, and then three of everything, and strange colors flashed in front of me and disappeared into people's faces.

"It's time! Quick, put 'is head back!"

I felt the two slave men grab my head and try and pull it back so that my mouth would open. Aunt Sarah stood over me with her new concoction. My vision and my coherence were fading fast.

The next time I opened my mouth wide enough to scream, she poured the thick liquid into my mouth. The slave closest to her slammed his palm down over my mouth so that I couldn't spit it out, and I swallowed it all in one gulp.

There were a few things about my new medicine that became immediately evident. First, it had a taste that would cause a tongue to jump out of its owner's mouth. Second, it numbed my throat as soon as it went down. The liquid seemed to hit my stomach, and then expand itself slowly throughout my entire body, like a peaceful fog. I realized I wasn't hearing myself scream anymore, and I could barely hear anyone else. I also didn't feel any pain whatsoever. There was a strange tingling sensation in my arms and legs, but the agony was gone. I began to giggle as the effects of Aunt Sarah's potion became stronger. People's heads began to blow up to huge sizes while their necks, chests, and legs shrunk, making them completely disproportionate. At first it was just the slave man that was closest to me, but soon enough, everyone's body had been transformed into these hilarious balloon-headed figures. I laughed so hard I began to urinate on myself. I would have tried to explain to them why I was laughing, but they wouldn't have understood me.

"Dis happen right?" Roka turned again to Aunt Sarah.

"Yeah, Roka, he on 'is way. He be fine."

The disproportionate people surrounding me continued to stare at me as I laughed, and then their skin began turning different colors. Roka's marble skin turned canary-yellow as I stared in wonder. Aunt Sarah looked as if someone had painted her in the brightest orange paint they could find. Bennie, Nessie, and Liza turned off and on like lightbulbs, alternating between green, blue, and red hues. I stopped laughing and covered my eyes as their skin grew increasingly brighter, as if they each had a bomb inside of them waiting to explode.

"You're too bright!" I tried to yell out to my observers. "You're hurting my eyes! Turn it down some!"

But all that came out was a mouthful of gibberish.

The light from each of them had gotten so bright that it began to burn through my skin. I looked down at my hands and saw the skin disintegrating from my fingertips. When I tried to look up at Aunt Sarah, her light shoved my head back down to the bed.

I was dissolving into nothingness. The dust that was left of my fingers blew around the room and disappeared. By this time, I could feel my arms and legs beginning to turn to sand and blow themselves around the room as well. I tried to scream out again, but the light had stolen my voice. When all that was left of me was my chest and head, Aunt Sarah walked back to me. She placed her hand on a shoulder that was almost gone and leaned into my rapidly disintegrating ear.

"Remember what you promised me..."

And then, in the last hurrah of the storm, an explosion of flurries blew themselves all around the room, and when they settled, I was gone.

I couldn't remember how I'd gotten here, but I was glad I'd arrived.

The Platinum Palace club was one of the most lavish I had ever seen, and I'd seen a lot of them. This one set itself apart, though. The door to enter the club was one-sided glass. Everyone inside could see who was trying to get in, but no one outside knew they were being watched and laughed at until they were permitted to enter. Tiny diamonds ran along the outline of the bar, as well as the tables in the VIP section, and there were plasma screen televisions that adorned the walls and showed a constant stream of provocative music videos.

None of that was what made the club so impressive to me, though.

I had just finished the last performance of my "Hoes In Da Attic" Tour, and I'd killed it. The crowd was crazy, the music was on point, and the energy in the stadium was so thick you could pour it on your pancakes. I came back on stage for two different encores, and even after the second one, the crowd stayed for another half-hour chanting my name, hoping to get a third blessing. People were already starting to call my show the best they'd ever been to on their Facebook and Twitter pages.

I didn't think things could get any better, but it turns out I was wrong. Deez Nutz Records had rented out the club, the Platinum Palace, to hold my afterparty. Without my knowing, they had directed the club owner to set up a motif for the venue that would celebrate the "Hoes In Da Attic" tour.

The entire club looked like a pimped-out cellar. Instead of chairs, everyone sat on shiny trunks that seemed to be lined with diamonds. The ceiling had been blocked off in a V-shape, to resemble an attic. Their were four large sets of stairs, two on either side of the space, that were set up to look as though they led to a lower level. Each set of stairs had a woman dancing on it that would give the most experienced video vixen a run for her money. There were cobwebs made of tiny silver chains and diamond spiders sprinkled randomly around the room, and there were golden storage boxes that seemed like someone had just tossed them and let them fall where they may.

It was the coolest thing I'd ever seen. I just couldn't remember how I'd gotten here.

I was drunk before I realized where the VIP section was, and by the time I got comfortable, there were four empty bottles of expensive vodka decorating the table in front of me. I looked around the spinning room to tell Brian to go and grab another one, and I realized that he wasn't here. None of the crew was here. Neither was SaTia.

"Wh...wait...where did...how did I...?"

That's when I realized there were three women around me. All of them had on little more than the tops and bottoms of lingerie sets, and the three of them together were enough to make a man cry. The first one was dark-skinned. She had an hourglass figure with more time at the top than on the bottom, short hair, and skin that glistened in the dim light. The second woman was brown-skinned, and had more time at the bottom than on the top. Her weave fell down to the small of her back, and when she flung it over her shoulders she looked like she was doing a shampoo commercial. The third one was light-skinned, and as close to perfect as I'd ever seen. Her curly hair fell to her shoulders, and her hourglass was as balanced as a scale.

The women crowded around me, and wouldn't let me move. They grinded on me and used their tongues to tease my skin. I was confused, but my hormones outweighed my distress. The light-skinned one stuck her tongue in my ear, and what inhibitions I had disappeared. When the women saw and felt my reaction, they stood up with smiles on their faces and led me to the back room.

I hadn't even noticed that there was a back room until they guided me toward the doors. Following the motif, the entrance looked like the folding doors of a closet. Had I had the use of all of my faculties, I would've known that this was no ordinary closet. Alcohol, having already taken its effect, however, I truthfully expected to see a small room of coats and scarves when we walked through. Instead I saw a large room with enough drugs in it to land us all in a federal prison.

"Hell yeah!" I drunkenly yelled out as the three women continued to lead me to a couch in the corner. A sober part of me heard my drunken outburst and warned my brain of just how stupid I sounded.

The three women lay me down gently on the couch, and then proceeded to slowly peel their lingerie off piece by piece.

I'd been in situations like this before. I'd been in hotel rooms full of video chicks who were either stimulating themselves while anticipating some action from me, or starting the party on the labia of one of their friends. I'd had more sex than a porn star.

So I couldn't figure out how I could be so enthralled with these women. I literally could not take my eyes off of them. Every paper-thin piece of lingerie that flew by my face made me less and less in control of myself, and before any of them had actually touched me, I had already moaned aloud and glued the crotch of my jeans...and it still didn't help! I was so aroused my breathing became short and I broke out into a sweat. Confused, embarrassed, and believing I was going to have a heart attack, I turned my head to compose myself.

The most perfect of the three women walked up to me and grabbed my chin. She turned my face until I was facing her, and then kissed me deeply, allowing her tongue to do jumping jacks in my mouth.

"Don't worry, Nigga," she said as she pulled away from my lips. "You can have every part of us, any way you want us. You'll never run out of it here..."

The other two women joined her by my side. All their clothes were off as they took turns showing me the parts of themselves that they wanted me to enter. Some guttural sound released itself from my throat as I exploded again, while slamming my hand against the couch repeatedly.

"Don't waste anymore, daddy," Brown-skin said. "We only getting started."

She reached down, unzipped the fly of my jeans, and began to reach into the abyss.

That was when I heard another woman clear her throat.

It stood out because it didn't have the tone of the other voices in the room. Hers was softer, more innocent. Even with a hand snaking itself around my genitals I had to look up to see where it had come from.

She was standing ten steps away, but directly in front of me. Her eggnog-colored skin and blonde pigtails seemed to shine through the darkness of the back room. She was as white and innocent as anyone I'd ever seen. Her yellow sundress with flower prints going around it swayed as she clasped her hands in front of her and rocked herself back and forth. Her ocean-blue eyes provided their own light. She could have stepped off the cover of a greeting card—leaving behind her mother to take apple pies out of the oven and place them on the windowsill by herself, opting instead to step into this den of sinfulness just to do what? To see me…

I signaled for all of the other women around me to leave as I kept my eyes focused on her. They seemed hesitant, but after sharp glances and a shove or two, they finally moved. Innocence stood staring back at me, bashful but visibly excited. I motioned for her to come to me, and she approached me slowly. When she was close enough for me to smell the sweet shampoo she'd used in her hair, I held out my hand and she sat down on my lap.

"What's your name, sweetheart?" I asked.

"Umm…I guess you can call me Miss." Her slight Southern drawl altered the words she spoke. She twirled the end of one of her pigtails with her index finger and thumb.

"Miss, huh? Well, Miss, what brings you up in here?"

She giggled before she answered and turned her head away. "Umm, you, Nigger…"

I shrugged off the unintentional insult. She obviously didn't know what she was saying.

"Me, huh? What you tryin' to do, babygirl?"

"This…"

She reached through the open zipper of my pants and pulled out a prize. My eyes fluttered like butterfly wings. She smiled sweetly and climbed off my lap and onto the floor, stroking me the entire time.

"O-M-G! I cannot believe I'm about to give The Nigger head!"

I started to say something, but she shoved her mouth down on me before I could utter a complete sentence.

"Said…ahh…my name wrong…mmm…"

She went up and down like her neck had a motor in it. When she finished, she giggled again, and climbed up on my lap and began to slide down on my instrument.

"Ooooo…oh, Nigger…you're as big as everyone said you'd be…oh my God…"

It felt as though someone was sliding me in and out of a bottle of sunshine, but I somehow forced my words to come out clearly. "Sweetheart…ahhh…you keep…sayin' my name wrong…"

Miss came up high, and then slammed herself back down on me. I thought I might explode again. She began inhaling and exhaling deeply as she spoke.

"OOO…oooo, no, no I'm not, Nigger. That's who…yes…you are. You're…mmm…my nigger…"

I stopped and opened my eyes, aware of her words, despite how good she felt. She kept rising and falling like clockwork. I'd never been so conflicted in my life.

"Say it…say it…say you're my nigger…say it…"

"You crazy…" My voice caught. I could have pushed her off of me, but I didn't want to.

"Yeah…oooo…yeah, you'll say it…I want you to say it…and then I…I…I want you to punch me. Take that big nigger fist and slam it against my skull!"

There were now two of me contained in one body. The first me was ready to impregnate her. The second me was ready to throw her to the ground. They cancelled one another out, and so I didn't do either. Instead I sat there, a torn man having the best sex of his life, being disrespected to the core the entire time.

"Yeeeaaaahhhh, Nigger...that's right...you make me bleed! You make this pure white pussy bleed, Nigger! And then, steal... my stuff...yeah...take it all! I want you to steal from me, Nigger! And...I'll bring you back...whatever...you want...and you can take steal it again...just be my nigger!"

She was moving up and down now as if she were operated by a hydraulic pump. It was faster than I ever thought anyone could move their body. And she continued to drip from her mouth.

"Oh my God...my God. You're so big...ohhhh...you...you can have me, Nigger! Take me away from...my parents...so I can go with you...yeeeaaaahhh! Uh...I wanna...sniff your powder...shoot your poison...let me follow you...'round like a dog, Nigger...I'll be...strung out...crack...whore... slut...heathen...don't worry... I want to...I want to! Just say...you're my nigger..."

Finally, something had to give. My two sides couldn't coexist inside my body anymore. I had reached the end of two different ropes, and I was either going to release inside her like a broken fire hydrant, or get her off of me anyway I could. My mind was no good. The electricity inside my brain had stopped firing correctly as soon as she mounted me. It would have to come down to instinct. I closed my eyes and decided to let it happen as it would.

My arms went up and shot out so quickly that the wind left Miss's body as I knocked her over. When she hit the ground, she started coughing and wheezing. Though she couldn't speak, she was clearly angry.

I stood from the couch completely sober of all the drugs that I had ingested earlier. I pulled up my jeans and fastened them tightly before I took another look at Miss on the ground.

She had stopped coughing. Standing to her feet, she took her innocent pose again, but her smile was dark and different.

"Are you crazy?" I screamed before she had the chance to say anything. "The hell is wrong with you? I'm not your or anybody else's nigger! My name is Da Nig..."

I couldn't say it. The words simply wouldn't come out of my mouth. I cleared my throat and tried again.

"My name is Da Nig...umm, it's Da Nig..."

It was as if my vocal chords had a fail-safe on them, and someone had flipped the switch each time I tried to finish my own name. What was wrong with me? I shook my head in denial and began to look around the room for some sort of explanation. The first person I saw was Miss. She was no longer smiling, and her hard, hateful expression made her seem like the star character in a teen psycho movie. The second person I saw was my dad. He stood about three steps behind her, and I couldn't shake the feeling that he had just arrived. He stared directly at me, as if no one else was in the room. He didn't smile, but his face glowed with pride, and he nodded his head in approval.

And everything went dark.

I musta passed out.

Those were the first thoughts that came to my mind as my consciousness began to reappear. I had the worst hangover in history, and so I kept my eyes closed while I stirred from my sleep. Immediately, a pair of hands assisted me in sitting up. I had a bad habit of inviting ugly groupies to the room when I was wasted, and I hoped that when I gathered the strength to open my eyes, I wouldn't want to slam them shut again.

Last night must have been crazy, I thought to myself. My entire body was sore, and it seemed to take forever, even with assistance, for me to sit upright. I tried to remember what had happened, and for a while all I got was flashes of a flower print dress and strobe lights. I tried to dig deeper into my thoughts, but the smell of nature began to disturb me. Whatever hotel room I was in smelled like the campgrounds that my Boy Scout troop used to visit.

"What the hell kind of hotel is this?" was what I meant to say, but all I managed was "Whhhaaaaahhhhmmmphis?"

I heard myself and laughed out loud. I must have gotten bombed last night. I don't know that I had ever been so hung over that I couldn't speak right.

Slowly, I began to open my eyes. I'd mentally prepared for the worst with the groupies, and besides, if I was in such bad shape that I couldn't talk right, I figured I should probably call SaTia in as soon as possible. It wouldn't be the first time I'd landed in the hospital after a wild night.

It took much longer than normal for my eyes to focus. No matter how much I blinked, rubbed my eyes, and shook my head, I couldn't erase the vision of myself in a one-room hut with two slave women beside me.

And then it all hit me. All at once. Where I was, how I'd gotten here, why my body felt like leftover animal parts squeezed in a Spam can. I had experienced half of this movie before. Now I remembered the beginning.

I tried to stand up and freak out, but my legs were held tightly in place. They had two wooden boards on either side and enough taut rope wrapped around them so I couldn't see from the middle of my thigh to my ankle. My arms were in makeshift slings, and had smaller wooden boards tied to them as well. I freaked out as best I could with my limited movement.

"I'm not supposed to be here," I tried to say. "I don't know how I got here. I'm not a damn slave—I'm a rap star. I'm famous. People love me. Nobody beats me. Nobody whips me. Nobody feeds me trash and makes me sleep in my own crap. I'm Da Nigga. You know—*Hoes In Da Attic?* I'm Da Nigga!"

All that came out of my mouth was incoherent mumbling, but I didn't care. I was confused and scared, and I resorted to the only side of me that could deal with those kinds of feelings. The slave women all stared at me. They couldn't understand what I'd said, but my disgust made them crumble.

"Who are you? Huh?" I turned and looked at each one of the women sitting around me. "Who da hell are you, huh? Ugly trick. Who are you? And you? Who are you? You know what? I don't care who the hell you are! 'Cause I'm Da Nigga! I'm da man 'round here. I'm..."

Just then the door to the cabin flew open, and two men walked inside. Immediately, it all started to come back to me. Nessie, Bennie, and Liza ran to the back of the hut and stood side by side with their faces to the ground. Aunt Sarah watched it all unfold.

I took one look at the two white men, then turned away, and urinated on myself. The hot liquid flowed down my thigh and onto the mattress I was lying on. I started crying enough tears to drown in.

Aunt Sarah stared at me in disbelief. One of the white men, Bradley, laughed with enough satisfaction to make me want to die.

"Eh, that's a good nigger..."

The slings and leg splints didn't matter. I was frozen. My muscles stood as terrified as I was. I couldn't even bring myself to look at their faces. I just sat where I was, moist with my own liquid waste, shaking and terrified by two men whom I knew could do with me as they pleased.

The other white man, Mr. Talbert, looked at Aunt Sarah with incredulousness pasted on his face. His sarcastic tone hid the slight fear behind his voice. "Are you sure it's safe to come now, Sarah?"

Aunt Sarah's expression changed from the disbelief to innocence as she looked at Mr. Talbert. "Yassah."

Bradley moved menacingly in Aunt Sarah's direction, but Mr. Talbert stopped him.

"She was looking you in the eye, sir," Bradley protested.

"She delivered both of my children, Bradley," Mr. Talbert said without looking at him. "I'll let this one slide."

Aunt Sarah never changed her demeanor. She stood the same way, with Bradley standing down, as she had when he was on the attack.

"Sarah," Mr. Talbert started again, "if I didn't know any better, I'd say you were trying to put one over on us with the nigger-disease you told us about."

Aunt Sarah maintained her innocent face.

"Oh, nawsah, nawsah! Nigger sick like he were—" she pointed to me "—and white folk come round and kill all da light in they soul! Sweet Jesus knowed!"

Mr. Talbert stood with a puzzled look on his face, likely deciding how much of Aunt Sarah's story he believed. Finally, he took a deep breath and gave up. "Well, he's cured for now anyways, right?"

"Yassah. He jus' waken two shakes befo' youse came in. Don' he look differen', sah?"

Mr. Talbert looked me over. My breathing turned shallow and my heart rate sped up. I thought I was going to pass out.

"He does look like a new nigger, even with the things on his arms and legs. And he seems to have learned a little respect, too. Looks like both of you did your jobs."

Bradley grinned at hearing Mr. Talbert's approval. Aunt Sarah nodded politely.

"Well, we just came by to let you know that there's been a lot of fuss in the town over that nigger. A lot of people believe Bradley's story about him being..." Mr. Talbert cleared his throat, embarrassed to even repeat the rumor. "Half-ape, and don't feel safe with him outside that cage. There's been talk of people coming around here to kill him, and I don't want to lose any of my property over this nonsense. I haven't had any problems with my niggers that Bradley or any of the others couldn't fix, and I don't plan to start now. So if any folks come around here to grab up that nigger, you give him over, hear? I don't want to hear about you trying to hide him or protect him or any other foolishness. You hand him over, and you go on about your business."

Aunt Sarah used everything in her to hide her concern. "Yassah."

"If he manages to survive through the week, he goes out in the field. No need in letting a good nigger go to waste."

"Yassah."

"Alright," Mr. Talbert said, and he and Bradley turned to leave.

"Sah?" Aunt Sarah called out softly.

"What is it, wench?" Bradley roughly answered.

"Yassah, sah what I do if da preacha come back 'round? He come time to time and check on da boy..."

Mr. Talbert stopped and thought deeply. "Well...you can't send him away on my orders, or I may have to suffer a penalty and he would surely have you hung. Damn that man and his father. Let him in, I guess."

Bradley couldn't contain his aggravation. "Sir..."

"No, Bradley, I'm not staking my business partnerships on making sure you get your pet nigger back! Whoever gets here first can have him. I'm tired of this whole thing. I'm washing my hands of it. The sooner he dies the sooner we can all get back to some degree of normalcy!"

Mr. Talbert stormed out, with Bradley right behind him.

Bennie, Nessie, and Liza began making their way back toward Aunt Sarah and me. Aunt Sarah turned around when the two men left and looked at me as if she was trying to figure out a calculus problem.

Even though the two men were gone, I still couldn't bring myself to move. I shook uncontrollably, and blinked to keep myself from bursting into tears again. The urine smell had begun to rise lightly through the air now, and the three apprentices began cleaning without being asked. It took all three of them to lift me, move me, and sit me gently on the floor so they could clean up the urine in the mattress. Aunt Sarah continued to stare at me. There were words sitting in her mouth that she couldn't bring herself to utter. Without warning, she turned and left out of her hut.

As I sat on the floor, watching three women clean up my waste, I had no doubt that I had died. I knew a world where I was once a king. Even if my royalty was false, enough people believed in it to make it true. I could pretend that my power was limitless, even though I was well aware of the boundaries I could and could not cross. But there was no pretending in this new world. There were no designer clothes or shiny jewelry to convince me that my life was something to be envied. I'd been beaten within inches of my life on countless occasions, and then thrown in a cage and left to rot and decompose like a dead carcass. But my heart was still beating, and my lungs were still drawing air. I was dead, yet my homicide was by way of spirit rather than flesh and I hadn't even known it. I now knew a race of men who controlled my very fate. Controlled my destiny. Controlled when I lived, how long I lived, and under what circumstances I would live, or die. This world was not mine for the taking. It had been taken already, and I was part of the spoils.

If I was trash in the world I came from, I didn't know it. In this world, I couldn't run from that understanding.

The door opened again and roused me from my depression. My bladder tightened in anticipation of another ruthless white man. Instead, Aunt Sarah returned, Roka with her.

And I realized then the irony of my situation. Aunt Sarah and Roka had saved my life in a world that I didn't want to live in. I couldn't figure out how to repay them for that sort of favor.

Roka walked up to me as I sat on the floor, and kneeled down to face me. He looked deeply into my eyes, around my face, at my nose, ears, neck, and forehead. Then he looked into my eyes.

"You lost," he said matter-of-factly.

There was no use in me responding. He wouldn't have understood it anyway.

"Them take you. Crush you. No same."

The man of so few words made perfect sense. He got up and turned to Aunt Sarah.

"He come back from spirits?"

"If he ain't, he be dead and buried long time 'go."

"Why he be broken?"

"Don't know exactly, Roka. Alls I can thinks—"

Roka cut her off with a panic in his voice. I saw his mouth move, but still had a hard time believing the words came from him. "Why he be broken, Sarah?"

"Breathe now, Roka...just calm down. Ain't no use gettin excited, now. Da spirit is funny sometimes. Listen now...a man could be rich and have all money 'n da world, but still thinks he po'. Work all his life like a po' man. Don' never know he be rich till somebody takes all dat money out the bank and lies it in front of 'im. See? Dat boy would've never got outta dat spirit world without being strong as a rock! It's inside 'im, just as sures I'm standin' 'ere..."

Aunt Sarah shook her head in bewilderment. "He must don't know it be there..."

"But see how talk to Bradley and Talbert! When first we saw him! He...!"

Aunt Sarah spoke, but didn't seem to comprehend the words she was saying.

"It mus' not a been real..."

Aunt Sarah slowly walked up to me, keeping her eyes focused on my face. She spoke like she was interrogating me. "Kinda world you come from, where a man can have dat much power in 'is words, but 'is spirit ain't real..."

If I could've spoken, I still wouldn't have been able to give her an answer.

Roka looked at Aunt Sarah, who was still looking down at me.

"But spirit still there?"

"Yea, it's gotta be or he be dead."

"So we fix him, like Elizabeth say."

Aunt Sarah diverted her gaze from me and looked at Roka.

"Ain't no easy task what you talkin' 'bout. Changin' a man spirit ain't—"

Roka cut her off again, this time with the same strong voice I was used to. "We fix him."

Aunt Sarah stared at him for a few seconds, and then nodded her head in acceptance. She motioned over to Bennie, Nessie, and Liza, who had been listening the entire time. "Get dis boy cleaned up and back in 'is bed, y'all. Me and Roka's got some talkin' to do…"

The ladies hurried over to pick me off of the floor, while Aunt Sarah and Roka stepped outside. I didn't understand the decision that had just been made, but I felt a bit like Frankenstein as the ladies scrubbed me, redressed my bandages, and laid me back down.

When Roka and Aunt Sarah came back into the hut, their sounds woke me from a troublesome sleep. My caretakers were scattered around the room, no doubt doing some task for the benefit of the hut. Again my body and bladder grew tight with the unknown of who had just entered, and only began to relax when I saw the matriarch and patriarch standing over my bed. I wondered how long I'd been asleep as Aunt Sarah started talking. "I'm gon ask you some questions, hear? You nod yo head yea o' no to answer. Dat alright?"

I nodded my head. Roka stood beside Aunt Sarah, paying close attention to her words and my actions.

"We's knowed yo ain't from here since we's first seen you. You remember where you come from?"

I nodded my head.

"Good. You remember how you got here?"

I shook my head.

"You from anywheres nearby?"

I shook my head.

"Yea, we's all figured dat. You gots no kinfolk 'round 'ere?"

I shook my head.

"So you here all by yourself?"

I nodded my head.

"How far aways you from?"

I looked at Aunt Sarah for a few seconds before she realized I couldn't answer her question with a head movement.

"Ahh, so's if I says sorta kinda far, real far, of far liken someplace me and Roka ain't never heard before, which is you from? Sorta kinda far?"

I kept my head still.

"Real far?"

I kept my head still.

"Someplace that we ain't never seen or heard of before?"

I nodded my head. Roka and Aunt Sarah glanced at one another before she continued. When they finished, Aunt Sarah leaned down so that her face was closer to mine, and almost whispered as she spoke.

"You a important man wheres you from, huh?"

I closed my eyes and nodded my head.

"Yea, I figured as much. You had most everything you wanted?"

I nodded my head.

"But somethin' 'side ya ain't real." She turned to face Roka, who was listening intently to the conversation, again.

"We thought he come 'ere wid somethin' in da insides and lose it, but ain't true. What he come 'ere wid wasn't never real. Shine high and bright like gold when you sees it first, but it's just a pretty rock."

Roka couldn't hide the confusion in his wrinkled eyebrows, even though he didn't speak.

"We seen how he talk to da white folks at first, and we believe his spirit be gold. We's thinkin' he must have a heart strong's dat oak tree outside. But he don't."

Had I had all my faculties about me, there's no telling what I would've done. Maybe I would've jumped up and run out of the one-room hut I had been rehabilitated in. Maybe I would've cursed out the person who had saved my life. Maybe I'd have even hit her, cocked back my fist with all the power and rage that self-realization can muster and brought it across Aunt Sarah's face, hoping she didn't try the same thing in return. But I was lying in a bed with both my arms and legs incapacitated, and my mouth unable to form any words that made sense. No matter how stomach-turning and fingernail-scraping Aunt Sarah's analysis of me was, I had no other choice, but sit there and bear it.

"He don't," Aunt Sarah continued. "S'all fake. All da heart and spirit he come here wid ain't real. It's good fo' show, but ain't da real thing. What stump me, though, is dat I gave 'im my roots, and he come back. Dem roots send you straight away to da spirit world. Ain't never seen nobody comes back save fo my daddy when I'se a girl. And da spirits don' lie. Dey cain't. So's gotta mean he jus' as strong's we thought in da beginning when we first seen 'im. He jus' ain't usin' it. Bet he don' even know its dere. You says you wants us to fix 'im?"

"Yes," Roka answered matter-of-factly. "We fix him."

"Den we's gots to show 'im da gold inside 'im. Da real gold."

Roka nodded his head in agreement. I tried to pretend that my world hadn't just been compacted like trash by someone else's conversation.

Aunt Sarah looked back down at me, but I couldn't face her. I kept my eyes trained on the ceiling as she spoke. "Where you come from, it's your talkin' makes you 'portant, right?"

I kept my head still, giving what little protest I could. When she realized I was refusing to answer, Aunt Sarah began to bend down to speak to me again, but Roka stopped her. Instead he bent down, and squatted so that we were face to face.

"No be angry 'bout truth. Save for lies."

He spoke as if he was giving me a life lesson, and I listened as if it was my first. When he finished, I exhaled my self-righteousness and looked back at Aunt Sarah. She repeated her question. "Where you come from, it's your talkin'...yo words makes you 'portant, right?"

I nodded my head.

"I figures. No matter what kinda heart you got, I know you got mo' words den all of us. It's yo words gonna save you here. Dem's da key to open ya true con'stution!

"What he do?" Roka wasn't sitting as close to me as before, but he was squatted down and his face was still level with mine.

"He gots to be talkin' 'gain. Can't waste no time. Every day, dis boy need to be talkin' 'is gibberish aloud tills it turn back into words 'gain. Every day, startin' now!"

Over the course of the next four days I ran my mouth like a marathon runner. Aunt Sarah and Roka would take shifts watching me. Aunt Sarah would take the daytime, since she didn't have to be out in the field. Whenever Roka finished, he'd come in and signal to Aunt Sarah, who would move from her spot to somewhere further away. Then Roka, sweaty and exhausted, would take over watching me. The deal was that I was not to allow the hut to fall silent, under any circumstance. I was to fill in all the blank spaces of silence with my gibberish until my gibberish turned itself back into coherent words. I was allowed a good night's sleep, but that was all. Any other time I was to be talking, or at least trying my best to. If the medicine woman was having a conversation in the hut, she would stop her conversation and come over to me if she ceased hearing my chatter in the background. Roka was always too tired to carry on any conversation with anyone. He just came, sat, nodded his head at me, and I knew to start my meaningless drawl.

Only, by halfway through day three, I realized that it wasn't meaningless drawl anymore. Nessie had just changed the dressing on the bed I was on, and I could feel the difference. I was already mouthing off random trash, but when I lay back on the sheets and pillow I smiled and turned to her. "Tank koo! Isss ealy nice."

All of us froze at the same time. I was so used to mouthing off gobbledy-gook just to make noise, I didn't realize my speech had gotten that much better. Nessie stood, shocked that she could now understand what it was that I was trying to say, and Aunt Sarah glanced at me with a quick smile before going back to her business.

For the rest of the time I had to talk nonstop, I did it eagerly. I put all my effort behind making my words clear. It was wearisome, and my jawbone locked up twice, but by the end of the fourth day, both Roka and Aunt Sarah paraded into the room in the evening. Nessie, Bennie, and Liza were behind them, and from the way things sounded, there was a crowd of people outside the door. I was still practicing my speech when they entered, and Aunt Sarah reached down and gently touched my lips, cutting my stream of words off altogether.

"I believes you c'stop now," the first lady said and I stopped talking. I was so used to not responding to anyone that all of us sat there quietly for minutes before Roka allowed his impatience to come through.

"You talk?" He motioned toward me with his hands, like he was encouraging a schoolchild to recite something onstage. "You talk now? Yes, you do. You talk."

This was my first conversation after learning how to speak again. I found myself nervous.

"I'ont know what to say," I said as I looked back and forth between the two of them.

I hadn't seen Roka smile since I'd gotten to this godforsaken world, but he held a smirk on his face that seemed as if it came from God tickling his sides.

"You sound almost same," he said as he nodded.

"How it feel?" Aunt Sarah asked as she grinned as well.

"Feel like I gotta learn how to talk again."

"Yea, but you work fo' dese words, chile. Da words you gots now, you gots to keep 'em close. Can't waste 'em. Y'hear?"

"Yes ma'am."

A commotion outside turned everyone's attention on the front door. A large amount of footsteps could be heard moving away quickly, and the excited chatter outside the hut died so quickly that Roka ran to the door to see for himself what was going on. When he returned, his face had reset itself with cold seriousness.

"Reverend Lewis outside."

Without warning, Nessie, Bennie, and Liza grabbed their things and ran out like the hut was on fire. Roka posted himself at the foot of my bed, poising himself for whatever might happen.

I broke into a cold sweat, began to see colored splotches, and hyperventilated without knowing it.

"Calm yourself, chile!" Aunt Sarah grabbed my chin and tilted my face upward so my eyes would meet hers. "Look at me! You jus' calm yourself down, alright?"

I tried to take a deep breath, but my lungs wouldn't allow it. All I could do was try and hyperventilate quieter.

"He come 'round here an dere to checks on you. Had 'im gone fo' 'while…" Aunt Sarah smirked briefly. "He were mo' 'fraid of dat nigger disease den Massa Talbert and Bradley! He come 'round 'gain 'cause he heard you betta and I can't hides you no mo'. Massa Talbert and Bradley done seen you. You gon' have to talks wid 'im."

I shook my head vigorously.

"Listen!" the woman giving orders barked her one word at me, and I stopped doing everything except trembling and breathing.

"You gon' have to talk to 'im, and I'se glad! Dese white folk ain't leavin' to go nowheres, baby! Lotta folk go runnin' scared when they comes round, but you can't be of 'em."

I shook as I stared at her.

"I be here wid you whole time, but you gots to find fire 'inside you. Gotta be stronger den us slaves…"

Reverend Lewis burst through the door as if he were backed by a royal court blowing trumpets and announcing his presence. He was clearly hesitant to be in the space, but saw me sitting upright and grinned. "There you are! Amazing grace, look at you! You don't look anything like when I first saw you in that cage!"

He began to make his way to the bed, likely assuming that Roka and Aunt Sarah would naturally move out of his way. When they did not, he stopped short.

"Leave this room at once!" he ordered with a touch of discomfort. "This nigger and I need to discuss business!"

If the two of them were to leave me, I would surely die. I begged Aunt Sarah with my eyes not to leave, and she nodded back ever so slightly before changing her demeanor like a shape-shifter.

"Oh, yassah! Yassah!" Her transformation was complete. "Yassah… 'cept we can't tell if da sickness all da ways gone yet, sah! He 'ave one mo' week fo' he clean completely, and we ain't want a good Christian man sufferin' da likes of a nigger plague, sah! If we stays, sah, we c'get you outta here soon's we see sumthin'…"

Reverend Lewis looked more cynical than Master Talbert had, but he weighed his options.

"Alright, you can stay, but you go over there to the corner. I don't want you around us."

The passive manipulator told me with her eyes that this was the best she could do, and she and Roka moved over to stand in the corner.

I sat on the bed with both my legs outstretched and in splints, both my shoulders in slings. The pastor sat down beside me and I could not look at him.

"Do you remember me?" he began in a soft tone, like meeting a dog for the first time. "I'm the one that got you out of your cage, nigger. I rescued you. Do you remember that?"

I nodded my head.

"I don't know if anyone has ever told you this, but you are a very special, God-given type of nigger. Fascinating, really! No one knows where you came from or how you got here."

I continued to stare at the floor, daring not to move or make any sound. I could feel my hands begin to tremble again. I looked up at Aunt Sarah and Roka, but their hard stares made me drop my gaze to the dirt.

"These crazy people down here are so stupid. God save them all, but they are just plain dumb. Some of them think you fell from the sky. Some of them think you climbed up from the dirt. All of them believe you are some kind of half-ape nigger that can smash buildings and kill livestock with your bare fingers. They want you dead. And you know the only person who can save you?"

Reverend Lewis paused and waited for me to respond. He didn't know terror had frozen my lips shut, and his patience wore thin with each passing second. Aunt Sarah tried to interject for me.

"He c'talks with you, sah, he jus—"

"SHUT UP!" Reverend Lewis jumped to his feet and pointed a long finger at Aunt Sarah. "HOW DARE YOU TALK TO ME! YOU SHUT UP!"

Startled, Aunt Sarah stepped back into the corner. Her face ran through a series of emotions, displaying each for only a second before moving on to the next.

Reverend Lewis sat back down, cleared his throat, and looked at me.

"I'm sorry...I've been letting my Southern gentleman come out more since I got here.

"Let's get back on topic, shall we? I am the only one who can save you from a growing mob of people who intend, at some point soon, to kill you. I can save you, and I will save you, but I need to know some things first. Are you willing to tell me those things?"

I heard his question, but found it hard to respond. His outburst toward Aunt Sarah had awakened a hesitant sort of anger in me. It wouldn't dare come out, though.

In the meantime, Reverend Lewis' lack of patience was beginning to show itself again. He began mumbling under his breath as he waited for my reply, and his face darkened in shades of red as the seconds turned to minutes. Finally, when he couldn't hold his peace any longer, he reached up with his arm and slapped me across the face.

"Listen, I didn't come here to waste my time, and I certainly will not sit around waiting for a nigger to open up his filthy mouth! Now I asked you a question, goddammit! So help me, I'll call those heathens in here to kill you myself! Answer me!"

Suddenly, I knew what to do. I didn't have the courage to talk to Reverend Lewis directly, and looking him in his eyes would've made my blood run cold. I was weak, and I felt as if I'd learned so for the first time right then. But at least I could vindicate a person who had what I didn't.

Slowly, almost painstakingly so, I lifted up my head and looked directly to the back corner of the room. When Reverend Lewis followed my gaze, he saw that I was looking directly at Aunt Sarah.

"What is the meaning of this?" he asked, on the verge of rage.

It took a willpower that I didn't know I had, but I opened up my mouth in the presence of that white man and said my first words. "I...I...I...I can talk to her."

Even as she stood in the corner, I saw the candlelight reflect off of the tear in her eye. It was gone before it had the chance to sprint down her cheek. Roka nodded at me in approval, and took a seat on the floor.

"You—nigger wench." Reverend Lewis stood again, but this time with less fire in his voice. "Come over here and talk to this nigger."

"Yas...sah..." Aunt Sarah said with hate in her voice. She walked slow and steady up to the bed, and then pulled up one of the benches that she used to work on. She sat directly in front of me, and until Reverend Lewis opened his mouth, it seemed as though the only two people in the room were the two of us.

"Ask him where he's from," commanded Reverend Lewis.

"Where you be from, chil?" Aunt Sarah said, soft and low, as if she was rocking me to sleep.

I closed my eyes and tried to remember a world gone by. "I'm from a place where there ain't no slaves."

My words seemed to suck the breath out of everyone's lungs. My eyes were still closed, but the silence I heard made me think everyone was dead. I finally heard Aunt Sarah take in a deep breath after holding it as long as she could. The air trembled as it came from her chest into her throat and then out into the atmosphere. She had a million questions, but she knew she couldn't ask them.

I wasn't sure why Reverend Lewis' breath got caught, but when he released it, it came out as a laugh.

"No slaves, huh? So you're from up north, from my neck of the woods?"

I didn't answer. It took a few seconds for him to recognize why I was silent. When he did, he was forced to swallow his pride and nod at Aunt Sarah for help.

"You be from da north?"

I shook my head. "No. I ain't from here at all."

Reverend Lewis narrowed his eyes.

"What do you mean, you're not from here?"

Aunt Sarah began to repeat the question, but I stopped her. I had felt some of my fear melt away. I still couldn't look at Reverend Lewis, but I opened my eyes and looked at Aunt Sarah as if my conversation was with her. Slowly, I swelled my chest, set my face hard, and answered the reverend's question.

"Wherever this place is, I ain't from here."

Again, everyone in the room ceased to breathe. Reverend Lewis broke the silence after some time. He spoke as if he had some sort of a secret to tell. "What year is it where you're from?"

"2010."

Aunt Sarah seemed to be hiding so many emotions on her face, I thought it might burst. I could hear Roka hit his head on something in the back corner where he was sitting. The thud was a reaction to his shock.

"My God…" Reverend Lewis stared at nothing with a blank face. "Do you know what this…" He stopped suddenly. "Wait… how do I know that you're from where you say are? What proof do you have?"

I was still staring at Aunt Sarah as I spoke. "All I got is my memories."

Reverend Lewis slammed his hand on the bed and stood up. He paced the room.

"Well, that is wonderful! All anybody is going to tell me is that I've gone down south and found a crazy nigger!" He paced the floor a few more steps, and then sat back down.

"Alright, let's hear some of these so-called memories."

Aunt Sarah's eyes lit up and went wider than I'd ever seen. She looked like a little girl, sitting at her mother's feet, waiting for her fairy tale. I closed my eyes again, and this time the memories came rushing back. They pounded my brain so hard that I felt my body rock back and forth with the motion. I could feel the excitement of my previous life beginning to fill up in my ribcage, and I smiled as I let it out.

"I…I was a rapper. I was THE rapper! I got all the clothes, money, and jewelry I wanted. Two platinum records, baby. Couldn't nobody touch me! Aww…man…I had so many hoes, dogg! Chicks would line up. Had a different female every night. And all the money I could spend. Moved my family out the hood and everything. Well…I tried at least. 'Cause that's the first thing you gotta do when you get some real money where I'm from…you try and get your fam up out the hood! Niggas'll kill you in the hood, man!"

I had forgotten where I was. Either that, or I didn't care. This was the first time since I'd gotten to this horrible place that I felt connected to a life I had before, and that connection took me over. I felt all the pain and terror rise to the surface of my skin and drip off like sweat. I laughed out loud as I remembered my old self, and allowed it to emerge.

Though my eyes were open, I forgot about Aunt Sarah and Roka and Reverend Lewis. I wasn't talking to them anymore. I was talking to the American public, to the fans who had tuned in to MTV specials about me. I spoke as if I was back on a private plane with the world under my feet and a camera in my face.

"See, what you gotta realize, before you learn anything else, is that I'm the best. Period. Niggas can't see me! That's why I'm Da Nigga! 'Cause cain't no other niggas touch what I spit! Nobody else in the game right now is doin' what I'm doin', y'know? But don't get this whole rap thing twisted. I'll put a nigga in the ground quick! Youngins like P. Silenzas think 'cause they got a record deal, I won't make a phone call and get they head split open! But it's all good...I'm not trippin'. We got mo' bottles than we can count up in here, man! And we got trees in da back! You ever been high at 30,000 feet, nigga? Ha! Yeah, I bet you ain't! You rockin' wid Da Nigga right now, baby! I'ma get you high just 'cause I can! Grab a glass so we can toast to the fact that we don't love these hoes, my nigga! Hahahahaha!"

I let the laughter reverberate throughout my body. I was Da Nigga again, and it felt like cocaine in my bloodstream.

"Lemme tell you somethin', my nigga...if Pac was still here, I'd be the only nigga he messed with! Pac woulda destroyed all these fake niggas in the game right now! He woulda torn 'em all apart! But Pac ain't here, and Biggie ain't here, and now all these fake niggas wanna turn the game to a ringtone contest. But you best believe I'ma hold it down. See this real hip-hop right here. You cain't get thrown off by the platinum chains, baby! I'm an artist at the end of the day! I take everything that the hood gave me, and I turn it into my music! I make music for the ghetto, you feel me? I seen niggas shoot each other in the head, so I rap 'bout shootin' niggas in the head! 'Cause that's what the streets taught me, know what I'm sayin'? I seen hoes in the street trying to get over on niggas, so I rap 'bout stanky hoes 'cause that's all I seen! If you ain't no hoe, then don't take no offense to it, feel me? Look...look...real talk, man, this is my art. This is what I does, and I does it well! I make smash hits and I dick down chicks!

Hahahahaha! Deez Nutz Records for life, baby! New album, *Hoes In Da Attic*, in stores right now! Go grab that! In the meantime, I'ma go say yes to some drugs! Holla!"

I laughed so hard I began to cry. I lay back onto the bed and let the bellows lunge out of my chest and bounce around in the air. Somewhere inside, I knew that when I stopped, I'd be returned to a foreign land, and I laughed until I coughed uncontrollably and my chest became tight and my throat felt as though it was on fire.

When I opened my eyes, I hoped to God that I'd see the ceiling in a privately chartered jet, but the mud and straw brought me back to reality. Instantly depressed, I blinked away tears as the power I had felt dissipated, and I returned back to the place where the white man beside me made me want to devour my own flesh.

I slowly leaned forward, and everyone seemed to come back into my view in slow motion. Three blurry figures surrounding me, encasing me as I tried to accept the weight of this world. Roka must have moved while I was under my own spell, because he was now standing five steps away from me and to my left. Aunt Sarah still sat in front of me, and Reverend Lewis was still to my right. I didn't pay attention to either of them as I dropped my head. I was too engulfed in my own emotions to pay attention to anyone else's. Having to bear the cross of this new reality was bad enough, but having it removed, if only for a moment, and then placed back onto my back was nearly unbearable. Desperate, I did the only thing I could think to do for support. I reached out for my lifeline. I looked up at Aunt Sarah.

If having to return to this world was a cross that I could barely carry, then Aunt Sarah's face became the lash of the whip and the crown of thorns that made me long for death. She stared at me with a mixture of extreme rage and utter sorrow. Single tears from both eyes came down her face, and I realized then that since I had come to this world, I had never seen her cry. I had never seen a break in the shell that allowed her to survive on Master Talbert's plantation. But she looked at me now like a loving daddy's girl who had just been told her father wasn't coming home anymore. She looked at me as if I had stolen something from her. As though I had taken her hopes and dreams and ground them up. She looked at me as if she hated me.

And then, just as soon as she was there, she turned her face away from me, got up, and left the hut.

"Aunt…Aunt Sarah…?"

It was as if she never heard me.

I turned to Roka for some sort of explanation, but his face was riddled with confusion. He had just heard a riddle from me that he couldn't figure out. He stared at me hard as he tried to decipher what I had said.

Unconsciously, I turned my head from Roka and back toward the door that Aunt Sarah had walked through. Before I knew what had happened, I'd come face to face with Reverend Lewis.

His grin was the ugliest thing I'd ever seen.

I cried out and turned my head away, as if his gaze would turn me to stone. He couldn't have cared less. He stood up from my bed, still grinning, and shook his head in disbelief.

"Jesus Christ in heaven—thank you for your blessings! I can't believe what I've found! A nigger from the future! I swear I didn't believe it—" he turned and looked at me "—until you spoke! You sound just like what I imagine a nigger from the future would sound like! It's amazing!"

Reverend Lewis' words were like a lightning bolt, and I began to understand why Aunt Sarah hated me now.

Reverend Lewis picked up his coat and hat and gleefully put

them on. When he was all set to leave, he turned around and looked at me again. He was still pleased, but seriousness coated his voice.

"Listen here, you belong to me now. You understand? I'm going to talk to Talbert right now. He won't be able to refuse. You get yourself ready to go traveling, nigger. I'm taking you back up north with me."

"You sayin' it wrong, sir."

I didn't know what I was doing. Roka looked at me as if I had given a death threat. I still couldn't lift my gaze from the floor, but I spoke desperately. The desire for redemption, no matter what form it took, was too strong for me to ignore.

Reverend Lewis' face went blank, and then the red began to come back to his cheeks. I could hear the tremble in his voice.

"What?"

"You...you sayin'...it wrong...sir. My name's Da Nig...Da Nig..."

I couldn't get the name out. My mouth refused to release it. And there was only one other name I could think of. "My name's Moses, sir."

I knew what was coming. Quickly, I turned to Roka, looked him dead in the eye, and shook my head.

"No..."

That was the only word I could get out before Reverend Lewis' boot came down across my face without warning. Unable to cover my mouth and nose, I fell back onto the bed and let the blood gush from my face. Reverend Lewis dove quickly on top of me and wrapped his hands around my throat. Out of the corner of my eye, I saw Roka twitch, and I gagged out one word before Reverend Lewis' hands cut my air off completely.

"No...!"

I began suffocating.

"You listen good, you dumb nigger...I don't give a damn what your name is! You ever talk to me like that again and I'll burn you alive myself! You think you're something special because of where you come from? A nigger's a nigger! You proved that just now. It doesn't matter how far you go in the future, a nigger will always be a nigger!"

He let go of my throat and sat on top of me as I coughed and choked. He cocked back his hand to hit me again, but a large commotion started outside of the hut. Horse hooves and men's voices filled the air, and Reverend Lewis jumped off of me to see what was happening. Roka, fearing the worst, immediately picked me up and carried me to the back shadows of the room.

Reverend Lewis stepped outside to a mob of about fifteen white men. Each one of them had probably endured a hard days' work and smelled of the slaves they had beaten in the daylight hours. I managed to raise myself and look out the window as best I could. The night sky was lit up by their torches, and the thick rope wrapped around Bradley's arm seemed to catch the light and shine brightly. The overseer led the pack with a determined countenance, and as soon as he saw Reverend Lewis, he lowered the barrel of his rifle.

The fourteen men behind him went quiet, and the silence seemed to last an eternity before one of the men in the mob yelled out to break it.

"We s'posed to be killin' that nigger, Bradley! Why you got the gun aimed at the Reverend?"

"Shut up!" Bradley called back behind him, and the man shut his mouth.

"I come for my nigger," Bradley said matter-of-factly.

"He's my nigger now," Reverend Lewis replied just as assuredly.

"Either I takes 'im with me or we hangs 'im tonight, but you ain't gettin' 'im. I kill you where you stand before I let that happen."

"You can't shoot me, Bradley. You can't shoot me because you know who I am, and you know who you are. One of these men behind you would probably shoot you before you even got in to grab the nigger. So why don't you put the gun down? We both know you aren't fooling anyone."

"You can't shoot the Reveren,' Bradley!" another one of the men behind him called out.

"Shut up!"

Bradley kept the gun trained for another thirty seconds, and then raised the barrel and shot into the air. "Goddamn you!" he screamed out as he fired.

Reverend Lewis looked contently at Bradley, and waited for him to lower his gun completely before he spoke again.

"Now, here's what's going to happen," the man of the cloth said, loud enough for the whole mob to hear. "None of you are going to lay a hand on that nigger in there. He belongs to me now."

"Hell he does!" Bradley screamed out.

"Would you like to go and discuss the matter with Mr. Talbert? I have a feeling that after I make my offer, he'll see things my way."

Bradley's head looked as if it was seconds away from exploding.

"Like I said," Reverend Lewis continued, "he belongs to me now. He is not to be touched. I'm taking him back north with me just as soon as the next train leaves out."

"Reverend," another man from the mob said. "Hopes you don't much mind me askin', but why you so fond a this here nigger? We comes up here to kill 'im before he heal on up and destroy the whole town. We gots wives and chirren, and ain't nobody safe till that ape nigger's dead."

The church leader spoke as if he was bored with the conversation. "I know all about your superstitions, gentlemen. I assure you they aren't true. Bradley here has been feeding you all lies. You want the real truth? The real truth is that my colleagues up north are worried about these niggers getting too much power if we end slavery—and what I've got in there is proof that no matter what, niggers will never be the kind of force that my colleagues worry about. It's just not in their genetics, nor will it ever be. It's impossible. And that nigger in there proves it. I don't imagine any of you know the political implications of proving that we can both civilize and industrialize our entire nation by ending slavery, and not worry about the niggers gaining unwanted power?"

The men in the mob turned and looked at each other for a translation of what had just been said. When no one said anything, Reverend Lewis nodded his head.

"That's what I thought. Bradley, I'm on my way to see Talbert. If anything happens to that nigger, I'll see to it that you are hung with the same rope you have around your shoulders. Good evening, gentlemen."

Reverend Lewis tipped his hat at the mob, and walked away whistling. The high-pitched noise echoed off of the trees even after he was out of sight.

Fifteen men sat on their horses out in front of Aunt Sarah's hut, looking around trying to figure out what to do.

"It's up to you, Bradley," the same one who had questioned Reverend Lewis said. "You got us out here. Whatcha want us to do?"

Bradley jumped down from his horse and ran up to the door of the hut. He stopped just short of knocking it in, and stood still in front of it as he tried to decide between his pride and his life.

"AAAAAAAAAHHHHHHHHHHH!"

Bradley let out a scream that seemed to shake the ground. Then, slowly, he turned back to the mob of men he had brought with him.

"Y'all go on home," he said with defeat in his tone. "Jus' go on home."

One by one, the men directed their horses away from Aunt Sarah's place, and rode off into the moonlight. Bradley was the last to leave. His horse trotted slowly as its rider swallowed his humiliation once again.

Roka and I heard everything, and the knowledge that a group of men had come to kill me settled itself into my bones. I didn't know if I'd ever sleep again.

Minutes passed after Bradley's horse left, and I assumed that I was safe for now. Just as Roka started to take me back over to the bed, the door to the hut flew open again. He dropped me down to the floor and stood in front of me, trying to protect me from whatever it was that had invaded the space.

This is it, I thought to myself. *They've come back to kill me. This is it.*

A figure stopped in front of Roka. It held a tiny candle, and used it to light a larger one that illuminated the room.

"Auntie Sarah say da white folks is gone. Says y'all come over to da cabin now."

I looked at the face in front of me and stopped blinking.

"SaTia...?"

I moved my right shoulder enough to loosen the tie on the sling, and used the free fingers from my left hand to pull it completely off. The pain was harsh, but unimportant, and Roka stood amazed as I reached out to her with my formerly incapacitated hand, letting it float in eternity.

12

She hadn't changed much. She still had the same beautiful brown skin, absent the artificial glow of makeup and moisturizers. The dirt on her face seemed to have scrubbed all her pretenses away. She stood in front of me pure, like a kindergartener in a grown woman's body. As she always did, if there was something serious going, she pressed her lips together.

Her dreads were gone; her hair hung in five different braids, and her roots were overgrown and exposed. In the world we had come from, she would've been mercilessly ridiculed. She would've been talked about because of her nappy hair. But staring at her now, with her fat braids and her thick cotton dress, her calloused hands wringing each other in nervousness, I was staring at perfection.

Roka bent down and picked me up again, and carried me about an eighth of a mile to a cabin that seemed to appear out of the darkness. I was afraid of turning away from my queen and returning my gaze to find that she was actually someone else, so I kept my eyes glued on her the entire journey. I cried out to Roka whenever he lagged too far behind her. Each time he took six or seven bounding steps and caught up to her. He was breathing heavily when we reached the cabin. Whatever he sensed in the air he had decided to take seriously.

Walking into the cabin, I assumed no one was in it. We followed

SaTia up the few steps and into a completely dark and quiet space. Yet, when SaTia gave the signal, three or four candles were lit simultaneously, and I realized we weren't alone after all. There were nine people in the cabin. Aunt Sarah sat on the opposite end of the room, and judging by her countenance, she was still unprepared to speak to me. SaTia walked over and sat down beside her, whispered something in her ear. Roka sat me down on the bed nearest to him and took a seat beside me. There were five other men in the room that I did not know, and after Roka gathered his wits, he stood again and pointed to each of them.

"That Sam," he said, pointing to the man closest to us. Sam nodded his head. "Tom, Law, Buck, Fred," he continued, pointing to the rest of the men. "All in field. This work cabin."

I nodded, understanding at once the odors and weariness that permeated this place. This was a cabin for the field slaves, and the men I'd just met were worked from sunup until sundown picking cotton for Master Talbert. Yet, I couldn't evoke the empathy that I should. My eyes and heart were fastened on SaTia as she sat beside Aunt Sarah and tried to avoid my gaze. How did she get here? How long had she been here? Had anybody hurt her? That last thought caused me to squeeze my fist until my knuckles went white. If anyone had laid a hand on her, I'd kill them. Except here I was, broken, both legs and one of my arms useless until the splints and slings came off. In reality, if anyone tried to hurt SaTia, I wouldn't be able to do anything to stop them.

No! No, my mind couldn't grasp that. My heart wouldn't allow me to accept it. What good was I in any world, and especially this world, if I couldn't protect the woman I loved. An issue was settled in my mind before I was even conscious of the decision. I turned to Roka with a determination I was sure he had never seen from me before.

"Roka, let me outta these bandages," I commanded. His face showed his shock. "Let me outta these bandages, man."

I repeated my command—respectful, but serious as well. Roka continued to look at me strangely.

"No off." He shook his head after processing my request. "Need more time."

"Roka," I said, looking him straight in the eye. "I need these bandages off."

"But…"

He turned and looked to Aunt Sarah for help, but she was in conversation with SaTia. She didn't even notice Roka. He looked around at the other slaves, and they all stared back with baffled looks on their faces. None of them wanted to be the one to make the decision.

Roka exhaled deeply and looked back at me.

"Your breaks no heal good," he warned.

"I got it, man. Now take these things off me."

Hesitation broke over Roka's face as he walked up to me. Slowly, he reached up and grabbed the sling that my arm was wrapped in, untied it, and threw it to the floor. As I began to stretch my other arm out, he reached down and to my right leg. He began working at the rope that was tied so tightly to keep the wooden planks in place. I could already feel the pressure lessen as he finished untying the last knot, and all it took was a few rotations of undoing the rope for the makeshift cast to fall to the floor. I immediately felt a throbbing pain as I tried to bend my knee back so that my heel could touch the side of the bed. My joints felt like they were unthawing from a deep freeze. By the time I had bent my knee completely, I'd broken out in a sweat.

By this time everyone in the cabin, including Aunt Sarah and Roka, was staring at me. Aunt Sarah yelled out while Roka made his way over to my other leg.

"What you think you doin'? Dem bones no ways healed yet! You gon' ruin dat boy's limbs!"

Roka spoke calmly while fingering the knot on the second splint. "He say let me out. No argue."

The splint for my left leg was removed easier than the one for my right. The knots were not tied as tightly, and the boards clattered against the wooden floor in half the time. I looked down at my arms and legs, finally freed, and then looked up at SaTia. Her face shone with awe and confusion. I had to go to her.

I stood up slowly from the bed and gritted my teeth. The pain in my legs was fierce, but I wouldn't let it stop me. I wouldn't be that weak in front of SaTia. I straightened my back and let my arms hang limp by my side, praying I wouldn't have to employ them. I disappointed them immediately by reaching down and grabbing a long, thick stick I had seen at the foot of the bed. I held the stick firmly with my right hand, and leaned as much weight on it as it could support. Then I took a step forward.

Everyone in the room gasped, thinking I would fall. But I refused to. Something inside of me kept me on my feet when everyone watching knew I should be flat on my face.

I took a second wobbly step, and then a third, making a straight line to the woman I thought I'd lost. She seemed scared as I approached her, and I wasn't sure if she thought I was going to stumble or if she was just nervous about what I'd say. It didn't matter, though. I knew I wouldn't fall, and I knew she had nothing but admissions of lifelong love and sworn oaths of protection in store for her. When I finally made it to her bedside, she held out her hands to take me and help me sit. I pushed them away, almost falling in the process, and navigated myself down to the bed. When I turned and saw her face right next to mine, staring back into my eyes, my voice caught in my throat. It took four deep breaths and a brief meditation to calm myself down.

Everyone in the room waited in anticipation for me to speak.

"SaTia...I...I don't know what ta say. I ain't never think I'd see you again. I got so many questions for you... like how in the hell did you get here? But I can't even ask 'em right now. All I wanna do is stare at you. Stare at you and remember where we came from."

SaTia stared back at me, listening intently. Her eyes smoldered like an inferno and lit up my body. She opened her mouth to speak and I closed my eyes to listen.

"My name ain't SaTia, sir. Ain't never met no girl got dat name. I'm Ella."

My eyes shot open as I tried to figure out who had just come and spoken in front of my face. I'd heard SaTia's voice since middle school. I knew SaTia's voice, and this was not it. The bastard must have been quick, I thought. I looked around for some kind of clue as to which one of the slaves it might have been.

SaTia opened her mouth to speak again, and this time I kept my eyes open, ready to catch the prankster.

"She must meant a lot to you, sir."

I stared at the woman in front of me for a long while, trying to figure out if I was in some sort of slave *Twilight Zone*. Finally, Aunt Sarah spoke up. She looked around the room as she spoke.

"Dis here be Ella," she said. "Massa Talbert buy 'er a few weeks 'go. She gon' work in da big house mos' time, but she gon' be comin' round here mo' now..."

I dropped my head and raised my aching arms to cover my face with my hands. How could this woman not be SaTia? She looked just like SaTia, walked just like her, even had the same facial expressions.

"I think I'm losin' my mind," I said while shaking my head.

"No you ain't." Ella quickly responded, just as SaTia would've done. "I seen the ways you look at me while we was in da hut.

And I knows you ain't from here, too. Seems I favor some gal gotcha heart somethin' powerful where you from, sir."

I nodded my head. "Yeah…SaTia…you look like SaTia."

"Was she yo' wife?"

"Naw…naw, she was my…umm, my manager."

Ella looked at me, confused. "S'cuse my ignorance, sir. Don't think I knows what dat is."

"It…it don't matter…"

I was having a hard time. My mind was trying to accept that this wasn't SaTia, but my eyes contradicted any reasoning. In my confusion, I asked her a question that I'd reserved for my lost love. "How…how'd you get here?"

"Well, they tells me Massa Talbert come up on some extra monies and fix 'is mind on gettin' a new wench fo' the cold nights." Ella's expression turned somber as she turned away from me. "I been able to 'void him so far, but…"

She shook her head, unable to finish her sentence. As the reality of what she'd said began to dawn on me, I turned to Aunt Sarah in disbelief. "Is that true?"

I could tell she didn't want to answer me, but the truth compelled her to speak.

"Yea. Da times Bradley spen' breakin' you, Massa Talbert ain't give 'im a red cent. Saved up enough money to buys Ella 'ere."

I looked back at SaTia's twin with a different kind of horror.

"He…he been rapin' you?"

"Naw, not yet," she said without looking at me.

It was all too much. Realizing the woman in front of me wasn't SaTia had been hard enough, but the thought of her getting raped nearly made me swallow my tongue. I used my makeshift cane and tried to stand up. Dizzy from all that had happened, and still weak from my healing bones, I fell back to the bed. Ella moved to help me, but I shrugged her off once again.

"No…no…you can't…I just…just need some air, man."

Roka came across the room and grabbed me by the arm. Effortlessly, he lifted me to my feet.

"I take."

With Roka holding up the majority of my weight, we made our way out of the door and into the night. Once we got down the steps, I pushed away from Roka, leaned against a tree and proceeded to vomit. My stomach balled itself into a fist and sprung open like five fingers as it forced its contents to the moist ground beneath me. When I was finished, I leaned my head back with my eyes closed and let the wind wash over me like a tsunami.

"Sick?"

Roka stood poised to take me wherever I needed to go.

"Naw, naw man, I'm okay. My head got a lil messed up, that's all. I think I'm good now."

"Know girl?"

I thought about that two-word question for a moment. It was a question I had to eventually answer by the time I walked back into the cabin. I needed to have decided whether I knew the woman inside, sitting on the bed, or not. It took me five minutes to figure it out. When I looked back at Roka, he had stopped expecting an answer altogether.

"You know what, man? Naw. Naw, I don't think I know her. She could be twins with a girl I knew back when. But naw, I don't know her."

Roka stared at me as I spoke, and grinned at me when I finished. "Yes, you do."

I looked back at him, dumbfounded.

"What? What you say?"

He walked up to me again and grabbed my arm. "Come. Talk inside."

"No! Why'd you say that?"

Roka tugged slightly on my arm. "Come. Talk inside."

Knowing that going down this road would eventually lead to Roka forcing me up the stairs in some way, I decided to cut my losses and move my feet.

No one had moved during the time we had been outside. The field slaves stood their ground, Aunt Sarah had stayed seated, and Ella continued to try and wipe the look of impending doom off of her face. Roka made sure I was seated comfortably, and then walked to the middle of the room and faced Aunt Sarah.

"Need tell him."

Aunt Sarah thought for a moment, probably trying to figure out what Roka was talking about. When the lightbulb flashed on, she whipped her head around to face Roka again and made her uncertainty clear. "You gonna tell 'im now? Wid all this hap'nin?"

"He ready."

Aunt Sarah turned her head to face me, and examined me from head to toe. Her gaze probed me like a metal detector.

"Yea, he might be," she conceded.

"Might be what?" Knowing they were talking about me, I broke into their conversation. "What you gotta tell me?"

Roka turned around and faced me.

"'Lizabeth gone now. Bradley kill her. She tell future 'fore she die."

"Okay..."

"Say man come to set free slaves. Say he look like slave, but free inside. Say when man come, freedom next come."

I looked at Roka as though he was telling me a riddle. "What are you talking about?"

"She say man come to set slaves free."

"Okay, and what does that got to do with..."

It was my turn to experience the flashing lightbulb. I looked from Roka to Aunt Sarah, and then to all the other faces in the room. "Wait a minute, y'all think I'm this guy she was talkin' about?"

Roka nodded his head.

"No *think*. *Know*."

"You know? How do you know?"

"Know inside."

I vigorously shook my head, which made my entire upper body hurt. Despite that, I kept shaking it. "I'm sorry, man, but y'all got this all wrong. Whatever dude you think I am, I ain't. I don't even know how the hell I got here, and y'all think I'm s'posed to get you out? Do you not see me right now? I can't tell my head from my toes! I piss myself whenever a white man come in the room, and I'm lookin' at a girl who I swear I'm in love with—just in another life—and you think I'm who?"

I had gotten angry without realizing it. My breathing became heavy and I started talking in spurts. My emotions were erratic as I sat there on top of the bed, and before I knew it, I had no control over them at all, and started breaking down in front a captivated audience.

My eyes blurred and my head shot back and forth. I laughed and cried and screamed and moaned with such randomness that even Roka took a step back. I began yelling at everyone like an angry coach. My eyes went twice as wide as normal and I flailed my arms around like a wild man. The adrenaline curbed the pain that I should have been feeling. "What the hell do you all want from me, man? I mean, really—what do you want? You want me to go back home and take y'all wid me? I would but guess what? I can't! I don't even know how the hell to get back home. You think if I did, I'd still be stuck here? I don't even know if I can get back home. I don't even know where my home is anymore.

Far as I can tell, I'm stuck here forever. I don't even know what's real anymore. Hey Moe, are you a rap star or you a slave? Do you run the town, or do you get whipped by stank white dudes? Who the hell are you, Moe? Who the hell are you? You confused, pissy lil' punk. Hahahahahahaha! Get back in your cage, boy. Git! Git! I'm the incredible, unbelievable ape nigger! Hahaha hahahaha! Pay a dime and you can cut my nuts off and hang 'em on top of your fireplace. Where the weed at, my nigga? Gimme an ounce and three bottles so we can keep the party poppin'. Hey, yo, Bradley. Lemme get blazed before you put da rope 'round my neck, my nigga. We give new meanin' to gettin' hung high. Hoes in da attic, baby! Hoes in da attic, hoes in da cabin, hoes in da shack. Hoes gettin' strung up and whipped on they back. I ain't met a hoe since I got here, what type of stuff is dat…hahaha… ahahahahahahaha…AHAHAHAHAHA!"

I threw myself back onto the bed and continued to laugh heartily.

By the time I was done, I had succeeded in making everyone question my sanity. The five field slaves looked at one another, trying to determine the best way to deal with me. Aunt Sarah and Ella sat beside each other, staring at me with a touch of fear in their eyes. Roka looked over at me from where he was standing, but kept his face as expressionless as stone.

Tom and Buck started to move forward, but Roka held out his arm to stop them.

"I take him." Roka stepped forward and paused to see if I'd react.

Aunt Sarah stood up from her seat. "I'll go on with y'all, see if da boy done lost 'is wits."

Roka nodded, and took two more steps in my direction. I continued to chuckle as I lay on the bed. Ella stood up next, and watched as Aunt Sarah began making her way toward me.

"I better head on back to da big house 'fore they starts lookin' for me," she said.

She gathered all of her things and prepared to leave, but stopped short of walking out of the door. She lingered in the corner, watching me.

Roka was up to the edge of the bed now. I stared at the ceiling, laughing at nothing. He spoke softly. "You…hear…?"

My light chuckles morphed into heavy breathing and a wide smile. "Yeah, Roka, I can hear you."

"Okay?"

It was a question I didn't exactly know how to answer. Was I okay? I'd felt as though I'd broken with reality for a moment, and it had given me a high. But I knew it wasn't real.

"Okay?" he repeated.

He was trying to make a decision about me. He and Aunt Sarah looked at me with different eyes now. Having a mental break, on top of everything else I'd been through, could be too much for even them to handle. They waited to see the extent of my lunacy.

I had stopped laughing and my smile was gone, but my head still felt as if it was in that five second period after it awakens from a beautiful dream, unsure of what's real and what's not. I had to decide which side to live in, and I had to decide now.

"You…"

"Yeah, yeah, Roka, I'm good, man. I'm good. I jus' need a second to get my head straight; that's all."

He seemed satisfied, and reached out his hand toward me. "Come. Take back."

I hesitated for a moment, but his hand never wavered. When I finally lifted my arm and stretched it out, he grabbed my hand with his gentle strength and pulled me to my feet. He held up most of my weight again as I made my way to the door. "Come. Rest. Know tomorrow more."

I focused my gaze on the room for the last time, and spotted Ella staring at me from the other side of the room. Shadows covered her hair and much of her face. All I could make out were her eyes. I'd looked into those eyes for as long as I could remember.

"That's SaTia, dogg. I swear to God, that's her."

She disappeared through the other door and back to the big house.

I didn't see Ella again for the next four days, but I thought about her so much that she may as well have been sitting beside me.

I could feel my bones and muscles getting stronger with each passing day. Still, they commanded me to stay in bed. I lay on the straw mattress and pillow, in between long, deep periods of sleep, and tried not to picture Ella's face. I tried not to imagine her body swaying sexily as she walked across the hard floor, or her sultry voice. My attempts at avoidance were to no avail, though, as her image embedded itself in my thoughts. I was hooked on her.

On the fourth day, Aunt Sarah made her way over to the side of my bed. She didn't speak; just sat looking at me long and hard. The truth was that I had longed to hear her voice over the last few days as well, but she'd lived in silence. This was the closest she had been to me since Reverend Lewis' presence turned the air sour. I sat patiently, hoping she would bless me.

She sat for over a half-hour, looking me in the eyes. It was during this time that I noticed Roka's absence. He had been acting as the liaison between us for the past few days, and I could have used him now.

"Where's Roka?" I asked, not expecting an answer. The matriarch kept staring at me. At times her gaze seemed to have a sharp edge and I diverted my stare. Most of the time, however, I prodded her to speak with my eyes. When she opened her mouth, I held my breath.

"Roka done got da lash today," she said. "Bradley whipped 'im some terrible. He in da other hut, restin' to break his fever…"

I felt like someone had thrown me in a football game without a helmet, but at least Aunt Sarah was speaking to me again. I counted my blessings when she opened her mouth once more.

"I spend most a my days 'ere at dis plantation," she continued, "Massa Talbert done had 'is way wid me mo' than I can count. But I neva been cut likes a few days ago when you say those things."

She spoke soft and solemn, reminiscent of someone giving remarks at a funeral. I was instantly saddened.

"Aunt Sarah…I ain't mean to hurt your feelings. I mean, you saved my life. Why would I want to hurt your feelings?"

"I knows you ain't mean to, baby. But you did jus' same. You did by showin' how you be in your own world."

My brow furrowed like a squirrel's tail. "What do you mean?"

Aunt Sarah sighed, showing how painful this conversation was for her.

"I understands most of what you says, even if it don't seems I do sometimes. You callin' yourself nigger where you from…I'm just confused. Why a man does somethin' like dat, I don't…I don't…"

As her voice trailed off, I understood her frustration a little better.

"Aunt Sarah, it's a name. Really. Just a stage name I use when

I perform. It's hard to understand, but everybody say it where I'm from. It's nigga—wid an A. It's like talkin' to a friend."

"White folk walkin' 'round callin' theyself nigger, too?"

I paused, knowing my honesty wouldn't help my argument.

"Well, naw, it's just the black people…"

She looked down and shook her head in disgust.

"It's really not that bad, Aunt Sarah. I call all my best friends my niggas—wid an A."

Aunt Sarah continued looking at the floor, as if she was searching for something. When she found it, she looked back up at me. "Lemme ask you a question, baby. You came 'ere back awhile now. And you been beat and broke harder than anybody I seen. You seen torment wid yo' own two eyes, and you knows what it be likes…"

I thought of the animal cage they'd locked me in and dropped my eyes. "Yes, ma'am."

"You seen any niggas since you got here?"

My eyes shot back up and I stared at Aunt Sarah. "What?"

"Ain't you seen niggas—with da A, like you say—since you got here?"

I kept my eyes on Aunt Sarah, searching myself for the right words to say to her, but none came. I had no answer for her. I diverted my eyes and looked around the room as if the solution to my conundrum was written on the walls. Still nothing.

"I…I…" I stammered.

As I sat there, drowning in a flabbergasted breath, I realized that I was stuck because I'd discovered the unthinkable. There were no niggas here.

Aunt Sarah's face showed more contentment than I'd ever seen from her. "I figure da…"

BOOM!

Aunt Sarah and I both jumped off of the bed as the door flew open. Mr. Talbert stormed into the hut, Bradley close at his heels. Mr. Talbert's anger was splattered over his face. I saw the two white men and my body almost went haywire again. I could control my bladder at least, but little else. I fell back against the table and lowered myself to the floor as best I could while my hands shook relentlessly. I looked straight at the ground as the two men approached us, and as their shadows moved closer, I tried to stop hyperventilating.

Aunt Sarah was standing by the bed. With a big grin, she threw on her invisible mask.

"Massa Talbert! You'se sure s'prise me! How can I'se help ya, sah?"

"This nigger has officially overstayed his welcome. I'm fed up!"

"I don't knows what you mean, sah," she said, playing the role of an idiot.

"Reverend Lewis has just forced, uh, demanded that I release this nigger to him in a week so that he can take him up to Massachusetts. Damn Northern bastards think they can come down here and take whatever they want."

I covered my mouth to keep from vomiting. Aunt Sarah lightly tapped her foot on the ground. She was telling me with the gesture to calm down.

"Why y'spose he wanna go and do dat, sah?"

"It doesn't matter one bit why he wants to. He's going to." Mr. Talbert turned to Bradley, who seemed surprised by the information. "He's making me take his ridiculous offer and sell him the nigger. Do you have any idea how much I could've gotten for a nigger that everyone thinks is as strong as an ape? I could've made a fortune. And now the Governor says I have to sell to that thief for the pennies he offered. There's not a damn thing fair in this world, Bradley. There you go. You want to be a businessman so bad—this is your first lesson. There's not a damn thing fair in this world."

Red in the face, Mr. Talbert caught his breath and stared at me with an intensity that felt like a burning cigarette being pressed into my flesh. I could feel it, even though I refused to look at him.

"I'll tell you one thing, though," he said through gritted teeth. "That nigger's not getting off of my plantation until he's worked the skin right off of his fingertips. I don't give a damn what Reverend Lewis says. By the time next week rolls around, he won't be any good to anybody."

"Da boy ain't 'pletely healed tho,' Massa Talbert," Aunt Sarah said. "Deys work to be done in 'ere and he—"

"Don't believe this wench no far than you can throw her, Mista Talbert," Bradley shouted. "This nigger's got 'nough work in 'im to go weeks. Dis nigger wench's been lyin', an I 'spect she been doin' it a while now."

Mr. Talbert looked at Bradley, then at Aunt Sarah. "Have you been lying to me, Sarah?"

"Naw, sah!" She shook her head so hard I thought it might spin right off of her neck.

Mr. Talbert stood quiet for a moment, looking between the two of them. Then he looked only at Bradley. "Take him over to the field hand cabin. Tomorrow he gets up and works like everyone else. If he has been getting special treatment, it ends tonight."

Mr. Talbert took a step closer to Bradley and attempted to whisper in his ear. I heard every word.

"Work him as hard as he'll go tomorrow. Let him know he's a slave, but don't permanently hurt him. Don't do anything serious. The last thing I need right now is Lewis breathing down my back. You understand?"

Bradley nodded his head, and Mister Talbert glanced at me once more. I could almost see the shadow of his gaze on the floor.

"Too much trouble for a damn nigger…"

He shook his head and walked out. Bradley looked at me and grinned as Mr. Talbert left. "Time I finish with you, you gon' wish you was still in that cage. Tomorrow mornin', you mine, boy. Now get up!"

I jumped to my feet before he came over, making sure to keep my eyes turned away.

"C'mon over here!"

As I walked toward the door, I looked at Aunt Sarah. A shadow seemed to fall over her face as I passed her. When I got to the exit, Bradley stepped behind me and kicked the back of my legs, forcing me to the ground.

"Jus' like old times, ain't it, nigger?" he said, laughing.

I slowly stood up. The unexpected fall had hurt my legs more than I'd have thought, and my knees buckled as I tried to get back up. As crazy as Bradley was, he wouldn't risk causing me any serious damage. He saw my struggle, and left me alone the rest of the way to the cabin.

When we arrived, Bradley yelled out to the slaves inside. "Y'all come get dis here nigger, goddammit!"

Sam, Law, and Buck all came out at the same time. They tried to hide the fear on their faces. They were all unsuccessful.

"Dis here's the ape nigger! He gon' be out with da rest of y'all come mornin. Take 'im and get the hell back inside."

Law slowly came down the steps and helped me up. When I turned around Bradley was gone.

"Dey gotcha workin' da field come mornin?" Law said as he led me into the cabin.

"Yeah."

"You ever work da field befo?"

"Naw."

"God save ya."

I tried to ignore the dread in his voice as I lay on the closest straw mattress I could find.

After I fell asleep morning came quickly. The loud clanging of the bells from the overseers tore me from my sleep just as the sun was poking over the horizon. I didn't realize how much sleep I'd been getting until now. I dragged myself off the mattress and found Sam standing at the door, looking at me.

"Best you hurry," he said and ran out of the cabin.

When I walked outside it felt as if I was in the Superdome after Katrina. I hadn't seen so many black people together since I'd first gotten here. They were crowded around three different tree stumps, while three black women who were dressed considerably nicer than the slaves poured some sort of thick, chunky liquid into wooden bowls. The crowd, despite its size, had obviously done this before. No one said a word, but they moved so efficiently it was hard to believe they weren't performing some sort of synchronized scene in a play.

I stepped down from the steps and immediately lost myself in the fray. Slaves passed me by, and after a while, I didn't know whether I was approaching the food or moving away from it. Buck passed me as he ravished his food, and when he noticed my confusion he stopped.

"Stay right 'ere."

I froze in place as he disappeared into the crowd, and within seconds, he emerged with an extra bowl of breakfast slop.

"Eat," he said.

Now that I had the concoction in my hands, I could tell by its stench that there was some sort of rotten meat in it. I looked at Buck with a raised brow. "I ain't eatin' this, dude. It's gone bad."

Buck looked at me for a few seconds, and then broke out laughing. "You 'spectin' steak?"

"Naw, man, I'm just sayin'…"

He held up his hand to stop me and finished laughing before he spoke to me again.

"Sometime, dis only food we get all day."

"What?"

"And dis be yo' first day. I find a way if I was you to eat it."

The slop tasted worse than it smelled, and I gagged on my first mouthful.

"You be alright," Buck said while he practically licked his bowl clean. "We's leavin' soon."

I thought for a second of how rich Mr. Talbert must be if he had all this land and all these slaves to work it, but my mind quickly moved from that thought to wondering exactly what was in store for me. The overseers were back and yelling again, and all of the slaves were beginning to disperse to different areas. Again, I looked around, confused, until Bradley rode up beside me. He had a shotgun over his shoulder and a burlap sack in his hand that I could've climbed into and pulled up over my head. Without warning, he threw the burlap sack at my face. The material felt as if it took pieces of my skin with it as it fell to the ground. I kept my eyes from looking at Bradley as he yelled out at me.

"You right over here, nigger. Right over here with me. We gon' have us some fun."

A group of slaves were moving in the same direction as Bradley had pointed, and I made my way toward them as they followed the path. We walked for about a half-mile, and when we finally broke out of the weeds and into the clearing, I was already tired.

The field stretched as far as my eyes could see, and was full of these plants that seemed to be covered by these white balls. I bent down to catch my breath, and reached out to touch one of the mysterious pieces of foliage.

"Hold up...is this cotton?"

"You niggers gidda work!" Bradley shouted. "Five bags apiece or you get the lash! Mista Talbert ain't putting up with yo' laziness no mo' and alls I needs is a reason to use me beauty." He held up the whip to remind us what he was talking about. "Now go!"

The slaves began to bend down and I looked around, confused. I had no idea what I was supposed to be doing. After a few seconds of trying to learn by example, I heard a crack beside my ear, followed by a sharp, stinging pain on the upper part of my shoulder that dropped me to my knees. I turned around to see Bradley with the famous grin pasted on his face.

"I told you we was gonna have us some fun," he said.

I stood up, making sure to keep my eyes focused on the moist earth.

"I...I...don't know...what to do..."

I could feel the slaves around me stop and look back and forth at one another.

"What you mean to tell me?" Bradley looked at me with his head cocked to the side. "You ain't never picked no cotton?"

I kept my gaze on the plants by my feet.

"Naw...uh...no, sir...I ain't never picked none."

Bradley continued to look sideways at me, then glanced at the two white men on horseback that were on either side of him. They shrugged, and when he turned back to look at me, he shook his head in disgust.

"Don't that beat all...a nigger that don't know how to pick no cotton." He turned back to his counterparts. "See? I would've turned this here nigger into the best worker anybody ever seen. He ruined is what he is, and he gon' stay that way now 'cause that bastard's stolen 'im from me. What the hell he gon' do up north?"

After agreement from his companions, he turned back to me. I dropped my head again.

"I tell you what, though. Today, nigger, you gon' pick me five bags a cotton, or I swear ta God, I'm gonna take the skin off yo' back."

Law must have taken Bradley's last words as permission of some kind, and run up to where I was kneeling. I didn't register his presence until he grabbed my arms and lifted me up.

"Look 'ere," he said. He bent down and grabbed the cotton from three different plants with one hand. Somehow, he separated the seeds and thorns with his fingertips as he picked it, so that what he put in the bag was almost 100% cotton. He did this repeatedly, until the bottom of my bag was completely covered with cotton, and then he looked back at me. "Okay?"

I nodded my head, and he went back to his section and returned to work.

I could feel Bradley looking at me, but didn't return his gaze. Slowly, I bent down and reached for a handful of cotton. Immediately, a thick thorn forced its way into my index finger, and I snatched my hand back in pain. I could hear Bradley laughing as I pulled the unusually large thorn out of my flesh, and sucked on the wound to try and slow the bleeding. When I reached out again for the same ball of cotton, I was extremely careful not to get stuck. Getting the seeds and all out of the ball, I found, was a lost cause. By the time I put my first ball of cotton into the sack, I was sure I wouldn't make it through the morning.

"Ha! There's a good nigger! And if that cotton's dirty, you got the lash to answer to!"

I bent down again and met a thorn that found its way into my palm.

Six hours later I was sure that death was around the corner for me. My hands had been reduced to bloody appendages. My fingers, gnarled and mangled, curled permanently into the position needed to pick the remaining cotton. I'd painted most of the cotton in my sack red with my blood.

The sun got hotter as the day wore on, and I could feel the cells of my skin dying as they succumbed to the ultraviolet rays. The slaves tried to help me, giving me their hats and cloths, but it was no use. I was already seeing triple by the time we broke for lunch, and now all the images and colors around me bled together like an ungodly watercolor. All of the bending over and standing up turned my back into a rusty door hinge. More and more frequently, it decided to stop operating, and caused me to collapse onto the dry ground. Bradley's whip would inevitably seek me out there, and steal pieces of my flesh until I found my way back to my feet. This process took longer and longer, until one time I fell and didn't even have the strength to yell out at the pain of the lash. It just kept coming, one slash after the other after the other, and I figured it wouldn't stop until I was dead.

At that point, Bradley realized the condition I was in. I couldn't move from off of the ground after he whipped me, and when he jumped down off of his horse to beat me some more, he found that my eyes had begun rolling back in my head. His fear of Reverend Lewis cut his torture short, and with great reluctance, he sent for water from inside the big house. I could feel the worry of the other slaves, but understood why they couldn't assist me.

A few of them had asked and had been met with the whip themselves. They struggled to figure out ways to help me, and I struggled to figure out a way to stay alive.

Suddenly, I heard Law's voice. It was barely audible at first, but got louder as he continued to go on. He was humming. A series of long, deep, dark notes came from behind his closed lips, and I recognized the song as "Swing Low, Sweet Chariot." One by one, other voices began to pick up the melody, and the entire field seemed like a choir.

It was fitting that Law would be the one to sing the first stirring words.

Swing low, sweet chariot
Coming for to carry me home
Swing low, sweet chariot
Coming for to carry me home

"Shut the hell up!" Bradley screamed, but none of the slaves listened. A rebellion was happening, and even in my state, I could feel the electricity in the air. It woke up something in my chest, even as I lay half dead in the scorching heat.

Someone ran up behind me and lifted my head and rested it on their lap. A few seconds later, I felt water rushing down my throat. I choked at first, spewing up the life-giving liquid, but then I relaxed and let it flow into my body. The more water I drank, the better my vision became, and I soon realized that I was laying in Ella's lap.

I looked up at her as she continued to give me water, her face etched with urgency. When she was done, she cradled my head in her arms, and I knew she loved me.

"I SAID SHUT UP, GODDAMMIT!" The rage in Bradley's voice was clear, and I knew what was going to happen before it occurred. I struggled to rise from Ella's lap, my back fighting against me. I made it upright just in time to see Bradley aim his gun and fire at Law.

The bullet struck Law in the shoulder, and he fell back onto the ground, groaning in pain.

Bradley turned to one of the white men beside him.

"I was aimin' for his goddamn head! Take 'im over to Sarah's. For all I care, he can die over there."

The overseer rode his horse over to where Law lay on the ground. After hopping down off the saddle, he grabbed Law by the arm he hadn't been shot in and yanked him up to his feet.

You could hear Law's teeth grinding, but he didn't scream.

The overseer took a rope off of his horse and tied one end of it around Law's neck. He took the other end and tied it to his own wrist. Then he hopped back onto his horse, and rode off toward Aunt Sarah's cabin, with Law being yanked and dragged the whole way.

"Now..." Bradley still had his gun in his hands. "Next time I'll shoot 'tween them nigger eyes! Nobody better make a sound."

I let my head fall back into the lap of my love. Law had made a wave that had the potential to be a tsunami, and the energy of it set my chest on fire. Now that it was gone, I didn't know what to do, and I felt my consciousness trying to leave me as my eyes fluttered closed.

And then I heard it.

O Mary
O Martha
O Mary, ring dem bells!
O Mary
O Martha
O Mary, ring dem bells!

It was coming from the other side of the field. It was too far to be able to pinpoint who it was, but it spread like the swine flu. By the time Bradley had instructed the other overseer to go find out who was singing, it had already made its way to our side.

I hear archangels rockin in Jerusalem
I hear archangels ringin them bells!
I hear archangels rockin in Jerusalem
I hear archangels ringin them bells!

My chest was aflame again. I sat up slowly, powered by the energy of the growing tsunami, and shakily made my way to my feet. Locking eyes with Ella, at that moment, I knew things would never be the same.

"I WILL KILL ALL OF YOU!" Bradley's rage had returned with a vengeance. He took turns aiming his rifle at each of us, and I believed every word he said. With an energy that I couldn't explain, and a background of slaves who were cracking open heaven with their voices, I looked Bradley in the eyes for the first time since he'd broken me. I did the only thing I could think to do. I did the only thing that felt right.

"I don't know how I got here, but all I know is
that you can kill the body, but can't kill the soul, it's
indestructible when my people confront you we be..."
Ringin them bells!

I turned around in disbelief. All the slaves had fallen in behind my rhyme, as if God had synchronized us. I turned around, my body pulsing with an unknown force, and I took a step toward my oppressor.

"I was lost at one time, but now I'm found
was on top of the world, but got knocked down
and now I'm standin' with a brand new crown, and now I'm..."
Ringin them bells!

I was rapping, but it didn't feel the same. This felt like I was trying to summon an earthquake with my rhymes. This felt like freedom.

"I got whipped, got chained up, and locked away
treated me like an animal, you put me in a cage
but now I'm out, and before I escape, you watch me…"
Ringin them bells!

I had made my way up to Bradley, and now I stood in front of him, screaming words that came into my head like they were being poured. The slaves had all stopped working, and had formed a group behind me. Bradley had his rifle aimed straight at my head, but he knew he couldn't pull the trigger. His rage turned the air around him to steam.

"I'M A MAN, YOU CAIN'T NEVER TELL ME ANY DIFFERENT!
I'LL STAND HERE AND TAKE YOUR BULLET, YOU DECIDE TO GIVE IT!
AND IF I DIE, BET A DUB YOU HEAR MY SPIRIT AS IT'S…!"
RINGIN THEM BELLS!

"I TOOK ALL THAT YOU GAVE, AND LOOK I'M STILL HERE!
LOOK YOU STRAIGHT IN THE EYES, I GOT NO FEAR!
GATHER THE SLAVES, TELL THEM LEND ME YOUR EARS, AND WE BE…!"
RINGIN THEM BELLS!

"THE NAME'S MOSES! I AM NOT NOBODY'S NIGGER!

THOUGHT YOU COULD BREAK ME? HOMIE, HOW YOU FIGURE?

YOU MUST BE DRUNK BUT I'M TAKIN' THE LIQUOR AND WE BE....!"

RINGIN THEM BELLS!

A blunt object came down across the back of my head, and I fell to the ground. Before I passed out, I made out the image of Reverend Lewis standing over me, holding a short wooden plank, and shaking his head.

"Damn, we're going to have to kill you."

My head fell to the side, and everything went black.

13

I knew before I opened my eyes that the old Moses Jenkins did not exist anymore. Standing in front of Bradley and speaking with complete freedom had done something that no drug or stadium crowd ever had or could. I felt an inferno within me even while I was unconscious, letting the warmth of the blaze lull me from darkness to peace.

When I finally opened my eyes, I thought I was in a *Matrix* movie. Things looked the same, but were somehow different, as is the case with a room in a house that's been slightly rearranged without the owner's knowledge. I imagine it's what Neo felt, seeing a wall one second, and a series of zeroes and ones the next. My head hurt from the blow I'd received, but it was a righteous pain that made me want to laugh more than wince. It was a pain that was worth it.

"I ain't believe it till now…"

I knew it was Aunt Sarah before I turned my head, which proved difficult because of the large knot and the blood caked on it.

If I hadn't known something was different about me before I'd awakened, I'd have definitely found out after I sat up. Aunt Sarah was at my bedside, but she wasn't nursing me. She hadn't bandaged my head, prepared any roots, or called Nessie, Bennie, and Liza in to attend to my needs. She just sat there and waited, like a soldier in limbo between wars.

Law, Buck, Sam, Fred, and Tom all stood behind her in various spots around the room. When I stirred awake they didn't move from their spots, but stood upright, squared their shoulders, and looked dead at me.

"Aunt Sarah, I..."

No. Something stopped me mid-sentence. A new voice that spoke through the fire in my chest. "She is not your Aunt," it said.

I nodded to no one in particular, beginning to understand what this difference really meant. I sat up straight, despite the nagging at the back of my head, and took in a deep breath.

"Sarah, what's goin' on? What's happened since I been out?"

My voice was different. Better. It was hard for Sarah to look at me now, as if I'd been infused with sunlight. She did anyway, though.

I could see her strength now, like those zeros and ones in *The Matrix*.

"Dey's meetin' up at da big house 'cause of what happen in da field. I figure they's fittin' punish all us fo' it, and hangs you at da dawn."

I had no more room for fear inside of me. The fire in my chest had taken up all available space. I nodded my head, hearing facts and nothing more.

"I gotta get up there. See what's goin' on. Can you fix this wound?"

I pointed to the back of my head, and she immediately produced the ingredients she needed to dress the wound. As she stood and began to work, I glanced around curiously, and then looked at the blood-stained bed where I had been lying.

"Why didn't you fix it while I was still knocked out?"

"You ain't ask me to. I know you wasn't dyin', and you a man now. Gotta give men dey choice."

She'd answered matter-of-factly, as if I'd asked her if the sun would shine tomorrow.

When she finished with me, I made my way to the door. I had a one-tracked mind—get up to the big house so I could find out what Talbert's plans were. They could do whatever they wanted to me, but I wouldn't allow the other slaves to suffer for my actions. If I knew what they were planning, I could figure out a way to get the slaves out of it. They could have me.

I was one step away from the door when Buck jumped in front of me and blocked it.

"Dey's got overseers out there. Dey's afraid a leavin' you alone."

I looked back at Sarah for confirmation. She nodded.

"Aight…look, Buck, is there any other way outta here?"

Sam stepped forward.

"Dere's a trap door in da flo' right here." He walked to the other side of the room and moved one of the cots, revealing the thin outline of a square big enough for a man to fit through.

I looked down at it, and then up at Sam in amazement. "How long this been here?"

"Be some years now. Cut it to help these two slaves run away a time 'go."

"And you ain't never thought to use it for yourself?"

Sam shook his head and Law shrugged his shoulders.

"Guess we been waitin' fo' you, even fo' we knowed you was comin'."

I looked at everyone in the room, making eye contact with each person as I did so, and nodded my head. Then I fumbled around on the floor until I found a way to lift up the trap door, and gave it a tug. It stubbornly opened.

"You be safe," Sarah said just before I jumped into the darkness.

"Yes, ma'am."

The space under the cabin seemed like an abyss. I felt things move against my feet and under my feet as I made my way to the daylight. I could vaguely hear the conversation of the two white men in front of the cabin, so I stepped lightly enough not to cause any attention. When I rose from the blackness, I stood up straight and squinted my eyes, happy to be back in the presence of sunlight. I took a deep breath, exhaled, and then sprinted forward.

The big house was about a mile and a half from the slave cabin. I didn't stop until the mansion was in my view.

There was a stream on Mr. Talbert's property that the slaves had told me about. It was shallow enough to walk across, they said, but large enough that you could hear it running from the house if it was quiet enough. Inside the stream was the jail yard line for field slaves. If you were caught going beyond it, under any circumstances, you were shot dead. The distinction between the two sides of the stream were clear—the slave friendly side had trees that stood side by side, swaying rhythmically with the calling of the wind. The other had two or three trees standing lonely and exposed, made to be envious of the freshly mowed lawn and flowerbeds that stood before them. I stood on the safe side of the stream, with my feet on the edge of my own mortality, and raised my head to take in this mythical abode. I faced the side windows, and from where I stood, any slave could stand and see glimpses of a life they couldn't have. They came in flashes as the Talbert family passed their display windows, making their existence a piece of clothing in a store where you weren't welcome. The large white house seemed to scream an invitation to other large white houses that stood erect with sunlight in its background. There was a homemade swing set sitting in the front yard, with accommodations for two little children with off-white skin and sundresses that smelled like honey. Any of the black children brazen enough to attempt fun would be thrown to the ground and beaten. A chimney complemented the roof of the house, while the small porch and shed in the back were only for the man of the house.

A picture of the house belonged on a postcard, I thought. Either that, or on the cover of a novel entitled "Don't Judge A Book..."

I kicked off my shoes, rolled my pants legs up, and began making my way across the stream. When I got to the other side, I quickly ran and sat behind the first tree I saw before I put my shoes back on. There wouldn't be many places to hide from here on out. There were one or two other trees, an outhouse, and a mound of dirt where I assumed someone or something had been buried. I took a second to get my breath once again, and peeked around the corner of the tree. When I didn't see anyone in the windows or around the house, I ducked down as low as I could and ran up behind the closest tree to the house.

From here, I could see people through the windows, but I couldn't clearly make them out. Still, I tried my best to get an accurate count. Resolved on what I had to do, I took a series of deep breaths. When I looked again, I was met with the image of Mrs. Talbert as she came out of the front door and made her way to the side of the house where I was hidden.

I jumped behind the tree, praying that she didn't see me. Sweat instantly formed on my brow, and I found myself too nervous to wipe it off. I hesitantly peeked around the tree again. Mrs. Talbert was about nine or ten feet from me, picking up her daughter's toys, singing softly to herself. I could tell that she hadn't seen me. I took a long look at her before ducking behind the tree. She looked as though she'd been radiant in her younger years, but life and children had taken their toll on her beauty. Her skin was beginning to sag like elastic from her face and neck.

I waited until her singing faded before I peeked out from the tree again. She was retreating back inside the house. My heart began to beat a little slower as a result. When she was back inside, and situated (I hoped), I took another series of deep breaths, then shot out from behind the tree. I tried to get even lower as I made my way across the field, and threw myself behind the outhouse.

The stench was a small price to pay for my safety. I sat on the ground and thanked God that I hadn't been caught. After a moment, I peeked out.

I was close enough now to get a good view of the inside of the house. The two windows closest to the front door looked on to the living room. Mr. Talbert, Bradley, Reverend Lewis, and two other well-dressed gentlemen were sitting on the couches and chairs, engaged in what looked to be an intense conversation.

"I've gotta get up there," I whispered. "I gotta know what they talkin' about."

The living room led to a dining room, bustling with a constant flow of traffic. I assumed the men would eat after they finished talking, because four different slave women were rushing in and out of the room setting up silverware and placemats. They bumped into and scooted around each other as they went hurriedly about their business.

Another window gave me a view to the kitchen; a lone woman was inside. My breath caught as I recognized Ella. She kept her eyes glued to a pan on the stove, as if she were frying up the key to her emancipation.

Suddenly, hearing the white men's conversation was secondary in my thoughts. I had to talk to Ella, no matter what it took.

I was close enough to make out the people inside the house,

but too far to hear anything that was being said. Each window was wide open, beckoning me to move closer, and I was too weak to resist. I gathered myself, ducked down, and sprinted to the mound of dirt that lay in the field. When I got there, I lay flat down beside it so anyone who happened to look out at it wouldn't see me.

I could only make out bits and pieces of the conversation now, but it was choppy at best. Frustrated, I decided that if I was going to jump in the water, it might as well be the deep end. Without thinking, I gathered myself once more and ran up to the side of the house, placing my back against the repainted white wooden panels. I was directly under the living room window, and if Mr. Talbert didn't kill me, my fear and nervousness would probably do the job.

Everyone inside sounded as if they were talking right above my head now. I forced my chest and lungs to still so I could listen.

"...so, again, I don't understand why this nigger has been allowed to cause all this trouble? Mr. Talbert, I've always known you to be a reasonable and rational man, which is why I find it hard to believe that you've let this spectacle continue for so long."

"Governor," Mr. Talbert said, with a voice that sounded like he was slightly under duress, "I assure you, my first inclination was to simply hang the nigger and be done with it. However, my employee here implored me to let him keep the nigger and break him as he saw fit. He made me a deal, and despite my better judgment, I allowed him to keep the nigger. Obviously, I regret that decision now, but it's not one I am at liberty to take back."

The other aristocrat sitting beside the Governor remained mute. He took notes, and occasionally leaned over to whisper something in the Governor's ear, but he never spoke himself.

"I'm sorry, Mr. Talbert," the Governor said, agitated and confused, "Why can't you take it back? What's preventing you from going and shooting the nigger in the head right now? Wouldn't that be simpler than calling this meeting during suppertime?"

"It would, sir, but I'm afraid Reverend Lewis is adamantly against the nigger's death."

The Governor turned an annoyed eye to Reverend Lewis, who sat self-assuredly in his seat.

"Why is this, Reverend Lewis?"

"Because I need him. The nigger is important to me."

"What could this nigger have that is of any importance to anyone in this room?"

"That nigger can prove that niggers will never be able to rival us. They will never pose a threat to white people, in this society or anyone to come."

"Reverend Lewis, I've yet to meet a nigger anywhere with any more intellect than the very couch I'm sitting on. You don't need this particular one to prove that to your friends up north...you can pick any one of them. Hell, take one of mine."

Reverend Lewis tried intently to maintain his calm as he spoke.

"Governor, my counterparts are significantly more humane and civilized than your Southern citizens. We've given niggers a chance to educate themselves, and in a few cases, seen miraculous results. We've seen niggers read and write right before our eyes."

"The hell you did!" Bradley said, spitting venom at Reverend Lewis. "Ain't never seen no nigger read and write, and I never will! It's just certain things a nigger can't do."

"Why, Bradley? You can't read, so how can a nigger know how, is that it?"

Bradley jumped out of his seat, breathing fire. "You goddamn nigger lovin' Yankee sonofa—!"

"That's enough!" The Governor yelled loud enough to cut the

argument short. When he was sure he had everyone's attention, he turned to Bradley and spoke with a soft, sympathetic voice. "I was inclined to your beliefs, too, until I took my last trip up north. It's true what he tells you. They have reading and writing and arithmetic-doing niggers up there. I don't know how they do it, but it's a few niggers that know more than a lot of white folk down here."

As Bradley fought that knowledge, the Governor turned to Reverend Lewis and his sympathy changed to contempt.

"But just because I've seen it, doesn't mean I agree with it. In fact, I absolutely abhor the idea of niggers getting educated. An educated nigger is no good to anybody. Hell—they're downright dangerous!"

Reverend Lewis interjected as if he was preaching a Sunday morning sermon. "But you see, that's why it's so important that I bring that nigger up to Massachusetts with me. He proves that the niggers aren't dangerous. No matter how much education they get, no matter how much they learn, they will be never be able to gain any power. They just can't. It's not in their blood!"

"And what makes you think this nigger can prove this to your friends?"

"Because he's from...he's from..."

The Governor sat back and placed his pipe in his mouth. "He's from where, Reverend Lewis?"

Reverend Lewis sighed, knowing that the chance of his being taken seriously was slim to none.

"He's from another place."

"We've figured that out, Reverend Lewis. Do you know where he's from, specifically? A territory we haven't discovered yet, perhaps?"

"He's from a place in the future."

The Governor almost choked on his pipe. "I'm sorry...did you say the future?"

The Governor burst into laughter, his notetaker following suit. However, they only laughed for a few seconds, before they realized that they were the only ones who found humor in Reverend Lewis' words. Mr. Talbert and Bradley both fell back into their seats, their faces carrying a somber fear. The Governor quickly composed himself, and then turned again to Mr. Talbert. "You believe this nonsense?"

"Honestly, Governor, I don't know what to believe anymore. I just want the nigger out of my hair. Whether Reverend Lewis takes him or we go and shoot him tonight, I want this entire situation done with."

The Governor stared at Mr. Talbert, a wrinkle in his brow. "What on Earth would make you think that nigger could be from the future?"

Mr. Talbert spoke as if he was telling a secret.

"When we first found him, Governor, he was dressed like nobody I'd ever seen—white or nigger. And the way he acted, it didn't seem like he belonged here."

"Then why did you take him?"

"Have you ever run across a nigger with no papers on the side of the road and left him, Governor?"

"Touché, Mr. Talbert. I don't believe it for a second, but I'll concede the point for the sake of this conversation. So what if the nigger is from the...ahem...the future? He's still a nigger, and my vote is still to kill him dead and go on with our lives."

"You can't do that." Reverend Lewis jumped to his feet. "I've already told you how important he is! You can't kill a nigger that can prove that white folk own the future! And you can't kill a nigger just because he makes you nervous. You can't."

"Sit down, Reverend Lewis."

The man of God looked around, and seeing that he was out-numbered by more than one person with wealth, reluctantly took his seat. The Governor moved to the edge of his seat, as if to pounce on the defeated reverend.

"I can do whatever I please, Reverend Lewis, and it's high time you learned that. Just because your father runs the largest corporation in this country of ours doesn't mean I won't go to war over my right to leave a nigger dead in a ditch!"

They stared at one another.

"Uh, sir, you thinks I can have a word?"

Bradley tried to disguise his dialect as he addressed the royalty in the room. The Governor responded while still staring at Reverend Lewis. "Sure, son."...

"Ahem...well, I been with this nigger lots since we first found 'im, and I agrees with Mr. Talbert that there's always been somethin' different 'bout 'im. But I broke 'im, sir. I broke 'im and broke 'im good. Ask anybody 'round these parts about when that nigger was in a cage and they'll tell you. That nigger over there—" he pointed across the stream where the slave quarters were, not knowing I was right underneath the window—"That ain't no nigger to be takin' up north, Mister Governor, sir. Nigger's got some kinda magic about him..."

"Oh, for heaven's sakes!" The Governor threw his hands up in exasperation. "First he's from the future, and now he's magic?"

Bradley, intimidated by the Governor's outburst, dropped his head. "Well, ain't for me to say, sir..."

The Governor put his hands down and composed himself again. "I'm sorry, son. That was rude of me. Please, continue with what you were saying."

Uncertain of what to do, Bradley looked at Mr. Talbert, who gave him a nod of approval before turning back to the Governor.

"Well, like I say, sir, it ain't for me to say, but I was out there today when he got to speakin' some crazy nigger voodoo talk, and I swear before God, he put all the other niggers under some kinda spell. I seen it with my own eyes, Mister Governor, sir. And I was sittin' there with my gun pointed at his head…and… and I couldn't pull the trigger. It was the damnest thing I ever felt in my life, sir."

Reverend Lewis threw Bradley a look of pure incredulity, but Bradley didn't catch it. Instead, he bathed in contentment, knowing that the Governor, who nodded his head reflectively, had taken his words seriously.

"Yes, I heard about this afternoon before I arrived. It seems that everything concerning this nigger manages to get around the town like wildfire. Do you think they would have revolted if Reverend Lewis hadn't showed up?"

Bradley looked earnestly at the Governor. "I think they woulda done whatever that nigger told 'im to."

The Governor turned to Reverend Lewis.

"You arrived in time to see this event taking place. What did you think of it?"

"I think Bradley lost all control of the slaves—simple as that."

"Bradley has been my lead overseer for over ten years now," Mr. Talbert said. "I've never known him to lose control of the niggers in the field. In fact, he's killed so many of my niggers for insubordination that I had to start taking it out of his wages."

"Reverend Lewis," the Governor said directly to him again, "was there a clear leader of the event that you saw this afternoon?"

"Yes, but I—"

"And who was that leader, Reverend Lewis?"

Reverend Lewis sighed and sat back in his chair, defeated.

"That's what I thought." The Governor placed the end of his pipe back in his mouth. "Gentlemen, this seems like a straightforward decision. We hang the nigger in the morning. We'll do it over by the post office, so everybody can come out and see. This way, we'll take care of the scared townspeople, and all of our issues will be resolved as well. Now..." He turned again to Reverend Lewis, who had his arms crossed in defiance across his chest. "We are all aware that your father's business buys up most of the cotton in this area. Is there any way we can convince you not to run home and tell your daddy about what's happened here?"

"No," Reverend Lewis said clearly and definitively. Everything was quiet in the room awhile, all the men looking back and forth amongst one another.

"Mr. Talbert, can you call your house wenches in here, please?" the Governor said after a moment.

Mr. Talbert, shocked by the request, fumbled his words. "Uh... umm...su...sure...we...I can...umm..."

"It's okay, Mr. Talbert. We're all men in this room. Send for your young wenches, please."

I knew Ella would be coming into the room. Against all my better judgment, I turned and peeked up through the window.

Five seconds later, Mr. Talbert returned with Ella and two other young female house slaves. He put them side-by-side in front of the Governor, who looked extensively at each of them. "Mr. Talbert, it seems you've been hiding your candy store..."

Mr. Talbert turned as red as a stoplight.

"Do you all know who I am?" the Governor said to the three young women.

Two of them shook their heads. Ella was the only one who responded. "Nawsah."

"I'm the Governor around here. I run this state...and most of the people in it..."

The Governor began groping on the first woman, saving the most beautiful for last.

Ella, obviously uncomfortable, diverted her gaze to certain landmarks around the room. Eventually she looked to the window. She saw me at the same time the Governor reached back and grabbed her behind, and she inhaled sharply.

"Ooooooooo, I like this one, Talbert..."

I wanted to cut the lust out of his throat.

Ella turned around quickly to face her owner.

"Massa Talbert, I'se wonderin' if I can get the flower tools from da shed in the back? Missus done said a few times she want da flowers fixed up nice."

Hints of jealousy had begun to appear at the corners of Mr. Talbert's eyes. He was all too happy to release her.

"Yes, go and fetch them. The rest of you go on back to work."

The three women scattered back behind the doors once again.

"You see, Reverend Lewis," the Governor began as he took a handkerchief from his coat pocket and dabbed his forehead and neck, "we do things a little different down here in the south. Now you can run home and tell your daddy about all that's happened with this nigger we got down here, and nobody will stop you. Your family is much too powerful for that. But, if I'm not mistaken, you've never owned any slaves before, have you?"

Now it was Reverend Lewis' turn to sweat. "No, I haven't."

"Well, you decide that you want to keep this little situation as our little secret, then I'll see to it personally that you get your pick of any three slaves in this entire town. Buck or wench, it doesn't matter. Nobody in Massachusetts has ever got to know about it. Hell, nobody in town has got to know about it. They'll be commissioned as slaves of the church, and that'll be that. Now, if that's something you would consider, let me know now so I can begin setting it up. If not, you can be on the first train out of here. What do you say?"

Reverend Lewis suddenly found it impossible to sit still. He shifted around in his seat as if there were hot coals under the cushions. "Uh...yes...that is something...something I would consider..."

"Good! Then our business is done. I expect to see a hanging bright and early tomorrow morning. Until then, I bid you gentlemen a good evening."

The Governor stood up quickly, with his notetaker directly behind him, shook each man's hand in the room, and exited through the front door.

I had once experienced a fear that seized my chest whenever white men entered the room. Now, I knew they planned to hang me in the morning and I didn't take an extra breath. I stayed there under the window, thinking about all I had heard, when something hit me that did cause my breathing to quicken.

The toolshed! Ella said she was going to the toolshed in the back!

I ducked down low and quickly scampered down the side of the house. When I got to the back corner, I squatted down as low as I could and peeked my head around the corner. Sure enough, Ella was standing there, shining in front of the shed. It was clear she had no intentions of getting any tools to work on flowers. Instead, she paced back and forth, looking all around her. When I stood up from where I was hiding and made myself known, she let out a cry that almost made my legs give way.

She ran up and hugged me like I was a returning veteran. She hugged me like we had been long lost loves—separated by time and space—and had just now found our way back to one another. And then she touched her lips to mine, and wouldn't pull them back.

I had expected a hesitant embrace—a longing stare in each other's eyes, maybe, but not this. This was a love that was meant to be in the future, but had found its way to the past. This was a destination, not a journey. We had somehow skipped all the steps needed to successfully connect two souls, as if we knew there wouldn't be much time.

At the moment, and from now on, I didn't care whether she was called SaTia or Ella. It was the same person. And I loved her.

When she finally pulled away, we were both sweating.

"I...I don't understand," she began. "I don't know how..."

"Don't worry," I said, wrapping my hands around her waist and pulling her close to me. "It'll all make sense soon."

She nodded and moaned simultaneously, and I bit down on my lip to contain myself.

"They gonna hang you in the mornin'." She wasn't trying to sound seductive, but she couldn't hide her passion as she spoke. She ended up making death sound like an orgasm.

"You let me worry about that," I softly responded. "If it's meant for them to get me, then they gonna get me no matter what. But I ain't goin' without no fight."

I was pushed back against the side of the house, and Ella stepped up and closed the space between us. She slid her hand down to my crotch and wrapped her fingers around me.

"It ain't fair," she whined and moaned. "We's just findin' out this is real..."

"Naw..." I managed to choke out in between inhalations. "I knew this was real years ago..."

I grabbed her shoulders and gently pushed her away from me so I could look in her eyes.

"I just...I wasn't ready for you. I couldn't handle you. And I ain't realize it until now."

She looked back at me, searching my face as she spoke.

"You talkin' so strange...but I understands you in a funny way. Like how you recognized me when you first seen me—it's like I finally recognize you. And now I can't stop thinkin' 'bout you. I can't help it."

"You don't have to," I said and pulled her back to me. "Not no more."

"It ain't fair," she said again, but this time her words filled with sadness. "They say you gotta die tomorrow mornin'…"

"I told you, let me worry about that," I said as I hugged her close. "I got a feelin' it's all gonna be okay; just let me worry 'bout it."

"Okay." She sounded like a child, trusting in me without any rational reason to. She rested her head directly below my chin, and I knew I would figure out a way to survive.

"Love?" she said.

The word sounded like cotton candy tastes. It took a second to realize it was for me.

"Yeah?"

"What's your name?"

I almost laughed out loud.

"Moses. My name's Moses."

"Like in the Bible?"

"Yeah, like in the Bible."

When Ella heard my name she hugged me even tighter than she had before. Slowly, the heat in her chest started to come back, and her tight embrace turned into warm, sensual fingers finding their way to my waist once again.

"Moses?"

"Yeah?"

"You say it was a time when you wasn't ready for me, right?"

"Yeah."

She turned so that her back was facing me, and slowly she grabbed my hands and navigated them under her dress. I realized that her underwear had disappeared when I saw a white heap on the ground about a foot from us. Later I would wonder how she managed to get them off without me knowing.

Before my hands struck gold, Ella turned and looked at me. Her eyes were narrow and she breathed as if we'd already started. "You ready for me now?"

I stood with my mouth open for what felt like forever, but when Ella called my name, my hands shot to the waist of my pants and began to pull them down. Neither of us heard the footsteps approaching the back door.

"Ella! Ella, you lazy wench, where the hell are you?"

In the four seconds that it took for Mrs. Talbert to get to the back door once she'd announced herself, I managed to frog leap from the back of the house to the side again, and was lying flat with my pants hovering somewhere between my knees and my ankles. Ella had managed to leap over to the tool shed, and put up a feigned struggle with the lock on the door. When Mrs. Talbert burst through the door, Ella was able to sell her performance, mostly because she was out of breath.

"Ella! We have been looking all over for you! I thought I told you to clean out the bathroom and wash the children's sheets?"

"I'm mighty sorry, Mrs. Talbert, ma'am! I come out here to get da tools to fix up your flowers, but this latch on the door be straight from da devil!"

"Mr. Talbert said he sent you out to get those tools quite a while ago. What has taken you so long?"

"Is dis here latch, ma'am! It's locked and I can't get it open!"

Mrs. Talbert looked at Ella suspiciously, then around the rest of the area. She pointed to Ella's underwear when she saw them on the ground. "What in the hell is that, Ella?"

"It's a rag I bring out here wid me, ma'am. I got so mad at da lock, I threw it on da ground. I'm mighty sorry, Mrs. Talbert, ma'am."

She'd been hanging around Sarah too long. Pretty soon she'd have Mrs. Talbert leaving her alone for fear of catching the nigger disease. Mrs. Talbert stared at her for a few more seconds, and then shook her head.

"Can't trust a nigger any further than you can throw them, I reckon. I don't know what kind of heathen, sinful actions you had going on out here, Ella, but you better come back in here now and do as I told you, or so help me God, I'll get the lash myself."

"Yes, ma'am! I'm leavin' my rag and rest of the things out here, then?"

"Heavens no, Ella! Pick up your things out here and report to the bathroom at once."

Mrs. Talbert, obviously fed up, stormed back inside. I crept up to the side of the house as Ella was running to retrieve her underwear. We met on our knees, and she kissed me and whispered to me in one breath.

"Come tonight, when all lights is out in da house, and I'll be back here waitin' for you."

"I'll be here."

She kissed me again, and ran back into the big house.

By the time I'd made my way back to the slave quarters, the overseers who had been assigned to watch me were in a drunken stupor. One of them had gotten his hands on a bottle of moonshine, and since, as far as he and the other overseers knew, I was still knocked out by Reverend Lewis' blow, they saw no reason to keep their senses. I practically walked through the front door of the cabin when I returned, which was a good thing. It's hard being stealthy with butterflies moving about in your stomach.

The slaves jumped up with excitement as I walked through the door. The fact that I had gone to the big house and come back alive was enough cause for celebration. They struggled to hold their peace and wait for me to speak.

"Did you hear 'em? What dey says?"

"Everybody sit down," I said calmly. "Y'all need to relax a lil bit. Everybody take a seat."

There were more people in the cabin than before I'd left. I hadn't noticed until then. The feel of Ella's lips had temporarily removed some of my senses. Now, though, I was fully alert. I stood in the middle of the floor and watched as my audience took their perspective seats around the room.

"You all are gonna be fine," I said matter-of-factly. "They not worried about y'all; they worried about me."

"Den, what about you?" Sam said with a surprising amount of worry in his voice. "What they gone do wid you?"

I took a deep breath and looked around the room. "They gonna hang me in the mornin'."

A collective wail went up among the slaves in the cabin and nearly brought me to tears. It was so loud and lasted for so long that, after a few moments, a series of erratic knocks sounded at the front door, followed by a drunken slur of words.

"…yousssseeee shuter niggggggers nasssssssssssssty damn it up!"

"quit…uh…quit 'cha….qu…quip…quite…errr…qui…qui…quiet…QUIET! Damn you!"

Amidst her own pain, Sarah gave a signal that caused all the slaves to lower their voices. When Law went and peeked out the door, the two overseers were on the ground, propped against a tree, snoring loudly once again.

"We…we can't let dat happen…"

Sarah found her voice amongst the mourners, and managed to grab their attention.

"Dis can't happen. Sure's a God restin' up in da heavens, we gonna' git you out from here tonight!"

The faces of the slaves began to shift from sorrowful to determined, and excited whispers of planning began to fill the room. I held up my hand for attention once again.

"Look, I know you wanna help me, but real talk, I don't want you to. Right now all Talbert and Bradley and the Governor can think about is gettin' rid of me. I ain't hear 'em say nothin' 'bout punishing y'all. If they can't find me in the morning, it's 'bout to be hell to pay, and I can't be responsible for none of y'all getting hurt. You been hurt enough already."

Sam, Buck, and Law all looked sideways at me before Buck stepped forward.

"What you gon' do then?"

"Don't know yet, man. If I'm not here in the mornin,' they gonna think y'all helped me outta here—even if you didn't. Best thing would probably be to wait till they come and get me, and try to find a way to escape before I get to da gallows."

Sarah stood up, her face indignant.

"And if you cain't?"

"Then I get hung."

She shook her head, unable to swallow what she'd heard.

"Naw…naw dat ain't it. Ain't your job to protect us, Moses! You done inspired us mo' than we ever been, and I'll choose dat over protection any day!"

The slaves in the cabin sounded out their agreement.

"We's heard yo' words, and we all respect 'em. You tell us not to do nothin and we won't do nothin. But if we get a 'scape route all laid out for you while white folks be sleepin', will you refuse it?"

I looked hard at Sarah, and then around the room. I realized that my freedom wasn't just my freedom anymore. It was the colored flag on the slave side of the field. They'd do anything they could to keep it from capture.

"No. If it's set up, I'm not gonna refuse it."

Sarah thanked me, and immediately began planning with a few of the other slaves. They were plotting my escape, but because I didn't know the backroads and deep forest, I felt acutely out-of-place during the conversation.

"Sarah?" I interrupted, and all of the slaves stopped talking and looked at me. "Roka still in the hut?"

"Yeah. He done took 'is beatin' hard dis time."

"I need to see him."

She nodded at me.

"Watch out. Dem white folk by da door…"

"Yes, ma'am."

I peeked out the door, saw the sleeping guards, and marched out into the evening. Before I got to Sarah's, I found my way to a clearing in the woods where you could get a clear view of the bighouse. Almost all of the lights were still on. My thoughts returned to Ella while butterflies danced in my gut and I experienced heart palpitations. I closed my eyes and tried to think of what tonight would be like. Just imagining Ella's sounds made my legs turn to clay, and I took a seat on the dirt and leaves for a while, trying to clear my head. I heard love songs that were popular in my previous life, and before I knew it, I was humming Luther Vandross to the sycamore tree in front of me. I caught myself, remembering who I was and all that was at stake, and I picked myself up off of the ground and began walking again.

Entering Sarah's hut was surreal. I could remember what the place had looked like when I was laid in there for so long, the walls and hard mattresses becoming my confidants and friends. Something was different about it now, though. My mind went back to the ones and zeros from *The Matrix* as I traced over a space that I was supposed to be familiar with. And then, as my eyes scanned over the beds, I saw Roka.

Sarah had understated his condition. He looked as though he'd been in a fight with a freight train. He lay on his stomach with cloth and roots on his back, covering his injuries. I could see the sweat soaking the mattress underneath him. For the first time since I'd woken up in the slave cabin, I began to feel fear. I had little to no concern for my own safety, but I felt as if Roka's broken condition somehow erased some of the strength he had given me. I slowly walked to him, contemplating whether or not to run away before he realized I was there.

"I knowed…"

The words seemed to come from the air itself. It didn't seem as if Roka had budged, and I'd had my eyes focused on him since I walked in. But, it was Roka's voice. Unmistakably. I watched him closely as he opened his eyes halfway and began stirring.

"I knowed."

"Know what, Roka?"

"Knowed it be you."

He began forcing his body up into a sitting position.

"Yo, Roka, lay back down, man. Ain't no need to be gettin' up."

He continued pushing himself up anyway, and finally reached the point where he could lift his head and look me in the eye.

"Look changed," he said with a smile he had to work for. "Fear go. Gone."

"Yeah." I knew Roka well enough to know he wasn't going to lay back down. I walked over and sat beside him. "I feel different."

"Like king?"

Roka's words struck me hard. He was absolutely right. I'd woken up this morning feeling like royalty.

"Yeah," I said, and nodded my head. "Like a king."

He nodded his head in response, trying to ignore the pain that came with his actions. Then he turned and looked at me hard, like he was trying to levitate me out the door. I held his look, unwilling to risk disturbing his thoughts with a question. We sat like that while the minutes passed, before Roka opened his mouth again.

"I don't much talk," he started.

"Yeah, no kidding."

His facial expression told me to shut up, and I did so.

"Long time, long time, long time...I wished was you. Wish me was you..."

I could tell he didn't want me to interrupt, but I couldn't help it.

"You wished you were me?"

"Yea."

"Why? Ain't nothin' special about me."

Roka looked at me as if he was tired of teaching me lessons. "You fool."

The insult caught me by surprise.

"I'm a fool?"

"Yea."

"Why I gotta be a fool?"

"Don't see inside heart. Inside brave."

For the first and last time, I saw Roka drop his head and gaze at the floor.

"Now...wish was you. Wish was strong and brave."

"Why you keep saying that? You the strongest man I ever met!

You see how much respect people give you 'round here? I ain't know what a real man was like till I seen you walk in a room."

"But, still fear. Still scared."

"Scared of what?"

"White people."

I shrugged off his comment like a bad joke. "You ain't scared of no white folk, Roka. I seen you around white folk."

"No see inside."

I shook my head in arrogant refusal.

"Naw, you ain't scared of no white folk, and you definitely don't need to be like me. I need to be like you."

Roka looked up from the floor and over at me. He had a pain and yearning in his eyes that made me want to hear my father's voice.

"First time came here, first day, I see you. I hear you. Talk white folk like dey ain't white. Talk da color outta dey skin."

I looked at my role model intently, not wanting to miss any syllable of this exchange.

"But, when I first got here, I was…different. I wasn't the same as I am now. How could you have wanted to be like that?"

"You always you. When first come and now—always you. You ain't know you, but I knew. Saw strong and brave like I wished for. Mine never come."

My understanding of his words made me want to weep. "And now?"

"Now you know you. Know self. Nothing same."

"Why couldn't you just tell me who I was when I first got here?"

"No listen. Finding self be journey, not lesson."

I took a breath and let all of his words sink in deeply. "So what do I do now?"

"What men do after dey find self."

"And what's that?"

"Find destiny."

I couldn't help but chuckle at the irony. "Well, that's a done deal. They gonna hang me tomorrow morning."

Roka heard this news and almost dropped his gaze again, which wiped the smile completely off of my face. At the last moment, he stopped, paused for a moment, and then lifted his eyes back to me. The fire in them burned intensely, and I'd never forget his next words even before he said them.

"If you die tomorrow, die well."

I nodded and sat there with my mentor for another half-hour. We didn't speak another word to each other, but seemed to be able to hear and understand each other's thoughts. When his pain began to overtake his will, I stood up as he was leaning over. He looked up at me and nodded once more, and then lay back on his stomach and closed his eyes. I stared at him for some minutes, wondering if this time would ever again repeat itself. After finding the courage to accept that is might not, I made my way out of the hut and into the cool night.

My thoughts were still in the space with Roka, so my instincts led my steps as I went trekking through the brush. Our conversation, both spoken and unspoken, echoed through my head, and I found myself mouthing some of the words he had said to me. "How...do you die well?"

The concept was a foreign one to me, and wouldn't have had a chance at making any sense on any other day but today. I couldn't help but imagine the heroes from many of the movies I'd seen who'd never made it to the final credits.

Had they died well? I thought. *Or is there something wrong about dying when everyone else figures out a way to live? And how do you find your destiny? Do you scrounge around for it like a misplaced wallet? Or*

do you wait for it to show up like a lost dog? And how do you tell your
destiny from a random cause that you've decided to fight for arbitrarily?

These and other questions bounced around in my head as I
walked the invisible paths around the slave quarters, not knowing
exactly where I was going. When I finally stopped, it was because
my foot had ran itself against a protruding rock coming out of
the ground. The pain brought me out of my stupor, and as I
jumped around on one foot cursing to myself, I realized that I
was in the clearing I had come to before. I looked out into the
distance and saw the big house, smiling back at me, with all the
lights in the windows turned out.

My mind shifted so fast that one or two thoughts got lost in the
process. My body felt a shock of electricity that literally caused
me to jump off of the ground, and when I landed again, I shook
my head in awe at the excitement I was feeling. Ella was waiting
for me. Just the thought alone made my hands tremble. My conversation with Roka was pushed further and further back into the
depths of my mind, and my hormones began to take over. I had
to get to her. I had to get to her as soon as I possibly could.

I began walking quickly through the woods, following the same
path I'd taken before, when a brand new set of worries began
popping into my head. How long had I been walking around
distracted, pondering my conversation with Roka? How long
had I stayed in the hut with Roka? How long had the lights been
off in the big house? Had Ella come outside already, waited for
me, and I hadn't showed? Had she been outside for a long time,
wondering where I was? Would she have to go back in because
someone inside noticed she was missing? Would she have to come
up with another excuse this time? Would they believe her? What
if they didn't?

My quick walk turned into a sprint, and I found myself leaping over logs and tree trunks so they wouldn't slow down my pace. By the time I was close enough to hear the stream, my acrobatics had become difficult. The sun was very much retired, and what had been the last traces of dusk had turned into pitch blackness. When I reached the stream, I thought about running right across it, but the splashing of the water would've been too risky. Instead I ran down to the far end of the stream, where I had been told there were large rocks, and prayed as I jumped onto the first one that I could feel around for the next ones. My prayers were not answered, and eventually I stepped quietly into the ankle-deep waters and began lightly stepping my way across. Once I had gotten to the other side, I took four running steps and then stopped abruptly, ducking and turning my head back to the sound of the stream. I'd heard a noise. It was slight, but in pitch blackness and dead quiet, a slight sound is heard through nature's microphone. I felt no fear, but disappointment instead, as I figured one of the overseers had followed me and I would now have to evade them rather than seeing Ella. But no one came. I waited for minutes, and the only sound I heard was one that had started far off in the distance that I had decided to be an animal that must have been trapped up ahead of me. I waited until I was satisfied that the sound from the stream was just another innocent animal, and I continued my sprinting.

There was a perimeter of tall grass that lay on the back side of the big house. I'd seen it on my earlier excursion into danger, and I knew that it was an extension of the cotton fields. I dove headlong into that grass, knowing that if I followed it, it would lead me straight to the person I was waiting for. I ducked down so that my head was only slightly below the blades that shielded me. I couldn't see in front of me, but I knew the house was up ahead, and that I was going in the right direction. I moved quicker and made more noise than I meant to, but by this time the excitement of what was about to happen had tightly gripped me. I felt as though I had taken a drug, and the effects grew more pronounced with each step that closed the distance between Ella and myself. I barely noticed the trapped animal anymore, even though it must have been trapped either close to or on the back area of the house, because the closer I got to Ella, the closer I got to it. After another few steps, I found myself hoping that Ella was tending to the dying animal.

I heard another sound behind me, and I whipped my head around again expecting to see someone, but no one was there. I wondered what had caused me to be so paranoid as I turned around. I could make out the silhouette of the big house now, and the fire within my body began to kindle itself once again. I moved even quicker, once again aware of the dying animal sound, but not caring. All I wanted was my Ella.

Finally, I reached the edge of the perimeter. I was grinning despite myself, and did the best I could to keep my composure. I'd never known what it was to want someone with your entire being before. It was like ecstasy and torture at the same time. I began trying to fix up my clothes, oblivious to the fact that I was wearing the same rags as all the other slaves. Holding my breath, I pushed the grass that was in front of me to the side, and beheld my queen.

There was no dying animal…

There was no dying animal. There was no dying animal. There was only Ella. There was Ella, with her face shoved into the dirt, her skin grinding against the ground like sandpaper. Pieces of her underwear lay strewn under her, and her dress lay in shreds underneath that.

Talbert kneeled behind her, shoving his pelvis into her so hard I could see the path in the dirt showing where he had begun to rape her, and follow it some fifteen feet to where they were now.

There was no dying animal. The sounds escaping from Ella were so horrific, I would have never guessed they belonged to a human being. She choked and suffocated, screamed and cried, convulsed and seized all at the same time. She sounded like a possessed woman, like some demon had taken over her body.

He rode her as if she was some god-forsaken horse. He used her hair as the reigns, and yanked her head up so she stopped moving forward from the force of his thrusts. Then he forced himself up through the front of her body, and slammed her face back into the dirt and laughed as she tried her best to keep her balance.

I shook behind the blades of grass. I shook so hard that the world became one big vibrating picture. The watercolors of the rape bled and blotched over everything else, and soon everything was rape. The trees, the grass, the bighouse, everything.

I could feel my mind when it snapped again. It felt like a rubber band when it's held with one finger and pulled back with another and then let go. Or like a twig when it's stepped on at the right place and gives way under your feet. I felt it. And once the water-colors had run their course, and things settled after God finished picking up and shaking my world like an Etch-A-Sketch, all I could think about was murder.

I stood straight up from the grass. I had no gun. I had no knife. But Talbert was a dead man. And that's all there was to it.

Before I could take my first step, one hand wrapped around my waist, and another around my mouth, and both my assailant and I fell backward into the grass. As soon as we hit the ground, he took his legs and hooked them around mine. I fought for ten seconds, and when I realized I couldn't move, I stopped and resolved that two people would die.

For a while we lay there quietly, the sounds of persecution echoing all around us. I silently lost my mind.

"No go," he whispered in my ear.

Roka! With renewed vigor I struggled against him, but to no avail.

"Shhhh! Massa hear us!"

I wanted to kill him. I wanted to wrap my hands around his throat while screaming out that I didn't give a damn. Talbert was going to die tonight. Him and Roka both. But my mouth was covered, and my body was locked up by Roka's, and I couldn't do anything but listen to the woman I loved as she was tortured.

"No go!" Roka whispered in my ear. "No, no now! Not right! She tell me! She tell me come! Please!"

Finally, the sounds stopped. I could hear Talbert standing up, putting his pants back on, and Ella writhing on the ground.

"Bra...Bradley!" Talbert called out with the little wind he had left, and footsteps came out of the far right corner.

"Yes, sir."

The voices stopped for a moment, magnifying Ella's.

"Why...why do you...have your gun out?"

"Thought I heard a noise in the grass ova there, sir, but ain't nothin'. Probably jus' 'coons. Thought 'bout comin' over to check, but..."

"It's a good thing...you didn't...Bradley..." Talbert still hadn't gotten his wind back. He wheezed out his words. "You... might've...disturbed my party..."

"Naw, wouldn't do nothin' like that, sir."

"Good."

Again, seconds passed without words. His belt buckled and shoes shuffled across the dirt. And a woman moaned.

"What you want me to do with the wench, sir?"

Mr. Talbert stopped moving. I could tell he was looking at Bradley. "You want her, too; don't you, Bradley?"

"Well, sir, I..."

"Get that thought out of your head, Bradley." Talbert quickly cut him off. "You can have any of the nigger wenches you want. You can even take Rosa from the kitchen if you like. But this one here...she's mine. Understood?"

"Yes, sir! I never even thought 'bout it."

"Yes, you did."

"So, umm, what you want me to do with the wench?"

"Leave her out here. She can make her way over to Sarah's when she's up for it. Those nigger roots will have her good as new in no time."

"Yes, sir."

I heard the door to the house open and shut, and everything was quiet.

Roka continued to hold me in place until he was sure Talbert and Bradley were squared away in the house, and then he loosened his grip. As soon as he did, I sprang up, turned around, wrapped my hands around his throat, and squeezed as hard as I could.

I can't imagine what my face must have looked like, but multicolored flashes went across my vision as I watched Roka's face go pale and his eyes go bloodshot. I squeezed so hard that I half-expected his throat to collapse in my hands. I could hear him choking and gurgling as I tried as hard as I could to squeeze the life out of him. But he never fought me back. He never raised his hands to push me away, or tried to move my fingers from his neck. He just lay there, staring at me as the life dripped from his body.

He's willing to die. The thought found its way into the madness of my mind. *He's going to let you kill him.* And just as I began to feel his tense body give up and go limp, I forced myself to let go. For several seconds he lay there, limp and lifeless. I just knew he was dead. But his body jerked up suddenly and he began to gasp and cough. I stared at him, partly in disbelief because I had almost killed my friend, and partly because I was terrified to turn around and face the woman lying on the ground. I watched as Roka's lungs reinflated, and he stumbled to make his way to one knee.

It suddenly hit me that he had already been hurt, and with what I'd done to him, it was a wonder he was still alive. Later I'd wonder how he found the strength to even follow me up to the big house, much less keep me confined after I'd seen Ella.

I still hated him, although I knew he'd saved my life. If I had come out from the grass, Bradley would have shot me. But Roka had also stopped me from saving Ella. And hearing her still moaning on the ground, I hated him even more.

We stared at each other long and hard in the dark. I watched him try and regain what little strength he could muster, and he watched me debate whether or not to kill him.

Finally, he took a deep breath and broke the silence.

"Her…" He spoke as if he had a tube in his throat. It was painful to hear him. "Help her…"

I turned around and began to hyperventilate while the rage found its way back into my bloodstream. Talbert's murder was still my number one priority, but to get him now meant walking past the woman I loved struggling to breathe on the ground. I tried to force myself to do it, to sprint right past her and though the door of the big house, up the stairs to whatever room Talbert was in, where I would shove the closest object I could find into his chest—but I couldn't. I couldn't leave Ella here.

Three steps and I would be completely out of the grass, and directly in front of her. The first two found my hands shaking and my lungs unable to take in a full breath. The last found my legs turned to a soft, bendable substance that was nearly impossible to walk on. But I made them. I made the three steps. And when my left and right foot stepped out of the grass and onto the dirt ground, I doubled over, suffering from a pain too unbearable to describe.

The side of Ella's face lay flat on the dirt. She hadn't been able to lift her head up. And just as when Talbert was tearing her apart, her knees searched, to no avail, for the strength to prop themselves up. Shaking uncontrollably, and muttering words that no interpreter of this world could ever understand, she went from lying flat on the ground, to making it up to one knee, and then falling back to the ground again.

I wept as I approached her. Still doubled over, my hands searched around me for something to brace myself on. Having found nothing by the time I reached her, it was all I could do to drop down to my knees.

"God...God...Ella..."

I hadn't seen the blood from where I had been. It was everywhere, as if someone had tried to paint her body and the ground beneath her. She heard my voice, and her groans grew louder. I stayed beside her, frozen.

"Take...take her..." Roka's voice still sounded like someone was carving it with a knife. "Take...her...to Sarah..."

I didn't move.

"Moses!"

It was the first time Roka had ever called my name. It snapped me into attention like a drill sergeant.

"Take...her...to Sarah."

I nodded through my tears, and turned Ella's body over. She flopped onto her back like a rag doll. The blood, sweat, and dirt had formed a plaster of Paris that hardened on the front of her body. The side of her face looked like a car had run it over. One of her eyes was caked shut with the hellish plaster as well. The other one seemed to search aimlessly for me, although I was right in front of her.

"Mo...Mo...Mo...Moses...Moses..."

My hands shook and I could barely breathe, but I felt Roka behind me, telling me to be strong without words. Slowly, I slid one arm under Ella's shoulders, and one arm underneath her knees, and hoisted her up. I thought her body would break into pieces and fall back to the dirt, but it stayed together long enough for me to stand up straight and bend my arms in slightly, letting my back take some of her weight. Ella's head lay back with her mouth open, and she began to gurgle on her own blood. I used my arm to tilt her head forward, and lean it upright against my bicep. She continued to mumble and gag, but she'd stopped choking.

Roka couldn't stand. I walked up to him with Ella cradled in my arms, and watched him raise up halfway and fall back down again. After the second time, he looked at me with an intensity that I could see through the darkness.

"Go!" He spat his venom at me, but I couldn't move.

"Roka..."

"Go!"

I was frozen. I looked at him, and I looked at Ella, and it was too much. I just couldn't do it anymore.

My legs began to weaken, and my knees started to buckle. I felt myself going down in slow motion, dropping to my knees in surrender. I didn't have anything left to give. I wasn't sure exactly what I was giving up on, but I was giving up.

And then, out of nowhere, came the slightest of noises. I looked over, and there in the dark I saw the silhouette of a slave girl, and then of another one. I didn't know how long they had been outside, but they stood there with a bucket of water and towels that I figured had to have been for Ella. I didn't know any of the other slave girls that worked in the big house, so I figured they had found a way to sneak themselves outside.

They both had a light with them, but I wouldn't realize until much later that neither one carried a candle.

One of them, the shorter of the two, began to dip her towel into the bucket. After she'd wrung it out, she walked up to Ella and slowly dabbed her forehead and face, cleaning the disgusting paste off of her. Then she approached Roka, and did the same. Finally, she approached me, and when the towel touched my face, I heard the stillest of voices come out from the darkness and speak to me. And after those few words, my legs found their strength again, and I worked my way back up to my feet, with Ella still in my arms. The slave girl placed the wet towel on Ella's chest as if she was playing an instrument.

Ella was quiet now. She was broken, but she was quiet.

The second of the two slave girls walked up to Roka. She reached into the darkness beside her, and gave Roka a white, wooden staff that must have been six feet tall and as thick as a soda can.

Even in the dark, I could see Roka's face go pale with shock.

Hesitantly, Roka grabbed the staff, and after two or three tries, he was able to use it to pull himself up to his feet. He was still staggering, but after he got set, he nodded to me, letting me know he was ready to move.

We turned at the same time to thank the slave girls, but they were gone.

Then, one step at a time, we made our way back across the stream.

14

"JESUS!"

Some of the slaves had seen us approaching before we actually reached Sarah's and informed her of our arrival. Even in the dark, I'm sure they took enough from how we were moving to tell her we didn't look so good.

She came rushing out to meet us. Roka, upon hitting her doorstep, collapsed to the ground. Ella had begun moaning softly again. She had bled the entire time we were walking. By the time Sarah saw us, she thought all three of us were dying.

She looked from Roka, to Ella, to me, and threw her hands up and yanked at her hair.

"AWW MY JESUS!"

Her eyes darted between the three of us as she tried to figure out which one to help first.

"Sarah!" I tried to wake her from the horrified trance she was in. "Sarah, get Roka up. He's hurt bad. Put him in that bed over there. I'll put Ella on this one over here."

"Is you hurt?"

"Naw, I'm not hurt. Help Roka, quick."

She hoisted Roka up enough to be able to duck under one of his armpits, and used all of her strength to stand and support him at the same time. Roka did his best to walk, but it was a real struggle. Sarah got him to the bed and watched him collapse once again.

She straightened his body and watched as he struggled to breathe.

I lay Ella down gently and when Sarah looked over at her, I saw tenderness in the older woman's eyes. She slowly walked over, and gently pushed me aside. She bent, and spent what seemed like forever just whispering in Ella's ear. Ella sobbed as Sarah poured herself out. Her quiet sobs turned to wails.

When they finally slowed, Sarah stood up again. She wiped her own tears and walked back to Roka.

"What you go out from 'ere for, Roka? What in da name o' God happened?"

"He followed me. I don't know how he knew where I was goin', but he followed me."

"Is...is...is da...is da sign!" I thought Roka had begun hallucinating, but with a shaking hand, he began to point at something. He lacked the strength to turn his head, but pointed his finger in a general direction. When I followed where he was motioning, the only thing of any significance was the white staff that the slave girl had given him.

Sarah looked at it for a moment, and then her legs almost gave out. She caught herself on the bed that Roka lay in, holding herself up with one arm as she stared intently at the staff lying on the ground. When she looked at Roka, he gave her a quick nod, as much of a smile as he had the power to make, and then he passed out. Sarah tried her best to get her legs back under her as she turned and looked at me.

"Is there...is there a cloth...?"

By this time, I was leaning over Ella. Her eyes were closed and I couldn't tell if she was conscious or not, but I let her broken body fuel my rage once again. I ignored Sarah as my vision began to shake and become static again.

"Is there a cloth, Moses?" Sarah sounded frantic now, as though she needed a cloth for something important. But she was disturbing my ritual. I was already on the brink of insanity, and I stared at Ella to purposely push me over the edge. Earlier when the slave girl wiped my brow, she had given me a peace that I did not desire. Now, as I smelled the sweat and stink of Talbert on the woman I loved, that peace faded. I began to feel the bloodlust that I felt in the grass, before Roka had stopped me from avenging my shattered reality. I thirsted for murder, and as I kneeled there, seeing Ella's hair stuck to her head and face with blood adhesive, I was determined to drink my fill.

I looked and saw the cloth Sarah was crying about lying on Ella's chest. It was the one the slave girl had given her. I picked it up and handed it to Sarah.

"Here. Take it."

I must have held my hand out for twenty seconds before I looked at Sarah. She didn't take the cloth from my hand, but stared at it, her eyes wide with a mixture of elation and terror.

"This...this be it...this da day..."

My rage decided it could wait no longer. I threw the towel on the floor and sprinted for the door. I wouldn't stop, I told myself. I wouldn't stop running until I got to the big house and had Talbert's heart in my fist, feeling its last beats before I crushed it in my palm. I wouldn't stop until he was dead. Until they were all dead.

Just as I approached the door, Sarah burst in front of me, knocking me back.

"Can't let you go," she said.

I couldn't read her face, but then again, I didn't want to. I would not be stopped again from what I needed to do. If Sarah didn't move, I would kill her. Simple as that.

"Get...out...of...my...way."

There was a demon in my chest that came out through my vocal chords. I hadn't yelled or screamed, but the blood drained from Sarah's face when she heard me. Her terror validated me. I smiled and growled at the same time.

Sarah knew there was something inside of me that I couldn't control. But she stayed in front of me anyway. Voice trembling... bottom lip quivering...she stood and looked me in the eye.

"I'm sorry, Moses, but I can't. Can't let ya leave. She told me not to."

It was resolved. Sarah would die. I balled up my fist and cocked my arm, knowing that after the first punch was thrown, I wouldn't stop until she was gone. Sarah stood her ground, braced her jaw, and prepared for impact.

"Mo...Moses!"

Ella called out my name from her bed. I still wanted to swing, wanted to fight my way through Sarah and take my insanity up to the big house, but I couldn't ignore Ella.

I dropped my fist, to which Sarah exhaled deeply and fell against the wall. Then I turned around.

"Come...come here!"

I walked up to the bed. Ella's eyes were open. They were blood-shot, but lucid. She spoke with a sandpaper rasp in her throat. "Where...where are...you goin'?"

"To kill Talbert."

She shook her head slightly.

"You don't...don't get to kill...Mr. Talbert."

"What are you talkin' about?"

"You don't...get to do dat. I do."

"But look at you!" My rage was still there, though it was diluted by Ella's words. "You can barely stand up. I'm going to kill 'im! That's it. That's all there is to it."

"No, you not!" she yelled, looking at me with a rage of her own. I cowered in response.

"So you saw…your woman gettin' raped, huh? So…so what? Did that white man force his way 'side you? Did he…did he infect ya from da inside out? Did he…did he slam yo'…yo' head 'gainst the gound? Did…did he take…take all da pure in yo' body and leave it…leave it lyin' bloody on da dirt? Did…did he leave his…his seed 'side you, so God forbid you haves a…a chile dat remind you 'bout how dirty you is….every time…every time you look at 'im? Naw! Naw…dat white man ain't done nuthin… nuthin ta you but hurt yo' pride…but takes…takes sumthin you thought belonged to you! You don't get ta kill 'im, damn you! I do! I do!"

My rage sat inside me like a bomb with nothing to destroy. Ella had contained it, but the power was still inside of me. It had to go somewhere. I just didn't know where yet.

When I turned around, Sarah was on her knees by the door, praying. She rocked back and forth with enough fervor to fuel a church revival, and when she was done, she stood and faced me.

"We gots the signs, Moses. I needs yo' permission ta have a church meetin'."

I looked at her strangely.

"Why you need my permission?"

"I jus' does."

I searched her face and could tell she was serious. She wouldn't make another move unless I said to do so.

Though I didn't know what I was doing, I knew it had something to do with the bomb in my chest. I looked at Ella, who was awaiting my answer as well, and then turned back to Sarah.

I spoke with the command of an army general as I nodded my head. My tone even took me by surprise. "Aight. Let's do it."

I could see the tears form in Sarah's eyes as she nodded her head in response, and then she moved out of the door.

I'm not sure what happened in the next half-hour. Sarah must have moved in and out of the hut a dozen times, each time quickly acknowledging me, and moving on to another task. I remained in the hut and tended to Ella, spending the entire time trying to get her to stay still when I touched her. One time, Sarah rushed in and ran back into her corner and mixed together some roots. When she was done, she brought them to Ella.

"We gon' be leavin' soon, baby. Dis' 'ere help with da pain."

Ella asked no questions, just took the paste on her fingertips and put her fingers in her mouth, sucking the paste off. She first reacted to the taste, and then to the texture in her throat. After a moment, her face relaxed and she began to look like her old self.

Sarah mixed some different herbs for Roka. Soon after taking them, he made the first noises I'd heard from him since we'd arrived.

Eight slave men came through the door. They had two make-shift stretchers ready to place both of the mattresses on.

"Is time." It was all Sarah said, and the slave men went four to each bed, moved the mattress over to the stretchers, and picked both Roka and Ella up. They each placed a corner of the stretcher on a shoulder, and proceeded with the rest of their mission.

I followed Sarah outside, and to my amazement, walked into the middle of a silent parade. I'd never seen so many people move so quietly. Sarah had managed to get all the slaves—not just the slaves from out part of the plantation—but all of Talbert's slaves and march them down to some place they all knew.

I turned to her in the darkness and silence. I was afraid to speak, but my questions were burning to be answered. "How did you do this?"

"We gots a system. Different folk knowed, it be meetin' time, and dey gets word out. Folks was already set to help you escape tonight. Jus' gave 'em differen' instructions." She paused. "Gotta tells you somethin'. You ain't gon' like what it is…"

I looked her in the eye. "Tell me."

"Roka…he be…he on 'is way home."

I looked at her strangely, not understanding, or not wanting to understand what she meant.

"What are you sayin', Sarah?"

She took in a deep breath, but still couldn't keep her voice from shaking.

"He dyin', Moses."

Her words knocked all the wind out of me.

"What are you talkin' about?! Roka's not dyin'. He can't die!"

"Yeah, he can, son."

"How do you know?"

"I knowed soon as I seen 'im back in da hut. His body was weak befo' he go wid you up to da big house. He's jus' pass his limit, now. Ain't nothin' else I can do but take da pain away."

I stopped walking, taking a knee in the dirt while the other slaves walked around me. Sarah stopped with me and took a hold of my shoulder.

"It's my fault." I could barely breathe. "If I hadn't…I almost killed him, Sarah."

"Naw, it ain't!" she said, adamant in her words. "Anything Roka do, he do 'cause he believe it be best. He knowed how weak he was befo' he follow you up da big house! You gots yourself a mighty work 'head a you, and last thing Roka want be fo' you to get down on yourself!"

I took a deep breath and stood up, staring Sarah in the eyes again. I knew she was right.

"How long he got?"

"Knowin' Roka? He won't go till da Lawd come in daflesh and snatch 'im!"

She smiled to herself, probably remembering all the good times they had shared. It was short lived, though. Her smile faded, and she looked back to me.

"I be suprised if he last 'nother day," she whispered.

We continued in silence as we trekked deeper into the woods. The news about Roka lay concentrated in my legs, and it became harder to move them. I had to keep going, though. The slaves surrounding me reminded me of that.

The big house was getting farther and farther in the distance behind us. Suddenly, I began to hear footsteps other than our own. I made sure I wasn't crazy, listening extra closely to the atmosphere surrounding us, before I grabbed Sarah by the shoulders.

"Sarah! I think we're being followed!"

She stopped and listened, and then shook her head.

"Naw, ain't no white folk. Clearin' be right 'tween three different plantations. You hearin' slave folk from da other two."

I looked around in amazement at all the different silhouettes that surrounded me.

"When's the last time y'all did this?"

"Last meetin' were called by 'Lizabeth. I was still in da big house, then. Talbert had' 'is ways wid me longs he wanted."

I'd heard her say it before, but I realized I never knew what it meant until now.

"Wait...Talbert raped you, too?"

Sarah looked at me like I was silly.

"Chile...Talbert done took me more den you or me c'count. At da place where I ain't even fights it no mo', jus' let 'im have me. Ella...did da girl stays on her knees?"

I had a flashback that literally made me gag and vomit. Sarah stopped with me, waiting for me to compose myself. When I stood back up, I nodded my head. "Yeah...yeah, she did."

"Good girl." Sarah nodded her approval. "You lays on ya belly or back, and he get to puttin' stuff inside ya. Had me a girl die once on account a somethin he put in her dat wouldn't come out. Told her when she got 'here—if he takes you, you stay on yo' knees! Don' lay down, no matter how bad it be, stays on yo knees!" Sarah nodded her head again. She was somber, but proud. "Dat's a good girl..."

We walked in silence again for a time. I had no more words.

Eventually, we reached an opening in the forest that had been set up like an outdoor theatre. There was a cleared circle, directly in the middle of the woods, that must have been the size of a one-bedroom apartment. There was a handmade podium in the middle and toward the front of the circle, and logs spread out all around the open space that a few of the slaves were sitting on. I barely recognized anyone, but as Sarah led me to the front, all I heard were whispers.

"Is dat 'im?"

"Dat be 'im?"

"Dey says he strong's three oxen!"

"I hear he can't die, no care how many times da white folk try and kill 'im!"

"Dey tells me he eats white folk, den throws 'em up 'cause he cain't keep 'em in 'is stomach!"

Different people began to light candles, and the circle became illuminated. Sarah and I stood at the front, looking over the masses. As the number of slaves in the space became more and more apparent with the light, my face must have shown more and more awe.

And then the slaves charged with carrying Ella and Roka came through the crowd and placed them at the front with us, and everything was put back into perspective.

Sarah walked up to the podium, and the crowd fell silent.

"Is been long time since we been 'ere last! Since God done spoke to 'Lizabeth, callin' her to bring us out 'ere, bringin' His spirit along wid her! Givin' us hope fo' tomorrow, makin' us feel like we more den jus' animals to be whipped and chained up! Makin' us feel like we mo' den property of white folk! Been long time…"

The clearing in the forest had turned into a church. People randomly called out to Sarah from the crowd. I could already feel the excitement building. The explosion—the bomb in my chest that I was charged with carrying since Ella forbade me to return to the big house—began to seep its way out through my pores and contaminate the air like radiation.

"Been so long dat some of us done forgot. Is folk dat was dere at that meetin' that ain't 'ere now on account of white folk…and is folk ain't 'ere on account of 'em not believin no more. I knows it's been a long time! Don't a soul 'ere know more den me! I done felt da lash more'n I can 'member! I done had Massa takes me mo' den I can 'member! I gots me five chirren somewheres dat I ain't seen since dey was took from my arms while dey was cryin' and screamin' my name! But I keep believin'! It's all I got to keep me from losin' my sense and mind! I keep believin and prayin' every night dat 'Lizabeth was right, and Jesus be sendin' somebody to deliver us! I prays so hard dat my knees bleed! I pray, and I pray, and I pray, and I pray, and I pray, and I pray, and I pray some more! And thank you, Lawd! Thank ya Lawd Jesus—you done heard me, and you'se sent your angel!"

Sarah pointed at me, and the crowd erupted. They let off a

sound like a filled football stadium. I felt confused, but my body continued telling me that this was right. That it was now my job to stand here and take it all in. I exhaled from the rage that had been caught inside my chest, relieved at being able to release it, if only a bit at a time. I knew the slaves were breathing it in now, and I wondered how it would affect them. Would they go crazy as I almost had? Would they go mad and start beating on each other? How would they be able to deal with the rage that I was releasing?

And then I inhaled, and I realized that it wasn't my rage in the air. It wasn't my anger being released into the atmosphere. It was theirs. It was the slaves'.

"I done seen what dis angel can do. I done heard it. Most y'all heard lies 'bout 'im, craziness done gone 'round…but I know now why 'Lizabeth pick me and Roka to give 'structions to you! 'Cause he come right in our house! He come right in, and showed us da power we got! Showed us how to stop bein' 'fraid all the time! And tonight, da very sign dat 'Lizabeth said done come to pass! So I ain't afraid no mo'! Lawd Jesus, I ain't afraid no mo'!"

The crowd continued to shout, but I barely heard them anymore. All I saw were flashes—memories. I looked out into the crowd, and every time a person looked at me—flash. The tall, skinny, man up front—flash—killed his wife and children, freeing them the only way he thought was possible. The woman to the far right—flash—pregnant sister tied up and had her belly cut open, seeing her fetus drop to the dirt before she died herself. The shorter man to the left—flash—castrated, genitals removed in front of the young white woman he was accused of staring at.

My rage was nothing. It was less than nothing. What I thought was horror, or pain, or suffering, was really nothing. I thought I was contaminating the air with my rage, but my rage would have flickered and died, like an ash that momentarily escapes from the fire before a gentle breeze puts it out. I wasn't here to contaminate them with my rage. I was here to get a taste of theirs.

I turned my head, trying not to look at anyone else's face. But it was too late. The memories flooded my brain. All I could do was bear them.

"Tonight be da night!" Sarah's voice echoed off the trees, projecting it to everyone among us. "We gots an angel—a leader be sent 'ere from God himself! He done come through time to show dat we mo' den what white folk say 'bout us! Done come through time to find himself, and thank da Lawd he found us in da process! Dis here is Moses! Moses bring da people outta Egypt! But dey ain't tell us dat us slaves is really Iz'realites! Dey ain't tell us us dat dese plantations, dese cotton fields and tobacco fields, dat dems really Egypt! But dey ain't got to tell us no mo', 'cause we gots Moses! We gots Moses! We gots Moses! And thank ya Lawd Jesus, I ain't scared no mo'!"

The crowd went into a frenzy. Big Mama would have called it catching the Holy Ghost.

"Moses?" Still bombarded with the memories of the people in front of me, I opened my eyes. Ella had worked her way to her feet. Even with her bruises and swelling, she was still beautiful. Whatever spirit had caught the rest of the slaves was trying to catch her, too, but she held out to talk to me. "Are you okay?"

I shook my head.

"No."

"I know it's hard, but dese folk here believe. They gonna follow whateva you tell 'em."

I looked down, and Roka was looking up at me, stern-faced, teaching me his last lesson. I nodded at him, and then looked back at Ella. She had taken a step back. I took a step forward. And another. And then I was standing beside Sarah, and the same spirit that had made everyone jump up and down, made them instantly quiet.

With their memories still fresh in my mind, I opened my mouth and gave them their rage back.

The sun was trying to poke its head over the horizon. It hadn't emerged yet, but the dark purple outline to the sky was beginning to announce its arrival. The cool air was a nice contrast to our warm bodies as we sat down, quiet, in the brush alongside of the road.

"Shhhhhh!"

I wasn't sure who'd said it, but it was overkill. Nobody was making a sound. Our nervousness hung around us in balls like Christmas ornaments, but we drew our strength from each other. When one of us saw uncertainty in another's eyes, we showed them our scars—our bare backs and missing limbs and gunshot wounds—and when the fire came back we nodded, clasped hands, and continued waiting.

None of us had slept, but it didn't matter. There was enough adrenaline in us to power our bodies for days. The time for sleep had ended five hours ago. When the slaves from the Smith plantation revealed that they knew the way to the town Armory, and how to get in. When Sarah revealed that there was only one path into and out of the Talbert plantation, and if the mob was coming to get me at daybreak, they would have to travel it. When the field hands from the Waller plantation presented a large box of hatchets and daggers that they'd stumbled across while hunting rabbits in the woods, no doubt misplaced by the soldiers that came through the town. The time for sleep had ended at the church meeting, when the slaves asked me to make a decision. When they begged me to lead them to freedom. How could I promise that, if we escaped, we wouldn't all be caught and returned and doomed to punishments worse than death? How could I promise them freedom with a catch? With a life of constant fear and uncertainty written in the fine print? I couldn't do it. Maybe Da Nigga could, but not Moses Jenkins. Moses Jenkins knew there was only one way, one sure way, to freedom.

The slaves asked me to make a decision. I decided they wouldn't be slaves anymore. Ever.

Lying there, crouched in the brush, a sound began to creep up through the dawn. I felt the fear ripple through the men and women surrounding me, and I turned around with the hatchet in my hand, prepared to hack anyone who would give us away. I met my eyes with each and every person surrounding me, repeating Roka's words silently. Destiny. Destiny. They nodded at me one by one, and steadied themselves for battle.

As the mob came over the hillside and made its way to the path to reach the Talbert plantation, I took a chance and poked up over the brush. What was supposed to be a mob had turned out to be a parade. No one knew exactly what would happen when the ape-nigger got hung, and intrigue was enough to bring out every man, woman, and child who was brave enough to risk it. I ducked back down into the brush, trying to hide the fear in my eyes, and turned to my right where Ella sat crouched beside me.

"There's more of 'em than I thought," I whispered to her.

She turned to me with a face as calm as still water. "So what?"

I stared at her, forgetting everything else. Then I leaned over and kissed her, and focused back on the road.

The mob was close now. We could smell the burning torches from where we were hidden. The crowd became more and more excited as they approached Talbert's property. Talbert, Bradley, Reverend Lewis, and the Governor led the crowd. They walked with purpose, feeling as if they were a part of something important.

Reverend Lewis was the first to see the object in the distance, sitting in the middle of the road.

My eyes watered as my mind went back to two hours ago.

"Mo…Mo…Moses…"

Roka had tugged at me, pulling the cuff of my pants to get my attention amongst all that was going on. I'd kneeled all the way down, putting my face almost to the dirt to hear him.

"No…no…long…now…"

I reached out to grab Roka's hand, and he yanked me over to him with a strength that wasn't his own.

"Last…last wish…"

"Anything, Roka. Whatever you want man."

He shared his request with me, and I denied it. But he gripped my arm until the circulation stopped, and wouldn't let it go until I agreed.

Crouched in the brush, I began to say a prayer for Roka, but I stopped. He didn't need it.

"What is that?"

Reverend Lewis drew everyone's attention to the object in the road, and tension began to build. The pace of the mob slowed, but they continued to inch forward. Not knowing what to expect, most of them had come prepared for anything, and the men, women and children pulled out rifles and muskets and took aim.

Bradley was the first to recognize the object in the road. "That... that's that nigger Roka!"

Roka sat in the middle of the road, propped up on a log that we had placed behind him. The rifle we had given him shook in his hand, but he kept his promise. He wouldn't let his spirit go until he'd fired his shot.

"Look here, nigger!" the Governor yelled out. They were close enough now for Roka to hear them clearly. "Drop that damn gun, or we'll..."

It seemed like the bullet hit the Governor before the sound came. His large body fell back against the man behind him.

"Kill that nigger!"

Countless guns began firing all at the same time, and Roka's body shook as the bullets filled in every space in his body. I turned my head away and bit my lip, desperately trying to stop my tears before any of the men and women around me saw them. But Roka's spirit scolded me, and I lifted my head and witnessed my mentor's death. When the bullets finally stopped, half of Roka's head was gone.

He sat there, in the middle of the road, with half a skull and a smile on his face.

"Goddamn nigg—!"

Bradley never had the chance to finish his statement. Sarah and I had split the slaves into two groups, and Sarah had taken hers and positioned them far enough down the road to ensure that they were behind the mob. Anticipating that everyone in the mob would be focusing on Roka being shot in front of them, Sarah had quietly snuck her group out of the brush and behind the group. No sooner had the last shot been fired into Roka, did

Sarah's group, armed with rifles and muskets from the Armory, begin firing into the crowd of white people.

We could hear the shouts of white men and the screams of white women and children clearly from where we were hidden. The plan was for us to wait until the first round of ammo was gone from the guns of the slaves, and then emerge from the brush, but the war had already started, and I couldn't wait anymore. I jumped out from the brush and sprinted across the road. Everyone at the front of the mob was now turned facing the back, trying to figure out who was firing at the back ranks of their group. The first person to turn around was a young white man, about my age. He had glanced behind him and did a double-take, not believing what he was seeing. I had my gun aimed at his head before he could raise his, and I blew his brains onto Talbert's shoulder.

The former slaves had taken my cue and run out of the brush on my heels. The men who took aim at me had been shot before they could pull their triggers. Ella had run out behind me as well, and had somehow gotten her hands on two different pistols. She'd killed six men and two women before they knew what had happened.

Everything was chaos now. The war cries of the slaves welcomed the sun into the sky. Gunshots echoed off the trees as slave and slavemaster alike fell dead on the road. The slaves that had run out of ammo had now adorned themselves with hatchets and knives, and were releasing their anger into the hearts and bellies of their enemies. The mob, having nowhere else to run, began frantically dispersing. Any unarmed person ran as fast as they could, praying to reach the woods before they were struck with a blade or a bullet. The slaves and the armed whites killed indiscriminately, screaming bloody murder at each other as they fought to the death. Bodies began to pile up on the ground, and pools of blood began to make clay out of the sandy dirt beneath them.

"MOSES!"

I heard Ella scream my name amongst the pandemonium, and looked around desperately while praying she was still alive. When I found her, she was covered in blood that was not her own. She pointed to two men running toward the big house, and I knew they were Bradley and Talbert.

I'd heard someone once, when describing an encounter they'd had with the police, say that they ran like a runaway slave. As I sprinted after those two white men, I was assured that that wasn't true.

By the time we reached the front door to the big house, we were close enough for me to stop, take aim, and fire at Bradley. My bullet struck him in the leg, and he limped inside as Ella and I followed. Bradley ducked off to the left, into the living room, while Talbert went right and up the stairs. Ella stopped, spat on the floor, took out her hatchet, and began to follow Talbert up the stairs.

"Ella…"

She turned around and looked at me, and her eyes stopped me cold.

"Either you can get this hatchet," the demon in her irises told me, "or he can."

Afraid to speak, I nodded slightly, and she began once more to stalk her prey.

I turned around to find a trail of Bradley's blood leading behind the couch.

"Bradley!"

I called out for him to show himself, but he stayed hidden.

"Bradley!"

"Goddamn you, nigger! Look what you done!"

"Stand up!"

"I shoulda listened to Mista Talbert…goddamn I shoulda listened to Mista Talbert! I shoulda hung you when I had the chance!"

Talbert screamed off in the distance, and Bradley cringed at the sounds of agony.

"Aw God! Aw God! Aw God!"

"This the last time I'm gonna ask you," I said. "Stand up!"

Bradley made his way to his feet, struggling, with the bullet in his leg, to stay standing. He looked at me as he limped, fear now overshadowing his contempt.

"You can't shoot me, nigger….if you shoots me, you goes to hell! You knows that, right? You can't shoot me, or God'll damn your soul to hell!"

I shot him in his mouth, hoping maybe he would shut the hell up, but he just kept moaning. So I shot him in the head twice. Then I thought about being locked up in that cage, and I shot him again.

I ran upstairs then, still afraid that Ella might be hurt, although it wasn't her screaming that reverberated throughout the house. As I walked around the corner, I picked up the pistol that Ella had dropped on the ground, and I was welcomed by the sight of Mrs. Talbert standing in the doorway of the washroom with a rifle of her own in hand. She was facing the inside of the wash-room, where it was clear the screaming from Mr. Talbert was coming from, and taking aim at Ella, who was so drunk with murdering Mr. Talbert that she hadn't even noticed. Without thinking I charged over and tackled Mrs. Talbert, knocking her back into the hallway. I ran into her hard enough for the rifle to come flying out of her hands, and when we landed on the floor in the hallway, I ended up on top of her. She fought me as I tried to hold her down and stand up at the same time, and finally I let go of the pistol and used all my weight to pin her arms to the floor and keep them there.

She looked up at me with perverted disgust.

"You're going to rape me, aren't you, you black heathen nigger? You're going to rape me, aren't you?"

I looked at her sideways for a split second, and then let go of her right hand so that I could grab the pistol.

"Naw," I said, and shot her in the chest.

The screaming coming from the washroom had died down a bit. I had reacted so quickly to seeing Mrs. Talbert that I hadn't even looked inside. When I did, I wished I hadn't.

Talbert lay on the floor, covered in blood. His entire body was mutilated. His penis lay on the tile beside his head, like a decoration. Ella sat on the floor, watching him die.

It wasn't too much longer. When she got up and faced me, the demon was gone from her gaze.

We were walking toward the stairs, when I heard a slight noise behind us. I turned, pistol ready, and ended up pointing the barrel at one of the two Talbert children. The oldest, the boy, stood there with his own rifle in hand, trembling.

I looked at him, and then at his sister, and finally at Ella.

"Go to your room," I commanded the children, and they ran off and slammed the door behind them.

We made our way down the stairs and into the living room, stepping over Bradley's dead body. The battle that had started down the road had moved itself, among other places, into Talbert's front yard. Sarah had just shoved her hatchet into an overseer's chest, and stood up triumphantly as I looked at her through the window.

I was just in time to watch one of the sheriff's men come up behind her and cut her throat.

She started to fall with grace as the blood spurted from the opening in her neck. Her eyes remained stuck on me the entire time. She dropped to her knees, her face showing a contentment with the inevitable, and then fell forward onto her face.

I leaned so far out the window that Ella had to grab me to keep me from falling.

"SARAH!"

"I'm going to help her," Ella said, and ran out of the living room and through the open front door.

The shotgun blast came quick. I knew before I turned around.

"NOOOOOOO! OH GOD NO!"

There she lay, her body forced back against the wall, with a hole in her chest the size of a basketball.

"Nigger! This is the Sheriff! You come out now with your hands up!"

I ran up to the door and slammed it shut. The Sheriff and his men began firing through the door, but I didn't care. I picked up Ella's body and carried it into the living room, cradling it as I sat down on the floor.

My tears blurred everything. Gunshots, shouts and cries and curses from people outside, they all bled together. I sat, rocking with the body of the woman I loved, cradled in my arms.

"Why did you bring me here?" I screamed at the sky, demanding an answer from God. "She's dead! Ella's dead! Sarah's dead! Roka's dead! Why did you do this to me?"

The gunshots stopped, and I heard the faintest whispers.

"What's his name?"

"Suh?"

"The nigger! What's his name?"

"Dey says 'is name be Moses, suh."

A man I took to be the Sheriff cleared his throat.

"Moses! Moses, come out with your hands up! This is the Sheriff!"

It was the first time since I'd woke up in the field that a white man had called me by my actual name.

I looked up at the sky after I'd gotten a hold of myself and nodded.

"Moses! You got until the count of ten, and then we're coming in!"

I kissed Ella's face, then gently moved her body to the side. I stood straight—as tall as I could make myself—and walked to the door with my head held high.

"Hands up!"

I slowly raised my hands.

"Is anyone else with you, boy?" The Sheriff was flanked by eleven people. Ten of them were his men, and they stood with their guns trained on me. The eleventh man was Law, one of the field hands I'd stayed with in the slave cabin.

"No," I said.

"Come down here slow, boy! Any sudden moves and I'll have these men send you to your maker!"

I slowly walked down the stairs, keeping my eyes trained on Law. He avoided my gaze.

"Is this him?" the Sheriff asked as he turned to the traitor. "Is this the nigger started all this?"

"Yassah," Law said.

The Sheriff turned again and looked me in the eye.

"You a dead-man walking, boy. What you got to say for yourself?"

"I—"

The bullet hit me in the back, forcing me two steps forward. The Sheriff's men, already frantic from the revolt, took no chances. They reacted quickly, and each of them had shot me before they realized I wasn't the one who's fired. I fell to the ground, flat on my back, numbed by my wound.

The feeling of dying felt strangely familiar.

I kept my vision long enough to see Mr. Talbert's two children walk out of the house behind me. The son held the same rifle I had seen him with earlier.

"Damn!" The Sheriff wiped his brow with his handkerchief, frazzled by the chain of events that had just happened, I imagine. As he regained his breath, I was slowly losing mine, and the last thing I heard was the Sheriff confronting the oldest Talbert boy. "What happened here, son?"

"I...I think the niggers got mad, sir..."

And everything went black.

PART THREE

15

I felt the silence before I opened my eyes. It hovered around me like a cloud, tickling my skin and caressing my arms and legs. Sweet fragrances filled my nose and lungs, danced around in my chest before I took a moment to exhale.

I'm in heaven, I thought to myself. *God…this is heaven.*

I intentionally kept my eyes closed, wondering what I would see when I gathered the courage to open them. Would there be pearly gates in front of me, or golden streets like those they sing about in the church? I hoped to God that Ella, Roka, and Sarah were here with me. How could I enjoy the afterlife without them?

I realized I was sprawled on what must have been a cloud. Everytime I moved, a thick mist adjusted to the contours of my body, molding itself to my frame. I hadn't even opened my eyes and already I wanted to return to sleep. And then I heard a sound—a *beep-beep-beep*, like a heartbeat, except more high-pitched. I wondered if it was the calls of angels? If instead of walking around with harps and wings, they just *beep-beep-beeped* all over heaven? I wondered if they were waiting to take me to God—and what kinds of questions would He ask me? I wondered if He would ask about the revolt.

Aight, I thought to myself, taking in a deep breath, *here we go.*

I opened my eyes and found Ella leaning over me, which made me certain I was in heaven. She looked down and caressed the top of my head. Tears formed in her eyes as she whispered words to me. I couldn't hear words. I just let the sound of her voice sprinkle over me like tiny raindrops.

Her hair had transformed. It sat on her head in locks now, falling back to her shoulders and neck. And I realized that the sweet aroma that I had smelled while my eyes were still closed was actually coming from her. The fragrance attached itself to memories I'd forgotten about—backstage powder rooms, studio sessions, award shows. A slow familiarity started to take hold of me.

It was akin to being hit by a car going two miles per hour. The blow wouldn't last, but it would eventually knock me over.

My eyes widened as I realized what was happening.

I looked away from Ella, and saw two women whose identities rushed back into my mind. Mama stood beside Ella, tears flowing freely down her face, and Big Mama stood beside her, raising her hands in praise to the Lord.

"Ella," I whispered hoarsely.

"Shhhhh…don't talk, Moe. Don't talk, okay? SaTia's here…I got you…you just rest."

I looked around the room in confusion. There seemed to be flowers everywhere. Cards, balloons, and candies were sprinkled about, and sunlight poured in through the window and illuminated my hospital bed.

"No…no…no…where's Ella? Where's Roka? Where's Sarah? I can't leave 'em! I can't!"

Big Mama made her way to me. She reached out slowly and grabbed the sides of my head, making me focus solely on her. She looked deeply into my eyes as she spoke.

"You're here now, baby. You hear me? You're here now…"

Without warning, the doors to my hospital room burst open. I looked up from Big Mama and saw three white men rushing toward me. Instinctively, I jumped out of the bed. All the women in my life screamed as I leaped and made myself into a barrier between the women and the white men.

Protect them, a voice in my head screamed. *It's not over.*

There was a letter opener sitting on the stand beside my bed. I deftly grabbed it and held it in my fist, ready to pierce the first white person who came close enough. The three white men, in their long coats, stopped in their tracks. One of them stumbled and fell as he saw me prepare to attack him. They made their way back to the door, their faces a mix of terror and awe as they rushed out.

In the next few minutes, things happened in flashes. The three white men returned to the doorway, a huge crowd gathered behind them, but they were content just staring at me as if I'd gone mad. I kept the women behind me, prepared at any moment to sacrifice myself for any one of their lives. I could hear their conversations dripping with confusion as I kept them to my rear, but I couldn't focus on that now. One of these white people was going to attack—I knew it. And when they did, I'd be ready.

I screamed at the white people with all the hate I could muster. Screamed at the pain of seeing Roka shot to hell. Screamed at the pain of seeing Sarah lying dead on her face, and holding Ella in my arms, her eyes and her chest wide open for the world to see. I screamed until the lunacy spilling out of my throat was the only thing that made sense to me. I didn't think I'd ever stop…

Time had become a blur. I'd overheard SaTia telling someone on the phone that it had been hours since I'd awoken, but it only felt like a few minutes. The security guards and the team from the psych ward had finally been called away, and the only people who remained were a pack of doctors outside that were trying to find their way into my room. SaTia forbade anyone from entering until she had some idea of what was happening.

I sat on the edge of my bed and stared out the window, trying to hold my sanity together. The window was my only solace. From where I sat, I could only look at the sky, and that became the only constant between where I was and where I'd been. The clouds crept slowly across a light blue background in the same way as they had on the Talbert plantation, and after watching the sky long enough, I almost convinced myself I was still there.

I feared that if I opened my mouth, my head would explode. Not symbolically or metaphorically, but that it would physically explode. I was having a hard enough time as it was restraining the stampede of my consciousness. I held the reigns for now, but one tug in the wrong direction—one pull with just a bit too much force, and the stampede would plunge itself into the depths of the sea, never to be seen again. And I would be lost for good. I knew that. And so I dared not make a sound.

SaTia, Mama, Big Mama and I sat silently in the room for what could have either been ten minutes or ten hours. The only sound to be heard was SaTia's BlackBerry incessantly going off. When it was nearly dead, and she stood to plug it into the wall charger, looking up to find all of us staring at her, she got the point, and placed it in her purse. She sat restlessly for a moment, only to jump up again, flailing her arms.

"I can't do this anymore!" she exclaimed, her voice teetering on the edge of a breakdown. "I can't! Moe, what's wrong with you? What's going on??"

"Nobody knows, baby," Big Mama said calmly. "All we can do is wait for Moses."

"Moses! Moses! Do your hear yourself, Mama Jenkins? It's Moses! Look!"

SaTia pointed at me as a tattle-telling child would. "He's here. He's up. Look! This time yesterday we didn't even know if he would live. Now he's up. He's back. Look!"

"SaTia...we know," Mama said, her voice about as strained as SaTia's. "We know, okay? You don't think I want to go over there and hug my son? Wrap my arms around him until my blood stops flowing? You don't think I've imagined this moment every second for the last six months?"

"Then go hug him! Go hug him, Ms. Jenkins!"

It was a bad piece of advice. Mama stood up with tears in her eyes and approached me. I looked at her face. I don't even know what emotions I was feeling, but I threw them all at her at the same time. She stopped, as if jerked by a chain attached to the wall, and made her way back to her seat and collapsed into a fit of tears.

"Moe...Moe..." SaTia was crying now too, releasing all of the chaos she'd let build within her over the last few hours. "Moe... you gotta give me something...please...Moe..."

I continued staring out the window into the clouds.

"Moe...please, you're killing me. I need to know you're still here, Moe."

Her voice echoed in the background behind me.

"Moe...Moe, please...Moses."

I finally turned to SaTia. Even through her tears she looked at me with realization written on her face. Wanting to test her theory, she walked to the other side of the room, away from my gaze and stood there for a few seconds. I turned my gaze back to the window, and she embarked on her experiment.

"Moe?" I heard her voice, but it didn't compel me to turn my head again.

"Moses?" I turned to face her, and she started slowly walking toward me. "You don't answer to Moe anymore?"

I stared at her, only partially understanding what she meant.

"Your...your name is Moses."

I nodded my head slightly, and turned back to the window.

"Moses, please..."

I looked at her once more, slightly annoyed. Why wouldn't she just let me get lost in my clouds again?

"Moses...you...you have to give me something, please. I've got a hallway full of doctors that either want to put you in a straight-jacket or run tests on you from now until God knows when. I've got record execs from Cosmos calling and wanting to know whether or not you're awake and whether or not you're insane. I've got an entire hospital that is getting ready to shut down because so many fans have bombarded this place that it's getting in the way of their other patients' treatments. And I don't know what's going on with you. I don't know what to tell people, because I don't know what's going on. What happened to you, Moses?"

I stared into her face, the face she shared with a woman I loved, and I had nothing to give her. I had so much to tell her, yet nothing to say.

Big Mama had quietly gotten out of her seat and was now making her way behind SaTia. She placed her hands on SaTia's shoulders, trying to provide all the comfort she could. Then she sat down on my bed.

She was on the other side, but just feeling her weight shift the mattress was enough to rattle my sanity again. I quickly turned my head to the window and focused on the moving clouds again.

"Look, child," Big Mama said to SaTia. "God does things in this life for a reason. And I'll tell you right now, one thing's for sure." She looked over at me, and I could feel her eyes prodding my skin. "That boy ain't the same as before. You can see it in his eyes, he done changed. What you got to decide is if you gonna love him no matter what. 'Cause that's what he needs right now. He needs love."

"Of course I'm gonna love him, Mama Jenkins. "

"Well, stop thinkin' 'bout yourself and start thinkin' 'bout him."

Humbled, SaTia nodded her head. Big Mama stood up from the bed and made her way back over to the seat she had designated as her own.

"Mama Jenkins, I'm still his manager, though. What do I do? What do I tell people?"

Big Mama slowly lowered herself to the seat, her muscles and joints rebelling against her.

"Child, them people outside don't know nothin' but what you tell 'em."

"So…I should lie to them?"

"You should figure out whether or not you believe my boy's gonna be okay. If you believe it, make them believe it."

Nodding her head again, SaTia thought for a second, and then walked over to grab her BlackBerry out of her purse. She made her way over to the outlet to plug it in, but stopped before she did and came and sat beside me on the bed. Her perfume hit my nostrils and I closed my eyes, using all of my strength to keep myself on this side of the asylum.

"I believe you're gonna be okay, Moe…I mean…Moses. I believe you're gonna be okay, Moses."

She sounded like Ella, and my heart began racing. I couldn't help myself. Slowly, I turned my head to face her.

"You do…you do look different. I can see it now…what Mama Jenkins was talking about. It's in your eyes," she said.

She was Ella. She was SaTia, but she was Ella, too. I could see it now the same way she could see the change in me. She was Ella without the pain trapped in her soul. But she was Ella nonetheless. I'd recognize her anywhere.

I felt the slightest tinge of hope as I stared at her.

"You're gonna be okay, Moses. Alright? You're gonna be okay."

I trusted her now, because I knew who she was. I nodded my head intently.

"Good. Now let's let the world know that you're back…"

More time passed. Either seconds or hours—I really couldn't tell the difference. Eventually my comforting sky began to change into shades of purple and red. I found myself standing up, pleading silently with the clouds to not disappear. They didn't listen. They waved goodbye, and then ducked into darkness.

SaTia's voice comforted me. Even while she talked nonstop on her BlackBerry, her voice soothed me in the absence of my daylight sky. She smiled at me as she told people that I was back and better than ever—that the coma had only made me more eager to get back into the studio and record new material for the fans that had prayed me through. She talked almost straight through the night, and I listened as long as her voice echoed through the hospital room. Mama and Big Mama had long since fallen asleep, but SaTia's phone kept going off, and she kept answering it. And every conversation reminded me more and more of who I had been.

"Mr. Longfire—Channel 7, right? Yes, yes, this is a very exciting time! A statement? Well, just that the man who the world knows as Da Nigga is alive and well! He has come out of his coma and is doing fine. We're staying here in the hospital for precautions, but as soon as he gets the okay, we'll be out of here and back in the studio. Have a great night."

And later…"Cindy Dawkins—how are you? How's the show going? Oh, you can get Moses on as a guest? Well, I can't promise anything now, Cindy. He's really just hanging out and getting back into the swing of things, but we'll definitely keep you in mind. Yes, Cindy, I know how big it would be, but we have to think about Moses first. He was almost shot during a television taping before his coma. We can't risk any sort of flashbacks. That's not a no—a let me get back to you, okay, sweetie? We'll be in touch."

I still hadn't said a word, but SaTia had been speaking enough for the both of us. She must have spoken to two hundred people before she finally sat down. Her eyes were heavy and her body looked limp.

"I think I'm done for the night," she mumbled as her phone rang one last time. But then she looked at the number, took a deep breath, and stood up, magically energizing herself again.

"This is the last one I take, and then I'm done. I'll be at it again in the morning." She put on a fake smile and hit the speaker button on her phone so that I could hear the other end as well.

"Hello?"

"Hello, Ms. Brooks. This is Mr. Rose from Cosmos Records."

"Hello, Mr. Rose!" SaTia feigned surprise at hearing who was on the other end of the line.

"Can you tell me what's going on, Ms. Brooks? I've heard a little bit of everything at this point."

I could see SaTia's eyes as she pondered how much information she wanted to share with the record executive. She paused before she answered, and Mr. Rose read her pause accurately.

"Ms. Brooks, listen…I understand you've been doing damage

control all day. Believe me when I tell you that all of us at Cosmos appreciate it more than you know. Moses is by far our highest-selling artist, and we're prepared to do whatever it takes to make sure he gets back to one hundred percent. But this is just you and me talking now, Ms. Brooks. The only way I can fix what's happening is if I know about it. You've got to tell me straight up—what's going on with our man?"

Mr. Rose's words stirred the ashes of the fire still within my chest. SaTia was too exhausted to have her usual filter, and gave in to Mr. Rose's sincere tone. I could see the resistance melt off of her face as she continued her conversation.

"Mr. Rose, I don't even know where to start…"

"Well, then, let me ask the questions, okay? First, is Moses out of his coma?"

"Yes, he is. He's sitting right here in front of me."

Mr. Rose could not hide his excitement.

"Thank God! Thank goodness!"

"I'd thought that was common knowledge after all of the news stories…"

"I hadn't heard from you, or from him, so I wasn't taking anything at face value. Now—is it true that he stabbed a doctor?"

The ridiculousness of the question caused SaTia to stumble over her tongue. "Wh…wh…I…what…what are you talking about?"

"That's one of the more prevalent rumors that's been going around."

"That Moses stabbed a doctor?"

"As ridiculous as it sounds, yes."

"I can't believe you would listen to that…"

"As I said before, Ms. Brooks, I hadn't spoken to you all day. All I had to go on were the news reports and the Internet."

"Umm…no, Mr. Rose, at no point did Moses ever stab one of the doctors, okay?"

"But he was enraged, right?"

"Yeah, you could say that."

"Great! Do you know how great that is? Da Nigga wakes up from his coma pissed off at the thugs who shot him. That's epic. The inner city is going to turn this guy into a super hero. Oh my God, this is amazing!"

SaTia looked at the phone incredulously.

"Why don't you tell me everything that happened after Moses woke up from his coma?"

"He…he had an episode. He had come out of the coma, and the doctors burst into the room! They must have frightened him. He jumped out of bed and acted as if he was trying to protect us."

"Wait…wait…so he did actually jump out of bed?"

"Yes."

"You're sure he didn't stumble? He jumped out of bed on his own?"

"Yeah, is there something wrong with that?"

"Well, that's been one of the rumors that has been going around, Ms. Brooks. So at least one of them is true."

"Why would him getting out of bed be a rumor, Mr. Rose?"

"It's not him getting out of bed, it's him *jumping* out of bed! I've seen at least fifteen doctors on the television this evening testifying that no one who is in a coma for six months should even be able to walk on their own—much less be able to leap out from under the sheets! I told you, these ghetto kids are going to turn him into a superhero…super Nigga! Hahaha!"

SaTia looked over at me, realizing the truth in Mr. Rose's words. I shouldn't have been able to jump out of bed. I shouldn't have been able to do much except open my eyes and maybe lift a finger or two. She looked strangely at me as the exec continued.

"So he's walking, talking, and doing everything else on his own, correct?"

"Well, not exactly…"

"What do you mean 'not exactly'? What's going on with him?"

"Well, frankly, he hasn't said a word since the episode earlier."

"So he's still upset from it? He's taking his time to calm down?"

"No, Mr. Rose, that's not it. He's not talking at all. It's been almost an entire day, and he hasn't spoken."

Mr. Rose's pause signaled that he'd reached the first significant problem since he'd been on the phone.

"Listen, SaMia—can I call you SaMia?"

"It's SaTia."

"I'm sorry, SaTia. Do you think this is something mental? Has he forgotten how to talk?"

"No, he spoke to us before the doctors came in earlier."

"So he could talk if he wanted to?"

"I don't know. It's hard to tell."

Another pause, and then Mr. Rose started to laugh.

"I'm sure this is a temporary thing. I'm sure he'll wake up in the morning and be talking his head off."

SaTia looked over at me again, and I looked back at her.

"I don't know, Mr. Rose. There's something different about him, now. I don't think he'll talk until he's ready."

"Well, when will he be ready?"

"I don't know, but honestly, I don't think it'll be tomorrow."

I listened as panic began to weigh down Mr. Rose's breathing.

"Okay…okay…let's not get too hysterical about this."

SaTia's act was amusing to watch. "Mr. Rose, what are you talking about?"

"Look, I'll send a shrink over tomorrow, okay? Best in the city.

He'll come in, turn Moses's head upside down, shake it a bit, and we'll have him back talking again in no time."

"I'm not letting Moe talk to a shrink! The only people who have been in this room in the last twenty-four hours have been myself and his family—and I think his head has been turned upside down enough as it is. No shrink."

"Well, then what do you suggest we do, SaTia?"

"We wait for him to come around. Wait for him to talk again on his own."

There was another moment of silence on Mr. Rose's end of the phone, and I found myself wondering what his face must have looked like on the other end.

"Maybe you don't understand the gravity of the situation at hand, SaTia, so let me explain it to you. We've had the biggest occurrence in hip-hop history, maybe even music history, happen to our artist. To a Cosmos recording artist! And this event, if played right, could be worth millions of dollars in revenue. And at the center of it all, we've got a rap artist who won't talk."

"I still don't understand the major problem, Mr. Rose."

Rose could no longer hide his frustration. His voice went up two octaves as he blasted back at SaTia. "If Moses won't talk, he won't rap! If he won't rap, then he might as well have stayed in the coma! He can't give interviews, he can't do movies, he can't do anything! How are you not seeing this?"

"Do you even care that he woke up from his coma today?"

"Of course I care! He's the biggest thing on every station! We've gotten reports that another hundred thousand units sold today alone because of this! Moses Jenkins is the most important man in my life right now! My job is to get him back to the public as quickly as possible so that he can generate more revenue. And he can't generate anything if he won't talk!"

"I don't understand why you can't leave him alone and let him get better? You said it yourself—the record sales are soaring. He's golden right now. Why not let him come around in his own time?"

"Because nobody has that kind of time, Ms. Brooks. Nobody has that kind of time! He is our artist. We don't wait for him. We tell him what to do and how to do it, and then we sit around and watch it get done! Right now we've got major networks, publishing companies, movie producers, clothing lines, I mean, we've got everyone lined up waiting for him to step one foot out of that hospital. Nike even wants to have him endorse a shoe! But none of that can happen if he stands in front of a television camera like a deaf mute. These inner-city kids aren't going to look up to a deaf mute, Ms. Brooks. They're going to emulate the guy who had his chest blown wide open, spent six months in a coma, refused to die, and then came back seeking vengeance on the people who shot him!"

My head began to spin as I took in Mr. Rose's words. SaTia stood quietly with the phone in her hand, trying to harness the anger I could see creeping onto her face. Mr. Rose's voice got softer as he continued to speak. "Look, SaTia, I apologize—I get a bit excited, okay? Listen, talk to Moses. Tell him about all the opportunities we have got laid out for him. Tell him the money he made after the diss record dropped is crumbs compared to what he could make now. I know my artist. Once he hears that there's a couple million dollars in it for him, he'll start running his mouth in no time. I'm lining up people now who can help him, in case he doesn't—"

"Then I feel obligated to remind you, Mr. Rose, that Moses hired me as his manager. You didn't. To that end, I have done and will continue to do everything in my power to make sure that everything that happens is in his best interest. You can line up all the psychologists and doctors you want to, but no one will set foot in this room until I determine that their presence and expertise is to his benefit. Moses needs time right now, Mr. Rose, and that's exactly what I plan to provide for him. As long as I'm his manager, he will have all the time he needs to get better."

"You're talking like we're on different sides, SaTia. We're not. We're on the same side. We both want to see Moe get better."

"No…we are on different sides. And by the way, his name is Moses. He doesn't answer to Moe anymore. You better hope the same rapper that went into the coma is the one that came out…"

"Who else would it be, Ms. Brooks?"

"It's late, Mr. Rose. I'm going to get some sleep."

"You do that. I'll have my people standing by whenever you come to your senses."

"Good night, Mr. Rose."

I let myself fall back onto the bed as SaTia hung up her phone call, and I began to feel my grip on reality weaken. I had begun to accept that I was back to my old world, back to the world that I knew before Talbert and Bradley and the plantation. But this wasn't the world I remembered. I remembered being a superstar. I remembered being adored and having fans screaming my name. I didn't remember being anyone's slave.

I turned over and buried my face in the pillow as madness crept into my head. Where had I come back to? This couldn't be right! I was a god where I was from! I was nobody's slave! This was not my home. I was Da Nigga, dammit! I was Da Nigga!

"HHHHHHHHIIIIIIIIIIIIIIII…AHHH…AHHHH… HHHHHHAAAAAAAA!"

I screamed into the pillow.

When the pillow wasn't good enough anymore, I slammed my fist against the wall behind the hospital bed instead.

The sound woke both my mother and Big Mama up, but SaTia

had already rushed over to the bed. She was terrified, but tried her best to hold it together as she attempted to calm me down.

"Moses…Moses, please…calm down! Please!"

SaTia's pleading was of no use. My mind spun around like a top, and I could barely tell up from down anymore. All my thoughts blended together, as if they were being melted into a large stew.

I continued screaming as long as my senses were still lost, and at this point, it seemed doubtful they would ever return. What I thought I was avoiding by not talking had crept up on me regardless. I felt my sanity begin to dissolve like cotton candy on a child's tongue.

The room was soundproof, one of the perks of being a VIP in a well-endowed hospital, so there were no orderlies or nurses to come rushing in. My mother ran up to the bed and knelt crying beside me. I don't know how her eardrums stood my screaming, but she wept and prayed. The sounds of both were drowned out by my screams.

I never even saw Big Mama come up to the bed. She walked up to me from my blind side, leaned over the bed close enough to be heard, and started to sing…

"O Mary, O Martha,
O Mary, Ring dem bells!"

She sang it softly, but the strength in her voice was enough to quiet my thoughts and shouts..

Big Mama never told me what made her sing that particular song, but she sang the madness right out of me as she leaned over my bed. SaTia, convinced that my grandmother had put me under some sort of trance, lay there beside me as I rocked back and forth ever so slightly.

"I hear archangels a rockin' Jerusalem!
I hear archangels a ringin' dem bells!"

I lay down and drifted into oblivion with those words ringing in my head. It was the first time I'd slept since I'd gotten up from my coma, and Big Mama's words echoed somewhere off in the near distance. They bounced around in my head, trying to attach themselves to every thought.

I slept hard and long, and dreamed of words I could not yet say.

The next morning I woke up and spent my first ten minutes wondering if I were dreaming or not. I could see my mother, Big Mama, and SaTia, but I kept expecting Roka and Sarah to come through the door. When the confusion became too much, and my mind began to give way once again, I slowly turned myself toward the window and continued staring out it just as I'd done yesterday.

"Do you think he'll be okay?"

Mama could never whisper well. She spoke to SaTia and Big Mama as if she were afraid I would hear her.

"He'll be fine," Big Mama answered her nonchalantly.

"How can you be so sure?"

"I jus' knows it."

Time was more defined for me now, which became increasingly scary. The minutes didn't turn into hours anymore, like they had the day before. They stayed minutes, and inched away one by one until I could no longer stand it. The bright sky was still a refuge, but I couldn't lose myself in it anymore. As I grabbed a hold of more and more sanity, my consciousness would force my mind to stay in the present.

After an hour of staring out the window, I stood up from the bed and began pacing back and forth across the room.

"Moe…I mean…Moses…are you okay?" SaTia said with uncertainty. I turned to her and nodded my head.

"Do you know where you are?"

I nodded once again.

"Do you remember everything that happened yesterday? Do you remember last night?"

Nod.

"Do you feel like…like you might need some help? Like, some professional help?"

I stopped pacing and looked at her, thinking hard about her question. She wanted to keep her hope that my recovery wasn't false. She was hoping that I could reassure her.

I shook my head and looked her straight in the eyes. I could still see the doubt on her face, so I walked up close to her. I could feel her nervousness as I approached her, but she didn't move. When I got close enough to kiss her, I stopped, looked her in her eyes again, and shook my head.

No, I said with my gaze. I'm okay now. Trust me.

She read my eyes and nodded her head in acknowledgement. "Okay then," she said, resolved. "Let's talk about what's going to happen today."

She walked over to where my mother and grandmother were sitting, pulled up a chair, and motioned for me to sit down. I did as instructed, and found myself seated directly across from her, with Big Mama on one side of me, her knitting equipment in her lap, and my mother on the other. They all looked at me, and then back at each other.

"It's good to have you back, Moses," Big Mama said as her hands went to work, and then she smiled so slightly that I believed I was the only one who saw it. "You lookin' a bit different this mornin'."

I nodded my head to my grandmother, and then looked back at SaTia.

Though she knew I wouldn't speak, SaTia still waited on my blessing to begin. I nodded, feeling bits and pieces of the man who had earned the trust of slaves coming back. She tried to hide her smirk.

"You do look different this morning," SaTia whispered, as if she was trying to sneak in a phrase without anyone hearing it. "Really different."

"You do, son." Mama backed up the other women in the room. "Something's changed."

I looked at each of the women and nodded appreciatively. Whatever strength I had gotten throughout the night was now visible, and knowing that made me feel even stronger.

I turned back to SaTia and willed her to start talking.

"Okay...first things first, this hospital," she began. "They've had to shut it down temporarily because so many people have tried to sneak in here to see you and it has jeopardized the welfare of other patients. I know you don't know this, because there's no way you could know, but you are literally the only patient in this hospital right now. That's causing a bit of a public outcry. So we need a timeline of when you'll be ready to get out of here. Any chance we could walk out of here today?"

I thought hard about SaTia's question, which again proved to me that I was finding my way back to the land of the sane. I was able to think rationally, but only in the context of being in the room with these three women. Overhearing a conversation might have thrown me into a psychotic break. God only knows what would happen if I tried to leave this room today.

I turned to SaTia and shook my head.

"Good," she quickly responded. "I wouldn't have let you leave today anyway. Just wanted to see where your head was. How about tomorrow?"

I thought about it again, and nodded my head slowly.

"I'll take that as a maybe. What do you think about me telling the press that we're leaving tomorrow? Believe me, no matter what, the hospital won't kick us out. You can still take all the time you need. It would just be a date for them to have."

I nodded my head. I couldn't hide in this hospital room forever. I'd have to face the world beyond its sliding doors eventually. It might as well be tomorrow...

"Remember," SaTia interjected into my thoughts, "it doesn't mean you have to leave tomorrow—just that that's what they'll be saying in the press. In the end, you leave whenever you're ready. Okay?"

I nodded my head again, grateful for her concern.

"Okay, next. The doctors are crying about it being against the law that you're being housed in a hospital but none of the doctors have been allowed to see you."

"Is it against the law?" My mother's curiosity got the best of her as she leaned forward in her seat.

"Yes, it is. I've been pulling strings to keep them out, but I won't be able to do it much longer. Moses, are you willing to let a doctor examine you?"

I flashed back to first waking up from my coma and having the white doctors charge toward me. I almost jumped out of my seat as I vigorously shook my head.

"Okay, okay, Moses, calm down..." SaTia saw my excitement and began to speak soothingly to me until I was sitting back in my seat once again. "God...Moses, I honestly don't know how much longer I'm going to be able to keep them out of here."

"Why don't you let 'im choose?"

We all looked at Big Mama, wondering what she meant.

"I'm sorry, Mama Jenkins?"

"Let him pick what doctor he want to look at him. Ask him if he wanna pick." She motioned to me while continuing her knitting.

"Moses, would it help if you could pick the doctor who looks at you?"

I nodded my head.

"If you picked out a doctor, would you let him examine you?"

See if you can find a doctor who can make Sarah's roots, I thought to myself as I nodded my head.

"Thank God!" SaTia threw her hands up. "Mama Jenkins, you're a genius!"

"Child, please…" Big Mama glanced up at SaTia incredulously, and went back to her knitting.

"Okay, I'm going to get some doctors in here as soon as we finish. The sooner we get you examined, the quicker I can get these lawyers and the medical board off my back. Just two other small things, okay?"

I nodded for her to continue.

"First, I want to expose you to some of what is beyond those doors today. Are you open to that?"

I nodded my head.

"Great. Second, Brian, Henry, and Ray have been blowing up my phone. They want to come see you tonight. I told them I'd get back to them. Do you think you're ready for that?"

My forehead wrinkled. I couldn't pinpoint it, but something was off. Brian…Henry…Ray…wasn't somebody missing?

"You're wondering about Orlando, aren't you?"

SaTia had read my thoughts once again. I looked at her solemnly and nodded my head.

"Orlando's in jail, Moses. He was working with P. Silenzas to set you up."

I knew it, but the words hit me like I didn't. I flashbacked to standing on my front porch and seeing his face before feeling my chest break apart like a dropped Lego tower.

Brian, Henry, Ray, and Orlando…my best friends from a different life. Would I even recognize them now? Would they recognize me?

I nodded to SaTia, telling her to go ahead and let them come. Maybe they could tell me who I was without my asking.

"Okay," she said while standing up from her seat. "I'll call them and let them know. Right now, though, I'm going to round up some doctors for you to choose from. The sooner we can get that over, the better."

SaTia walked briskly over to the double sliding doors, but stopped before she walked under the censor.

"Moses...come here."

I stood and walked up beside her.

"There are two sliding doors to this room. You have to walk through the first set, and then take about four steps and walk through the second set. By the time the doors to the hallway open, the first set have already closed. As the VIP room, it's built that way on purpose, so that no one looking in from the outside hallway can see straight into the room."

I looked at her, wondering why she couldn't have told me this while I was sitting down.

"I'm telling you this because it's time you saw what's on the other side of this room. You need to know what you'll be walking into, whenever you decide to leave. Come with me."

We took a step forward and the double doors in front of us opened, revealing the short hallway and the next set of doors a few feet ahead of us.

"You wait here. When I step up and open those doors, you step back from these doors. It'll be about a two second delay before they close, and the reporters on the other end have gotten so used to seeing me come out that they don't even lift their cameras anymore. You won't have a long time, but take a good look at what's out there. I'll be right back with the doctors."

SaTia looked over at me as I nodded to her one last time, and then she stepped forward. Once I heard the doors in front of me begin to move, I tried to step back from the doors that I was standing in, but I couldn't. The scene in front of me was mesmerizing. There were people all crowded into the cramped space of the hallway like sardines in a can. I couldn't see the walls anywhere. Every spot had a body blocking it.

It was like a parade had decided to march into the hospital. The cameramen waved their cameras while the reporters did tricks with their microphones. Various journalists had found unused gurneys lying around, and turned the portable beds into their own temporary office spaces. Papers lay scattered around like litter in a public park, and the tapping of laptop keyboards seemed to fill the air with a rhythmic cadence that you could almost dance to.

It was just a matter of time, I guessed, before it would happen.

"Oh my God...it's him. It's him!!!!"

And just that quickly, my comical parade turned into an unrelenting stampede. I couldn't even tell the different people apart anymore. Before my eyes, they all meshed together into one huge, ferocious beast that galloped toward me, shaking the very foundation of the building as it bounded ahead. The sheer force of what was coming toward me forced me back a step, but when I looked up again and saw how close it was, my body froze in the fear of impending death.

Finally, when the beast had gotten so close that I could just about smell the bloodlust on its breath, the first set of double doors slid shut, as did the set that I was standing in front of, and before I knew what had happened, I was back in my solitude, surrounded by peace and quiet once again.

"Moses, baby, you okay?"

My mom saw me standing at the doors, still frozen from the few seconds that had passed. She walked over and placed one hand on my arm and the other around my waist, leading me back toward the bed.

"You rest now." She sat me down and glanced at my pale face. "You'll be fine; you just rest."

Thirty minutes later, SaTia walked back through the door. Exhausted from my brush with death, I had fallen into a fitful sleep on the bed. The sound of the double doors opening again jarred me awake, however, and I jumped up with wide, darting eyes.

"Calm down, Moses. It's just me." SaTia walked up to the bed and sat down at the foot of it. "You didn't see me looking back at you, but I saw what happened. I hope you can understand why I had to make you do that. Nothing I said could have prepared you to come face to face with them. You had to see them for yourself."

I nodded my head, understanding what she was trying to do, but traumatized nonetheless.

"Whenever you're ready, Moses, I have doctors waiting right outside the door."

I nodded again, and closed my eyes to try and shake off the fear from earlier. Once I calmed myself down, I moved over to the edge of the bed, took a deep breath, and motioned for SaTia to continue. Mama and Big Mama sat quietly in the corner, spectating.

"Okay," SaTia said, "so I pretty much rounded up all the doctors I could find. I'll bring them in three at a time."

Immediately I became defensive. The thought of my room being crowded with people I didn't know made me uncomfortable enough to stand and ready myself for battle once again. SaTia saw my face change and my body tense up as I rose to my feet. "Moses, what…?"

"I think you better bring them doctors in one by one," Big Mama said. And before SaTia could respond she added, "or else you gon' get one'a them doctors hurt."

SaTia looked at Big Mama, then me. "Moses…look, I'll bring them in one by one, okay? Only one at a time. But if I do, you gotta sit down and try not to look like you want to murder them. Deal?"

She waited for my response. Slowly, I lowered myself back down to the bed and tried to calm myself.

"Good. Thank God! Okay, one by one. You ready?"

I nodded again, and SaTia made her way over to the door. When it opened, she motioned to the first doctor, who was an older white man with a gray beard. He came in with a smile, but lost it when he saw the hate in my eyes.

I didn't even have to shake my head. SaTia ushered him out just as soon as he had come in.

That was the routine for the better part of an hour. SaTia would usher in white doctors of all varieties—tall and short, male and female, fat and skinny, tanned and pale, and I'd reject all of them in the same manner. Every once in a while there was an Asian or Middle Eastern doctor thrown into the mix, and the room would become quiet as everyone watched my face soften a bit, but in the end, I'd shake my head for them as well. They were still strangers to me.

SaTia never lost hope. She continued to bring more doctors in, and I continued to turn them away. Just as she began to show a little crack in her armor, and cut her eyes at me with the slightest look of exasperation, she invited in a middle-aged man with bifocal glasses and a crisp shape-up.

Visibly nervous, his white coat shook slightly and contrasted with his dark tan skin. He'd set his face hard. He wouldn't let it betray him. He'd been broken before. I could tell by his eyes. He'd been broken and had somehow found his way back, just as I had.

I turned to SaTia and nodded.

"Are...are you serious? You're okay with him? Really?"

"Well, what's wrong with him?" Big Mama said from the corner.

"Nothing, Mama Jenkins. I just can't believe Moses finally made a choice. So..."

SaTia turned to me again, hesitant. She was scared I would change my mind, but it was made up. "You're okay with him? We can start your exam?"

I nodded my head once again. SaTia paused a moment and turned her head up to the ceiling. "Thank goodness!"

"Wasn't too hard to figure out the puzzle after while, girl," Big Mama interjected. "Seems you went and rounded up all the white doctors you could find."

SaTia looked at Big Mama with words on her tongue that she knew she couldn't say, then looked back at the doctor.

"Moses, this is Doctor—"

"Bail..." the doctor's voice cracked like a broken cell phone screen. I, along with my army of women, couldn't help but smirk. His embarrassment had sufficiently lightened the mood in the room. I was already happy I'd picked him.

He cleared his throat and tried again. "...Bailey. My name is Dr. Bailey. And if you don't mind, Mr. Jenkins, we're gonna see just how healthy you are today."

Mr. Jenkins. If I'd ever been called that before, I hadn't cared enough to note it. Now it made all the difference in the world.

"Shall we begin?"

One more nod, and we were under way.

An hour later and Dr. Bailey was wrapping up. I hadn't said anything during the examination, but he'd gotten over his nervousness and become light-hearted and jovial enough for me to consider him a potential friend by the time we were done. Every once in a while he'd look at me curiously, as if there was something he just couldn't figure out, and then he'd shrug his shoulders and start out with the next part of the exam. There was only one point in the exam where he was perplexed enough to stop the process and pull me to the side.

"I know you aren't talking just yet, Mr. Jenkins, but I have to ask you something."

I looked at him curiously, wondering what he was going to say.

"Are you aware there's something wrong with your back?"

I looked at him as if he had spoken Mandarin.

"Nothing's broken but you have some significant markings on it. I reviewed your file thoroughly before I came in here, and none of the doctors or nurses reported this kind of scarring being present while you were in your coma. And I know for a fact that you didn't come in here with that kind of scar tissue, so I've got to ask, how did it happen?"

I reached around, under my hospital robe, and ran my thumb over the skin of my back. I'd brought a gift back from the Talbert plantation, it seemed. The mountains and ridges formed in my flesh whispered to me as I caressed them. I closed my eyes, knowing now that I could never forget, and let my pain swell my chest before opening my eyes again.

"Did someone from the hospital give you those scars? If they did, you need to let me know immediately. Do you know where the scars came from?"

I nodded my head.

"Did someone from the hospital give them to you?"

I shook my head.

Dr. Bailey stood in front of me, unsure of how to proceed. I looked at him, then over to my family, and back to him again. I shook my head slightly so that the women across the room wouldn't notice.

"Don't worry, Mr. Jenkins, I won't tell anyone. I'll even leave it out of the report I give to the board—but under one condition. I'd be remiss if I didn't immediately recognize what the scars on your back look like, and frankly, I'm baffled. When you're feeling more comfortable, you've got to promise to find me and let know how you got them."

I offered my hand. He extended his as well, and we shook on our agreement.

With that done, he placed his stethoscope around his neck, took in a long breath, and spoke loud enough for everyone in the room to hear. "Well, I've got good news and bad news for you, Mr. Jenkins."

Mama and Big Mama stopped what they were doing and focused solely on the medical professional in the room. SaTia almost fell out of her seat.

"Oh my God, there's bad news?"

I looked Dr. Bailey in the eye, waiting for his diagnosis.

"Well, let me start with the good news first, Ms. Brooks. The good news is that there's absolutely nothing wrong with Mr. Jenkins. He's in perfect health."

SaTia stopped pacing the floor and faced Dr. Bailey.

"Okay...so what's the bad news?"

"The bad news is that there's absolutely nothing wrong with Mr. Jenkins. He's in perfect health."

Even I looked at the doctor as if he had grown two heads.

"I'm sorry, Dr. Bailey, are you trying to make some sort of a joke?" SaTia narrowed her eyes, and I saw her attitude building. "Because if this is all funny to you, you can—"

"No, no, Ms. Brooks, it's not a joke. It really is good news and bad news."

"How?"

"Well, it's good for obvious reasons. He's not carrying any symptoms that people usually experience after spending so much time in a coma. In fact, physiologically, it's as though he was never in a coma at all. It's bad because I've never seen or heard of anyone coming out of a six-month coma and having full use and function of all their muscles and limbs. Mr. Jenkins is now officially a medical miracle, and there are two things I know for sure. One: after they see my report, the other doctors will question it and try and discredit it. Two: they will want to run extensive tests on him for the next couple of weeks. Maybe even months."

SaTia bounced around, frantic. "We can't stay in here for that long! Are you serious? Moses wouldn't let a white doctor anywhere near him. There's no way he's going to let them all run in here poking and prodding him. They're crazy."

She was right. Just the thought of all those white men bursting in my room made me want to slit someone's throat. I listened intently to Dr. Bailey, wondering as his lips moved if I should prepare myself for war once again.

SaTia turned back to Dr. Bailey, all the attitude drained out of her beautiful face. "What can we do?"

"Well, he has to give consent."

"I'm sorry?"

"Moses has to give consent to the tests before any of them can be performed."

"And if he doesn't give his consent?"

"Well, now that I've already declared him healthy, he would be able to leave whenever he wants to. And without expressed consent, the doctors can't do anything but watch him leave out of the door."

SaTia turned to me with a big smile replacing her once tormented face.

"Okay, then that's settled. Moses, will you give your consent to the doctors doing any other tests on you?"

I shook my head. Hell no.

"Alright, then. Moses, we leave when you're ready, and that's the end of it."

Dr. Bailey spoke up, reluctant to kill the premature good mood.

"Actually, there's one other thing. With Moses still not speaking, the doctors can try and have him declared mentally unfit. If the ruling passes, then they can do whatever they feel is in his best interest."

"And we don't have any say about that?"

"Not unless one of you has his power of attorney."

SaTia dropped her head in defeat.

"None of us do," she said quietly. "He never declared one."

SaTia's head was still down, and so she couldn't see the urgent look on my face as I stood up and tapped her on the shoulder. When she looked at me, I lifted my arm and pointed a finger at my mother, who was pretending not to pay attention.

"Umm, Ms. Jenkins?"

"Yes?"

"Do you have Moses' power of attorney?"

"Yes, I do."

SaTia looked at me with her mouth gaping open.

"Why didn't you ever tell me?"

She was looking at me when she asked the question, but my mother answered.

"I didn't even know I had it. While he was still in the coma, when the doctors didn't think he would make it, they asked me to come and step outside. They said that I held his power of attorney, and that I could make the decision to end his suffering. I told them to go to hell, and I came in and sat back down by his bed. I almost forgot about the whole thing."

SaTia turned around and looked at me, smirking. "You sly bastard."

I smirked back.

"So," she said, and turned and looked at Dr. Bailey again. "Moses' mother has his power of attorney."

"Then he's covered, and you all don't have anything to worry about."

Dr. Bailey stood up, preparing to leave.

"S'cuse me, doctor…"

Big Mama had placed her knitting material on the floor, and was now looking up and focusing on the physician. "We just wanna thank you for all your help, sir. You a mighty kind man to let us know what them doctors was gonna try and do."

"Oh God, yes," SaTia said. "Thank you so much, Dr. Bailey. I'd ask why you did it, but I think I already know…you must be a fan of Da Nigga."

"Actually, no." Dr. Bailey stopped in mid-stride and turned around. "I'm not a fan of his at all. Truthfully, I hate his music. I really do."

SaTia's mouth dropped open for the second time in less than an hour. Mama looked up, her attention now piqued, while SaTia stumbled over her words. "You…you hate his music? If you hate his music so much, then why did you help him?"

"Honestly?"

"Yes, Doctor. Honestly."

He raised his hand and pointed directly at me. He never touched me, but the tip of his finger made me rock back and forth on my toes.

"That's not the same guy I've seen in all the videos and all over the news."

His words pushed me back onto the bed. The room fell silent.

"Well, I better get going," he went on. "I'm sure the last hour in here has probably turned me into an instant celebrity. Let me go out and greet my adoring fans."

He walked briskly through both doors, and the sound of the harassment of reporters echoed back into the room before the doors closed once again.

Two hours later, Dr. Bailey's words were still echoing in my head. SaTia had been in and out of the room several times, assuring the press and media that Dr. Bailey's exam was not falsified. She reiterated each time she went out that she'd been present during the exam and it was absolutely legit. Despite her assurances, the head doctors in the hospital did exactly what Dr. Bailey said they would—they demanded that they be able to give their own battery of tests to determine Moses Jenkins' health. SaTia heard their request, denied it, and wished each of them a wonderful evening before she retired to the room.

As the excitement of the morning died down, and the afternoon began to lay its claim on the sky, Mama and Big Mama finally put their knitting equipment down and went their separate ways. Big Mama stayed in the corner, sitting peacefully, reading her

Bible, while Mama went back and forth between a magazine and an iPod.

SaTia came back for a final time, looking tired but resolved. She crumbled on the bed beside me and took deep breaths.

"These idiots never quit," she vented. "I don't how many times I have to say the same thing. No, we didn't fake the test. No, you won't do any more tests. No, picking the only black doctor in the hospital does not prove that Moses Jenkins is mentally disturbed. I'm done! I'm not going back out there anytime soon. They're going to make me lose it."

I looked over at SaTia with a sad appreciation. She was driving herself crazy, trying to save a reputation that I didn't want anymore. If people like Dr. Bailey hated my music, what kind of people liked it?

SaTia sat up from the bed and looked at me. I could see her armor begin to crack. "Moses...do you think we can get out of here tomorrow? I've tried to keep this from you as long as I could, but this place is starting to drive me nuts. The days are starting to run together. You know I'll stay in here with you as long as you need me to. But too much longer and they may have to admit me, you know?"

I nodded my head to show that I understood.

"Don't force that boy to make no decision he ain't ready for," Big Mama said without looking up from her Bible. "You might not like the consequences."

"Mama Jenkins, I don't want Moses to do anything he's not ready to do." SaTia looked directly at my grandmother as she spoke, and then toward me. "I don't want you to leave here until you're ready, Moses. But as soon as you say the word, we're getting out of this place if we have to jump out the window to do it. If it's tomorrow, great. But you know I'll wait for you."

I looked at SaTia, knowing that I'd do anything for her. It must have shown on my face, because she looked away with guilt.

I resolved then that we'd be leaving tomorrow. Even if I wasn't one hundred percent, I was strong enough to make sure that SaTia got some peace.

Realizing what she had done, SaTia stood up from the bed and stared at me. Her lapse in strength had made my decision for me. She pondered a way to make the situation right.

"Moses, have you noticed that we haven't had the television on at all?"

It was an odd question on many different levels. First, I had to struggle and remember what a television was. I looked up at the large black box hanging from the wall with the screen on the front, and recall took over. Second, why would I have noticed that the television wasn't on? I vaguely remembered the part of my life when television would entertain me for hours on end, but it seemed so long ago that the question seemed lost in time. I shook my head at SaTia.

No, I wanted so badly to tell her. *No, I didn't notice that we hadn't watched television. Is that important? Does that make me crazy?*

"I talked to your mother and grandmother very soon after you woke from your coma, and we made an agreement about the television," she explained.

"Wait..." Mama had stopped listening to her music to offer her thoughts. "You want to show him now?"

"You sure this is a good idea?" Big Mama stopped reading and looked up.

"No, ma'am, I'm not sure it's a good idea," answered SaTia. "But it's the only way to see if he's ready or not. I know Moses. He's going to agree to leave tomorrow because he wants to protect me. Maybe he'll change his mind once he sees what's really out there. You were right, Mama Jenkins. I don't want him making a decision that he isn't ready for."

I jumped up from the bed, looking at everyone with confusion.

"I'm going to turn on the television, Moses," SaTia said as if she was my psychiatrist. "I'm going to turn it on, and I want you to watch it."

"I know it don't seem like a big thing, Moses, but she showed us the news right after you woke up, and it was nothing but craziness with you all up, down, around, and through it. That's why we decided to keep it off in the room."

"So why are we turning it on again?" Mama asked.

"'Cause she wanna see if Moses ready to go home or not. She figure if he can take all the foolishness on TV, then he ready to get outta here."

Mama thought about it for a moment, then shrugged her shoulders and sat back down. She kept her headphones off, however, and watched me very closely.

I still failed to understand the importance of turning on the television. I turned around slowly and grabbed the remote before SaTia had a chance to grab it.

"Moses, no," she protested. "Let me."

I motioned for her to calm down, and with a steady hand, raised the remote to the television and hit the Power button.

…rapper Moses Jenkins, otherwise known as Da Nigga, remains a mystery as he continues his seclusion in the hospital. The only fact that this network can confirm is that he is, in fact, out of his coma as of yesterday. The rumor mill has been in overdrive since news of his emergence from the dead became public, the most rampant rumor being that he has had some sort of psychotic break and is no longer mentally stable…

The station was showing footage from my last Grammy awards performance, and I barely recognized myself. I had on a huge pair of shades, with three or four thick chains around my neck. As I watched the footage, the memory of buying each of the chains specifically for the performance came back to me. The most expensive one would've bought Mr. Talbert's plantation and all the slaves that came with it. I had to pull my pants up every few seconds or so while I was performing because they kept falling. I had a grill in my mouth, and everytime I knew the camera was close enough, I opened up and pressed my teeth together, showing off the gold and platinum.

"Hoes in da attic, yeah! Hoes in da attic, yeah! Come on to my crib; I keeps some hoes in da attic, yeah!"

I was high. I had to have been, because I kept randomly laughing in the middle of my lyrics. Nobody cared, though. I remembered seeing other artists who were just as wasted as I was, either coming offstage or going on.

"HOES IN DA ATTIC, YEAH! HOES IN DA ATTIC, YEAH! COME ON TO MY CRIB; I KEEPS SOME HOES IN DA ATTIC, YEAH!"

The crowd was screaming and chanting along with me. I jumped around onstage with Brian, Henry, Ray and Orlando acting like fools behind me. Suddenly I remembered what happened after that performance. I remembered all the industry heads telling me I had done a great job. I remembered getting even higher back in the limo before we all came back out and took our seats in the audience. I remembered all these things clearly, but something was different now. Those ones and zeroes from *The Matrix*, the same ones that had changed my vision on the Talbert plantation, had now altered my vision here. I'd found a pair of 3-D glasses while in my coma. I'd dug them up from the earth underneath the Talbert plantation. And now, with my new lenses, I could see all the things that I wasn't able to see before. I could see the older white men in the audience laughing at us—pointing and mimicking us as if we were a minstrel act. I could see the older black women in the audience, with skin and hair that reminded me of Sarah's, looking uncomfortably at the very scantily clad dancers we had onstage with us. I could see the older black men, stone-faced, looking at our performance, shaking their heads so slightly that only a keen eye could catch it. I could see embarrassment now where I once only saw a smile of enjoyment. I could see the eye roll that came after the thumbs up; the look of disappointment that came after the applause. A movie that was once a light-hearted comedy had turned to a deep, deep, drama—and it hurt to watch.

Figuring that this was the worst it could get, my thumb searched frantically for the channel button and I changed the station.

Moses Jenkins, otherwise known as Da Nigga, remains in the hospital this evening after emerging from a coma. Witnesses say Da Nigga immediately began biting himself and screaming hysterically before trying to attack a group of doctors who were on their way in to make sure he was in good health. It is said that only his manager, Ms. SaTia Brooks, and his mother and grandmother can keep him calm. Anyone else whom Da Nigga sees is at risk of being attacked…

I turned and looked at SaTia. The disgust must have been evident, because she immediately shot out her hands toward me, symbolizing deflection of any blame. "I don't control the media, Moses! This is why I've been saying we need to get out of here."

Mama and Big Mama were standing on either side of me now. Big Mama kept her hand on her Bible.

"Lawd, I knew you was all over the TV, but I ain't know they was saying stuff like this."

"SaTia, they can't just lie on the news like this, can they?" Frustration was beginning to build in Mama's voice.

"Until we come out of here and prove otherwise, they can take information from whatever source they choose. So...yeah, yeah they can lie on the news like that."

"Why didn't you tell us it had gotten this bad?"

"Because it wouldn't have done any good before now."

Big Mama sat down on the bed and grabbed my hand, putting it in between hers.

"Lawd Jesus..."

I felt my mind trying to slip away again, but I wouldn't let it. I was too angry. I grabbed the horns of my sanity and yanked it back every time it tried to leave. Eventually, it just stopped trying.

I flipped the channel. This time, the report ran with one of my music videos playing in the background. I stood shirtless with an array of chains around my neck. A Lamborghini that never belonged to me was parked behind me with the driver's side door up. Three young ladies in bikinis and hair that clearly was not their own groped and grabbed at me as I rapped. At one point, I took the prettiest of the three, bent her over the hood of the Lamborghini and stuffed a hundred dollar bill in her g-string.

I turned away as the news report continued.

...amidst allegations that SaTia Brooks, Mr. Jenkins's manager, has been providing false information, including getting a doctor whose credentials are now in question to perform a dummy medical exam that declared her client to be in perfect health. In the end, no matter what rumors you subscribe to, whether you believe he's mentally unstable, still in the coma, or being held hostage by his manager, mother, and grandmother, everyone in America right now is asking themselves— what's wrong with Da Nigga?

The bull tried to get loose again. I threw the remote control onto the bed and began pacing around the room. If I let my anger go, it would consume me, and I couldn't allow that. But the bomb in my chest that had introduced itself to me after Ella's rape now found its way back, and I struggled to control it. SaTia, Mama, and Big Mama all followed me closely, watching to see what I would do. They knew, and I knew, that if I lost it again, I might not come back. The bull kicked and butted, charged and jerked me around, but I wouldn't let it go. I couldn't let it go. SaTia was right. She'd been right all along. We had to get out of here.

I grabbed the notebook that had been left on the counter by the sink, and the pen that had been left beside my bed, and I wrote three words on the paper. I handed it to SaTia, who tried to hide her smile. She handed it to my mother, who nodded in approval, and then to my grandmother, who took a look at it and then dropped it on the floor, where it landed face up.

Tomorrow we're gone, it read.

Big Mama walked back to her seat, grabbing things as she moved, already starting to pack up. "You Moses, ain't you?" she looked at me as she began stuffing her crochet equipment into her bag. "Hell...I go where you go."

16

"They're on their way up."

SaTia had just gotten off the phone, and she looked at me as if she was worried about my health. "I'm warning you…they're really excited. They sounded like they were sprinting through the halls. I wasn't sure about letting them up at first, but we're leaving today. Having a few extra people around you for protection can't hurt."

Everything in the room that didn't belong to the hospital had been packed up neatly and set off to the side. I hadn't realized how much decorating the ladies had done until we had to take it all down. The room looked dank now. The white paint that had looked vibrant as the backdrop for well-wishing posters and balloons now looked dreary. Even the windows, which had been my gateway to sanity for a time, looked depressed without the colorful reflections and get-well cards taped to it. The ladies in my family had managed to disguise the type of room that this really was. Now that I saw its true nature for myself, I couldn't wait to leave.

I stood up from the bed and walked over to the window, trying not to count the seconds. All the reporters, SaTia had told me, were on alert because this was the day she had announced we'd be leaving. She believed the best time to leave would be either early in the morning or late at night. Unfortunately, she'd forgotten about all the precautions that would have to be taken, and so it was 10 a.m. and we were waiting for the team of bodyguards who would escort me to the limo.

I managed to hold both my nervousness and my excitement at bay without exploding. I wasn't sure how much of me was the same and how much was different, but I agreed with Dr. Bailey—I wasn't the same person from all of the music videos and performances they showed on the television. I had met Master Talbert and Bradley, and Roka, and Sarah, and Ella—how could I be the same after that?

I heard the large doors to my room slide open and close while I continued to ponder my new life. I turned around to ask SaTia a question, and came face to face with my past. Brian, Ray, and Henry stood side by side, staring at me.

They each looked at me as if I was a man who'd had his chest blown open right in front of them. They looked at me as if I was a miracle. And I knew then that whoever I turned out to be, I had to keep them with me. For their sake and mine.

Henry was the first one to break rank. He slowly walked up to me, with every step as if he was contemplating taking off down the hallway. Finally, when he got close enough, he held out his hand to give me some dap. "Yo, what's up, homie?"

The greeting was familiar, but didn't seem appropriate for conveying my emotions. I pushed his hand away and threw my arms around him, giving him a hug. I could feel his hesitation in embracing me, but I decided I wouldn't let him go.

"Awww hell naw," Brian said his voice shaky and cracking, "we ain't gonna be doin' all this, man. Y'all niggas ain't 'bout to have me cryin' up here, dogg. Real talk, man, I'll go wait outside or something."

He never moved. When I looked up from embracing Henry and over at Brian and Ray, they both made their way forward as well. I hugged each one of my friends as if I'd just come back from war. Twenty minutes later the guys sat in front of me with a million and one questions written on their faces.

"So...you cain't talk or you don't wanna talk?"

"Yo, why you look so different, son?"

"You ain't really try and kill nobody, right?"

"Why they got all dis craziness on the news 'bout you?"

"So...if I, like, punched you in yo' jaw, you'd just sit there quiet, right?"

"Yo, you know how many records you done sold, homie?"

"Man, niggas walkin' 'round head to toe in Da Nigga gear!"

I nodded and moved my head from side to side like a bobble-head doll, but hearing that last statement, made me look over to SaTia for some clarity.

"Oh...I forgot to tell you...Mr. Rose and the execs preapproved a line of clothing and apparel to memorialize you once you died. Except...you didn't die. So they've taken all the designs and released them in the wake of your coming out of the coma."

Mama looked up from her packing in the corner. "It's only been a day, SaTia. How so fast?"

"They already had one shirt ready to go, Ms. Jenkins. They were set to hit stores next week, but Mr. Rose and the other guys at Cosmos pulled some major strings and got them delivered and released yesterday."

"Da streets is feelin' you right now, dogg," Ray said. "Everybody in the hood right now walkin' 'round with da same shirt 'I Am Da Nigga.' Da block is on fire, waitin' for you, man!"

"And don't worry," SaTia cut back in. "We get a percentage of all the sales. You've managed to make quite a bit of money since you've been in this place."

My face must have spoken for me. All the laughing stopped and smiles faded as I looked at everyone in the room as though they had gone insane.

"Yo, what's wrong, homie? What's good?"

Brian tried to comfort me, but it was too late. I jumped up from my chair and ran over to the window, resisting the urge to punch through it. The thought of people wearing shirts labeling themselves as Da Nigga, because of me, made me want to throw up the little bit of food I had eaten.

While I was at the window, SaTia made her way over to my friends. She spoke softly.

"You guys ran over here so quickly that I didn't have the chance to fill you in on a few things. Moses has gone through some... umm...changes, since the last time you saw him."

"Moses?" Ray glanced at me, and then back at SaTia. "Since when anybody 'cept his Mama call 'im Moses?"

"Since he stopped responding to anything else."

"Hey, Moe!" Henry yelled at me. "Moe! What's she talking 'bout, son?"

I didn't turn around.

"Moe!"

The people in the window on the other side of the building were having some sort of party. It seemed as though they were having a good time.

"Moses!"

I turned around and faced Henry, wondering what he wanted. He looked at me strangely as he spoke. "Damn...you really ain't hear me, huh?"

"I tried to tell you," SaTia said. "Also, and I'm not sure how far or how deep this goes, but he seems not to like white people around him very much."

My three-man entourage looked at each other, and then burst into laughter.

"Hold up...wait, wait, wait..." Brian managed to choke out his words through his cackling. "You mean this nigga comes back from da brink of death, only to find out he ain't got no love for white people? Son, you better get over that quick...you know they run the world!"

The three of them continued to laugh, but as they looked at my stoic face, their laughter ceased. Before long, an awkward silence had embraced the room.

"Yo, Moses," Everything was serious now. No more joking or laughter. Henry spoke up hesitantly, unsure of his words. "You know you can't leave out this room talkin' 'bout you don't like white folks, right?"

"He's right, dogg," Ray chimed in. "How serious is you 'bout this whole thing? I mean, you turn Muslim while you was in yo' coma or somethin'? You 'bout to start rappin' 'bout white devils on the corner? What's good?"

I didn't have an answer for him. Even if I could talk, I wouldn't have had an answer. I took a step back, realizing this was what I'd asked for. I wanted to know if I was the same person or not. Now I was finding out.

"So what if he does begin rhyming about white devils on the corner?" SaTia stepped up and placed herself in the conversation. "Where will you be?"

"Me?" Ray pointed to himself, as if he was surprised to get the attention. "I'm gonna be right here wid my homie. I mean, I ain't goin' on stage talkin' 'bout all dat black power stuff, 'cause it ain't me. But as long as he still want me in da crew, I'ma be in da crew."

"Real talk," Brian interjected. "I'm the same way, dude. My man just came outta coma, feel me? I ain't leavin' no matter what. Jus' wanna know what we dealin' with."

"Same," Henry said, and gestured toward himself. "I'm here till he tell me I gotta go."

I looked appreciatively at each one of my friends, and then walked back over to the window. Even amid the room's new dreary appearance, the window still helped to center me.

"Alright guys, look." The tone of SaTia's voice hinted that she had mentally switched gears. "We can finish up this conversation later. For now, we have to worry about leaving. The security personnel just texted me and let me know they're on their way up, and the limo has been here for the past hour. Are you ready to get out of here?"

She sounded as if she was asking everyone, but when I looked up, SaTia was looking directly at me. "Are you ready to get out of here?" she repeated.

I looked around the room. My mother and Big Mama were putting the last of their belongings into their bags. Ray, Henry, and Brian were discussing how they would shield me from the press outside when we left, and SaTia was searching my eyes for any hint that we should stay. I didn't give her one.

I stood erect and nodded my head. Inside my head, I was mentally screaming, *Let's go!*

SaTia stared at me until her phone went off once again and brought her back to reality. She looked at her message, gathered herself, and then walked forward and went out the door. Several seconds later, she returned with eight men behind her, all dressed in black suits, black ties, dark sunglasses and earpieces in their ears. They were all my complexion or darker.

I took one look at them, and then looked at SaTia. This time, she nodded at me.

"I got you," she said, and smirked.

"Yo..." Henry looked the guards up and down. "These cats look pretty serious."

"They should." SaTia gathered up the last of her things as well. "They're military contractors."

"What? Contractors? So what, like, they fix up houses for the soldiers?" Ray, in his curiosity, had invaded one of the guard's personal space. The guard never said a word, just cocked his head slightly and lowered his right hand closer to his sidearm.

"They mercenaries, you dummy!" Brian looked up to see the interaction between his friend and a killer. "Like in da video games. And I suggest you move back, son. If he blast you, you ain't goin' in no coma..."

Ray, heeding his friend's advice, took more than a few steps back, and the guard moved his hand away from his pistol.

Mama looked at the men with uncertainty. "How did you manage to get eight black mercenaries?" she asked SaTia.

"The National Guard wouldn't let me pick and choose who I wanted, so I decided to take my business elsewhere."

"Ma'am." One of the guards stepped forward and presented himself to SaTia. The room fell quiet as he spoke. "It is my understanding that we are to protect Mr. Jenkins at any and all costs. Is that correct?"

"Yes, it is."

"And our first order of business is to get him from this room to his grandmother's residence unharmed, correct?"

"Correct."

"Alright, here's the situation. There are more news cameras out there than could've been anticipated. We can only guarantee that he will not be touched or harmed. We cannot guarantee that he will not be seen or photographed."

"We'll take care of that," Henry said, nodding to the guard.

"Fine. If you guarantee that he won't be seen, we'll guarantee his safety. We will depart from this room in five minutes, at exactly 10:47 a.m. It will take between eighteen and twenty-four minutes to get to the limo, depending on resistance from the crowd and media. After Mr. Jenkins is in the limousine, one of our men will stay in the vehicle with him, while the rest of us provide cover from the SUVs on the road. The residence, which is 11.82 miles away, should take twenty-two minutes to reach. If a situation occurs on the road, we will divert our course to the address of a predetermined safehouse. If all goes well, when we arrive at the grandmother's residence, we'll take position around the house. With the owner's permission, we'd like to keep a man inside the house at all times as well. Is that acceptable?"

SaTia looked at Mama and Big Mama for approval. They nodded nonchalantly, seemingly caught up in the mystique of these eight black men who could likely overthrow a government.

"That is acceptable," SaTia responded.

"Excellent. We depart in four minutes and thirty-eight seconds."

Four minutes and thirty-eight seconds later, the doors to my room slid open and the press found themselves looking at a human wall. The hired men had made a circle around me, and even though there wasn't enough space in the hallway for the people congregated there, my guards still managed to bully their way through the crowd at a steady pace. In fact, they were shoving and manhandling people with such force that after a while, as an exercise in self-preservation, many of the reporters and media personnel just moved out of the way.

Inside the moving fortress that the mercenaries made was Mama, Big Mama, Henry, Brian, and Ray, all standing very close together as instructed. And I stood in the middle of them, hunched over slightly, wearing a large hoodie that Henry had brought for me. The hood was pulled up tightly over my head, and the shades that went with it made me seem like I was on my way to rob a corner store. I barely recognized myself.

Still, even with all of the security entourage, and family surrounding me, I almost passed out as I was taking those first steps out of the door. The terror was indescribable. It was as if I stepped out into a building full of people who wanted to kill me.

It didn't even seem like the same place once I'd left my room. I found myself tumbling around in an abyss. Each camera flash was like a spring on a pinball machine. I'd look one way and—*ping*—get bounced back, only to have it happen again and again. And the noise was deafening, like out-of-tune wind instruments being blown in my ear. Henry tried to check up on me a few times as we were walking, but it was of no use. I couldn't hear what he was trying to say.

I glanced over at Mama and Big Mama, and could tell immediately from their faces that they were unprepared for this assault as well. I stopped our progress to check on them, but noticed that SaTia was keeping both of their heads down and leading them calmly along with me. Comforted that they were taken care of, I began to focus once again on myself.

After several seconds, my entire sense of direction was gone. Either Ray, Henry, or Brian ended up spinning me to the left or right to get me back facing the right direction.

By the time we got to the limo, we were all exhausted. Even my security was breathing heavy as they blocked off the crowd and allowed us to enter the vehicle. As promised, one of them stayed with us, and the rest got into two SUVs, one in front of us and one behind us.

I sat down on the long seat and let my head fall back onto the leather.

"Moses, you good?" Henry tried to check up on me, but I was already asleep.

THUD!

I jerked awake, wondering what was going on.

THUD! THUD! THUD!

The sounds were coming in rapid succession. The world was out of focus as I looked around, but even with blurry eyes, I recognized everyone I'd left the hospital with. They were all watching me and making sure I was okay.

As my vision sharpened and the world became clearer, I recognized where I was. I was back in my old neighborhood, no more than two blocks from my house. The basketball courts and corner stores tried to welcome me back, but the people surrounding the limo and SUVs stole all their glory.

THUD! THUD! THUD!

The palms of fans slammed against the windows of the limousine, rocking it back and forth as we crept through the crowd. There were so many people that the banging of their palms began to sound like heavy rain.

I watched as SaTia read the worry on Mama and Big Mama's faces.

"Don't worry, Mama Jenkins. The police have a perimeter set

up around your house, and your street is blocked off to anyone who doesn't live on it. Plus, our very own private security will be posted around the house. You don't have anything to worry about."

"Baby, ain't no road block or none of these here men gon' stop these people if they decide to run in my house. Only one protectin' me is the Lawd! All these other folks jus' helpin'."

SaTia couldn't argue if she wanted to. "Yes ma'am," she said, and pushed back in her seat, making herself comfortable enough to ponder her elder's words.

"All these people are here for Moses?" Mama asked nervously.

"Yes, ma'am," Henry said. "A lot of 'em been here since SaTia announced y'all were leaving today. They figured this'd be the only place he'd wanna go."

"Maybe we should have gone somewhere else. This is crazy."

"I know it seem like that, Ms. Jenkins, but these people love Moe...ahh...Moses. These people love Moses. I mean, a bunch of 'em was camped out last night, like this was a concert or somethin'. I ain't never seen so many people hyped up like this before."

Henry's words made me think as I looked out the window. I saw one man press his arm up to the window, revealing a tattoo of my last album cover on his upper shoulder. I saw at least four or five different people in tears, screaming my name as if I'd turned water to wine. There were signs with my face plastered on them, welcoming me home, and everyone had on one of the shirts that SaTia had warned me about. The people who couldn't lay hands on the limo just pointed to their T-shirts and jumped up and down.

"I Am Da Nigga." It was on everyone's chest, like a Superman mark.

Finally, the limo and SUVs were let past the blockade that the police put up, and the world was still again. I saw the house that

I'd grown up in, and my first instinct was to jump out through the sunroof and dive onto the front lawn.

One of the military contractors, the same one who had introduced himself and his team to us, began moving to exit the car. As he did, I was taken aback, realizing that I hadn't noticed him sitting in the limo with us. He'd faded into the background, like a man standing in distant shadows. Now that he moved, it was as if a ghost had reappeared. He motioned for me to stay put, and I easily followed the direction.

Spilling out from the two SUVs, the private security team came together as a group. The soldier who was in our limo gave orders for all of ten seconds, and then the team scattered like illuminated roaches. If they had been any other group of people, I'd be sure that they had all left and gone about their business. As it was, after ten minutes had passed, they all reappeared in the same thirty-second timeframe, checking in with their leader. After they'd all returned, the commander gave one last set of orders, and then most of them took positions around the house.

The one in charge came back and opened the door.

"You all are free to enter the house."

First, Big Mama and Mama got out and made their way to the door. Next, SaTia emerged, and then Ray, Henry, and Brian. They each waited by the door after they'd gotten out.

When I stepped out of the limo, thunder filled the air. The crowd of people was far enough away so as to not pose a threat, but close enough that I felt as though their collective roar could knock me over.

At that moment, I wanted to go back to the old me. It would've been so easy. A crowd of people were putting themselves in physical harm just to be able to lay eyes on me. I lifted an arm in a half-wave, and the roar seemed to make the sidewalk shake.

Why not go back? I thought to myself. *I'm a god here. Every woman in the crowd wants to screw me, and every guy wants to be me. I'm young, I'm rich, I'm black, and I got it all. Why does the old me have to die? Talbert's plantation was just a dream. Roka and Sarah and Bradley…that was all a dream. This is real.*

And then the chanting began. It started low, one person in the crowd at first. A familiar song whistled from a distance that I couldn't quite put my finger on. As it grew louder, I began to recognize it, even though I didn't want to. It began as a song and turned into an alarm.

DA NIGGA! DA NIGGA! DA NIGGA! DA NIGGA!

And just like that, I knew I was fooling myself. There was no turning back now. I didn't have to make the decision whether or not to let the old me die—he was already dead.

Sad but reassured, I started to walk toward my home. The leader of the soldiers had waited for me before he entered the house himself, and I realized that he was studying my face. As I studied his in return, I saw his confusion at the situation. All these people cheering for me, and yet I probably appeared melancholy at best. We looked at each other like intricate pieces of art, until I got close enough to him that it felt uncomfortable, and we both had to divert our gaze as we walked into the house.

"Okay, we made it!" Mama and Big Mama, happy to be back in their home, headed upstairs to rest. The rest of us sat in the living room, watching SaTia as she attempted to chart our course. "Huge hurdle down," she said. "But where do we go from here?"

"That's all up to Moe…Moses. Right now, everybody's waitin' on him." Brian motioned over to me, putting me on the spot.

"That's real talk," Henry said. "We can't do nothin' without 'im."

Everyone looked at me. I was unable to respond, because I was enthralled with a house that I felt as though I hadn't seen in decades. I felt as if I was being taken back in time. I looked in the kitchen and remembered playing with a toy firetruck while I sat on the floor. I looked at the dining room table and remembered sitting on my father's lap, helping him eat a ham sandwich before he ran out of the house. Every inch of the wallpaper and carpeting brought back a separate memory that held my full attention.

My gaze darted across the room, and again, out of thin air, I saw the commander standing in the corner, silent. I wasn't so much taken aback this time, as I wondered how he continued to pull the same trick, and as my eyes moved past him to the house adornments around him, my mind quickly left the commander and returned to the memories of my youth.

"Moses?"

SaTia called me out of my trance, and I looked at her as if I wished she hadn't. "Moses, are you okay?"

I let my eyes wander away from her as I nodded my head. It was clear that something had me preoccupied, and my friends just sat looking at me in silence until they could figure out what it was. Eventually, I stood up from the couch and allowed myself to walk around my long lost house. I was eager to find new memories that didn't involve me being whipped. I explored every room on the floor. I crawled along the carpets and sat on the counters and let the mist from the refrigerator cool my frame. I knew this was my home, but it would never be my only one. It would never wipe out the memory of a plantation where I was broken and set free. Even in the house where I'd grown up, a part of me was still stuck back there, never to return.

I came back to the couch and sat down amongst my friends. SaTia took a look at my long face and stood to address everyone.

"Okay, guys. Let's do this. Let's everyone go home for the evening. We'll come back tomorrow morning at 9 a.m. and revisit everything."

"Naw, that's not cool, SaTia," Ray said. "There's people out there, they want Da Nigga! I mean, like they want 'im now! Hell, he could step off da front steps and probably make a million. I know my nigga, aight? Ain't no way he'd wanna jus' sleep till da mornin' when it's so much money to be made!"

I looked at Ray, and then at the rest of my squad. I could tell they were inclined to agree with him. SaTia calmly sat down on the sofa, and motioned her hand toward me. "Why don't you ask Moses?"

"Moses cain't talk, SaTia."

"That doesn't mean he can't hear you. Ask him."

Ray took a deep breath and then turned his head to meet my gaze. "Moses, do you—"

I decided not to let him finish. I stood up while he was talking and made my way over to the steps. After I'd gotten to the top, I walked to my room, opened the door, and fell down on my bed.

I could hear SaTia's voice faintly from downstairs.

"So," she said. "like I said, let's all go home and meet up tomorrow morning."

I heard them all stand up, but I was asleep before the front door announced their departure.

I knew where I was immediately. Even before my vision had the chance to focus itself, I could already recognize the difference.

The feeling of breathing fresh air, of sunlight that had already been filtered into its purest form, made the location clear to me. I stood and looked straight at the Talbert house, the bullet holes still decorating the walls and the front door. I could still see the legs of Ella's dead body poking around the corner, and when I looked down to avoid the vision, I was greeted by my own frame lying dead under my feet.

"AHHHH!"

I jumped high enough that I figured I'd land on the roof, but instead I came down just inches to the left of my own limp arm. I noticed, however, that it didn't move. My full body weight leaping off of it hadn't caused it to budge. As I tried to get over the shock of seeing my own dead body lying beside my feet, I noticed that my feet were in the same white Nikes I'd worn out of the hospital. The dead body beside me was dressed in the same hard cotton shirt and burlap-like pants that I'd worn most of the time on the plantation. But I stood there in fresh, custom-made white Nikes, True Religion jeans, and an Armani T-shirt.

"Was it worth it?"

I swung around, expecting to see a white man with a pistol aimed at my face. How stupid was I to not pick up the first gun I saw lying on the ground? I hadn't been back on the plantation sixty seconds and I already saw how soft Da Nigga's life had made me.

If he miss me, he's dead, I thought to myself as my head swung around in slow motion. But there was no white man behind me. There was only my father.

"Dad?"

"How are you, son?"

He spoke, and it was as if all the emotion from everything I'd gone through, both on Talbert's plantation and back in the hospital, bubbled up to the surface of my skin at the same time. I swung my arms around his neck and squeezed him.

"It's okay, son. It'll be alright."

"Dad…" I choked the word out. It was barely audible.

"I told you, son, it's okay."

"No, no it's not, Dad. Look…"

I separated from him and pointed at the ground, where my dead body lay. He looked down at it, and then looked up at me calmly.

"You're not really here, son."

"Wh…what? What are you talkin' about?"

"You're not really here. You're asleep in our house back home."

"But I'm lying there dead on the ground!"

"Yes, and you're standing here talking to me. It mustn't be a surprise that you can be two places at once by now." ·

I looked around again and realized that everything was frozen in place. The Talbert children and the Sheriff were stuck in the same position, and the dead bodies lying on the ground had ceased decomposing. My father and I moved freely in a world frozen in time.

"Why am I back here?" I looked my father in the eye as we began walking.

"You brought yourself back here."

"I didn't bring myself back here, Dad. Why would I do that?"

"Because you needed to be reminded. It's easy to forget in a designer T-shirt."

I wanted to respond, but looked down at myself and decided to shut up. A few steps later and I was eyeing my dad once again. I was at once grateful for his presence and eager for his answers.

"Again, why am I back here?"

"I told you, because you need to be reminded."

"I don't need to be reminded. I never forgot."

"Just because you didn't forget, doesn't mean you don't need reminding."

"What? Why are you talking like that?"

"Like what?"

"Like you're auditioning to play The Riddler."

"It's the only way you'll understand me."

"I don't understand you, though, so your logic is off somewhere."

My father laughed out loud.

"You were always a smart kid. I knew you'd make it. There were times when I held my breath, but I knew you'd eventually make it."

"How come you weren't there?"

The question took both of us by surprise.

"What was that, son?"

I cleared my throat and pushed the words out like a newborn. "How come you weren't there?"

"I just couldn't be, son. I wish I was. I watched you the whole time."

"But you weren't there."

"Yes, I know."

We walked in silence for another moment, stepping over the dead bodies of both blacks and whites as we moved along. This time, my dad broke the silence. "So...was it worth it?"

"I don't know. I don't really know who I am anymore."

"That's a lie."

"What do you mean, it's a lie?"

"I mean, it's a lie. It's fake. It's a falsehood. It's not true."

"How do you know?"

"Because I'm your dad."

I realized that there was no better answer to the question.

"So was it worth it?"

"I don't know, Dad. I really don't know."

"Listen!"

My father grabbed me by the shoulders so suddenly that I almost jumped out of his grasp.

"I would die a thousand deaths if I could've died like you. A thousand deaths."

And then he turned and walked off into the haze of the Southern day.

"DAD!"

I had been yelling out for my father in my sleep, and the sound of my own voice woke me. I sat up on my bed, and tried to rub the image of my father fading into the distance from my eyes. Slowly, I stood and paced back and forth across my room. I felt as if he was standing somewhere in the room, and the feeling made the hair on my forearms stand up.

"Was it worth it?"

I heard the words, and even though I felt my mouth move, I knew I wasn't the one speaking. I ran over to the door and left the room before I had the chance to turn pale.

I wasn't sure of the time, but the sun was no longer in the sky. I could hear Big Mama, Mama, and SaTia's voices echoing off the walls in the living room. As I made my way down the stairs, I looked at all the familiar pictures on the wall. Big Mama had always kept a bunch of old, black and white photos on the wall. They'd been there since I was young, and I'd long since ignored them. Now, though, I stopped and looked at each one. They each seemed to call out to me, as if the pictures knew something about me that I didn't. I stared at each photo, trying to figure out why they were drawing me closer. And then, five steps from the bottom, I saw it. Hanging there on the wall, where it had always been, I saw it and my mouth fell open. I stared at the small photo, in a frame no larger than my shoe, and allowed the color to drain from my face. The photo contained two women, adorned in dresses and clearly tired from a hard day's work. The woman on the left I did not recognize, but the woman on the right almost stopped my heart cold.

It was Sarah.

With my hands shaking, I took the picture off the wall and walked slowly into the living room. The women fell silent when they saw me. I could see the concern on each of their faces.

"Baby?" Big Mama reached out to grab my hand. "You gon' be alright?"

Instead of grabbing her hand, I put the picture down on her palm and pointed to it.

"This thing here?" She laughed, holding the picture in front of her face. "Lawd, I cain't tell you how long it's been since my mama gave me that! Now the lady on the right, I never knew who she was. Nobody ever told me. But the one on the left, that's my Aunt Elizabeth. She was Mama's great-great-aunt. They says she was a powerful woman. Say she gave prophecies to slaves."

I looked at Big Mama, then at the picture she grasped in her hand, and I knew it was time. I felt Roka and Sarah nudge me on the back of my shoulder blades.

"Big Mama...Mama...SaTia..."

At the sound of my voice, Mama dropped the full cup of coffee she held in her hand..

SaTia probably didn't know how to feel. She sat there with her mouth open and her face contorted in a mass of unclear emotions.

Big Mama just smiled and shook her head. She looked back at Mama and SaTia with a grin on her face. "Told y'all she was a powerful woman..."

I smiled at my grandmother, and then turned to face them all once again. It was the first time they'd heard me speak since I'd first come out of my coma.

"Big Mama…Mama…SaTia…I'm ready to tell y'all what happened to me."

I turned around so that my back was facing them and took off my shirt, revealing the scars from Bradley's whip. My gift from the Talbert plantation.

SaTia became instantly enraged. "Who did this to you? Was it somebody from the hospital? Who did this?"

"Jesus…" Mama looked at my back in horror.

I noticed after a few seconds that I didn't hear Big Mama's reaction. When I turned to see her, she had her rough, calloused hand over her mouth. As her hand began to shake, tears formed and dripped from her eyes like a leaky faucet. It was my first time seeing her cry.

"I know exactly what them are," she said, choking out the words.

In that moment, the empty space beside Big Mama on the couch was the only one that felt comfortable. I sat down and grabbed Big Mama's hand.

"Speak, child," she whispered, and looked me dead in my face.

I took a deep breath and looked around the room at the ladies. Again, like clockwork, I saw the commander standing in the corner, in the distance behind my mother. He looked intently at me, and I could tell he had seen the scars on my back as well.

As I sat back, I kept Big Mama's hand in mine.

"After I got shot, out there, on the porch…well…I woke up in a field…"

As the sounds of the night played on, I relived my past life.

17

The afternoon sun tiptoed across my face as my eyes fluttered open. The world was becoming more concrete by the second. I didn't wonder where I was, or how I'd gotten here; instead, my thoughts raced back to last night. To the faces of my family as I'd described to them all that I'd been through. They'd hardly blinked as I'd described what it was like to be caged and fed garbage, or to have my bones broken in order for them to heal properly, or to urinate on myself whenever a white person came into the room.

I could tell they didn't want to believe me. To chalk the whole story up to some psychotic break would have been easier for everyone, including me. But they'd sat by my bedside and been with me every second I'd been awake from my coma. They knew, though they may not have wanted to, that there was no explanation for the marks on my back except that my story was true.

We'd been up all night. I'd gone from not uttering a single word, to talking for almost six hours without interruption. I turned over every detail of my alternate life and exposed it. There were times when I looked up and everyone was weeping, and I realized I was shedding tears as well. Other times I had to catch myself, realizing that I was shouting at the top of my lungs. When I finished, I was too weak to move, but so were my family members. They'd taken a portion of my cross and borne it on their own backs. Eventually it was the commander who—as the birds sang the credit music to my story—took each of us and led us to our respective rooms.

If he was tired, he didn't show it. I figured he'd been trained not to. But as he silently helped me up the stairs, I had the chance to glance in his eyes. I could tell he'd taken a piece of my cross, too.

I'd slept straight through to the afternoon, and now that I was awake, I wondered what to do? Where do I go? Who do I talk to? I'd finally told someone about what had happened to me, but that was just the first part. I still didn't know who I was yet. I only knew who I wasn't.

It suddenly occurred to me that I could make the decision to just stay in my room for the rest of my life. That way I'd have all the time I could ever want to figure myself out. As soon as I stepped out my door, however, I knew everyone would expect that I knew who I was. No doubt Big Mama, Mama, and SaTia had come to their own conclusions about who I was—or who I should be—now that they knew what had happened. And everyone outside of the house was still expecting the same man who'd gotten shot on the porch to emerge better than ever.

I decided I wouldn't leave the room until I had some idea of the person I had become. It would be too dangerous. Preparing mentally to stay confined in my room for an undetermined amount of time, I walked over to the window. I wondered how long it would be until I lay my feet on the small patch of grass outside, and then I turned my head, realizing I was depressing myself.

And that's when I saw it.

It lay underneath the desk, in the shadows cast down by the open drawer. I would have never noticed it, except the sunlight was coming into the room just at the right angle to reflect off of its screen. Slowly I walked over and reached down, closing the drawer, revealing the iPod lying there on the ground. After turning it on and entering the code, I scrolled through the music. It had every last one of my albums on it, from the first one I'd done with the local studio, to *Hoes In Da Attic*.

I could hear the whisper of Sarah's voice through the touch screen.

"You can't knowed who you is till you knowed who you was befo.'"

I put the headphones in my ears and scrolled up to the very first album under my name. Hitting play, I let the familiar bassline wash over me, and studied every word like a chemistry book.

Some hours later, I emerged from my room with my head spinning and my chest tight. My own words had tried to suffocate me. I stumbled down the steps with my lyrics buzzing in my ears around me. I swatted at them like flies and hoped that no one saw me.

It was early evening by now, but because of the late night we'd all had, the smell of bacon, eggs, and pancakes still met me at the doorway. I stopped briefly before I entered, wondering how my family would treat me now that they knew the truth, and then threw caution to the wind and stepped inside.

My family members looked like robots. They moved mechanically around the kitchen, doing tasks that were only completed because they were second nature to them. Their eyes still had the same distant glaze from the night prior, and they didn't utter a word to one another. Big Mama went back and forth between the different eyes of the stove as if she'd been programmed to do so. Mama set the table and started the coffeemaker as if she was a wind-up doll, and SaTia just sat at the table, staring into space. They all looked at me as I came into the room, and I could tell they had everything and nothing to say at the same time. I sat down beside SaTia as Big Mama began putting pancakes on everyone's plate and Mama poured coffee.

"I wanna have a press conference today," I said assuredly to SaTia, waking her from her daze. "I wanna call back all the news people who was out here yesterday, and I wanna talk to 'em."

"Are you sure that's the best idea, Moses? Maybe you should think a little about what you want to say first."

"I been up in my room for the last couple hours doin' nothin' but thinkin', SaTia. Now that I'm startin' to know who I am, I wanna tell people. I wanna let people know."

"Alright," she said, picking up her cell phone. "It's done. They'll be outside in two hours."

"Also, can you contact Dr. Bailey for me? You know, from the hospital? I wanna talk to him."

"That's not a problem. Anything else?"

"Yeah. I wanna take you on a date."

The last line caught everyone's attention. I heard the snap of Mama and Big Mama's necks as they whipped their heads around to stare at me. SaTia dropped her BlackBerry in her pancake syrup.

"You…what?" she said.

"I wanna take you on a date. I'd ask you to marry me, but I think you need to get to know me first. I ain't the same person I used to be."

Mama laughed out loud as SaTia looked at me as if I was a newfound fool.

"Moses, do we need to take you back to the hospital? Are you feeling okay?"

"I'm fine, SaTia. You don't have to ask me that anymore, okay?

Look, I love you. I've loved you since high school. And if you ain't love me, you wouldn't have put up with me for as long as you have."

Big Mama set the hot skillet on top of the table to listen to our conversation. I ignored the smell of the burning tablecloth as I went on.

"I wasn't ready for you before. Now I am. So let me take you out."

I watched SaTia transform in front of my eyes. She began with the shocked eyes and mouth wide open look that I'd expected. But as she slowly sat back in her chair, the realization that I was serious seemed to fall over her like a fog, and before I knew it, she had reached into a hidden place inside herself and brought Ella out to meet me.

"You were hiding her," I said as if I'd just seen a magic trick.

By the time SaTia got relaxed and comfortable, she didn't have to say a word. Her eyes, her moves, and her body said it all.

This was the SaTia that Da Nigga never got to see.

"What makes you think you're ready for me now?" Her voice sounded like sex on a bed full of roses. I had to remind myself that my mother and grandmother were still in the room.

"It's not a thought," I responded matter-of-factly. "It's a promise. I can handle whatever you got, and still be your king when the sun comes up."

She was impressed. I could tell by the notes in her laughter and the shift of her legs.

"So, you gonna let me take you out?" I pressed.

"Yeah, I guess," she said nonchalantly, as if the subject had suddenly become unimportant. "I don't have anything else to do."

"Actually, you do. You gotta manage the career of the biggest rap star in the world during a transition that'll probably make 'im lose all his fans."

"Yeah, well, I've got that…but that's it."

I leaned forward to her and lost myself. "Marry me."

"Why?"

"Cause you're my mic."

"What happened to waiting?"

"Who has the time?"

"You've been in a coma for six months."

"Exactly."

"You said I didn't know you anymore."

"I was wrong."

"I know you were."

"Why didn't you tell me?"

"Where would the fun have been in that? I'd have missed you bending over backwards trying to introduce me to someone I already knew."

I shook my head, amazed by the woman.

"Marry me," I repeated.

"I married you when I took this job, Moses. You just never bought the ring."

She leaned forward and laid her lips on mine. For a moment, I thought I'd been shot in the chest again.

When she pulled away, I could see the vulnerability in her eyes.

"If you hurt me…"

"Then you'd survive, 'cause you're that strong. I wouldn't. So I can't."

"Moses…"

"I told you, you're my mic. No one hears me unless I'm with you."

"Is that enough?"

"It is now."

THUD! THUD! THUD!

Three solid strikes sounded at the front door, and I saw a blur pass outside the kitchen window and head toward the front door.

The mercenary, I thought to myself. *Man, he was there the whole time!*

Instantly, SaTia and I fell back into our normal roles.

"Oh! Moses, I forgot to tell you that the guys were coming back over. I had planned to tell you at the table but I forgot."

"It's cool. Is that them?"

"I hope so."

I got up and walked out of the kitchen. My protector was standing off to the side of the door. He held his pistol with one hand, and moved the cover to the peephole with the other as he cautiously looked through.

"It's your colleagues from yesterday, sir. The same three men."

"Okay, they can come in."

The soldier swiftly opened the door, letting Ray, Brian, and Henry back into the house, and then stepped off to the side and talked into his radio.

"Packman, this is Alpha, come in."

"Packman here."

"Why was I not notified of the three men coming to the door?"

"1800 hours, Alpha. We off the clock and ready to roll. Waitin' for you in the truck."

The soldier they called Alpha held the radio up to his mouth, but didn't say anything. The news had taken him by surprise, and it seemed as if he was struggling to decide what to do. I looked at him for a while, and then followed my friends back into the living room. SaTia sat with her laptop out, ready to take notes. When I walked in, she kept her eyes on her computer screen.

Brian got comfortable on the couch and looked up at SaTia.

"How's Moses doin'?"

"I'm good," I answered.

Ray stood too fast and ended up falling backward out of his seat. Henry missed his chair entirely. They both hit the ground and popped right up together.

"What the hell!" They sounded like a duet.

"Yeah, he started talking last night, fellas," SaTia said. "He's actually had a lot to say since the last time you saw him."

Brian hadn't quite closed his mouth yet. He looked at me as if he was looking at a ghost.

"Mo...Moses?"

"Yeah, dogg, it's me. You seen me yesterday; why y'all actin' so crazy?"

"Nigga, you wasn't talkin' yesterday! You was goin' around pointin' at stuff like a retard!"

I felt the red lines coming back into my vision, but SaTia grabbed my arm and massaged my hand.

"He doesn't know, Moses," she whispered.

She was right. I closed my eyes and felt my anger fade.

"You aight, man?" Brian noticed that something was bothering me. "Yo, I ain't mean nothin' serious by the retard thing, man. I'm jus' sayin'...it's...it's good to hear your voice again, my nigga... that's all."

I had to laugh at him. He meant well. "It's all good."

"Yo!" Henry made his way to the middle of the floor with excitement written all over his face. "Yo, we can hit da streets for real now, cuz! My mans is back and in full effect! Yo, we 'bout ta turn dis whole world upside down!"

"Slow down, homie, slow down!" I stood and placed my hand on Henry's shoulder. "We gotta talk first, man. Things ain't da same as they used to be."

"What's changed?" My friends' excitement quickly turned into nervous curiosity as they sat down.

"Well, first, I can't do—"

"Ah, excuse me, sir."

I looked over to see that the lead soldier was standing directly to my left. I was too curious to be annoyed. "Yeah, what's up?"

"I...ahh...well..."

It was weird seeing him stumble over his words as if I was watching a law of nature being broken.

"Ah...the contract that you all had with my company...the time has expired on it."

"Oh, yes, I know," SaTia said, and turned around and looked at the soldier from her seat. "I've got another outfit on the way. They aren't as impressive, but they're a lot less expensive. I just wanted to make sure that we had over and above what we needed getting out of the hospital and staying our first night in the house. Tell Mr. Tooley I said thank you, and that you all did an outstanding job."

"Yes, ma'am."

We all waited in awkward silence as the soldier refused to move. SaTia pulled up the contract on her laptop and looked it over one last time. "Did I forget anything?" she asked.

"No, ma'am." The soldier continued to look uneasy.

"Well...can we help you with anything else?"

The commander took a deep breath.

"Ma'am, as soldiers we're trained to follow our instincts. No matter what happens, if our guts tell us something, we listen to them. I've lived and operated under that premise, and it's kept me alive more times than I can count."

"Okay?" I knew he was going somewhere, but I couldn't figure it out.

"I heard your story last night."

It was my turn to take a deep breath. This was the first time anyone had brought it up directly since I'd told it. "I know."

422 R. KAYEEN THOMAS

"I didn't want to believe you."

I laughed.

"I don't think they wanted to believe me, either," I said, motioning toward my mother, Big Mama, and SaTia.

"Was it true, sir?"

I looked in his eyes and saw the same conflict that I'd seen when he'd spoken with his fellow soldiers over the radio.

"Yeah, yeah, it was true."

The soldier nodded and his eyes focused on the floor. Finally, as he resolved in his mind what he wanted, he straightened his back, lifted his head, and turned into a stone wall again. "Sir, I'd like to stay on your detail."

"What? What are you talkin' about?"

SaTia pulled my arm.

"I think he's saying he wants to stay here and keep protecting you."

I looked at the soldier with disbelief. "That's not what you're saying, is it?"

"Yes, sir, it is."

"But you gotta get orders from your boss, right?"

"I'd like to work for you exclusively, sir."

"So, you want me to hire you?"

"Yes, sir."

"And you're gonna quit your job?"

"Yes, sir."

"Don't you have a family or somethin' that you need to discuss this with?"

The soldier's eyes glazed over as he tried to focus on something else in the room.

"No. No, sir, I don't."

He was trying to hide his sadness, but I'd seen too much of it on the plantation not to recognize it. I quickly asked another question.

"Well, how you know I can afford you?"

"It doesn't matter, sir. I'm following my gut, as I was trained to do. My gut tells me that you need me here. And, well, that I need to be here."

"Why do you need to be here?"

"I don't know yet, sir. You remind me of someone."

I looked at SaTia, who shrugged her shoulders and shook her head, and then I returned my focus to the mercenary.

"I'm not sure what you tryin' to do, man."

"I'm choosing my own mission, sir. You can accept or decline as you see fit, but I'm offering my services."

Everyone was quiet as I thought it through. This could easily be some kind of trap or set up, and if it was, I was falling right into it. But if it wasn't, then this guy, whoever he was, connected with my story. It had struck him enough to want to be a part of whatever I was doing.

I decided that he was worth taking a chance on. "Aight then," I replied to the soldier. "I accept."

"Thank you, sir."

The soldier picked up his radio.

"Alpha to Packman, come in."

"Packman here. Still waiting on you, Alpha."

"Not coming. Tell Tooley I quit."

"Come again, Alpha?"

"You boys leave without me. I got another outfit now. Over."

"Okay, Alpha...so you just want us to leave you here, over?"

"Affirmative. Go home. It was a pleasure working with you."

"Red Eagle, Alpha! Red Eagle!"

"No! Red Eagle is docked and locked! I am not in distress. Repeat, not in distress!"

"Don't understand Alpha, over."

"You won't. It's code green, here. You boys leave now; that's an order."

There was silence on the other end for a while before the uncertain voice came through once more.

"Departing now, over. Hope you know what you're doing, Alpha."

The soldier put his radio down and looked at me. "Should I go back to post, sir?"

"Well, no, hold up a minute. If you're gonna work for me, then we gotta know each other's names. I cain't get with all that 'sir' stuff. I'm Moses."

"I'm Xavier, sir. Xavier Turner."

"It's good to meet you. Stop calling me sir."

"Yes, sss…ah…okay."

I turned and looked at Ray, Henry, and Brian. "Looks like we got another squad member," I said.

Ray sat up in his seat with his nose turned up.

"Whateva, I don't know dat nigga."

I slammed my hand down on the table without realizing it, and everyone in the room jumped except for Xavier.

"Aight, look." My anger came so quickly that my voice surprised me.

"Calm down, Moses," SaTia tried to whisper, but it wasn't an effective effort.

"Now's a great time to talk 'bout what things is the same, and what things is different," I said. I had a hard time trying to get the fire out of my voice, but the flames eventually died down to embers. "First off, don't nobody use the word nigga in my presence no more."

"Hold on, what?" Henry sat up in his seat and scratched his head. "Don't say nigga? That don't make no sense!"

"Look, you don't know what happened, aight? When I was in the coma…"

I started to reach for the back of my shirt, and then stopped. I looked into Ray, Brian, and Henry's eyes as they looked back at me with various emotions ink-blotted on their faces. I realized they wouldn't understand my explanation. I could talk another whole day about where I'd been and what had happened to me, but in the end, they wouldn't get it. They'd hear my story, and maybe even believe it, but they wouldn't understand it.

It was then that I realized how valuable Xavier really was.

Sadly, I dropped the back of my shirt, covering my scars up once again.

"Look, I just ain't with the word no more, aight? I'm not tryin' to hear it no more."

"But how you jus' gonna up and say we can't say nigga no more?" Brian chimed in with slight agitation. "It's your name, man!'"

"Look, you can say whatever you wanna say when you not 'round me." I looked at Brian, unmoved by his sentiment. "When I'm around, though, you can't say it. Like I said, I ain't feelin' it no more."

"Moses, come on, man…" Ray stood up to address me, but before he could get fully to his feet, Xavier stepped forward and made himself known. He didn't say a word, but Ray, clearly thrown off by this new force, sat back down.

"It's like that now, Moses?" he said as he sat gingerly back in his seat.

I looked at Ray, and then back at Xavier. I hadn't turned to anyone else, but I knew they were all watching me, anxious to see what I was going to do.

As I took account of myself, I realized I was not inclined at all to say anything to Xavier. I knew that Ray wasn't going to do anything after he stood up but say his piece and sit back down, but the man had just quit his job to protect me. Who was I to stand in his way?

"Look," I said, and stood up in the place where Ray would have been. "I told y'all, some things is gonna have ta change. Y'all my homies, man. We been through a lot together…and I understand if you can't get with the new changes, but if you gonna stay with me, then you gotta."

I looked around at their serious faces.

"I'm just being real, y'all. Take some time to think 'bout it. If it wasn't no money involved, would you still put up with it? 'Cause I'm tellin' you, I can't do things how I used to, dogg. If it costs me some money, then so be it. And it probably will."

"Hold up," Brian looked around the room, confused, and then back at me. "You sayin' dat with all dis money you could be makin' right now, you 'bout to do somethin' that could make you go broke?"

"I'm sayin' that, in all seriousness, don't nobody in this room know where we gon' be at in six months. You stick with me, then yeah, you could end up goin' broke. That's not the plan, but it's a possibility. In order for this to keep goin', you gotta be here for more than the money."

"More than the money?" Henry looked like a priest who'd heard a curse word. "The hell is wrong wid you, man? What's more important in this life than money?"

"This…"

I turned my back to them and lifted up my shirt, showing them my scarred flesh.

"Damn!"

"Yo, what the hell!"

"Who did that to you, man?"

"It doesn't matter," I replied, and turned around. "Y'all go home. Come through tomorrow mornin' and let me know what's good. Real talk, I'd much rather see y'all roll out now and we stay friends than later on and we ain't even talkin' to each other."

"Yo, you kickin us out, homie?" The hurt in Ray's voice almost made me feel bad.

"Naw. You can stay if you want, but I gotta press conference." I stopped for a moment, and then looked at SaTia. "Right?"

"It's already taken care of."

"Cool." I turned around. "After that, I gotta get some rest, so we can hook up later."

"I can't believe this, yo!" Brian said as he stood up. "You know what we s'posed to be doin' tonight? It's like, ten clubs in the city all havin' 'Welcome Home Da Nigga' parties! We s'posed to be hittin' all of 'em! We s'posed to be gettin' twisted and layin' pipe in some shorties and hittin' the studio. Dis nigga—yeah, I said it—dis nigga come outta coma after six months, and all he wanna do is sleep and not say nigga no more!"

I shook my head and smirked. "Naw, that's not all I wanna do."

"Really? So what...you tryin' to go out tonight?"

"Naw, I'm good. I'm chillin. Y'all hit the parties for me. I'll see you tomorrow."

"Whatever, man."

Brian walked out the door, with Ray and Henry on his heels. I let the weight of disappointment fall over me as they walked out the gate and past the police officers on duty.

"Sir," Xavier started, but I cut him off.

"Moses. It's Moses."

"Sorry, sir. Moses?"

"Yeah?"

"I don't trust them."

I didn't want to hear his truth so I walked away, then stopped and turned back. "Well, I trust *you*, and I just met you, so give them a chance. Okay?"

"Yes, sir."

It wasn't worth correcting him again. I dropped down to the couch and tried to convince myself that I hadn't lost my three best friends.

Two hours later, I stood a few feet from the front door, listening to the hustle and bustle on the other side. SaTia had instructed the police to only allow the press past the front gate, and now my front lawn was standing-room-only. Peeping through the window, the scene reminded me of my floor at the hospital over-run with reporters. They were everywhere, from cameramen to news reporters to journalists, all falling over one another trying to get as close as they could to the podium that had been set up on the front porch.

Xavier stood beside me, his face stern and calculating. I'd counted at least six different firearms on his person as he was loading up, but now you couldn't tell that he was armed at all. Even though the sun was down, he still wore a dark pair of sunglasses, hiding his suspicions from the rest of the world.

"SaTia, is that a JumboTron outside?"

She was finishing a phone conversation, and moved the phone away from her mouth. "I never cleared a JumboTron, so no, it shouldn't be. This isn't a concert, it's a press conference. It's probably just some new piece of satellite news equipment."

"I don't know, SaTia. It looks like a JumboTron."

I was in a dark pair of jeans and a dark T-shirt. No shades, no grills, no expensive jewelry that could have afforded one of the reporters an early retirement if I'd given it to them.

SaTia walked up beside me. She paused, then pivoted on her heels and wound up standing directly in front of me. Instinctively, I kissed her.

"Still not going to tell me what you're going to say for the press conference, huh?" she said breathlessly after we parted.

"Nope. Why ruin the surprise?"

"Well, how do you know I'll be here when you finish?"

"'Cause you were here when I started."

The look of confusion on her face quickly changed into a smirk.

"You must've been chained up with some slick-talkin' slaves," she said, shaking her head.

I threw my head back and laughed like a fat man before a quick knock at the door cut my bellows short.

"One of the policemen," SaTia said. "I told him to knock when they sealed off the front yard." She looked into my eyes, and I could tell she was proud of me, though she didn't know what I was about to do.

"It's time," she said, and stepped to the side.

"You're not going out there with me?"

"No. I look a mess."

"That never mattered before."

"I wasn't marrying you before."

I thought for a half-second, and then nodded my head.

"Yeah, I guess you're right."

"You've got Xavier now, and he'll protect you more than I ever could. I don't want the world to see me as your manager anymore."

"You want me to fire you?"

"No, dummy…nobody else could handle you right anyway. It's just…you know how you want the world to know you're not the same person? Well, I want them to know I'm not the same person either."

I looked in her eyes and kicked myself for the years of foolishness. "I feel you. It's done."

She smiled, and I walk past her with Xavier at my side.

"Forgive me if I don't hear your statement, sir."

My hand stopped short of the doorknob as I looked at Xavier.

"It's Moses. You plan on shooting anyone?"

"If I have to, sir…Moses."

"Better them than me, I guess."

"Would you mind filling me in if I don't hear it, sir?"

"It's Moses. Hear what? The statement?"

"Yes."

"Why do you…" I stopped short, denying my curiosity. "Yeah, I'll definitely fill you in." I grabbed the doorknob and turned it, but only opened it slightly before I turned back to Xavier and let my curiosity win out. "Why do you care, Xavier?"

The question stopped the soldier cold. He stood still for a moment, and then removed his shades and looked me in the eye. "I've only heard your story, sir. You haven't heard mine."

I shrugged my shoulders and raised my eyebrows, conceding his point. "Guess we need to talk then."

"Yes, sir"

"Xavier…"

"Yes, sir?"

"It's Moses."

I threw the door open before he could respond. The flashing lights that met us would have given a little child a seizure. Xavier immediately stepped in front of me, shielding me from the direct onslaught of the lights, and leading me to the podium that had been set up.

There was a three-second delay from when I walked out, and when the tsunami of noise hit us, but I had expected it. In almost all of my previous pictures, videos, and interviews, I'd been covered from head to toe in accessories. This was probably the first time any of the reporters had ever seen my eyes. It took them the three seconds to realize it was really me. After the realization hit, everything turned to chaos.

The press started screaming out questions. Their noise alone would have been enough to make me want to cover my ears, but a sea of fans, who had taken a cue from the television cameras, gathered beyond the perimeter drawn by the police. Even though they could barely see me, they cheered as if I was walking through their crowd.

Xavier stood shoulder to shoulder with me as I lowered the microphone to my mouth.

"Thank y'all..."

I hadn't anticipated two things: the loudness of the microphone or the revelation that what I'd seen outside was in fact a Jumbo-Tron, and that it was set up just outside my front yard. SaTia must have had the same thought, because as soon as I saw it, she was running through the front door, pulling me away from the podium.

"I don't know who cleared that damn JumboTron, but somebody is catching hell for it! This was never supposed to be this big, Moses. You don't have to do this if you don't want to."

She was screaming, but I'd just barely heard her over the noise.

"It's okay. Go on back inside. I'll be fine."

"You sure?"

"Yeah, it's all good. Go on back."

As she ducked and made her way back inside, I stood up at the podium. Feeling as if I was about to give an announcement in a football stadium during the Super Bowl. It literally felt as though the ground was shaking.

"Thank y'all. Please, calm down. Calm down."

I lifted both of my arms and waved my hands, signaling for the crowd to be quiet. The noise dropped slowly, taking several minutes before I was able to speak.

"Thank you. Thank you everybody for coming out. Thank you for all your love and your prayers over the last six months."

"WE LOVE YOU, NIGGA!"

Random women yelled from the crowd positioned behind the press, igniting another wave of cheers and screams. I just decided to wait this one out.

Xavier had unholstered one of his pistols and was holding it behind his back and out of view. I could see his eyes darting back and forth over the crowd behind his sunglasses.

Another several minutes passed before they got the hint that I wasn't speaking again until there was a moderate amount of order. Finally, they began to settle down.

"I called this conference 'cause I wanted to clear some things up. There's been a lot of rumors goin' around, and I know people wonderin' what's been goin' on with me, 'specially since I came out of the coma. First, let me promise y'all that I'm not crazy. Matter-of-fact, I'm feelin' better than I've ever felt. Bein' in that coma changed my life."

I looked around at all the eyes focused on me, and I knew it was time. There were sporadic cheers here and there, but it was quiet enough for me to think straight. I took a deep breath and cleared my throat as I continued.

"Da Nigga is dead. He died while I was in the coma. Everything he stood for, everything he did, everything he was, is dead. My name is Moses Jenkins. It is no longer Da Nigga, and as such, I don't 'spect to be called that anymore. All y'all out there wid Da Nigga T-shirts and everything on, y'all reppin' a dead man. It ain't me no more. I ain't nobody's nigga."

I saw jaws drop.

"From now on, I will take being called Da Nigga as a personal offense. To all my fans, if you really are my fans, take them damn shirts off! Shouldn't nobody in the hood be walkin' 'round wid no shirt with 'I am Da Nigga' on it! I ain't makin' no more music under the name Da Nigga, and if I can find a way to, I'll have all my old music destroyed. You ain't heard this from my record company, 'cause they don't know yet. I ain't discussed it with 'em, nor do I plan to. From now on, I ain't nobody's nigga and I ain't nobody's slave!"

The initial shock of my words had worn off, and the press members were working feverishly, making sure they got every word of what would undoubtedly be the story of the century. Cameramen fell over each other trying to shoot me from different angles, and the crowd behind the press had started a low murmur of whispers amongst themselves. I paused up at the podium, soaking in the reactions, and suddenly felt a sense of calm. I relaxed with both my hands on the podium, and laughed quietly into the microphone. This night would change my life forever. I just wanted to make sure I remembered it clearly.

"You know…" I started speaking again and the noise died back down. "I got up outta bed and I listened to all my music. I listened to every record I ever released. And, well, y'all don't know who Roka is, but Roka woulda punched me in the mouth. I'm sure of it. He may have even broken a few of my bones. And Sarah, oh my God, Sarah woulda probably hung me from a tree! They'd probably took turns killin' me if they heard some of the stuff I said. I jus'…I can't make music like that no more. Honestly, I can't. I tried to rap along with the lyrics earlier…and I couldn't. It was like I ain't even write 'em. Somebody else did."

I felt SaTia's stare and glanced over my shoulder. She was standing in the doorway and nodded for me to continue.

"It was always easy for me before, you know? Get a lil high, get a lil drunk, and the words, they just fell right out. I never had to think about what I was sayin', jus' about how well it all flowed. Long as the flow was nice, everything was straight. But now I gotta think about it. Hell, I gotta think about everything…"

A few people in the crowd of fans started to boo loud enough for me to hear it up on the podium. I stood my ground, expecting for the boos to grow. Instead, a larger crowd of people yelled their support, and after realizing how outnumbered they were, the objectors held their peace and fell silent once again.

"I wanna tell y'all I'm sorry. I know this is gonna disappoint some of y'all. I know a lotta people love my music. Though now, I can't really tell why. I mean, it was like all I did was bash y'all over the head lyrically. 'I'll put a dick in yo' chick an' leave you payin' her rent'? Who wants to hear that? I'm 'bout to get married. I don't wanna hear about nobody screwin' my wife."

Hands began to shoot up in the press section, and I knew the firestorm had started. I ignored them as I tried to finish.

"Anyway, I don't know what my music'll sound like from here on out. All I can do is promise you one thing…it ain't gonna sound like Da Nigga. It can't, after all. Da Nigga's dead. Thank y'all for comin' out."

All of the press, even the cameramen, managed to throw their hands up and yell my name at the same time. I took a step back from the podium, and Xavier immediately dove in front of me, blocking me again from the camera flashes and media assault. A couple of people tried to make their way up onto the porch, but the police stopped them and forced them back. One person, a taller, stocky gentleman, managed to force his way past the officers and sprinted toward me for questions. I barely noticed Xavier move before I saw the man flying through the air and landing on his back. I wasn't sure if the cracking sound was the man's bones or the wood underneath him.

Having dealt with the man, Xavier quickly directed me back into the house and shut the door behind us. Mama and Big Mama were in the living room, looking at me as I came back in. SaTia was standing in the hallway with the BlackBerry up to her ear and a smirk on her face.

"It's Mr. Rose," she said. "He says you're dropped from the label if you don't get down to the office right now."

"Tell him I'll be there tomorrow at 10 a.m. If that's not good enough, then go 'head and drop me."

SaTia relayed the message with pride, while a furious Mr. Rose burst back through the telephone receiver. After a ten-minute rant, he hung up on SaTia, who looked at me with the same grin.

"He says he'll see you tomorrow at ten."

I saw Xavier smirk for the first time since we'd met, and I turned and headed up the stairs.

Déjà vu is a strange phenomenon, especially when you've found yourself having traveled back in time.

I sat in a very comfortable chair, with a very familiar looking woman staring sternly at my face and trying to figure out what to do with it. She hadn't changed at all since the last time I'd seen her, except for maybe having added more Botox to her already numb face.

"What do we do with you this time, Mr. Jenkins?"

Her voice had the raspy tenor of a long time cigarette smoker, and her perfume proved no match for the nicotine aroma on her clothes. Still, I appreciated her. She reminded me of a time long gone.

"Your face has changed. I don't think it needs much makeup, just a slight brush here and there, and you should be fine."

She glanced uncomfortably at the man with midnight black shades standing to my right.

"Don't worry, he won't hurt you," I told her.

"That's not what the papers say."

"You don't believe everything you read in the papers, do you?"

I turned and cut a smirk at Xavier, who stood stoically by my side, watching the makeup woman closely as she reached for her brush and began lightly tapping my face.

"X, you gotta stop scaring people everywhere we go, man."

"Can't help it."

"Yeah, you can. You gotta start carrying around a box of kittens or somethin'."

Xavier averted his eyes from the makeup artist and looked at me. I couldn't see his eyes, but I knew him well enough by now to know that he was silently telling me to shut up. I laughed out loud and turned back so that the woman could finish her job.

It had been almost a year since the press conference, though it seemed as if it was just yesterday. Life had been nothing short of a rollercoaster ride since. And here I was, sitting back in the exact same chair, being beautified by the exact same woman at the *Phil Winters Show*. So much was still the same, but so much more was different.

SaTia made a grand entrance into the room. She no longer burst in all frantic as she used to. Now she made every step count.

Her transformation had drawn so much attention that she'd been offered four or five modeling gigs in the last six months, but she'd turned them all down. The only thing she modeled was her ring, and she did that for free.

Her heels clicked across the floor as she walked up and, to the dismay of the makeup artist, kissed me deeply.

"Hey, baby."

"Hey. What's up? I thought you were waitin' in the audience?"

"I wanted to come back here and let you know what was up."

"Where's Danielle? Isn't that what you hired her for? You s'posed to be sittin' down and lookin' pretty."

"Danielle's running around making sure everything else is straight. I wanted to come back here myself."

"Okay, what's going on?"

"Phil Winters is still a bit shook because of what happened last time you were on his show. He's beefed up his security and got the network to have plainclothes cops in the audience."

I turned to Xavier. "We still got our plainclothes guys in the audience, too, right?" I asked.

"Yeah. One in every section."

"Damn! Half the people in the audience gonna have guns!" I laughed nervously.

"I wouldn't worry about it, baby. Everybody's here for your protection. Winters' audience seats almost three hundred people. We need all the security we can get."

I took a deep breath and tried to calm down.

"Is that it, babe?"

"Almost. Winters also got the network to shell out for bullet-proof glass. The cameras won't catch it, but there'll be a clear shield around you all. The only people behind it will be you and Winters."

I turned to SaTia with concern in my eyes.

"What about X?"

"Winters said he'd feel much more comfortable if Xavier stayed on the other side of the glass."

"Naw, that's not gonna work. I told Phil months ago, if I'm gonna do the show, X has got to be with me onstage. If he feels that uncomfortable with it, we can just cancel."

"I told him that already, and he's not willing to cancel. He knows how much revenue this show is going to bring in. He asked me to come in and ask you how you felt about it."

"It's X or no show."

"Alright. X, please don't shoot Phil Winters during the interview, okay?" she said playfully as she leaned down and kissed my forehead.

"Okay," he nonchalantly responded.

My beauty queen turned and walked back to the door with inaudible theme music playing to her stride.

"See you out there," she called, and walked out.

Almost immediately afterwards a skinny brown girl with a short ponytail rushed into the room.

"Mr. Jenkins! Mr. Jenkins, they're ready for you!"

"Danielle, we've talked about this. Calm down, okay? They not about to do the show without us."

"Okay…" She bent over and took several deep breaths. "Alright… I'm calm. Mr. Jenkins, they're ready for you on set."

"Thanks, Danielle."

I let the makeup guru dab my face one more time, and then stood and made my way to the door. Xavier had long since quit the formalities of escorting me places. Everywhere we went now, we went side by side.

I spent more on legal fees for him than I did for myself, but I couldn't complain. The man was good at his job, and I never went anywhere without him.

We walked down the hallway as though we owned the entire studio. All of the pandemonium in the hallway stopped as we made our way through, and everyone stood frozen in place. We could smell the fear of some of the staff members as they trembled in our shadows. Others stared at us in awe, as if we were superheroes on our way to go and save the world. Either way, no one dared to stand in our path. We walked undisturbed straight through to the set.

As we were getting ready to walk out, Phil Winters came and met us at the door. He was sweating so much that he'd commissioned one of the staff members to do nothing but follow him around and dab his face and forehead. He was flushed and bright red as he shook our hands.

"Yo, Phil, you don't look so good, man."

"I'm fine, I'm fine. Just a little nervous about the show. I still have nightmares about the last time you were here…no offense."

"None taken. Did you talk to SaTia?"

"I did." He turned to Xavier as his lapdog found more sweat on his eyebrow to wipe clean. "Please don't shoot me, okay?"

Unlike SaTia, Phil was being as serious as the heart attack he looked as if he was on the verge of having. Xavier nodded his head.

"Okay."

"Okay? Okay…that makes me feel a little bit better." Phil was still jittery as he turned to face me again. "The show's getting ready to start. I'm going to skip the jokes and go right into your introduction. Is that okay?"

"Yeah, that's great."

"Alright, see you on set."

He walked away with his staffer bounding behind him, trying to wipe the back of his neck. I waited until he was far enough away, then turned to Xavier myself. "Seriously, man, don't shoot him. Okay?"

"I'm not going to shoot him. I don't have a reason to."

"Yeah, but he might try and nudge me on the arm or something, you know? Just for fun."

"No, he won't. He's too scared. He won't move from his seat."

"Yeah, you probably right."

"Everyone I've shot has been trying to attack you. I don't know why people think everywhere I go I'm going to shoot somebody."

"You know the media blow stuff outta proportion, X. Don't let it bother you. You know I got your back. Long as you never pull a gun on me again, we good."

"Moses, I…"

"Naw, no more apologies. We good, aight? If I had the story you had, I'd probably pull a gun on everybody I saw."

Xavier nodded his head guiltily.

"'Sides, you wasn't ever 'bout to shoot me, right?"

"No, I wasn't going to shoot you. You might have had to help me clean James up, though."

I laughed and gave Xavier dap as the applause from the audience began and Phil walked out onstage. True to his word, he went immediately into my introduction.

"Ladies and Gentlemen, tonight's show will be a historic one. For the first time since his earth-shattering press conference held almost a year ago, Moses Jenkins will be interviewed tonight here on this show! The last time he was here was eventful to say the least, but when my producers found out that he was willing to come on our show yet again, considering all that happened before and especially all that's happened since, we decided it was an opportunity that we could not pass up. I know that many of you at home, as well as many of you in the audience, have mixed emotions about our guest today. Rumors have spread like the plague since he's come out of his coma, and it's safe to say that he is now the topic of international conversation and debate. Tonight, for the first time since standing on his front porch and shocking the world, he will speak for himself. Ladies and gentlemen, please welcome Mr. Moses Jenkins."

I couldn't tell the boos from the cheers and applause. It all faded together into a white noise that I'd become used to. I walked out onto the set with Xavier right beside me, and he made his way to the back of the couch and stood tall behind me as I shook Phil's hand and took a seat on the couch.

Every once in a while, the boos would get louder than the cheers and vice versa, the crowd engaged in a noise war over which faction could be heard the loudest over the other. Eventually, the uniformed officers standing in the audience intervened, and the audio soldiers died down and eventually fell silent.

"Mr. Jenkins, welcome back."

"Thanks for havin' me, Phil."

"I don't even know where to start. We could spend all night talking about what's happened to you."

"Yeah, I know. You ain't got that kinda time, though."

"Tell me about it. Let's start with the question that everyone seems to be asking: Are you crazy? Have you lost your mind?"

I laughed whenever people asked me that, as if there were no other explanation for how I was acting.

"No, Phil, I'm not crazy."

"What happened while you were in your coma?"

"I had a revelation. An epiphany. I just couldn't do things the same way anymore."

"Okay, so tell me what happened with Cosmos Records?"

"I went to the execs at Cosmos and I told 'em I wanted all my old stuff taken out the stores. I ain't want it sold no more. They refused, of course, 'cause of the money they would lose. So for my next album, I went back, used the same beats from all my previous projects, and changed all the lyrics. According to my contract I still owed them records, so that is the record they got."

"And they've accepted it?"

"They have to! I wasn't makin' anything else till I went over and re-recorded all my old stuff. I can't take my old albums away, but at least I can give the fans a choice, you know?"

"They threatened a lawsuit, didn't they?"

"Yeah. They tried to say I violated my contract by using the same beats, but it was all bull."

"So how do you think the new album will perform?"

"It'll be crazy! For every fan I lose here in the U.S., I believe I'll gain ten overseas!"

"But will you lose fans here in the U.S.?"

"I'd imagine. Some people just can't feel what I'm tryin' to do, and that's cool. You can't force 'em."

"Yes, but you have to admit, Moses, some of your new lyrics that have been leaked are a bit controversial…"

"Like which ones?"

"Let me see…" Phil went flipping through some of the papers he had on his desk. "Here's one."

Subconsciously, here's what this CD is
Lyrically stopping racists from ever having a kid
I give 'em the biz
Like a slave fed up to his ears
And blowing off his master's powdered wig
I stayed small till my people needed me to get big

Till they needed my words to wipe away their tears
And if it takes for you to die for them to live
Then say goodbye to your family, thank the Lord for your years

"I mean, you're talking about killing people here, right?" he asked.

"I'm talkin' 'bout killing people who were tryin' to kill me or my ancestors back in the day. If you ain't a racist, then these lyrics shouldn't bother you."

"And if a person is a racist?"

"Then they need to stay away from me. You know, it's crazy since the new music leaked how many people act offended by my lyrics. When I was talkin' 'bout shootin' other black folk in the head, nobody cared. I talk about killin' racists in one song and all of a sudden I'm a hatemonger and a terrorist. White folks is somethin' else, man."

Phil made an innocent face at me. "Well, I'm white, Moses…"

"Then you somethin' else, Phil."

We shared a laugh, while the audience remained tense.

"No, really Moses, come on. You've gotta admit that some of these new lyrics are problematic." He shuffled more sheets and started to read again.

I am the insurrectionist
I stay smacking in sense
And fighting against
This white power
And this black ignorance

"Honestly, Moses, what white power are you talking about? This isn't the sixties anymore."

"Phil, if you gotta ask, then that's all the inspiration I need to keep making music."

"And look, here, at this one," he continued.

If you're offended by my obvious spite
Then I suggest
you go upstairs and turn on the light
and if it just so happens
that your skin is white
then I can understand why this music
may cause you fright
I guess that
Symbolically I'm lookin' you in the face
And hocking up mucus and spitting it
In the name of my race
But you can't honestly tell me your place
In history's space
Doesn't justify the spit on your face

"Come on, Moses! You're talking about spitting in my face, here! How am I not supposed to take offense to that?"

"First of all, I said symbolically."

"Oh yes, that changes everything."

"Second, if you really look at the history of slaves in this country, ain't no reason why white folk don't deserve some metaphorical mucus."

"Come on, Moses. This is racist! This is racist against white people!"

"How is it racist? I ain't callin' white folks names or tryin' to hang 'em from trees! All I'm sayin' is that I'm still pissed about my history. You got no idea what it's like to…well, I'm just still pissed off! And I got every right to put it in my music."

"But what point are you trying to make by putting out music like this?"

"I didn't have a point when I started, just wanted to get a lot of stuff off my chest. Once the album drops, though, a point will kinda make itself. It's obviously cool to talk about killing people in rap songs, as long as you not talkin' 'bout killing white people."

"Why do you hate white people so much? I mean, do you really want to kill us like you say in your songs?"

"Not anymore."

"Not anymore?"

"Hey, look, I'm tryin' to be honest here. Couple months ago, yeah, I kinda did wanna kill some white folk. I had to go through some counselin', you know, see a shrink and all, and now I'm past all that. I just let it all out in my music."

"I've heard you make it a point to have as little contact with white people as possible."

"Yeah, that's true. That's just for my own sanity, you know?"

"Who goes into a coma and comes out hating white people, Moses?"

"I don't hate white people anymore."

"What happened while you were in your coma?"

"I told you, I had a revelation."

"But specifically, what happened?"

"I can't talk about it."

"You can't, or you don't want to?"

"Both."

"Something must have happened. You're a completely different person than when I interviewed you last."

"I had a revelation, Phil. Let's leave it at that."

Phil sat back in his seat, debating whether or not he wanted to push the issue. I hoped, for his sake, that he didn't. I could already feel Xavier getting fidgety behind me.

"Alright, let's move on. Tell me about your newfound wealth."

"Well, it turns out that I made more money while I was in the coma than I ever had before. The sales of my records and merchandise and everything. Since I wasn't spendin' any of it, it just all piled up in an account. So, my beautiful wife—"

"Who we will come back to, because that's yet another unexpected turn in the life of Moses Jenkins."

"I wouldn't say it was unexpected, but anyways, my wife suggested I invest it. I bought a lil bit of real estate here and there, you know, but then I found out about AudioTech."

"The music software company?"

"Yeah. They had a product they said changed the way people heard music. First, I was like whatever, you know, they just fakin', but then I heard it, and I was sold. They needed money, so I gave 'em some."

"I think you're downplaying the situation a bit, Mr. Jenkins. Didn't you become part owner of the company?"

"Yeah."

"So then what happened?"

"We got bought out."

"I love the way you can talk about this like it's just not that big of a deal."

I shrugged my shoulders. "I mean, it is what it is."

"So who bought you all out?"

"Microsoft."

"For how much?"

"I'm not really at liberty to say, Phil."

"Well…can you give us a hint?"

"Let's put it this way—between the money I made from the deal, and the money I'm still bringin' in from the music and stuff, I'm s'posed to make the bottom of the *Forbes* list in a couple months."

"For the richest people in the country?"

"Yep."

"I didn't know that."

"Yeah, they jus' called me last week. They said I'll probably be the most controversial person they've ever had on it."

Phil looked genuinely amazed as he shook his head. "To make the *Forbes* list, you've gotta be...wow..."

"Phil, chill out, man."

"So you're a billionaire hatemonger?"

I laughed out loud.

"I'm not a hatemonger, Phil. If I was a billionaire hatemonger, though, which I'm not, I wouldn't be the only one out here. I'd just be the only black one. But like I said, I'm not a hatemonger."

He stared in awe for another second, then shook himself out of his stupor. "How does your wife feel about this? Your wife and former manager."

"Oh, she's still my manager. She don't trust nobody else with the job. She jus' got some staff now."

"She looks like she had an extreme makeover."

"Y'all act like she was ugly before! SaTia wasn't never ugly, she jus' dressed like she was always on the job."

"And now?"

"Well, you can see for yourself."

A picture flashed on the screen of SaTia in one of her more elegant dresses, one she'd worn to the Grammy Awards.

"She looks like a model, Moses. Seriously."

"Yeah, I know. I put that ring on her finger and it was all downhill from there."

"Does she act different now that you're married?"

"Naw, not really. Matter of fact, she stronger than ever. You know she runs the organizations, right?"

"Yes, I do, and I wanted to talk to you about that. I'm glad you brought it up. In the last year, you've started two organizations, correct?"

"Yeah. There's Pride Roka, and Sarah's Seeds, both of which my wife oversees. One is for men, and the other for women."

"And…this has been another source of controversy, correct?"

"It's whatever…I mean, it has, but it's all bullsh…I can't say that on the air, can I?"

"No."

"Okay, well, it's all lies. We only got twenty-four people, twelve men and twelve women, and people already talkin' 'bout we teachin' hate. All we talk 'bout is lovin' ourselves and knowin' where we came from."

"What about the two young men from Pride Roka that assaulted the group of white men downtown?"

"The way I was told, them white guys called my two guys niggers. Say what you want 'bout my organization, but I got no problem sayin'—you call anybody from Pride Roka or Sarah's Seeds a nigger, you be lucky to just get beat down. Real talk."

A faction of the audience burst into cheers and applause, while the rest began booing and screaming. We stopped talking for a while as the police struggled to get order back amongst the crowd. Four people were escorted out and after five minutes, we were able to continue.

"And this isn't hate speech to you at all, Mr. Jenkins?" Phil continued.

"Hell no, this ain't hate speech! If you gonna get on my folks for reactin' if somebody calls them nigger, then tell the Jews stop gettin' people fired and blackballed for bein' anti-Semitic! Tell the Irish to quit fightin' people over they heritage. Why every time black folk stand up and be proud, we always gotta be seen as bein' violent and hateful, huh? If y'all scared of us, jus' say y'all scared of us and let's take it from there, but stop tryin' to say that we violent jus' 'cause we love our people!"

"And I guess your new rap lyrics aren't hate speech either, right?"

"What I spit in my songs is truth; no more and no less."

"Well…" Phil began gathering up the papers around his desk. "I think it's safe to say that you've established yourself as one of the most controversial, and maybe even dangerous, people in this country."

I shook my head. "See, Phil, that's what I'm talkin' 'bout. I'm dangerous 'cause I want black folk to be proud of themselves, huh?"

"No, you're dangerous because you convince black people to hate white people."

"That's not true. I've never, not in a song, not in my organization, ever told anyone to hate white people. I tell people to know they history."

"Do you know your history, Moses? Do you know that white people have championed the causes of African-Americans in this country for decades? White people were doing sit-ins with blacks, white people marched on Washington with Dr. King, white people got killed fighting for civil rights the same way blacks did! Do you know your history, Mr. Jenkins?"

"I've lived it, Phil."

"What do you mean?"

"I mean, I've lived my history. So you can't tell me a damn thing."

Phil looked around in a panic, knowing that I'd just cursed on live national television. He looked over at one of his producers, who gave him the signal to keep on going, and then quickly composed himself.

"Well, I don't know what you mean by saying you've lived your history, but we obviously see differently on many different things."

"Yeah, we do, and that's cool. It's some stuff you jus' ain't gonna understand 'cause you ain't black. It is what it is, you know?"

"No I don't know, Mr. Jenkins. And according to you, I never will."

"Exactly. Finally, we agree on something."

"So…what are your plans for the future?"

"I'm jus' tryin' to reach as many people as I can. As many people who will listen."

"And what's your message, if you could sum it up?"

I looked down at the floor and thought long and hard.

"To question your society is to question your reality."

Phil turned and faced me. "That's it?"

"That's it, Phil."

Phil stared at me, confused for a moment, and then turned his head toward the camera.

"There you have it…a man transformed from an ordinary rapper into something…well, something else. We're out of time tonight, but you can leave us your comments about the show on www. philwintersshow.com or email us at comments@philwintersshow .com. Tonight's interview has been eye-opening to say the least, and we'd love to hear from you about it. I'd like to thank our guest, Mr. Moses Jenkins, for being with us on today's show, and we'll see you all next time. Good night."

"What happens now?"

The three of us, SaTia, Xavier, and myself, had all climbed into the black Escalade that was to take us back to the hotel. The rest of the security team was following in an SUV behind us. SaTia looked at me with a curious interest written all over her face. "The world knows what you're about now. What do you plan to do?"

I couldn't answer her immediately. Instead I looked out the

window at the passing cars and buildings, wondering if this world was real. I still vividly remembered my time on the Talbert plantation. It played over and over in my head like a repeated Blu-ray disc. The colors were bright, the sound was clear, and the pain sometimes woke me up at night.

SaTia had told me a while ago that sometimes I screamed out in my sleep. She could never wake me when I did, but took to singing "Ringin' Dem Bells" in my ear whenever it happened. Only then would the scars on my back stop burning, and I'd fall back into resting.

"Moses?"

"I heard you, baby."

I turned away from the window and looked at her.

"Sorry. I got caught up in my thoughts."

"That's okay."

"She's right, you know." Xavier took his shades off. "I overheard one of the producers on the way out. The show broke all kinds of records for viewership, national and international. The whole world really does know what you're about now. What's your plan?"

I shrugged my shoulders and looked back out the window.

"I guess I gotta change it."

SaTia sat up.

"Change what? The world?"

"No doubt."

SaTia looked at me, then at Xavier, before sitting back in her seat. Xavier slipped his shades on, and we rode off into the city's horizon.

Epilogue

"I heard you'll be on the *Phil Winters Show* next week."

Dr. Bailey, who I'd called James since we sat down and talked after my defining press conference, made his way into the headquarters for Pride Roka, a three-story mansion right outside the city that'd we'd converted into a combination of offices, auditoriums, and outreach centers.

"With all that money you have, I figured you'd just rent out a couple floors downtown."

"Naw…this here is more homelike, you know? I mean, you gotta travel to get here, but if you dedicated, then it ain't no problem. We pay for all the members to get back and forth anyways."

"Sounds good. I hear you're trying to save lives out here."

"That ain't what the papers is sayin'."

"The papers are going to say what they want, Moses. You should know that by now."

"I do. That don't mean I gotta like it."

We made our way into the auditorium space, where Xavier was teaching a martial arts class to five guys in their twenties. He'd overseen the security specifications to the house when we had it overhauled, with a promise from me that money would not be an issue. In return, I got an estate that looked totally normal from the outside, but had windows that could stop sniper bullets, walls reinforced so thick that a stick of C4 could explode in one room and leave the other rooms unaffected, and an information center in the basement that ran a background check on anyone who came through the front gate. This house, and my own home, which had very similar work done, were the only places he felt comfortable leaving my side.

"X, how's it going?"

Xavier waved at James, and then turned to his class and called them to attention. After bowing, he dismissed them, and then ran over to meet us.

"James, what brings you down here?"

"Wanted to talk to Moses about something."

"James, would you mind if X came along?" I knew Xavier had some free time, and wanted him to stick around. If what James wanted to talk about was as important as he made it out to be, then I'd need someone to talk with afterward.

"Not at all. As a matter of fact, I was going to ask that he come."

"Cool. Let's go to the back office."

We made our way through the house, greeting all the guys as we passed them. When we got to the office in the back, each of us took a seat.

"So…James, what's so important that it brought you away from your job?"

"You ever heard of Nathan Freeman?"

"Naw…I never heard of him."

"I have." Xavier's eyes went dark as he looked sideways at James. "What do you know about Nathan Freeman?"

"Hold up, hold up…who is Nathan Freeman?" I interjected, beginning to feel left out.

Xavier looked at James for a few moments longer, and then turned to me.

"Nathan Freeman died a couple of years back. He was wanted for murder."

"What's that got to do with me?"

"Xavier, how long ago did you start working with that contracting firm?"

"Why?"

"It was right after Freeman died, wasn't it?"

"How do you know about him?"

"Come on, man, y'all sound like some schoolgirls. What the hell is goin' on with this Nathan Freeman dude?"

Xavier stood as if he was getting ready to exit the room, and before any of us knew what was happening, he had his pistol out and pointed at James' head. James jumped back in his seat and screamed.

I didn't even know Xavier had a pistol on him.

"You've got five seconds to tell me how you know about Nathan Freeman, or so help me God, I'll kill you right here."

"Whoa!" I jumped up out of my seat. "X, what the hell are you doin', man?"

"One…"

James sat frozen in his chair, mumbling over his words and not sure of how to react.

"Two…"

"X, put the goddamn gun down, man!"

"Three…"

"X!" I reached out to grab the gun, and Xavier's arm was a blur. I noticed that it wasn't pointed at James anymore at the same time I noticed it was pointed at me.

"Moses…you know I put my life on the line for you every day, and I count it an honor to do it. But you have got to stay out of this, please."

Xavier's hands trembled as he spoke. I raised my hands with my palms up. He turned the weapon back on James and resumed his countdown.

"Four…"

"James, you better tell this man somethin'."

"He sent me his blood, okay!"

Xavier lowered his gun slightly.

"What?"

"He sent me his blood! I met him once, when he was still teaching. Two days before he died, he sent me his blood. He asked me if I could see what was wrong with him."

Xavier lowered his gun to his side.

"Do you still have it?"

"Yes, but I can't do anything with it in public labs. I was going to ask if Moses could fund my research. I've been putting together pieces of information on Nathan ever since he died. I know that you two knew each other, but I don't know how…"

"Why didn't you just say that in the beginning?"

"I thought if I worked you a little bit, I could get a little more information. I didn't know you'd pull a gun on me, for Chrissakes!"

Xavier sat down in his chair. His face was white and sweat leaked down from his forehead.

I'd always seen the craziness in Xavier's eyes but I'd learned to ignore it. Now that it had come out, I found myself just as scared as James.

"Yo…X, you…you pulled a gun on me, man! You had a damn gun pointed at my face!"

Xavier spoke with a voice that didn't sound like his. "I'm sorry."

Everyone in the room regained their composure except me.

"Somebody better tell me what the hell is goin' on!" I screamed.

"Alright. I owe you that much." Xavier looked at me with tears in his eyes. "I...never told you this. Hell...I never told anyone this. And anyone who knows probably thinks I'm dead...but...I had a family. I had a wife and two children."

"Damn!" I said while both James and I sat on the edge of our seats. "What...what happened, man?"

"I met Nathan Freeman..."

The wind rustled the trees as the sun began its descent, but neither James nor I noticed. Instead we sat captivated as Xavier poured his pain out inside the four walls surrounding us.

About the Author

R. Kayeen Thomas is one of Washington, D.C.'s hottest writers. Having lived in the nation's capital since the age of three, he self-published his first book, *Light: Stories of Urban Resurrection*, during his junior year at Carleton College in Northfield, MN. Upon coming home to D.C. to market his first work, Thomas sold 1,000 copies of his book in the Washington metropolitan area before returning to college to finish his undergraduate studies. Now, at age 27, he is an author, poet, playwright, hip-hop artist, journalist, and social justice advocate. He resides in Southeast, D.C. with his wife and daughter.

IF YOU ENJOYED "ANTEBELLUM,"
BE SURE TO CHECK OUT

THE SEVEN DAYS

BY R. KAYEEN THOMAS
COMING IN SPRING 2013 FROM STREBOR BOOKS

Nathan and Xavier are black men from two different sides of the track. Nathan is a failed academic. Having written a book that that he believed would change the black community forever, he is crushed by the fact that it only gained a white readership and no black people seem to care about it. His marriage is slowly fading away, and his once-beloved son is now strung out and desolate.

Xavier is an ex-special forces commando who has given up war to be at home and raise a family. He loves his wife passionately and is adored by his children. His wife being an executive, he collects a check from the military and spends most of his time doing martial arts training at home, and pondering on how to be a better husband and father.

When a series of murders leave the lives of these two men shattered, they will find that their pain is the beginning of a perilous journey from which neither will emerge the same…

CHAPTER TWO

The night sky is peaceful, as if God himself had put everything to rest after the sun had set. The stars shined bright in their set places in the sky, as the wind hummed the nocturnal soundtrack that would continue to play until the slightest of light rays broke the through the darkness. The air up here is thin, like a strand of thread, and for a while it sits undisturbed in the peaceful dark, until first a sound, growing louder and louder, and then an object, pierces through it. Only something manmade could disturb such serenity.

The plane continues to make its way through the dark clouds, going several hundred miles an hour. The occupants of the plane are mysterious figures, with equipment hiding their faces as if they are ashamed of their purpose. The two pilots, sitting in the cockpit, direct their attention constantly from one gauge to another to another, making sure that all elements of the flight and the plane are conducive to the mission. The three men in the back sit still, clearing their minds of everything else except the task at hand. This is how they were trained; to ignore all else, and focus solely on the successful completion of the objective. Attached to their clothing is tactical weaponry, and these men have mastered the use of each one of them. They have trained for countless hours in every environment imaginable, enduring conditions that would have easily broken any lesser of men. But these three have survived, and have shown themselves worthy of the task set before them. Even their slow, steady breathing reflects the hours of training they have completed. They are weapons, human robots programmed over and over again with the same simple command—complete the mission. Ask no questions, think no thoughts, feel no emotions, just complete the mission. For now, they have no mothers, no fathers, no girlfriends, and no pets. They have no favorite movies or songs, no recreational hobbies, no favorite soft drink. For now, their lives only have one meaning—completing the objective. Successfully finishing the mission. This is how they were programmed. This is how they were trained.

When the GPS system in the cockpit shows that the plane has reached its destination, one of the pilots gets up from his seat and walks toward the back. He tells the three men that it's time, but they've anticipated it, and have already re-checked their equipment to ensure that everything is in order. As if on cue, all three of the men stand together, and when the pilot remaining in the cockpit is given the word, he presses the flashing, bright red button in front of him, and the back hatch to the plane opens, revealing a night sky that now seems as though it's out of a horror movie. The wind, obviously angry, charges through the compartment with incredible force, but the three men withstand it. They have been trained to. After going through the necessary preparation procedures, each of the men mechanically walk to the edge of the hatch, and one after the other, jump from the plane.

Their stomachs rise into their throats as they fall rapidly toward the earth. They put their bodies in the right aerial position to slow their descent, and after reaching the correct altitude, they pull a string attached to their clothing and deploy their parachutes. They are now low enough to get a good view of their target. The bunker is well-lit, and although they are still airborne, with the night vision equipment they can make out security personnel on patrol around the building. They land softly, expertly, in the brush on the outskirts of the bunker, and it is only after removing the equipment that is no longer necessary that one could make out the differences between the three men. Two of them stand out, their skin tone contrasting with the darkness. The other blends in perfectly.

They move through the brush with stealth, weapons drawn, and faces tight. They walk low enough to avoid being seen by any of the security, but high enough to keep aware of their surroundings. When they come into close proximity of the first guard, the first of the three signals to the other two to stop and wait. Then he sneaks up behind the guard, who has been daydreaming for the past hour, and quickly snaps his neck. After lying the guard down silently on the ground, he signals for the other two to continue following him. They are now at the target building, and each of them covers a particular direction, so as to make sure that all of their sides are covered. They make their way up the stairs and along the makeshift balcony. This is the entrance route with the least resistance, as they have already determined, and the door on the far side of the walkway is where they plan to enter. Everything is going according to plan, but just as they reach the ladder that marks the halfway point between the steps and the entrance, two guards unexpectedly emerge out of the door.

Initially the guards had been laughing, lightening the mood of the night, but as soon as they see the three men, they immediately open fire. The three operatives take cover positions and fire back, dropping the two guards quickly, surmising that the gunfire is sure to draw more guards to their location. They run for the door, knowing they must complete the mission as quickly as possible now or the remaining guards will kill them. After entering the door, they make their way down the stone stairs and stop at the corner. They can all hear footsteps approaching, and again, as if by cue, they each peek around the corner and take out the approaching guards. They then start making their way down the hallway, toward the metal door that should have been at the end of it, but before they can get there, a dozen guards seem to come out of nowhere and begin to open fire. They each duck around the corner, narrowly avoiding the bullets aimed at them. The guards, after they stop firing, begin screaming something in a language the men don't understand, and slowly make their way up to the corner. Two of the three men keep their backs against the wall and hold on tightly to their guns, but the third one, the one that could fade into the night, throws his gun on the ground.

"X, what the hell are you doing?"

Xavier doesn't answer; he just waits for the right moment. And when the guards are close enough, he comes from around the corner and strikes the first one in the throat, crushing his larynx. Then he begins attacking the rest of them, rendering most of them dead with one blow. Xavier kicks one in the knee, popping it out of place, then punches one in the ribcage, puncturing the heart, then back-fists one on the side of the head. For a reason foreign to the combatant, none of the guards are shooting at him. They're all trying to attack him, and he's flooring them one after another. He's not tired, he's not fatigued; he's just doing as he was trained. And he sidekicks one of the guards in the nose, then turns around and grabs another guard's arm, maneuvers around, and breaks it. Then he pops out another one's elbow, turns around and breaks his neck. More guards are coming out from everywhere now, but Xavier could go on fighting forever. He smiles, knowing he is perfect in his combat, and there is no way he can be beaten. But as he reaches the peak of his pride, he realizes something, and everything stops in its tracks. The guards stop attacking, and he stands there, as if time itself stops to pay homage to his revelation.

Xavier realizes that he doesn't know what he's fighting for.

He knows what the mission is, he knows what he's supposed to do, but he doesn't know why he's doing it. Horrified, he stands there and wracks his brain, trying to figure out the question thudding at his head. He drops to his knees and strikes his head against the floor, hoping to trigger some thought; some memory of inspiration or reason or purpose, but nothing comes. And when he looks up again, he realizes, with the deepest feeling of despair, that there is no reason. And that there never was.

And at that exact second, each one of the guards surrounding him pulls out a gun, and fires into him at the same time.

Soaked in sweat, Xavier jerks awake.

As his eyes adjust to being open, the first thing Xavier notices is the sunlight racing in through the window. It illuminates the entire room, but the beautiful dresser that faces the curtains gets most of its attention. The pictures on top of the dresser are illuminated as well, and Xavier stares for a while at the pictures of him smiling, embracing his family. The room smells of pleasant scents that attach themselves to marriage; potpourri, baby powder, perfume, and fresh laundry. The bed sheets, which have absorbed most of Xavier's sweat, are adorned with flower prints. The colors match the carpet, which has been very well kept, and matches the paint on the walls. The entire scene is like a freeze frame from a cliché made-for-TV movie. There are two or three pictures on the wall, all depicting some form of nature at its most complacent, and all matching the color scheme. The books placed at the head of the bed give the room an air of intellect; while the tulips, placed in a vase to the side, give it an air of romance. There are children's toys strewn around the carpet as well. A little Barbie doll lays face-down beside a toy truck in the middle of the room, and an open children's book sits beside the mirror, waiting to be resumed. The toys fit in the room, as if they sprouted themselves up from the carpet. In fact, everything in the room seems to fit into place.

Everything except the gun, hidden under a stack of magazines, in the small drawer on Xavier's side of the bed. It has never fit.

Xavier feels a hand caressing his arm, and turns to face the beautiful woman lying in the bed next to him. The concern on her face asks Xavier what is wrong before she even opens her mouth. He just shakes his head and breathes deeply, trying to forget about the dream that woke him so violently. She leans forward and lightly kisses him on his cheek, and then on his arm, where her hand had just been. She speaks softly.

"Was it another nightmare?"

"I don't know, Theresa. I don't know. Everything was fine, and then… and then it got all screwed up."

"It was about your days in the military again?"

"Yeah."

Theresa sighs deeply.

"You keep having these dreams about what you used to do, baby. I know you don't like talking about the military, but maybe we should. I want to be able to help you."

"It's nothing."

Theresa stays silent for a few moments, then speaks again, hesitantly.

"I know you miss it. I know it's a part of you; what you used to do. I know you loved it…"

"I love you all more." Xavier cuts her off quickly, looking into her eyes. "I love you all more."

Theresa drops her head, not knowing what to believe.

"Listen," Xavier says as he gently lifts her head back up. "I got out for a reason. I married you for a reason. We had kids for a reason. That time in my life is over. I'm a husband and a father now. Nothing is going to change that."

Xavier leans forward and kisses Theresa, but she draws back slightly after a moment.

"I just want you to be happy," she says regretfully.

Before Xavier can respond, there are two sets of light knocks at the door. Despite the seriousness of the conversation, Xavier smiles. He knows that, for the tiny hands doing the knocking, they had mustered about as much strength as they could to give those cute little knocks. He looks at Theresa to make sure that she is okay with ending the conversation for the time being, and when she nods her head, he yells to come in. The two children burst into the room and start running around screaming with such joy in their voices that Xavier and Theresa can't help but to laugh. They pick up the children and play around with them on the bed, tickling them and rolling them around until everyone is tired. Then they all lay down, with Theresa holding their son, Xavier, Jr., and Xavier holding their daughter, Felicia.

"Daddy." XJ looks over to him. "Can I get a tattoo?"

"What? Heck no, you can't get a tattoo!"

"Why not, Daddy?"

"Well, first of all, you're too young. What would you look like going into kindergarten with a tattoo?"

"But you have tattoos!!!"

"Yes, that's because I'm an adult."

"But my friend Dante, at school, his brother has a tattoo and he's not an adult."

"Well, that's Dante's family; not mine."

"And," interjects Felicia, "If he can get a tattoo, then Mommy can buy me some makeup."

Theresa rolls her eyes. "I'm not buying you any makeup. Who wears makeup in the second grade, Felicia? Where did this whole makeup thing come from, anyway?"

"Tasha's mom lets her wear makeup some days."

"Tasha's mom is a hoe."

Xavier immediately looks over at Theresa, who has realized that she's just made a mistake.

"You know what's coming next." Xavier laughs, and Felicia is the first to inquire the inevitable.

"What's a hoe, Mommy?"

XJ follows up quickly. "Yeah, Daddy, what's a hoe?"

"Alright, it's time for you two to get ready for school." Xavier starts pushing his daughter off of the bed and toward the door. Theresa does the same thing to their son. "Go wash up and put your clothes on."

"But…"

"But nothing. Go wash up, put your clothes on, and get ready for school. I'm not going to say it again."

The two children, after hearing the warning, quickly get up and run out of the room.

"Thanks for the save." Theresa laughs when the kids are out of earshot.

"Don't thank me." Xavier laughs. "You still have to worry about little Tasha's mom calling you about that hoe comment. You know Felicia's going to tell her when she gets to school."

"Ugh, you're right." Theresa curses herself as she starts getting dressed. "I guess I'll figure out some way to apologize later."

"Apologize for what? We all know she's a hoe. It's no secret."

"Still, apologizing is the right thing to do," Theresa says as she starts to make her way out the door. "I'm going to fix breakfast. Are you going to eat?"

"Yeah, I'll be down in a minute."

As Xavier hears his wife's footsteps echoing off the walls, he lies back in bed and tries to relax. Memories of his dream come to him as soon as he closes his eyes, though, and he decides to keep them open. Slowly, he gets out of bed, stretches, and makes his way to the bathroom for a shower.

Fifteen minutes later, Xavier begins to walk down the stairs. He can smell the eggs, bacon, pancakes, and potatoes cooking in the kitchen, and congratulates himself for marrying a woman that can cook. His children are already sitting at the table, eating their eggs and waiting for their pancakes to be served. They smile at him as he walks into the room, and he begins to think, as he so often does, that he doesn't deserve what he has. He walks up and kisses Theresa on the cheek, then takes his seat at the table. When he hears his children laughing, he looks up and sees that his wife has made smiley faces with the syrup on their pancakes. When she gives Xavier his plate, his pancakes have "I love you" written just big enough to fit. He laughs along with his children, then gets up and kisses Theresa again, this time on the lips.

"Ewwwww!" The children react as if a jar full of bugs have entered the kitchen.

Theresa laughs, then starts to wash her hands.

"Come on, kids," she says. "I don't want to be late for work."

As the children start to eat faster, Xavier grumbles slightly under his breath, just loud enough for Theresa to hear.

"What is it, baby?"

"You know I don't like you working. I mean, we can get by on the money I'm still getting from the military. Why not just stay home with the kids?"

"Because I don't want to," Theresa replies. "I love my job, and I'm doing just fine at being a mother and a working woman. You have a problem with that?"

"No. I just don't understand why you'd work, if you don't have to."

"Well, I'll explain it later. Right now I have to drop off the kids and get to the office."

Theresa rushes the children away from the table and tells them to get their bags and coats. Then she sidesteps Xavier and starts gathering papers from the nearby desk and puts them into a briefcase.

"Nobody tries to hit on you at your job, do they?" asks Xavier playfully.

"No, they wouldn't do that."

"Why not?"

"Because I'd fire them."

Xavier walks up behind Theresa and slides his hands around her waist.

"You know I like a take charge kinda woman, right?"

Theresa turns around and smiles. "Well then, you'll love me tonight. I've been reading up some stuff in that book we got for our anniversary.

"Really…? And you can't take the day off to show me?"

"No, I can't. You'll just have to wait until tonight."

Xavier turns around, playfully disappointed, but Theresa grabs his shoulders and makes him face her again. When he looks at her face, it is dead serious, and she stares deeply into his eyes, preparing to say words originating from her soul.

"I love you, Xavier."

Whenever she says it like that, Xavier can never think of a way to respond in kind. He always tells her that he loves her back, but it never seems as powerful coming from him as it does from her.

"I love you, too."

She stares into his eyes for one more second, then relaxes her demeanor and smiles. "Good. 'Cause I'd beat your ass if you didn't."

Before Xavier can come back, the children rush downstairs with their things and yell to their mother that they are ready to go. Theresa throws on her coat, kisses Xavier goodbye, and makes her way toward the door.

"Bye, Daddy!" the children call out as Theresa opens the door.

"I'll see you all later."

The door closes, and after a while Xavier hears the car starting, then pulling out from the driveway, and the family is gone.

Xavier sits down and finishes his breakfast, taking in the silence. He doesn't especially enjoy it. It reminds him of times past, where silence and darkness were his primary weapons. His house does a good job of overpowering these reminders, though. He can look up at the refrigerator and see pictures drawn by his children, of birds and pink flowers. He can taste the syrup that his wife wrote "I love you" on the pancake with. He can see his daughter's tiny shoes on the floor, with a picture of a female cartoon character on the sides and the bottom. His wife was right. There was a part of him, a big part of him, that missed his past. But it didn't compare to what he had now, and as long as nothing changed, he knew he would never go back.

WHO IS R. KAYEEN THOMAS?

Check him out at
www.whoisrkayeenthomas.com
and download his new hip-hop mixtape
"Heretic: The Nat Calling Project"
FREE!